PRAISE FOR DAWN MILLER'S
GRITTY, AND AUTHENTIC WC
FICTION—ONE OF THE GREAT A
NOVELS OF OUR

The Journal of
Callie Wade

"The historical novel at its best. . . . Its tenderness, grit, gumption, and amazing characters will captivate. . . . Like Laura Ingalls Wilder, Dawn Miller gives voice to a generation of pioneer women . . . [and] re-creates a bygone era with imagery that illuminates the reality of the wagon train era. . . . A beautifully realistic novel told in journal form in the clear voice of one extraordinary girl."

—*Romantic Times*

"Lovely and heartwarming . . . a poignant, hopeful love story. . . . Callie Wade will remain with you long after you close the covers of her journal. She puts the history of the American journey west into very tender, human terms."

—Cathy Cash Spellman, *New York Times*
bestselling author of *Bless the Child*

"Hardships of leaving behind familiar surroundings, friends, and beloved household items are told with poignant elegance by Miller."

—*Library Journal*

"Miller adds a feminine touch to the frontier."

—*Publishers Weekly*

"Miller's narrative offers a realistic sense of time and place."

—*Kirkus Reviews*

"[A] smashing debut by a new superstar."

—*Affaire de Coeur*

"One of the most poignant and unforgettable stories of the era. . . ."

—Tanzey Cutter, editor, *The Old Book Barn Gazette*

ALSO BY DAWN MILLER

The Journal of Callie Wade

Published by Pocket Books

Letters to Callie

Jack Wade's story

Dawn Miller

POCKET BOOKS

New York   London   Toronto   Sydney   Singapore

This book is a work of fiction. Names, characters, places and incidents are products of the author's imagination or are used fictitiously. Any resemblance to actual events or locales or persons, living or dead, is entirely coincidental.

An *Original* Publication of POCKET BOOKS

 POCKET BOOKS, a division of Simon & Schuster, Inc.
1230 Avenue of the Americas, New York, NY 10020

ISBN: 0-671-52102-0

First Pocket Books trade paperback printing August 2001

10 9 8 7 6 5 4 3 2 1

POCKET and colophon are registered trademarks of Simon & Schuster, Inc.

Cover design by Carolyn Lechter
Front cover photo by Rosanne Olson / Tony Stone Images

Designed by Jaime Putorti

Printed in the U.S.A.

This book is dedicated to my brother

SHAWN MICHAEL BECKER
1968–1995

Words can't describe how much I miss you.

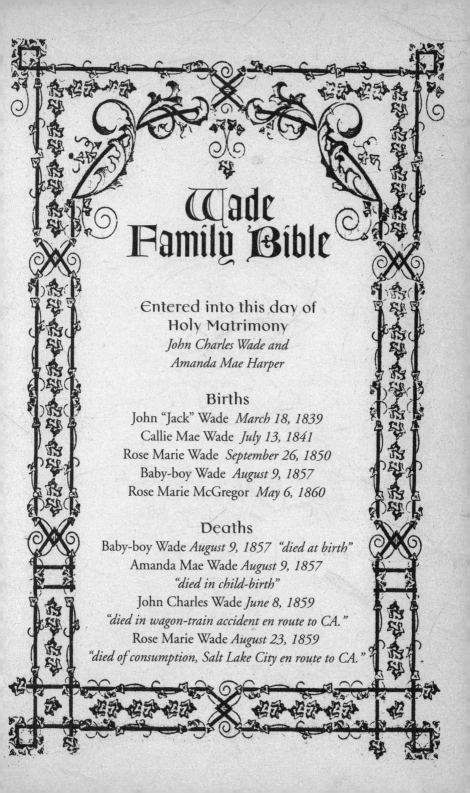

Wade
Family Bible

Entered into this day of
Holy Matrimony
*John Charles Wade and
Amanda Mae Harper*

Births
John "Jack" Wade *March 18, 1839*
Callie Mae Wade *July 13, 1841*
Rose Marie Wade *September 26, 1850*
Baby-boy Wade *August 9, 1857*
Rose Marie McGregor *May 6, 1860*

Deaths
Baby-boy Wade *August 9, 1857 "died at birth"*
Amanda Mae Wade *August 9, 1857*
"died in child-birth"
John Charles Wade *June 8, 1859*
"died in wagon-train accident en route to CA."
Rose Marie Wade *August 23, 1859*
"died of consumption, Salt Lake City en route to CA."

Journal Entry

~

March 18, 1864

It has been so long since I dared to open our family Bible, but for some reason I was drawn to it tonight. As I traced my fingers over the names, it seemed so strange that they could be gone now, all except for me and Jack. Looking at Mama's flowery print, I couldn't help imagining her excitement as she recorded the beginnings of her new life with Pa and the birth of her first child. I wondered, too, if she was fretting up there in heaven like I am for Jack. I wonder, does God let you fret in heaven? I know at the very least she is thinking of him as I am, today being his birthday. How long I stared at the day of his birth in our Bible, I can't recall, but staring at it made me feel as if I could bring Jack closer to me somehow. Foolishness most likely, but I am so worried about him. Those letters from Colorado painted such a lonely life, always moving, another town, another game—but even they were some comfort. Christmas has already come and gone, the new year, now his birthday and still no word.

Could it really be five years since I last saw his face? As long as I live, I will never forget the day Jack rode away from our wagon train back on that dusty road in Salt Lake. How very alone he looked. I remember Quinn telling me that he thought Jack was searching for a life for himself out there but I wonder. What kind of a life does a gambler have? When I look at the sleeping faces of my own family—my husband Quinn, our little Rose—I think of how very blessed I am, but I also think of my brother and how I yearn for the same kind of life for him. He's my family, too, after all—and my history.

There aren't enough miles or time that could sever the ties that the good Lord weaves together to make families. Our memories . . . the laughter, the trials . . . even the tears have bound us together, as has our love.

So, my handsome, reckless brother, I am lighting a candle for you tonight and as I blow it out, I'm making your birthday wish for you. I wish for this to be a year of new beginnings for you, Jack; I wish for you laughter and love and a family. And I pray with all my heart that no matter where you are, you'll somehow know I am thinking of you.

Callie Wade-McGregor
Plumas City, California

Mrs. Callie McGregor
Plumas City, California

Dear Callie,

Ignorance ain't a sin, but it ain't a blessing, either—remember Pa always saying that?

I don't know why I'm writing this but for some reason, you have been strong on my mind this night. Pa, too. Those words of his were stuck in my head for the worst side of two months as I rode alongside a crooked gambler named Jude—and on through to the night I caught the marshall standing outside our door with his guns drawn. See, when Jude invited me to ride the gambling circuit with him, he forgot to mention he was wanted by the law for robbing some folks. But I never asked him anything, either. I guess that's what Pa meant by ignorance. Course, I don't think Pa figured me learning my lesson much like this—or maybe he did. Pa could be real sharp that way.

Whatever I'm guilty of, Sis, it wasn't what that marshall thought, but I ain't the fool to stand and argue the point. I'll spare you the details, but let's just say it's not the first time those guns our ol' friend Grace gave me were put to use. And I ain't killed nobody if that's what you're thinking. I've only had to buffalo a fellow or two, until that marshall. I did wound him. But it was plain self-defense. I guess even that might shock you. But if I can't tell you the truth, who can I tell? In any case, that's the short of how I've ended up out here in the middle of nowhere, with just the clothes on my back. It still sticks in my craw that I had to leave all my things behind. Grub's getting low, too. If I hadn't caught this fish it would've been biscuits and water for two days going. The kick of it is, if my figurin' is right, I think it just might be my birthday. Heck of a way to celebrate, ain't it?

At least the view ain't bad.

"God's backyard" I've heard some call this place. I ain't sure what I expected, but I tell you, it is a sight to come across this land, all wide and open, more sky than anything else. Seems like I've studied the sky for days and still ain't seen all of it. The first few days of travel wasn't so bad, you know, just me and nature. But the silence has become a derned aggravation lately. That and the loneliness.

The loneliness is worse at night; all my thoughts and worries being my only company—and bad company at that. You know, it don't matter how tired I am, I can't seem to escape the brainwork. I guess all this empty land can make a person crazy after a while. I've mostly tried to keep my mind fixed on something—you, Quinn, or little Rose. And I guess there ain't a day that goes by that I don't wish for a dose of our ol' trailboss Stem's advice. But about the only thing that helps is writing. Until I stop scribbling, it's almost like you're here.

As fickle a bunch as we humans can be, we can't seem to live without each other, can we, Sis?

Callie, I know this letter might worry you but I'm telling you, don't. I expect I have as much sense as I ever did. Well, I'm alive ain't I? I guess I'll end it with that. This letter is longer than I planned, but I've been putting off going to sleep. The bugs out here are something. Some's so healthy they could pass for small birds. I guess I'd rather come up against a snake than a bunch of these bugs. I do hope Virginia City treats me better—they say there's a gold boom going on. I figure I'm about a day's ride away and I don't mind admitting I'm itching to get there.

Jack

Part One

❧

Virginia City, Montana

"Falling down doesn't make you a failure.
Staying down does."

—*Jack Wade*

One

Virginia City,
Montana Territory
March 19, 1864

Mrs. Callie McGregor
Plumas City, California

Dear Callie,

Well, I'm here and Virginia City ain't exactly pretty. But she is a sight for these sore eyes.

It's fourteen crowded miles of miner's sin here, as Ma would call it, more saloons, gambling dens, and dance halls than I ever saw. And slapped up quick, too. If it weren't for the mountains, I'd think a good wind might blow it all away—but I'm hoping it won't. I have a hunch if I play my cards right, this place just might be my ticket to a new start.

And truth is, I don't know how many of them tickets I have left.

I swear, I ain't ever seen so much coming and going since we joined that wagon train back in Independence. By God, but it is good to see people again! Makes me think I ought to stay here awhile. I guess I'm just sick to death of being on the run. I imagine I'm far enough from the trouble I wrote you of, too. Even if I ain't, this *would be one hard place to find someone who didn't want to be found. If I can just fade into these crowds for awhile, I might buy enough time to sort things out. Might be I can hit some paydirt, too—mine the miners, so the saying goes. I swear, you can almost smell the gold on the fellows walking by.*

Well, if Lady Luck's finally invited me to the party, I guess I ought to quit this letter for now and scrounge up a room so I can clean myself up for the doings. Ain't no time like the present to dust off and get back to living.

Funny. You know what I keep thinking about? Remember what Grandma Wade said to me that time that bully tried to get the better of me? She said, "Jack, you lay down once and you'll end up stayin' there. Next thing you know some feller's tossin' dirt over you." Well, I got up— just like the old lady expected—and I aim to this time, too.

I guess it's in the blood, Sis. We Wades ain't made to stay down long.

Jack

If women and whiskey were at a premium in Virginia City, rooms were worth the mother lode and a lot harder to find. Jack rubbed the shadow of a beard on his face and considered his dilemma as he watched the fracas going on along the bog of mud and manure that was Jackson Street. With the sun fading behind the mountains, the gulch seemed to come alive quick like a shaky drunk after downing his first drink of the night. The street was jammed with even more people, if that was possible; prospectors and cowhands, ladies both painted and proper, sharing leg room with the horses, oxen, and stray hogs that stood in the road, driving up the mud and the stink.

Still, it was life, Jack figured. And underneath all that raunch was opportunity.

But it was more the sounds that drew him in every time; the raucous laughter that spilled from the doorways, the arguing and the crack of gunfire, the call for a new game—it all helped him to drown out his failings for awhile. And whatever he won in gambling just helped him to keep moving and forgetting. The risks were worth it as long as he could forget.

Time alone hadn't been much of a healer.

Jack's eyes strayed for only a moment to the other side of town, the side he figured to stay clear of, where there were finer buildings, houses, and a school and all. It was the comfortable side, with its families that reminded him so sharply of Callie and the little sister he'd failed. Somewhere—probably when he'd left the wagon train behind in Salt Lake, after he'd built the coffin for little Rose with his own two hands—he'd given up that part of himself, his history. Sorrows could kill a man quicker than anything he knew if he gave in to them.

He knew most folks looking at him never would have guessed his history because of the mask he hid behind, always good for a story or joke to make them laugh. It didn't take long to figure out that it was better for the game to keep up a cheerful outlook. It was only in his heart where nobody could see that he kept his distance. He had learned all too well that it never paid to get too close because what you cared for could be lost. Which was why he preferred poker, he thought, looking around. Money wasn't so hard to lose—and he rarely did.

Jack was pulled from his thoughts as another squabble suddenly erupted in the street. This time, it appeared to be between a scrawny auctioneer who hogged a good part of the street with his animals and a big fellow who had been trying his best to park his rig. The black man was about the tallest Jack had ever seen and had arms as big around as small trees. Jack watched with interest as the black man quietly pondered his dilemma, then promptly halted his team dead center of the selling, stepped off into the ankle-deep mud, and solemnly trudged by. The auctioneer had been ready for a fight until he realized the man's size. So, he waited to holler until the man got far enough down the plank walk, then put himself into a lather that was comical, drawing more of the crowd's attention.

"If you're looking for civilization, mister, it's two streets over," came a sudden female voice, causing a healthy roar of laughter from the crowd. "If not, come on in and try your luck. We're the only place around that'll guarantee you a square deal."

Jack craned his neck and saw the woman standing just inside the doorway of a ramshackle affair with a sign overhead dubbing it "Pair-O-Dice." She was small but built generous with a fine head of brown curls piled high and a nice smile that faded as the hawker carried on about *Negroes* and *not having brains enough to think*.

"I guess you're right," she called. "Had the man been *thinkin'*, he'd have just shot you."

The little auctioneer looked startled.

"Ain't no woman that would've mouthed me like that back home," he declared, but Jack hardly paid any attention. He was watching the woman as she turned back into the saloon with the rough bunch of lean, gaunt-faced miners trailing behind her like schoolboys. She had to have sand to handle a crowd like that, he thought admiringly. These were the kind of people who worked hard and played harder. As he watched the last of the crowd file in, he felt the familiar rush of a new game build in him.

". . . *No* woman," the little man repeated loudly as he set to gathering the animals that he'd been hawking. Jack grinned at him, suddenly feeling in better spirits.

"Well, if you ain't goin' to take the lady up on the invite to play I guess I should," he said, proceeding into the Pair-O-Dice. Hesitating queered the luck as far as he was concerned—and that was just how he felt, lucky. Stepping through the batwings, he heard a fiddler strike up a lively tune somewhere in the crowded tobacco haze. A smallish bartender with a sorrowful expression glanced up and Jack saw his eyes rest briefly on the tied-down holsters before he went back to mopping the bar. A ragged dove smiled an invitation, but when she saw he wasn't interested, the light in her eyes faded and she tottered on back through the crowd. Jack heard the familiar husky female laugh then, followed by the constant clack of chips being shuffled, and he moved in closer to the faro layout at the back of the room.

"Remember boys, it's all about faith. The more you bet, the more you're likely to win," the lady dealer said, smiling as she drew winners and losers from the case box. "Reverend Webb, you of all people should know that."

The men all laughed at the sally, but Jack couldn't help to notice how far off the lady dealer seemed in spite of her friendliness. Up close, her face was fair and distractingly pretty with a pair of large blue eyes that appeared set on a thought of somewhere else, though the other boys didn't seem to notice. He guessed more than half of them were there just to look at her. She was fresh looking—that alone could do it in a place where most women appeared dried up or wilted.

He watched the game for a bit as she calmly called winner or loser, then stepped forward and slid a chip to the seven, coppering it at the last minute with the token that marked it to lose. She glanced up at him briefly, her eyes staying on him a bit longer than he expected, then drew a five of clubs, loser, and ten of diamonds, winner. He shrugged off the loss as minor and studied the dealer as she collected his chips off the table. He noticed the mending done in her silk dress and thought she couldn't be getting much of the rake-off. But the stubborn set of her chin said she wanted more. There seemed something lonely about her too, he saw, but he was quick to brush the thought aside.

"Last bid, gentlemen," she announced, drawing down to the hock, "all or nothing."

"Wouldn't none of us be standin' here if we didn't want it all," Jack said and a few of the men chuckled, not noticing he was looking at the dealer and not at the table. The woman they called Lillie was no fool, though. He saw her eyes go a bit wider, but she quickly recovered and gave him a grin that caused the dimples in her cheeks to appear.

"Wantin' and gettin' is two different things," she said finally. Lillie shuffled the cards easy then laid them before Jack to cut. After he did, she set them in the case box and Jack slid a chip to the ace of hearts. She pulled a six and a queen and slid Jack's chips off of the layout. She then drew the two of clubs for him, loser, then the ace of hearts, winner. Lillie gave him a wry smile that said, *You see?*

Jack grunted. The thing was, he didn't see. He had had the gut feeling when he stepped through the door that his luck was about to change. The first time he didn't so much mind it, but the second time he'd felt sure and his feelings weren't usually wrong. Faro had never been his best game—not like poker or three-card monte—but he wasn't a slouch at it, either.

By the time she took the third round of wagers, Jack suspected she had an edge of some kind, but he was hard put to figure out what. As close as he looked, he saw no sign of the usual cheats: spring or sliding plate. When he finally glanced up and their eyes met again, it was with silent regard, like two war-weary soldiers who had come face to face only to realize they were fighting for the same thing.

Survival.

She grinned and Jack smiled in return. But he was forced to step back from the faro layout just the same. He'd had a mind to stay in her game until he figured it out, but his funds wouldn't allow it. Nothing aggravated him more than having to be cautious—especially when a challenge had been laid down.

He felt her curious eyes stay on him as he felt for the small wad of greenbacks tucked inside the money belt beneath his vest. He had sold his saddle and rifle for a lot less than their worth, but he had figured it to be enough to get into a poker game. The rest would take care of itself. He winked at Lillie to let her know he wasn't finished, then started back across the room.

He had no problem finding a game. The three miners were a

friendly bunch who appeared tired of their own company and quickly offered him a chair. One of the miners who sat across from him was so caught up in asking Jack about his travels that he kept spitting tobacco on the floor instead of in the spittoon that was provided. Jack had no more dealt the cards when he saw the sorrowful-looking bartender march toward them, his thin face turning red clear to the bald area on his head. The bartender grabbed the closest spittoon and dropped it so hard that it bounced once and sloshed over a bit before resting next to the miner's mud-caked boot, then he stalked off.

The old miner didn't seem to take offense.

"Ely's got bad nerves," he confided solemnly, then smiled. "But he's the only feller I know that'll believe an outright lie when ya want to tell one."

"Why, that's the best kind of fellow to have around," Jack chuckled, grateful for the bartender's nerves; the miner's endless questions were starting to make him uneasy. His hand was called then and he peered over his cards, at ease again. "Well, boys, as my sainted Pa used to say, the safest bets are the ones you don't make." Jack laid his cards down, displaying his flush, and the men laughed amiably. They even laughed when he won the second hand—they cursed too, of course, but it was good-natured cursing.

"Where're you from?" the curious miner asked again, as the dove served them another round of drinks. Jack saw his friend kick him under the table to silence him, his eyes darting to the guns, and he smiled slightly.

"Oh, here and there," he replied softly, glancing back to the lady dealer again. She had kept his interest throughout the evening and he had found it more and more of a burden to keep his eyes from straying over to her table for a look. Not that he was interested in another go at faro—he preferred games where the odds were more in his favor, he thought, brushing the fattened bankroll in his vest. There was just something about her. . . .

"She a sport?" Jack asked finally, inclining his head toward Lillie. The old fellow glanced at Lillie then grunted and let loose a stream of tobacco, this time careful to aim it into the spittoon.

"Only when she wants to be," he replied disgustedly, as if she were a disgrace to her profession, but he immediately became contrite. "Most every feller in here's tried for her. Harm here oiled his hair and turned his paper collar twice in one week. I, myself, even offered to marry her," he sighed. "She's a challenge."

Jack raked in the third pot with a thoughtful expression on his face. He had always liked a challenge.

He smiled a bit as his eyes slid over to the lady dealer again, thinking Virginia City might just have more possibilities than he thought, after all.

There were only a few stragglers left in the saloon by the time Jack dealt the last card to Lillie: Ely, the bartender, the dove he'd seen earlier, and the fiddler. The fiddler, who had turned to song after drinking all night, had passed out in mid-chorus of "I Miss My Sainted Mother, Now that She's Dead and Gone to Heaven" and was still lying on the floor where he dropped. Ely swept around him as if he were a permanent fixture, while the dove called Mabel picked through the broken glass and clumps of mud for loose change or dust that had fallen from the miners' pockets.

Jack glanced at Lillie, who sat across the table from him. She had a distant look on her face, but he had seen a difference in her when she had won the first hand; she had looked almost like a young girl and had even laughed outright. As lonely as he had been, he almost wanted her to win just to see that expression again. Jack had a feeling she wanted it as well but for different reasons; she had already sent the bartender to her room twice for money and she had begun to look hesitant as he dealt them another round.

He himself hadn't drawn a bad card since they sat down together, and the relief to be back on familiar ground made him bold. He was sometimes shocked at his own thoughts, but the truth was he didn't relish another night sleeping on the ground—or the loss of good company.

"How 'bout we add to the stakes and make this interesting," he offered. "You win, you get the pot, naturally. But if *I* win, I get to spend the night in your room."

Mabel cackled loudly in the quiet of the room, but Ely looked almost sick with worry. "You want me to get your money, Lillie?" he asked, setting his broom down on the floor, but Lillie waved him off.

She had no intention of sending Ely up to her room again. She hadn't made do with old dresses and no jewelry just to see all of her money fall into the hands of a handsome stranger. Her money was her one hope of making a different life for herself. She studied her hand, then glanced across the table at Jack, who was grinning his challenge. She smiled herself, the heavy anticipation in the room biting into her boredom.

"Fine by me," she said finally, and Jack slid the hundred in gold dust to the center of the table and called her hand.

Lillie laid her hand on the table face up: four kings and an ace. She moved to take the pot, but the expression on Jack's face stopped her. He was looking at her with something like regret.

"Sorry, sugar," he said low and spread his own cards on the table. Her eyes froze on the four perfect aces, and the realization seeped in that she'd duped herself with a joker that had been a dangerous twin to the ace of spades.

"It was a good game, Lillie," Jack said, and she smiled.

"Not good enough. I must be going blind not to realize I laid down that cutter."

Lillie sat quiet, allowing the loss to settle in. Fate was a curious thing, she thought. She had figured if she were careful, she might avoid it. The last time she wasn't careful, fate had tricked her and her quick decision about a man had been a bad one.

Lillie studied Jack. He was a big man by most standards, dressed in the dark clothes of a gambler—a bit trail worn but cared for. He was handsome too, not the frail kind of handsome she'd seen in other gamblers, but strong. And there was something in his green eyes that made her think he had been alone too long. After all, he had ridden all of his winnings on the chance to stay the night with her. If that wasn't lonely, she didn't know what was.

"My room's upstairs," she said finally, then managed a smile. "But I guess you already know that." When her eyes met Jack's, she saw him hesitate and she drew her shoulders back and pushed away from the table.

"You won fair and square, Jack," she said, abruptly rising from her chair. "I may be a lot of things, but one thing I'm not is a poor loser."

As she climbed the stairs to her room, Jack following a short distance behind, Lillie glanced back toward the bar. She saw Ely standing in the center of the room, his face frozen in a part shocked, part sorrowful expression. The rag he was holding was dripping large drops of water on the floor. "You're gonna warp them boards," she said, smiling a bit to cheer him, but Ely just stood there like he hadn't heard a word she spoke.

Ely didn't know what to make of it. Although he was usually slow to talk, for the most part he had no problem with his opinions. But he couldn't seem to form one as he watched the stranger climb the stairs to Lillie's room.

It *had* given him a queer feeling, seeing how Lillie had just taken up with the fellow. But it still didn't help him on how he should approach the situation. Being short and skinny to the point of awkward had always provoked a shyness in him that made it hard to get his point across at first. Sometimes his nerves pushed him, but thinking of speaking to the man with the fancy guns and haunted eyes made his throat clog.

Ely suddenly felt weak but resisted the urge to take to his bed, as he usually did when aggravated. He had to think of Lillie.

Lillie was, after all, why the boys came to his place night after night. The very fact that he had found her had perked up his confidence amongst the fellows enough to carry on a conversation every once in awhile. The sudden thought that he might lose Lillie brought on such a wave of protectiveness that he figured to speak his mind in spite of the danger.

Hey, fella! Just you remember, Lillie ain't no sport. Not really. She's just trying to get by like the rest of us.

But he'd only thought it, not said it aloud, and a deep sense of loss that he couldn't explain filled him as he watched the door to Lillie's room close behind the stranger.

Jack glanced around the room. It wasn't much: a little cubicle just wide enough for the rough lumber bed, its shuck mattress and an old three-legged stool perched just beneath the window. Folks back east would have considered it hellish, but Jack had seen worse—heck, he had *lived* in worse. When he glanced up, he found Lillie watching him.

"You won a night in my room," she said quietly. "But just so you know, that's all you won."

The look in her eyes seemed so wounded that he thought better than to try to tease her. Truth was, he was pretty sure there would be *nothing more* long before he laid his last hand down. Just as sure as he was now that it didn't matter.

"I guess I'll take that spot on the floor if you think you can scare up a blanket or two," he said finally, grinning to cut the awkwardness between them. But in spite of his effort, she kept herself stiff as she plucked up the blanket folded at the end of her bed.

"If you knew the floor was all you won, why did you play?" Lillie asked, handing him a scratchy wool affair but keeping her distance, as if she still wasn't sure what to expect.

"I chanced it for the company," he said truthfully. "I don't know anyone who doesn't like a little company once in awhile."

Lillie looked at him funny for a long moment. "Well, one thing this town isn't short on is people," she said finally. "I guess we're all just *rich* that way."

The way she said it made Jack think maybe she understood what he was really saying better than what she was letting on. But instead of letting it go at that, he felt his curiosity start to get the better of him, wanting some kind of response from her that wasn't so businesslike. He didn't even know why he felt the need for it—maybe it was just to outrun the silence that had hounded him on the trail or maybe it was something else. He gave a sigh and sat down on the bed.

"You ever just miss hearin' someone else breathing when you're falling off to sleep?" he asked and saw her surprise as she went still for a moment. Just when he thought she was about to answer, she turned to the cracked piece of looking glass and began to let her hair down. Jack squirmed a bit. For some reason, it almost seemed too personal—her letting her hair down in front of him. But the real surprise came when she had wiped the last of the paint from her face and he was put back to see how young she looked, how out of place.

"Whatever brought you here, Lillie?" he asked suddenly, watching her in the reflection as a smile played bitter on her lips.

"Life," she answered simply and he saw in her eyes something akin to memories—or maybe regret. Jack understood that look, if he didn't any other. He did something that shocked him then: He reached out and pulled her down to sit next to him and he held her hand. She appeared shocked too, and they both fell silent for a bit.

"Simple word. But it ain't simple, is it?" Jack asked finally, wondering if he was just filling the silence again, but when he looked at Lillie there seemed to be a change in her.

"No." Lillie said, stealing a side glance at him as if to check if he was making fun. She sighed, then stood with a determined look on her face.

"Guess I ought to get some sleep. It'll be another long day tomorrow."

As he watched her climb into her bed, it took everything he had not to chuckle as she nervously turned down the patched cover and slipped primly underneath, fully clothed. He then spread out his own blanket, untying the holster strapped to his thigh but making sure his guns were in easy reach before he slipped his boots off.

Just as he tucked his hands under his head, Lillie leaned over to turn her lantern down. When their eyes met, her stare lingered and he saw the loneliness looming large as his own in her blue eyes. But she quickly turned the wick down and before either of them could think to say anything, the room was painted black.

In the dark, Jack wondered if maybe he imagined the look, and the feeling that seemed to come with it; as if something deep within the two of them had recognized each other in some way neither was able to understand just yet.

"Jack?" came Lillie's voice in the dark.

"Yeah?"

"I lied—I mean about company. I knew what you meant . . . I just . . . I haven't been around any real company in a long time," she said in a quiet voice and he smiled softly.

"Me either," he said just as quiet. "You know, ol' Ely says the room next door will be free tomorrow. Who knows? We might just end up bein' neighbors for awhile."

"Neighbors?" Lillie chuckled as if the thought tickled her and he joined her, glad to hear the humor in her voice again. "I guess stranger things have happened."

As silence filled the room again, Jack waited for his eyes to adjust to the dark, then he turned his head and watched the door. He would have gladly given the night's winnings if he could just pull

Lillie toward him and drift off to sleep against her warm skin and not think of anything for awhile, maybe just talk and talk until they both fell asleep. Talk so the silence couldn't haunt him.

He had been through it before, running from what haunted him; time and again, town after town, until his recollections were a tired blur of seedy rooms and faces without names. At least in towns the stretches of silence were shorter. But they still came, and with it his thoughts of his time on the wagon train with his family: hearing the cows bawling, the clack of their horns hitting against each other, wagons rumbling along, laughter, his two sisters picking wildflowers along the trail. Long days and shorter nights. In his mind's eye, he saw again his sister Callie's tear-streaked face when they buried first their pa, then their sister, Rose.

Rose. Good God, would he ever be able to wrestle the demon that put her tired little face before his eyes when he tried to go to sleep? Did he want to be free? Free of remembering Rose's hope for a new home, of his failure at giving her nothing but a pine box in a town that never knew her name? If not pain, what did he have left of her?

But he could only bear the pain for so long. So, he pushed it down again and let it be someone else's life for awhile, someone else's pain. Feeling took too much out of him, he thought; it was the doing that counted.

Only now, Jack thought wearily, there was one more thing to outrun. His letter to Callie hadn't been all truth, but he hadn't wanted her to worry. *What if the law does come for me before I can clear my name? What if, like that marshall, they don't believe I didn't rob that bank with Jude?* he wondered, the endless possibilities of what could happen rolling through his mind. *How did it ever come to this?* he wondered. *How did I end up here?*

Jack sighed and glanced up to where Lillie lay sleeping on her bed, listening to the steady rise and fall of her breathing. For the first time in a long while, he wished he knew her better, wished more than anything she was awake so he could ask her if she ever wondered the same about her own life.

Lillie sat on the little stool next to the window and gazed out. Mid-morning was about the only time she could tolerate the view. The lowered sun had a way of painting the gulch pretty; warm oranges and yellows gilded the clapboard buildings that sagged and leaned against each other and retouched the barren hillsides, scalped of every last tree. But like giving a sporting gal a coat to wear over her bloomers, it only lasted for a little while.

Like most good things.

Lillie bit her lip as she glanced over at Jack, who had finally found sleep, and she couldn't help wondering how long he'd be around. A gambler was what he'd called himself and said no more. But she'd sensed from the first that he was skirting trouble. Had been for awhile, from the look of it, she thought, studying the long, lean body sprawled out on the floor.

Still, there was something about him that made her want to give in to her loneliness in spite of the misgivings, made her want to know more about him. He had made her laugh. How long had it been since she'd laughed like that?

How did you end up here? she recalled him asking, and for just a moment it almost sounded like he'd cared about the answer. No one had ever asked her that question before. Of course, most men didn't talk much anyway.

And he had held her hand. That had been a shock, too. *You're a peculiar one, alright,* she thought. *But I'll keep my past to myself. It's about the only thing I have left that's mine alone.*

It seemed like another lifetime, her past. Her pa had been wrong, of course, to hit her ma like he did in front of everyone. But her ma's desertion the next morning along with another miner was more punishment than her pa could bear. Stripping away a man's pride can make them do fool-headed things they wouldn't normally do.

Leaving their claim in Colorado was his first mistake—getting the fever had been his last. By the time they finally made it to Virginia City, they were out of money and luck.

Lillie could see her pa as clear as if it were yesterday, trudging ahead of her through the large drifts of snow that had settled over the town, each step making him weaker. Still, up and down the gulch they had drifted. There were plenty who had offered to take Lillie in, but her pa's fevered eyes and flushed face scared folks into being cruel and greedy. "Got any money?" they'd ask, over and over. Her pa would pull his billfold out and open it up, frown at it being empty, then stick it back in his coat only to pull it out a few moments later as if the effort could produce the miraculous. Again and again, she watched him do that until it hurt too much to look. It was maybe a few hours later that he stopped abruptly in the center of the street and looked back at her. "Ain't nothin' free, Lillie," he said and fell down face first in the snow and died.

Not long after, she'd been led to being a kept woman—reluctantly maybe—but not blindly.

No family, no food, and a winter wind biting your backside tended to open a person's eyes. Morals, she'd learned, were only for those who could afford them.

"Morning," Jack said. Lillie felt the memories being brushed away by his voice as he came up behind her and she was grateful for it. Remembering sometimes made her feel scattered.

Jack seemed to study her hard for a moment, then he moved to the window. He had his trousers on, but his shirt was off and she noticed a graze wound on his side as he leaned and looked out, an odd, searching look on his face.

In spite of herself, she looked too, half expecting to see Jack studying some unsuspecting soul, but his eyes were fixed beyond the town, past the bare slopes of sage and cactus to somewhere in the distance. For some reason it made her uneasy—how quick he was to give all of his attention, then be drawn away just as fast. Like he was standing there but really gone.

"I sure hope there's more fish in the pond today," he murmured suddenly and she felt a rush of relief to be on familiar ground.

"It's Sunday," she answered, as if that explained it all. There was no such thing as a quiet Sunday in the gulch. Already, she could hear the stir of life: men's laughter, ripping and sawing of new buildings, the clatter of wagons, pounding stamps and dull booms of blasting that she'd come to know as well as her own heartbeat. Lillie glanced at Jack and was glad to see the fuss had caught his attention. "The boys will be packing the house for a game. They're rough as cobs, though. Think you're ready?"

"What say you introduce me to the fattest of the flock and I'll take it from there," Jack said, excitement building in his eyes.

"You looking for someone to clean you?"

"No, just to make it interesting. I can hardly tolerate boredom." Jack turned to her and grinned. "I promise you won't regret it, Lillie. I don't usually lose."

"We'll soon find out," Lillie sniffed, but she felt an odd tingle of excitement run through her anyway.

She even found herself enjoying watching the town come awake with him. Instead of wanting him to leave and let her alone—like she had with her customers at the tables—she felt herself wishing he could stay for a little while longer.

Of course, it wouldn't pay to trust so soon. She'd done that before. Frank Monroe had seemed like the sure, good-natured type at first, breezing into her life that first long winter when she'd been so scared. He'd been the one who taught her to deal—a joke really, until she got good. It wasn't long after that he'd turned mean. Lillie had allowed the meanness for a time because she thought being lonely was worse. It didn't take long though for her to change her mind.

Jack didn't seem like Frank. Elusive maybe, but not cruel. And he did have a way of talking of dreams so's a person might almost believe they'd come true, Lillie thought. And even if they didn't, she had the feeling that his way of chasing them would be a lot more fun than hers.

Some days just weren't what folks chalked them up to being, Ely thought, wiping a table that didn't need it, trying to appear casual as he glanced over at Lillie and the gambler who'd seated themselves close together.

The racket he'd created in the kitchen earlier had drawn them down, he knew. He wasn't usually so brash, banging pots and pans around like a woman, but he was curious—and maybe a bit put out. He'd thought Lillie was through with sporting after Frank; she had even agreed to quit when she got good at dealing. She *had* looked lonely lately. But laws, everyone *looked* lonely in the gulch.

Loneliness makes quick bedfellows, Mabel was forever chirping. Ely glanced over at the sport he'd recently acquired and she grinned mean, as if she knew what he was thinking. Mabel, who was only half-filled with laudanum, had enough curiosity left in her to prop up near the bar so she could watch, too—in spite of the dirty looks he'd given her.

"You're a sour one this morning," Lillie said suddenly and he practically dropped the plates of bacon and hard biscuits on their table. She looked too cheerful and flushed and Ely felt her words prick him. He was half in love with her even if she didn't know it.

"I'm usually not so sour, but my nerves are bad," Ely said defensively. "I think if I could just shoot someone I'd feel better." Life was chancy, anyway, he told himself. Still, he watched nervously for the gambler's reaction.

If Jack had understood his meaning, he didn't show it. The cautious look the gambler had most of the time was gone, and Ely thought he looked plain friendly, sitting there like he was with Lillie. Ely noticed he had shaved the shadow of a beard off his face.

"Ely, your nerves are always bad. And you can't shoot besides," Lillie said, looking at him curiously. But it was Jack's fleeting glance that made him testy again.

"If I was worked up enough I guess I could," Ely replied, like an old dog hanging onto a bone with his last tooth. But he could see the threats were no use, so he silently prayed the gambler would just leave and let them get back to their normal routine.

"Hey, Ely," Jack called suddenly, causing him to start a bit. "Lillie and I've been talkin' and I think we've come up with a pretty good plan to have us all sittin' pretty in no time. If you can spare that room you told me about?"

"Sure, Jack," Ely said cautiously. He turned his back to them then, avoiding his own reflection as he stared into the long mirror behind his bar, considering the gambler's offer. It *would* be nice to get some extra cash coming in, he thought. Besides, seeing the new spark in Lillie's eyes and the familiar way the gambler rested his arm on the back of her chair, he knew there was no sense hoping for things getting back to normal anytime soon.

If ever.

Virginia City,
Montana Territory
March 30, 1864

Mrs. Callie McGregor
Plumas City, California

Dear Callie,
Just finished reading your letter and knowing you like I do, I fig-
ured to drop you a line and let you know I've found a place to stay. See,
me and the owner of a saloon here have struck a deal. Ely (a fine fellow

too in spite of being a bit wispy) has decided that he can get more of a draw with a resident gambler. I took him up on it. Even if there was a room to be had—and there ain't—this place is pricey. Most shacks rent $20 to $30 a week and hotels $125 a week. It's a good thing I'm a gambler and not a miner; I'd never afford it here. I've made a few friends in the bargain, too. One friend (a lady dealer) is showing me the ropes. You might find it funny that the lady beat your ol' bro' down at the faro tables.

Underneath all the mud and muck, Virginia City is pretty much what I figured it to be. One thing it's not is quiet; ripping and sawing of new buildings, miners blasting, then drunk again for another night. If you close your eyes, you'd swear the sun never sets the way they carry on. Ely says it's a test of some kind. He says it's like God Himself took an old broom and swept us together to see what would happen. I told him God might not be too pleased, but I guess He won't get bored trying to fix it, either.

A town of schemers and seekers, that's for sure. Miners, gamblers, barkeeps, even the doves are all scrambling for their share. Makes me think it's a good thing for the West, Sis. I don't imagine half of us would survive the rules back East. I know I couldn't.

You asked what it feels like: the gambling, moving from town to town. Easiest way I can explain it is being free. There ain't no one counting on me out here, Callie. No one but me, and if I disappoint myself, well, that ain't so bad a pill to swallow. There are times I look around and think, "What are you looking for, Jack? And how are you going to know if you find it?" I think of Pa, too, and what a decent, hard-working man he was and how maybe he might've wished I was more like him. But I can't be what I'm not. If I've learned anything these past years, it's that.

One thing I'll tell you, Sis, I had the oddest feeling when I set eyes on these mountains out here, on this country and the sky that goes on past. It was like I knew, like I felt down deep somewhere that this land would make me.

Life can be funny, can't it? If I hadn't hooked up with that crook Jude, I'd never have come here. I guess you can plan all you want but that don't mean you'll end up where you figured.

'Course, if we knew the road ahead of time, who's to say we'd walk it?

Jack

P.S. And tell our buddy Stem to just keep looking out for you like he has. Tell him I ain't as green as he thinks. There's trouble in every mining town, sure. But that don't mean I aim to go and find it.

Two

*J*ack studied the men hunched around the poker table, feeling trouble brewing just beneath the surface. It had been his experience that the best way to know a man was to sit across a card table from him and what he saw in two of the three men didn't set well. Rumor was, they had blown in with a rough bunch from Salt Lake. *To look at them, though,* he thought, *you wouldn't expect much:* an older gent, with a tobacco-stained beard, kept his eyes on the door, and an angry, tow-head kid, fifteen if he was a day. They didn't appear to be much. But then, things weren't always as they first appeared.

The last two weeks of making the rounds with Lillie convinced him of that.

True to her word, she'd led them to his table. Miners mostly, taking their losses cheerfully, used to living by chance like they did. But the old guy and the kid weren't miners, and it was clear they didn't like losing. As a matter of fact, they seemed put out that *he* wasn't losing. Then there was the third man.

Jack watched the older man's angry eyes dart from him to the big black man dressed in a soldier's coat and an old slouch hat sitting across from them.

"I've played against sharps before. Ain't never played no Negro, though," Ned Wayne speculated, talking around a wad of tobacco as he surveyed the stack of chips in front of the black man. "This ain't no pebble toss. How do we know you got any money, boy?"

"I gots de money, massa, sho' as I's black," the man parroted sarcastically. Amused, Jack watched him as he leaned back in his chair and brought out a sizable bag of dust from beneath his jacket and set it on the table. His gaze never wavered from the two men. "See, the *old* master didn't need it where he was going."

Jack chuckled, studying the man with interest. Lillie hadn't told him much about him, except his name was Duel—and that he'd made enough smithing during the first rush to grubstake half the miners in the gulch. He recalled his first day in Virginia City, seeing him trudge past the auctioneer, quiet but strong.

"I think he's sassin' us, Pa," the younger of the two said, and Jack could see the boy was fairly trembling to start trouble. Jack didn't say a word but laid his pistol on the table within easy reach. The boy's eyes narrowed.

"I guess I should be scared, huh?" he sneered and Ned gave him an elbow to the ribs.

"Shesh, boy." He gave his son a sharp look, then focused on his hand. "I'll stay," he said finally, furrow between his brow. If Jack had liked the man, he would have advised him not to play poker. But he didn't. He hadn't missed the old timer's eyes shifting greedily to Duel's sack of dust on the table—or the prick of warning that ran up his neck.

The boy was nervous for some reason, pulling his top card off his hand and shoving it to the bottom, waiting for Jack to move. He did it over and over and with every pass, Jack caught the corner of each card. It wasn't long before he knew his hand. Although he prided himself on playing a square game more often than not, Jack figured he would never be too proud to take the edge if it was handed to him outright.

He gave the bet a hoist. Duel folded and Ned lost his bluff the second time around but the kid hung in. When Jack raised again, he felt the rush of winning closing in. He glanced briefly to the table where Lillie was busy dealing and when he looked back, he was caught by the steady gaze of coffee eyes that held a glint of humor. Duel raised a thick eyebrow. Jack grinned and laid his cards face up on the table.

"Sorry, boys," he said as all three stared at his flush in silence. Angry, the kid rose from the table and stalked over to the bar. Ned tossed his cards across the table.

"Third time he's cleaned me. It ain't natural," he declared and Duel chuckled, trying to ease the tension.

"Ain't nothin' *natural* about it," he said. "Ol' Lady Luck's chosen her beau is all." The black man's smile dimmed though, seeing the dislike spread across the older man's features—a look that said, *Know your place, boy.*

It was a look that Duel would never forget, even though it had been more than ten years since he'd made his way west. He'd survived by learning and escaping. The traveling preacher's wife had been first—boredom causing her to throw caution to the wind. It'd amused her how fast Duel had learned to write his own name—until he'd figured it was time to move on and left his signature as an IOU for the beans and bacon he'd taken with him. Then there was the trapper, more interested in a slave than a partner. But Duel had learned and once again moved on. They were little things that he'd learned. But all together, they'd taught him how to stay alive.

Now here he was in a card game gone wrong with two jaspers bent on trouble and a gambler with a reputation; word was Jack Wade's skill with cards fell second only to the way he handled a gun and that was as good as an open invite in the territory. The thought had no more come to mind when the kid started in.

"You ain't all that great, Wade," he called out. "I guess buffalo dung would look good if enough folks said it was. But it's still just *crap.*"

The silence that followed was jarred by the rough scrape of a chair dragging back across the floor.

"Live and let live's always been my motto, son," Jack said, rising slowly. "But now you've gone and made me doubt myself. You best get." A few of the regular customers chuckled, but most of the crowd began to scuttle for cover.

Duel saw the gambler smile, but he saw the muscle working under his jaw, too, and he knew if it came down to it, he'd back Wade. There was something about him—the solid way he squared off against a threat, as if he'd been through more than his share and figured to win the next time around. Something that Duel understood all too well.

The kid didn't see it that way, though. His face was tight with fear, but he'd gone too far to back down in front of the crowd. "I ain't listenin' to no piece of dung cheat," he declared. Ned Wayne cackled and the sound seemed to bolster the boy's resolve and he puffed up like a bandy rooster.

Before the kid's gun was halfway out of the frayed waistband of his trousers, Jack and Duel were on their feet with both holsters cleared. Jack's shot found its mark first, knocking the six-shooter from the kid's grip. As the kid howled in agony, Duel swung around and drew on Ned Wayne, who dropped his guns to the floor with a look of pure hatred.

Acrid smoke filled the room as the boy made to rise and to Jack's amazement, Duel smoothly flipped his pistol over and knocked the kid square on the skull with the butt of it. As the kid slumped to the floor, Ned joined him, raising his shaking hands over his head.

"Think maybe we ought to just kill them?" Jack asked, as if remarking on the weather. He saw a smile for the first time spread across Duel's face.

"I can't rightly see killing a man for being an aggravation. I'd have to kill half this town," Duel said casually. " 'Course, we could just kill the kid."

"I'm for the Negro's idea," Ned piped up, his voice muffled against the floorboards. "He's a right smart feller. Boy ain't been nothin' but a trial, anyhow."

"You're a piece of work, ain't you, Ned?" Jack said, and Duel nudged him as the kid had chosen that moment to come to. As he sat up and felt the blood on his powder-burned hand, his face went milky white. "I ain't going to forget you, nigger," he said, hatred in his voice. Then he glanced at Jack. "You neither."

"You'd do best not to," Jack replied calmly, but the threat was there just beneath the surface. "Unless you and your *pa* here want to try your hand, you'll both hightail it out of here."

Jack watched the two hesitate briefly, weighing their chances, and his smile went hard. "I'll lay odds you'd lose." Ned quickly helped the boy to his feet, cuffing him before he pushed him on through the crowd.

"That's about as rough a pair as I ever saw," Jack said, shaking his head.

"Welcome to Virginia City," Duel offered, his tone wry. He took the hand Jack offered him, his grip strong but friendly. When their eyes met, Jack felt an odd kind of kinship forge between him and the big man.

"You know, I didn't trust either of those jaybirds when I first laid eyes on them. But the kid, I guess I figured he was too wet behind the ears to cause much trouble," Jack confided, a bit amused at himself. And he'd believed himself a sharp judge of character. If the old trailboss Stem could've seen him, he would've laughed—either that or brained him with his wooden leg. Duel went easy enough on him, though.

"Young ain't always innocent," he said with a shrug of his buffalo shoulders. "I wouldn't take the old fellow lightly either. Their kind don't cotton to bein' put down. It ain't over is all I'll say." Duel shook his head. "Your kind of luck don't leave much room for friends, does it?"

"Know any luck that does?" Jack returned. They shared a knowing kind of grin; men that knew too much bad luck made folks uneasy, but too much good just made them mad.

Duel chuckled. "Guess I don't," he said. He made to go then but paused at the door of the saloon. As if on impulse, he turned back to Jack and reached inside his jacket, producing a frayed playing card that he held out as an offering.

"What's this?" Jack asked, taking the card.

Duel smiled slightly. "A reminder," he said. "Only way I've gotten through life is to remember mostly the joke'll be on me."

Jack turned the card over in his hands as Duel walked away. A slow grin appeared on his face as he carefully tucked the joker with its dog-eared edges in the pocket of his vest. Watching the mammoth figure disappear into the crowds along the street, he felt a tug of interest. The fellow was a curiosity. A loner like him—he'd gathered that much. Close up, he had realized them to be about the same age, but Jack felt younger for some reason, as if Duel knew things he didn't. *An old soul,* his mama would have called him.

Jack sat back down at the table, flexing his fingers to ease the tension the ruckus had caused. His hands paused for a moment over the stack of cards as he glanced toward the door of the saloon, thinking of the man who had backed him up without question. *Everyone* had a story, Jack thought. He just couldn't help but wonder what Duel's was. . . .

Duel Harper stopped at the end of the boardwalk and glanced back at the Pair-O-Dice. It was a strange feeling he'd had around Jack Wade. Rare was the man who could understand you without a word spoken, he thought. But it was more than that, more than the feeling that only chance had brought them together. Much like the same feeling he'd had when he had met his wife, Celie. *"We're going*

to teach each other 'bout life," he remembered promising her that day. *"Blind leading the blind,"* Celie had laughed.

But they *had* taught each other so much.

Duel glanced at the sun fading behind the mountains and started off again. He always liked to get his fire going before it got too dark. Ever since he'd lost his Celie, he made it a point to stay outdoors, their little cabin being too quiet, too empty.

Lately, being there had become a burden. Even a tussle like the one at the Pair-O-Dice was a welcome change in comparison.

Maybe he and the gambler did have a reason to be thrown together, Duel thought, feeling a new spring to his step as he climbed into his rig and headed his team down the stretch of road that would take him to the darkened cabin perched in the hills.

Or maybe he was just tired of being alone.

"Bringin' trouble right in my front door is what he's doin'," Ely griped as he drew up alongside Lillie's table. "Live by the gun, die by the gun is what I always say." Lillie could see he was trying to appear pious, table rag draped over his arm but the rag was dirty. As far as she was concerned, you couldn't be too pious when you weren't lavish with the soap.

"You ain't never said nothin' of the kind," Lillie scolded over her shoulder as she dealt, worry making her snappish. The next card she drew was the hock. She pulled the deck from the case box , shuffling as she gazed through the crowd and smoke to the poker table where Jack was playing. She had a bad feeling about the men he and Duel had stood up against—especially Ned Wayne. There was something familiar about him she couldn't shake. Lillie sighed as Ely walked off to join the crowd of spectators milling around Jack's table. She knew Ely was worried, too. In spite of what he said, she'd seen him develop a grudging kind of friendship with Jack over the weeks. Jack had charmed him same as her. Same as everyone for that matter.

Jack was always good for a show; the fast way his hands moved over a pack, the shuffle that seemed more like art. An appreciative murmur went up and Lillie saw Jack shake with two fellows who had thrown in their hands. The last fellow left at the table remained sitting. It was clear he'd lost a pile. Lillie had seen the look of shock many times. The miner sat stock-still for a bit, looked down at his cards again, then to Jack.

"Jack, if you lend me ten, I'll go to the claim and stay there till I get some sense," he said finally, and the crowd tittered.

"Well, if you're goin' to stay there that long, Harm, I'd best give ya twenty," Jack ribbed, sliding some half eagles across the table. Harm laughed outright along with the rest of the boys.

Lillie couldn't help smiling. Jack was fast becoming a favorite. Which was why she had yet to figure out why he hadn't gone for the big gaming houses like Burch and Clark or The Mammoth, where fortunes were won and lost regular. Few men had the natural-born talent he did; his way of reading a face before most could blink or the good-old-boy charm that usually took the sting out of his winning.

Usually, she thought. Life had been about as good as she could ask for except for the constant worry that Jack would one night push his luck too far.

As if reading her thoughts, their eyes met briefly across the room, Jack's saying, *Don't worry,* that grin of his nearly taking her breath away. Then, as always, he drew his attention back to the game.

But even a moment was something, she convinced herself. Most men she knew couldn't look a woman straight in the eye at all—as if they avoided looking, then they could avoid what they'd done later on when they went home and prayed over their beans and smiled across the table at their women thick with child.

Jack was different alright. Eyes that always searched and a hungry look that seemed to speak of a past that wouldn't stay buried and a future just beyond his reach.

Lillie knew all about that kind of hunger.

She chanced a look over at Mabel, the sport Ely had recently rescued from a hog ranch along the Bozeman. Mabel with her sparse yellow hair and the dose of too much rouge and powder that failed to hide the sagging lines of her face . . . and those eyes glossed over by laudanum.

Mabel, who had just celebrated her twenty-first birthday.

She had a feeling Mabel didn't care much for her, even though all Lillie felt for her was pity—that and a thread of fear for what she herself might become unless something changed.

It was maybe a few hours later that she watched as Jack raked in his winnings. She saw him look up and when he found her watching from across the room, he grinned easily. She hoped for his sake as well as hers there would be no more trouble. *Just let everything turn out right,* she silently prayed. *Just this once, God.*

Lillie felt suddenly uneasy about asking. She hadn't prayed since she was a child. She had to wonder if He even listened to people like her.

"Looks like I'll be stayin' here awhile, Lillie," Jack called out. When the men burst into a round of raucous laughter, Lillie just smiled, a thoughtful expression on her face.

Virginia City,
Montana Territory
April 18, 1864

Mrs. Callie McGregor
Plumas City, California

Dear Callie,
Well, I tell you, it sure was a surprise getting Mama's Bible in the mail. I don't mind admitting I felt a bit like a kid with his hand caught in the candy jar when I unwrapped the Good Book while standing smack in the middle of the saloon. Made me wonder if someone wasn't

trying to tell me something. I do thank you, even though I'm apt to think it would've been in better hands had you kept it. An old saddle-tramp like me has a hard time holding on to things, let alone something as important as that.

In any case, all is well here, except for a minor run-in I had with some jug-head kid who tried to get the better of me a few days back. I might've done some things I ain't proud of, but dirty talking another man ain't one of them. It appears I've been dealt a reputation of sorts—not a good thing in a town where every wrathy jaybird with a pistol is looking to make a name for himself. Ely says he's never seen a fellow as fast with a gun—but I ain't sure he meant it as good. He also claims the whole mess has "dimmed his cheerful nature." I kind of think he enjoyed the show—even if he did stay ducked down behind his bar most of the time. Truth is, if I hadn't had the help of a big colored fella by the name of Duel, it might not have turned out so good.

I think you would like Duel, Callie. He's got a different turn—tough but kind—and a peace about him I admit I envy. I've heard he likes to stay outdoors for all but gambling—rain or shine. Some say he's odd, that they've seen him kneel in the high grass just to brush his hands through it and when it rains, he tilts his head back and drinks the water, right from the sky. But I think I understand. He's tasting free-dom.

Most of all, I think he ain't afraid to stand up for what's right and that's more than I can say for some around here. The only code most of these fellows follow is to come out of it alive any way they can. I guess I'm just lucky, Sis. Remember what Grandma Wade used to say? "The Lord gave Jack a lot of luck on account of the messes he gets into." Then she'd slap me on the back so hard it'd sting. Remember? Hard enough to get your attention, but not so hard you'd forget she cared. I sure miss that old gal.

And don't ever think I don't miss you, Callie. Who else knows me like you—and is fool enough to bother anyway?

Jack

P.S. In case you think I forgot your question—I didn't. The lady dealer's name is Lillie. A little slip of a thing, too, but sharp as a tack when it comes to dealing. She's seen hard times, Sis, like the rest of us, maybe done things in some folks' eyes that ain't proper but I hope you won't judge her too harshly. I don't. I consider her a friend.

Virginia City,
Montana Territory
May 8, 1864

Mrs. Callie McGregor
Plumas City, California

Dear Callie,

You say you wonder what it would be like being a lady dealer. If it weren't so rough, I'd have you come for a visit and have Lillie show you. Wouldn't that be a kick? There are plenty of other working ladies here. There's a lady who shoes for Bart the blacksmith and another who tends the stage station. I guess it's no shock for you to hear of wives working side by side on a claim, skirts hiked and shoveling tailings. These gals are a hardy breed.

They don't take no guff, neither. I will tell you what happened just today.

You see, there's a big horse race near every Sunday here. Monte, who owns the livery, holds them on the top of a ridge about three miles from town on this flat between the Madison and Stinkingwater (it's the only place that ain't been dug up). The race was a fine one—I ended up with a tidy sum. But the miners weren't satisfied and decided to hold some races of their own between each other.

Well, Ely caught the fever somewhere along the second race and when some of the miners proposed a race between man and mule, Ely stepped up. I can't recall if I told you before, but Ely is a small man. But these fellows will bet on anything. Anyway, the mule was in a froth but was still the favorite until the final push, then Ely went and upset the odds by winning—even though he collapsed at the finish line. The shock came when Mabel, who works for Ely, pushed through the crowd.

"Ely, if you're figuring suicide," she said, hands on her hips, "you ought to have just drank yerself t'death in town. It's easier on the joints." Whose "joints" I ain't sure, for the next thing we knew, the fair Mabel had helped ol' Ely up and was practically carrying him back to town herself.

"Just like a woman," I said then, and Lillie gives me a look and says, "To have to pick up the slack." Duel thinks the remark is the funniest he has ever heard and repeats it even though I told him to quit.

Women ain't so easy to figure. But I guess you already knew that.

Jack

P.S. Speaking of women, tell Little Rose happy birthday for me. The ring I'm sending for her is made of Virginia City gold—or at least that's what the fellow I won it off said. Oh, and no, I don't mind your "harping" as you put it—it just seems like old times—but I do mind your worrying. If I ain't, why should you?

Three

*J*ack hated to worry. Especially on such a fine day, he thought, looking out across the high country. The sun had burned off most of the snow from a sudden squall and everything looked sharpened; the deep browns and greens of the wet land seeming blanketed by the wide clear blue of the sky. *"Mother nature is as fickle as the only gal at a dance in the spring,"* Duel had told him, grinning as they rode out. *"But when she dances, she cuts a rug."* Jack smiled. Duel was right. Once you got out of the gulch, past the treeless, rooted-up heaps of earth, there was some fine scenery: long valleys and mountains bristled with trees and caps of snow. Truth was, most *everything* had been fine as not; he had made a tidy sum at the tables— enough to send Callie and Quinn some extra for the new baby on the way—and he couldn't ask for a better gal than Lillie. Still, there had been that nagging feeling the past few days that he always got when things got too good: Something bad was bound to come up.

The worry over wounding that marshall weighed heaviest on him lately. He couldn't count the times he'd surveyed the posters while standing in line at the post office or how many nights he'd lain awake, staring at the door. Jack studied the figure of Duel as he rode ahead on his sorrel. There was something about Duel that reminded him a bit of his pa; honorable and good, the kind of man you could trust, he thought. He spurred Big Black into a quick lope to catch up to him.

"Got something I'd like to run by you, Duel," Jack said, reining up alongside his friend.

"Just so it ain't cards or women. I think you've pretty well sewed up that area," Duel said, chuckling. "Pick up the slack," he chuckled again, shaking his head as they rode along. He enjoyed ribbing Jack to no end about what Lillie had said, and most of the time Jack went along with it. Duel had a way of making him want to laugh, with those eyes of his, sometimes deep with seriousness, sometimes just a smile at the edges. Today they were brimming with laughter. Jack attempted a smile, but the effort was difficult and Duel must have noticed, for he steered his horse closer to Jack's, a look of concern coming over his face. "That serious?"

" 'Law's looking for me over in Colorado," Jack announced abruptly. He then dismounted without looking back. As he heard Duel's horse come to a halt, he gazed toward the mountains and the wide sky above, then lit his Hilt's Best and drew on it before going on. "I was ridin' with a fellow who was a pretty hard case, I guess. Didn't know it at the time. Leastways, not until the law appeared. I guess the marshall figured I was in on whatever he'd done." Jack looked back at Duel, his smile wry. "He didn't exactly take the time to ask."

"The law ain't always what it's cracked up to be," Duel said as he dismounted. "Ain't much in the way of it here, anyway. I guess you couldn't have picked a better place to come to. More'n half this town settled here to escape one thing or the other, be it the war, the law, or maybe just a bad-tempered wife." Duel smiled. " 'Sides, Lady Luck's takin' a shine to you here. Must mean you're to stay."

Jack heard the hopeful note in Duel's voice and he was cheered by it. Maybe he could stay. He thought it odd that Duel didn't ask if he'd killed the marshall but seemed to just assume he hadn't. *A true friend,* he thought. His last true friend had been Stem and that was a lifetime ago. How many towns and faces had he been through without that feeling? The mountains seemed to bring out friendship like nowhere else, Jack thought. Far from the opinions and rules back east, folks were free to be who they really were and feelings tended to run truer because of it. Jack thought of Lillie. In some ways, she was more than a friend. But she was a woman, too, and women counted on things men didn't. Jack wasn't sure he had it in him to give—or how long he'd be able to stick around if he could. The whole thing made him feel like he was on tenterhooks: He knew Lillie deserved better than that but the selfish part of him didn't want to give her up.

"Speaking of ladies, Miss Lillie know any of this?" Duel asked almost as if he'd read Jack's thoughts.

"No, I ain't told her," he answered warily. "Figured it best if she didn't know too much in case I have to take off and someone comes around wantin' answers." Jack hesitated a moment, looking at Duel. "Lillie's a fine gal, but I ain't going to make promises I can't keep."

"Good thing," Duel said finally. They both mounted up then, turning their horses back toward town. "Women's got real long recall on things like that."

Shabby. It was the first word that came to Lillie's mind when she glanced around Jack's room lit by the hazy afternoon sun. In spite of the throbbing in her back and arms from a long night of dealing, she was determined to spiffy the place up. Everything seemed ready to fall apart. Even the crates Ely had scrounged up and fashioned into a kind of a chest appeared wobbly as she poured water into the bowl and set the pitcher back. *Funny that I would even worry over what his room is like,* she thought, wringing out the rag she used to wipe down the dusty furniture. But she did. For some reason she wanted Jack to feel comfortable. She knew she hadn't ever really been comfortable living at Ely's. Maybe she had just gotten used to it—like she had the never-ending noise and the closed-in smells of unwashed bodies and whiskey fumes, the stale smell of tobacco smoke that stayed in spite of Ely burning all the sweet-grass he could find.

Something's changed, Lillie thought. *I don't want to just go along with the way things are anymore. I want it to be different.* She didn't know why it mattered suddenly, other than the thought had come to her that morning after Jack and Duel had ridden out to the mountain country beyond the gulch. Seeing Jack ride away on that large black horse of his had started her thinking. The horse was the largest she'd ever seen and fine looking. It had occurred to Lillie then that maybe Jack might like nice things around, that he might be used to it. The way he was forever scribbling letters to that sister of his said something. Only good family bothered writing each other.

She glanced at the Bible he had set on one of the crates and Lillie suddenly felt uneasy. Family wasn't something she knew much about. But she had begun to think it might be nice to be a part of one. She thought of the night her mother had left without so much as a good-bye, just packed up and took off with some miner. Of her pa dying. Lillie shook off the unwelcome thoughts and looked about the room again. The shirt Jack had tossed on the floor was all that was left of the mess and she scooped it up, holding it to her. It smelled of Jack and she kept it to her nose for a moment, feeling something like longing stir within her.

Don't, her mind told her. Lillie noticed the sun slanting low through the window and hurried to place the little doilies she'd bought off a peddler about the room, topping one with a tin cup full of wildflowers. Jack would be coming back soon for another round at the tables; he had been winning—and big—over the past few weeks. Her cut hadn't been so bad, either.

She stepped back to admire her handiwork and she couldn't help wondering what Jack would think of the room. She felt a bit like a kid at Christmas. It wasn't long before the familiar sound of boots hitting the stairs came and she took a last peek around the room, quickly turning the chipped side of the bowl and pitcher around to the back just as the door swung open. Jack let out a whistle as he took in the change, and she tried to smile, a bit surprised at the nervous jitter in her stomach.

"Why, I'd say you've been busy," he observed.

He took his hat off and raked a hand through the dark shank of hair that curled up at his collar, looking at her from beneath thick, dark lashes with those green eyes that turned down at the corners like half-moons. For just a moment he appeared to hesitate as he looked about the room again. She might have imagined it, though, for when their eyes met again, he seemed like he didn't have a care in the world and tossed his hat on the bed.

"Real homey. You goin' human on me, Lillie?" He grinned, the kind of slow grin that took her will and sank it in the palm of his hand. It was always that way with him, she thought. She would have it in her head how things would be, then Jack would turn it, teetering her between the urge of wanting to hug his neck one minute and wring it the next.

"What would you know about bein' human?" Lillie retorted. She started to turn away but Jack caught her arm and pulled her down next to him. He laughed and tugged at the pins in her hair and she slapped his hands away. It had been this way between them over the past few weeks, laughing and teasing and somehow with it, he had gotten under her skin.

"Aw, Lillie, don't get so het up. I was only funnin' you."

"It ain't like it's a house or somethin'," she said calmer, more to herself than to Jack. "Fixin' up this old room ain't nothin' special." Lillie glanced at him as he twirled a long curl that had fallen loose around his finger. His face suddenly turned more thoughtful. She felt her heart twist, knowing deep down that he was about to kiss her.

"Maybe not," he said quietly. "But you are."

He leaned over and kissed her softly, so softly and tenderly that it nearly startled her to tears. The rare show of real feeling warmed her, and she tried to imagine what might have provoked it. Lillie thought if she were granted any wish right then it would have been to know that.

Jack seemed to have read her thoughts as he finally pulled away. He smiled again, but this time it was the smile he gave when he sat at the tables. She saw his eyes go distant, hooded, and she knew as he leaned in to kiss her again that at least for now, he wasn't going to give her the opportunity to find out.

"Concentrate, Lillie," Jack said, smoke from the cheroot trailing from his lips. A large blast from the mines rumbled the ground beneath them and shook the table a bit but Lillie remained mute, studying her hand as Jack smiled inwardly. Her poker face was getting better but she still had a *tell;* the dimple that appeared when she bit the inside of her cheek usually marked a good hand if he wasn't mistaken.

"I guess you thought you had me," Lillie said, laying the flush face up on the table with the flourish of a born gambler. Jack laughed.

"Maybe next time you won't be so stingy with the ante."

"I ain't stingy, just careful," she said pertly, her face flushed from winning. "Do you want to talk or play another hand?"

Her sass pleased Jack; she appeared sure of herself, brighter when she won a fair pot of her own. Sometimes he had seen her look lost, and although he pretended not to notice, he understood why. And it made him think twice about anything other than stealing a kiss or two. Jack leaned back in his chair and studied Lillie a bit as she dealt them another round. Lillie caught his eye, swiping a stray curl from her forehead. She grinned and Jack felt something in him soften.

Sometimes she was just like a kid, wanting to please, Jack thought. Other times she was full of opinion and stubborn to boot. But she was *real*—more than any schoolmarm, dealer, or two-bit dove he'd ever come across. And she had made it easy for him to stay. He had endured Virginia City longer than anywhere since leaving the wagon train because of their time together being so pleasant.

Lillie laid her cards down once again: four deuces to his pair. He hadn't intended on her winning the second hand, but it was his own fault for not paying attention.

"I think this is somethin' I could get good at," Lillie laughed as Jack took a long look at her. There was something in the way she said it that had called up memories of Callie and a long-ago night on the trail when they had shared a game.

"Not if I can help it," he said, acting sour. Lillie came to his side, putting her arms around his neck as she planted a kiss on his nose.

"Well, that's one way to take the sting out," he sallied with a slow grin. " 'Course, I don't think I'll try it. The fellows might not appreciate my efforts."

They both laughed and the sound caught Ely off guard. It sounded so free and genuine that he glanced up from the piece of Brussels carpeting he'd pulled out from under the scales, bringing his inspection for gold flakes in the deep nap to a halt. He saw Lillie and Jack grin at each other like fools, and in spite of a brief twinge, he couldn't help smiling himself. He had an affection for Lillie: brother, protector, wishful lover. Whatever it was, he had hopes for her.

Ely glanced to where Mabel perched and saw that she had been watching, too. Her lips were pursed in thought and when she found Ely studying her, she appeared to hesitate. "Gonna be hard on that girl when the fairy tale ends," she said in explanation, but there wasn't any rancor in her voice. Since Mabel had quit taking laudanum and gotten over the shakes, she wasn't so mean anymore and she didn't look nearly as used up as she once did, he thought. But she was often guarded like a stray dog that had been kicked too often.

"Aw, you oughten be so full of gloom, Mabel," he said. He was through wishing them ill. His last effort at trying to impress Lillie had been at the race when he had wound up with Mabel carting him off. What was the point? Ely sidled himself next to Mabel as he poured her a small drink—just enough to steady her hands—and she smiled gratefully.

Jack had shuffled and was tossing cards when Ely eyed him again. Ely had recently decided he liked Jack. Business seemed better with him around—safer too—especially when that Negro friend of his showed up. They both had reputations as pistolmen and most of the boys decided not to try them. There was something to be said for reputations, Ely thought. He hadn't had a nerve spell to speak of in nearly two weeks.

Mabel did have a point, though; gamblers were gamblers, after all. He had seen enough of them himself to know they didn't stay put long and some gals could take a man's leaving real hard. Alder Rose was one of those. She walked the gulch every night, same dress on two years running, the rose her beau had left her tucked behind one ear. The actual rose had crumbled after a few months, but she had made one of silk that was sturdier to the elements.

Talk was the fellow had left her after hearing rumor of a strike up north and that he didn't cotton to excess baggage.

Ely stared hard at Jack, as if he might be able to figure out his intentions. Nothing came of the effort, so he was left to wonder what it would be that would cause the gambler to pull up stakes and leave. And he worried what would become of Lillie when he did.

She looked like Rose, maybe a bit older, but even in the crowded smoky haze of the room Jack couldn't help see the resemblance to his baby sister who had died while on the wagon train. Of course, Rose hadn't ever had cotton sack for a dress, he thought, but there was that dark hair with a bit of red and something about her eyes and the thoughtful way they appeared to look at things. She cleared her throat once, but the miners were playing "fly-lu" at the bar, laying bets for which lump of sugar the fly would land on first. They were so intent on the game that none of them noticed her standing there as she hitched the baby up on her hip and looked around the room. When her eyes met his, though, Jack realized it was more than the fact she looked like Rose; there was a cold stir low in his belly and the little hairs on his neck raised up like they always did when danger was near.

Jack frowned at the notion and forced himself to study his hand. He knew he was being foolish and he had a poor hand besides, but it seemed better to study on it than the alternative. He stalled as long as he could but after the two miners he and Duel were playing had folded, he had no choice but to follow.

"Well, that's a first," Duel said, shocked to be raking in the pot for once. "You losin' your touch?" Jack's eyes flicked over Duel's shoulder for only a moment, and he saw that Lillie had abandoned the faro table and was talking in earnest to the girl. Something in his expression caused Duel to turn around and glance toward the bar.

"Someone you know?" Duel asked when he turned back around. He seemed to take the kid's appearance as natural so Jack just shrugged.

"Puts me to mind of someone I once knew," he answered but said no more. But the strange feeling stayed, making it hard for him to concentrate; his hands were clumsy on the deck and he wondered briefly if it was an omen of some kind. Lillie then appeared at the table, looking worried.

"That kid's in a bad fix," she said, looking between Jack and Duel. "She says her pa went off to deliver a team or somethin' and ain't come back. She's done run out of the milk tins her pa left for the babe two days back."

"What about takin' up a collection?" Duel asked.

"Well, that'd be fine if there was milk to be bought," she said with a sigh. "Mail ain't the only thing runnin' behind with the weather like it's been." Lillie glanced at Jack, who had remained silent, and saw that his usual grin was gone and covered by a look of wariness. His wariness shocked her a bit; Jack was known to be a soft touch for those down on their luck. She'd seen him not be able to eat a lick of food until he returned a diamond necklace to a lady after her husband lost it in a game. Whenever he heard of a miner who'd gotten injured or lost his job, he was always the first to tuck money in an envelope and send it off.

"I figure if we all put our heads together we might be able to come up with a plan to help this kid," she said, still watching Jack. She saw him squirm in his chair a bit, as if he felt her eyes on him.

"Well, what is there to do?" Jack asked finally, not bothering to look at her directly. Lillie felt her frustration rise. For reasons she couldn't figure, Jack could act almost *too* careless at times, as if he worked hard at not caring for some reason.

It was Duel who finally rose from his chair and walked slowly to the center of the room. The men turned their heads his way, his size alone commanding their attention.

"Ain't none of us strangers to hunger pains," Duel said to all those in the room. "But most of us got that way by choice. Ain't a man alive that'd leave a dig that's showed glitter." Many of the miners nodded. Some laughed, but it was a hollow laugh of knowing the price. Duel's eyes traveled slow to the little girl, to the way she held her little sister to her chest as if to protect her. In the silence of the room, the baby's weak, mewling cries jarred even the hardest of hearts. "I don't guess a little one would understand it, though."

Lillie was pleased to see it took hardly any time at all after Duel's simple speech before a wary Jack, along with the rest of the sour little group, had come up with a plan.

Virginia City,
Montana Territory
May 20, 1864

Mrs. Callie McGregor
Plumas City, California

Dear Callie,

You'd think a saloon would be the last place for a kid to show up in. I did, until a few days back. I'd just sat down to a game with Duel and some fellows when here this kid shows up at Ely's with a baby on her hip. She tells us her pa left a few days back to deliver a team of mules he'd sold and she'd run out of milk for the babe. She'd appreciate the help, but no charity. "Name's Nell," she says. "If you're needin' work to be done, I'm for the job." I guess it would've been funny if it weren't so sad.

Some people have no business coming out here—or bringing their kids, either. Lillie says it happens a lot; folks getting so crazy about gold that they forget about their kids or wives. She says back in December three little girls came to town begging for food, dressed in nothing but slips. She remembered them because they had names like birds: Canary, the oldest (she thinks her name was Martha or Mary Jane), wasn't more than twelve and Lillie said she wouldn't ever forget her because she looked old already. I guess that's why this one upset her and made her want to do something. I admit I was a bit edgy—the kid showing up like that brought back memories I'd thought buried, if you know what I mean, and gave me a bad feeling in my gut. I know it sounds crazy, but all I could think to do was give the kid money and hurry her on out. But it wasn't that easy since there ain't no milk in town to be bought.

Lillie shamed us into action—she and Duel. You would've laughed if you saw us pacing the saloon, trying to figure out where to get the baby some milk. Then someone—I can't remember who—recalled a range cow that likes to wander around just outside town. I ended up chasing that poor cow clear up one hill and down another, everyone laughing like drunks when I finally hog-tied her. And all I got was a pint of thin milk for my effort, too. Tonight Ely told us he got a hold of a fellow who has promised to bring some store-bought back from Salt Lake.

Which is just as well, since every time that poor cow spots me now, her tail goes up in the air and she runs like heck for the woods.

Jack

P.S. I guess you'd say I shouldn't be so standoffish, but I've had a queer feeling since that kid came in the door—like I'm being led to trouble. Maybe because she looked like our Rose. The past ain't that easy a package to lay away, is it, Sis?

Four

Lillie wasn't sure why she agreed to ride out with Jack. Maybe because he had seemed so *haunted* lately. But something in him seemed to settle after one of his rides—though it was beyond her how. There was always something about the wide open spaces that made her think of her past, and the helpless feeling that came along with it unnerved her. Town, with all its madness, had become a security to her, a wall of sorts that was always there to hold back her fear of loneliness.

It was odd how you could be so scared of one thing until another event forces you to stare it right in the face, she thought, glancing over at Jack as they let their horses foot aimlessly over the wrinkles and rolling hills that led out of town. Jack's bouts of silence and the lone rides out of town since the day the girl appeared at the door of the saloon had made her want to get him away from it all and get them back on solid ground . . . somehow. Then he had gone and put the chance in her lap early that morning, waking her by pounding on her door until she answered and greeting her with one of those smiles of his, telling her to dress warmly.

While most gamblers preferred to sleep until noon because of the late nights they kept, Jack was always up shortly after morning dawned. *You can take the boy off the farm, Lillie,* he'd told her once, grinning, *but derned if them hours ain't still in my blood.*

Lillie pulled the stiff overcoat Ely had loaned her close to her body, wishing the wind would settle. Truth was, she knew Jack had taken to craving his rides out in the countryside those first hours of morning like other men might crave a good meal or cigar. She watched the land tug at him over and over as he stood at her window, like some kid doggedly yanking on his sleeve for attention until he gave in.

Now that she was here with him, she saw why; the restlessness in Jack eased as he stared at what seemed a particular point near the mountains—as if he'd drawn a bit closer to that place he searched for. A place that seemed real enough that she found herself looking, too. When Jack caught her eye, he sidled his horse close to hers.

"I swear, Lillie, if they moved the town out here, I think half the fellows would sober just for this view," he said, smiling that big easy smile of his.

"Might be bad for business," she teased and Jack laughed. Lillie felt her heart ache with gladness just to hear him laugh again. Somewhere along the way she'd fallen for him. It was the little things he'd done that caused it: brushing her hair back from her forehead and kissing it, hugging her close to him when he won a game. She felt so safe with him at those times. Lillie wondered, though, if he even knew he was doing it.

Lillie drew in a deep breath and smiled anyway as she let her horse fall in step next to Jack's. "God does put on a good show when He's in the mood though, doesn't He?" she said and saw a change come over Jack's face, as if he'd been woken out of a good dream and she felt bad she'd somehow spoiled it.

"When He's got a mind to," Jack said, suddenly quiet.

Lillie tried to figure out if it was anger that she saw in Jack's eyes. She almost asked him but then thought better of it. Maybe Jack had a good reason to feel put out at God. She figured she had a time or two.

What really surprised her was that she'd said anything at all. Sometimes, like today, she felt like a kid again and would blurt out whatever came to mind. Funny thing was, when she was a kid, the beauty of things had made her angry, for she'd figured God spent too much time making the scenery pretty but not the people. Lillie stopped thinking and decided to ride quietly the rest of the time as they headed back for town. *Can't put a foot in a shut mouth,* the old saying went, and she figured it was a wise one.

"There's Duel," Jack announced. She squinted until she spotted a speck in the distance and she felt rather than saw Jack's mood lighten.

Jack offered Lillie a smile before he nudged Big Black on. It wasn't her fault that what she'd said had struck such a sour chord in him. In spite of his raising, he hadn't really allowed himself to think much about God since Rose died. Mostly because he had it figured that God had turned a deaf ear to him. Jack loped on, steering Big Black carefully around the open mining pits that pocked the ground near the wagon where Duel's sorrel was tethered.

" 'I God, Duel, I never figured you for a piker," Jack called, swinging his leg over the pommel as he dismounted. He found Duel on the other side of the wagon, holding a scrawny baby in his arms like a father would and looking a bit embarrassed to be found out.

"Well, Jack," was all he said, handing the baby back to Nell, the same girl who stepped into Ely's asking for help. She looked at Jack, then back to Duel.

"I thank ya for helpin' me, mister. When my pa gets back, I expect he'll pay ya in kind," she said, speaking surer than she looked.

"She ain't got a pot to piss in," Duel said low, moving closer to Jack so Nell couldn't hear. "Brought what I could to tide her over, but that babe looks poor." Duel's gaze shifted to the girl, kindly but worried. "Can't imagine a daddy leavin' his own this long."

"None would, least not on purpose," Lillie said as she came up to where they stood.

Jack felt a tightening across his chest. There would be no good come of them getting involved, he thought. Caring got you in trouble as far as he was concerned and more often than not didn't change anything. He had cared for both his pa and Rose more than his own life and yet it hadn't been enough. The memories of that, after all the years that had passed, still hadn't lost their sting.

"It'd be fine, if she'd go," Duel said, looking at him with those serious coffee eyes. "She won't go."

"She can't stay here alone," Jack said, avoiding looking at Duel or the girl. "She won't make it."

"My pa told me to stay put and that's what I reckon to do till he comes and fetches us," Nell interrupted. "We'll make it just fine." She sounded tired but there was a dogged stubbornness in the set of her jaw.

"Sure you will, honey," Lillie said. Jack watched as she put her hand out to the girl's shoulder to comfort her. Nell jerked away though, and he saw something in Lillie's face that he'd never seen, a look of understanding . . . and pain. He felt an odd catch in his heart then, like opening an old trunk that had been stored in the attic.

"That's right, honey," he heard Lillie whisper to the girl. "You stay mad. If nothin' else, mad keeps you alive."

Jack tensed. He hadn't bargained for any of this, he thought, hadn't *wanted* it.

"Derned foolishness. She wants to stay, let her stay," he muttered angrily, but the anxiety in his voice bubbled through the anger and Lillie and Duel stared at him curiously. Jack snatched up the reins of his horse and quickly mounted.

"We best go, Lillie," he said abruptly, surprising Lillie so that she remained next to Duel for a moment as they watched Jack ride off.

"What was *that* all about?" Lillie asked, turning to Duel. Jack's moods were as quick changing as the weather in the Territory lately, she thought, watching his figure getting smaller and smaller with distance.

"Been my experience, those that feel the most hurt the most," Duel said almost to himself. When his dark eyes met hers, she had the sudden sense that Duel spoke more out of knowing. "Most folks do about anything to get away from that feeling, Miss Lillie."

Lillie shook her head, wondering where Jack's hurt came from. But maybe it didn't matter where. Hurt was hurt and Duel had been right about one thing: When a person felt it he'd do anything to escape. She'd been there herself, hating the hurt so bad that she'd chosen not to feel at all. Funny thing was, it was Jack who made her think that putting the bad away allowed you to feel the good when it came along.

Lillie sighed with all of the sadness of knowing the road Jack chose and all of the frustration of not being able to stop him from going down it.

Jack played the tables like his life depended on it that night, accepting the drinks the miners shoved at him but showing little or no effect by the way he won. Not until he'd headed upstairs to his room, Lillie thought, staring off into the night from her stool perched by the window. She had had to help him up the stairs, with him blustering all the way that he didn't need her help. He had changed his tune once he was lying on the rickety bed in his room, asking her in a quiet voice that she had never heard if she would just stay until he fell asleep.

When she'd heard his steady breathing, she realized there would be no talk coming this time and she was filled with a low feeling. She'd hoped he'd let her into that part of him he kept walled off, that maybe he'd want to talk about what troubled him. Or that he'd want to know about her, too. He had asked in the beginning, but she hadn't been ready. Now that she was, he seemed to want to back off from anything too personal. Lillie wondered what Jack thought of her. She knew how most folks thought, that her kind didn't care for nothing, that she'd do anything for the turn of a coin. But she'd been someone else before. *Just like you, Jack . . . Duel, too,* she thought, remembering the sad look in Duel's eyes. *We were all someone else before life got to us.*

It was a long while before she crept back to her own bed and finally fell into a troubled sleep.

She was lying in the wagon alone, the mountain fever sweating her into a kind of half-wakefulness. Lillie felt a tug at her sleeve and looked down to see the mice playing along the arm of her nightgown. She felt the hopelessness snake through her when she realized she was too weak to shake them off. "Pa!" she croaked through fevered lips but then realized her pa had died weeks ago. Tears of frustration leaked out of the corners of her eyes. Then Frank Monroe was there, his head peeking through the back curtain of the wagon, and she remembered he was one of the fellows her pa had asked for help. Lillie tried kicking at him but her legs wouldn't seem to work right. She saw Ely's face next. Ely seemed to understand.

"That's right, honey," he said softly. "You stay mad. If nothing else, mad keeps you alive."

The words had taught her some . . . but not enough. Not enough to keep the anger. But maybe Ely didn't know much of the foolish trust of a woman's heart.

Lillie's dream shifted and she saw again Frank Monroe's face before her, then Jack's. She wondered in her dreaming which was worse: a man who'd hurt you for the hell of it, or one who didn't care enough to know he was hurting you.

Jack hated waking up when all he wanted to do was sleep away the troubled thoughts that plagued him. What he hated even more though was hearing the whimpering sounds that seeped through the thin walls that separated him and Lillie. He could hear the rustling of her tossing and then came the sudden sound of a small cry that undid him.

With a heavy sigh, Jack got up and headed for the room next to his, no longer caring what anyone thought as he slipped into the bed next to Lillie, taking her sleeping form in his arms, and pushing back the long curls of hair that hid her face. He couldn't help thinking how in sleep, she looked so small, so helpless. But thoughts such as those would be of no use; anything he'd cared too much for he lost, he repeated in his mind like a litany. And he had gotten good at not caring.

In spite of his resolve, Jack suddenly drew Lillie tight to his chest, rocking her until the whimpering stopped.

What is it that haunts you, gal? he wondered in the still quiet of the room. After awhile, he leaned his head back against the wall and closed his eyes. Everything was getting too close, too personal. It was easier when they had just shared the game.

He would have to leave soon, he decided. He'd have to leave before fate turned up again like a bad penny and gave him no choice in the matter.

Virginia City,
Montana Territory
May 26, 1864

Mrs. Callie McGregor
Plumas City, California

Dear Callie,

It's morning but there ain't no sun to be had. Just rain. I haven't slept yet as I just got in from a friendly game with Ely. We played for whiskey. I won.

I sure wish you were here for me to bend your ear a bit. Callie, I'm thinking of quitting this place. I don't know how to explain it other than that gut feeling our family tends to get when something bad is ready to come down the pike. We saw that little gal again—her pa ain't back yet. He ought to be shot. The West ain't for kids. Sometimes I wonder if it's for anyone with all the trouble I've seen.

Ely told me that trouble finds you no matter where you are, but he was drunk and had to take to his bed shortly after he'd said it. So, I'm not sure how handy that advice is. I haven't mentioned leaving to Duel or Lillie just yet. Truth is, this is the first time I've been so undecided. Ain't that a kick? I can't remember the last time I couldn't just pick up and go if I wanted.

I guess I ought to go to bed. I don't know why I'm even writing this. Maybe it's this rain. You know as well as I do that rain has always made me restless. . . .

Jack

Five

The crowd of men shouted, cramming themselves into the post office with a kind of frenzy Jack had usually seen reserved for fights, not tardy mail. The heavy spring rain had turned the streets to mud, not the light kind, either, but the swampy stuff that sucked down wheels and brought teams to a halt. The rain had finally let up enough for the mail stages bound from Snake River to get through, but not enough so as he could make good time in leaving. Or at least that was what he had convinced himself of, Jack thought, as he felt the crowd jostle him toward the window where a fellow, small as a twig, stood sorting mail. The bundle appeared to have been chewed and spit out, half frozen, but it could have been the mother lode for all the ruckus.

"Some's ain't yet thawed," the frazzled postmaster announced. "But I kin see there'll be no waitin'. I guess if you boys want to break your dern teeth tearing them open, go to it. Might just improve yer sorry looks."

Boisterous laughter filled the musty room and with it, a final push for the window. Jack was shoved into a pair of men ahead of him and glared at the miners behind him, annoyed. The men, so caught in their jawing, didn't seem to notice, but as he righted himself, Jack caught a snip of their conversation and he recognized the voice of the one man as being the old troublemaker he and Duel had dealt with.

"Been working for Frank," Ned Wayne was saying. Jack saw the second fellow glance at him sharply.

"Didn't know he was hirin'," he said, surprised.

"If ye can do the job he is," Ned boasted. "Got us a team of mules by chance a few days back. Frank says if I sold 'em quick, I'd git extra. So, me and Riley took 'em down to ol' Pete's and tolt him I'd sell 'em to him for a steal. The ol' codger says to me if he knowed me right, it wasn't him that'd be doin' the stealin'."

Both of the men chuckled

"Ol' Pete bought 'em?"

"Wouldn't tech 'em," Ned replied disgustedly. "But he nearly got a load of buckshot for *sassin'* me—them's Riley's words."

Jack felt the little hairs on his neck raise up. Seemed like he recalled little Nell's pa had went off with a team—and still wasn't back. Of course, teams were bought and sold nearly everyday in the streets. But he knew deep down it was no coincidence. Not with a character like Ned Wayne.

An hour later, he found Lillie. She looked fresh in spite of the jammed house, smiling as she added a chip to a young miner's dwindling pile. The boy appeared ready and willing to chuck in the last of his earnings for another smile until Jack caught her attention. As if sensing something, her smile dimmed abruptly, and without a word she moved toward him through the hazy din of the saloon. As Jack repeated the conversation he'd overheard, he watched the growing alarm on her face.

"I don't know nothin' about these fellows, Lillie, 'cept for the feeling they're up to no good," he finished. Lillie nodded but her mind raced ahead with fear. *Frank,* Jack said they called him and she knew it was Frank Monroe. She'd been a first-rate fool to think he'd finished of Virginia City when they parted ways. She thought of little Nell and the baby, of them being without their pa and a hammering started in her chest. She'd never known Frank to pass up a deal—at any cost.

Lillie caught Ely gesturing for her to get back to the faro table. The miners were getting edgy and Ely looked desperate. There'd be no help there, she thought. If anything, Ely'd probably take to his bed, sure that they were doomed for getting into Frank's business.

"You've got to get a hold of Duel, Jack," she whispered urgently. "He'll know what to do." She didn't think it right to mention Duel was part of the vigilantes that had formed to keep peace after the sheriff died. The vigilantes were a closed-mouth bunch that didn't cotton to folks knowing too much. And with Jack just being the messenger, he didn't *need* to know.

Jack appeared as if he suddenly regretted getting involved, but she pleaded with her eyes and she saw something in him finally give.

"Might be that girl's pa is lyin' up somewhere hurt," she said softly. She saw a doubtful look come to Jack's face before he headed out the door—the look of a man who knew sometimes life wasn't kind enough to leave it up to chance.

He had no one to blame but himself, Jack thought as he loped off towards Duel's cabin. Instead of telling Lillie they ought to keep their noses out of the whole affair—as his head told him—he'd saddled up and headed out to Duel's anyway. *"We're doin' the right thing,"* she had said, following him out to the livery. He had laughed harshly. *"The right thing?"* he told her. *"Who is it that decides what's right? Because I'd sure like to have a talk with him sometime."* But the hurt look in her eyes had caused him to mount up anyway. She had made him feel responsible, as if it was his duty, and it stuck in his craw that he had allowed it. *Like being pulled along by an invisible rope and no way to cut free....*

Jack glanced up as he neared the little cabin perched on the hill-

side, and he eased Big Black to a walk. If he hadn't heard about
Duel's dead wife, Jack would have figured it out for himself. The
place looked like a *home:* the start-ups of dozens of little flowers
clung to each side of a stone walk, the curtains, the wind chime,
tiny pebbles of all shapes and sizes strung up like pearls that chinked
together in the wind. As fine as it all was, Jack felt the uneasiness in
him that had started days ago heighten.

Even the little decisions can change a man's life, his pa had always
warned, and Jack couldn't help wondering as he rapped on Duel's
door where this one would lead him.

"Bad business," Duel said simply after Jack finished his story. "Don't
mind me for sayin' you don't look none too happy to be the bearer,
either." They were both hunched near the fire where Duel had been
cleaning fish when Jack had found him out beyond the back of the
cabin. Ely had told him of talk that Duel hadn't set foot in the place
since his wife died but he hadn't believed it. Now that he had seen it,
he chose not to say anything. He figured Duel's reasons were his own.

"I don't guess I had much of a choice," Jack grumbled and was
surprised to hear the black man chuckle as he rolled the fish in meal
and set them over the fire.

"Women can be an aggravation like that, can't they?" Duel said,
offering the pan of fish to Jack after awhile. " 'Specially when they're
right."

"How is it that they don't have to say a word, just look at you
and make you feel low unless you do like they want?" Jack suddenly
felt undermined and thought of saying more about the fearful look
he'd seen in Lillie's eyes but decided just to eat his fish.

"I reckon if we was to know all the answers, they'd quit bein'
fun," Duel speculated as he chewed. "Women's chancy creatures,
Jack, you ought to know that."

"I know I've seen better odds at cards," Jack said around a

mouthful of fish. Duel laughed again, but his face sobered some as he stood and brushed himself off.

"Hope the odds are for that little gal's pa, tho' I doubt it if it's who I think that's went after him. Guess I should round up some of the boys. Ain't no sense goin' in outnumbered." With that Duel picked up his saddle and headed for his horse, then rode off without another word.

Being that as it was, Jack took it that he was meant to wait, so he stretched his long legs out and pulled his hat down and tried not to think of Lillie or the thought that there was more to her fear for the girl's pa than what met the eye. The anxious way she'd looked had jarred loose old memories—memories he'd gambled down or rode away from until now.

No sooner than he'd thought it, a stiff breeze came and pushed away his ponderings. Jack shouldered himself against another gust and glanced at the darkened cabin, entertaining the thought of holing up inside until Duel returned. He stared a bit longer, then thought better of it and scooted closer to the fire.

It didn't take long for Duel to come back or for Jack to figure the group of men who rode up with him were the vigilantes that everyone spoke of. Jack stood and pushed his hat back, studying the weather-hardened faces lit by the fire. A few he recognized, being some of the miners who frequented the Pair-O-Dice. Their usual mischievous expressions were somber though—the look of men who'd tired of the constant fear of being robbed everytime they left town—and expected to be taken seriously.

Hell, anyone'd be a fool not to take them seriously, Jack thought. Everyone in the Territory had heard of their notice to the outlaws by now: 3-7-77 scrawled with charcoal on a tent or cabin, warning them to "Get out or get hung." No one really knew what the numbers meant—except they spoke business.

They got down to the business at hand quickly, asking Jack to repeat what he had overheard.

"That'd be Frank Monroe's bunch, alright," one of the miners spoke up. "Last I heard they were holed up near Dempsey's Ranch. It wouldn't surprise me none if they did the fellow in."

"Ain't nothin' like a stout rope and a good drop to cure such as that," another man intoned.

"So you fellows the law, then?" Jack asked. A few of the men around the five snorted, one of the fellows in the back calling out, "What asylum is he from?"

"You ain't been here long, have you?" the miner said politely. "We jes' make the law as we go—but we ain't the *law*." The last statement allowed Jack to breathe easy again; he'd heard as much from Duel but had just wanted to make sure. Without another word, the men went into action, grabbing weapons, and Jack felt himself pulled along once again.

"What was it that happened to the sheriff, Duel?" Jack asked as they mounted up. "Recall you sayin' he was dead but never said how."

"Oh, he was hung awhile back," Duel explained with that quiet way of his. " 'Tweren't no great loss. Plummer was just a killer wearin' a badge."

Duel looked speculatively over at Jack, whose face looked grim. "You ready to ride?"

"What I should do is ride for the next town," Jack said, then looked a little put out as if he had voiced his thoughts aloud. When he spoke again, Duel heard a weariness in his voice—the kind that knows the road ahead. "All we're going to be bringing that kid is disappointment."

Duel watched his friend closely and wondered if anyone else saw through the smoke Jack put up. He had a feeling most thought Jack the typical gambler: a showman, frivolous and shallow. But Duel sensed Jack's game was more to get him through town after town, to keep him from gambling the one thing he couldn't. Jack wasn't cold; he was just haunted. *Dark nights of the soul* is what his

Celie used to call them. He had spent many such nights alone himself and he knew Jack probably would, too. Knowing this gave him a compassion for Jack; the rare kind between men that runs deep as blood. If he'd had the words to give Jack help, he would, but Duel knew well enough that you just had to stumble through the blackness until you found light again.

Duel pushed his hat down, spurring his sorrel into a pace to catch the riders ahead, and he knew without looking back that Jack was following.

The men were as nearly given out as their horses by the time they crossed Wisconsin Creek, camping seven miles below Dempsey's. Jack sat next to Duel almost on top of the fire they had built, trying to thaw; the creek had been frozen but the ice hadn't been strong enough to hold the weight of men and horses and they had all emerged half-drowned, cased in suits of frosted clothes.

"I think I'd rather burn than freeze to death," Jack said after thawing a bit. "I ain't ever felt cold like that, not in Missouri or anywhere else." He tried to smooth his mustache but it felt hard, like it might break off, so he pulled out his whiskey flask and took a long swallow before offering it to Duel.

"I don't know," Duel speculated. "Seems burnin' would take longer. I've heard them Apaches can burn ya long—keep you goin' to watch your own skin melt off." Duel shook his head and took a modest swallow from the flask before handing it back to Jack. "No, sir, if I go, I prefer it be quick—with all my skin still on."

Jack chuckled. The warmth of the whiskey soaking through his body had taken some of the edginess of his feelings away. It lulled Duel, too, and they sat quiet for awhile listening to the night sounds. After awhile, Duel got up and stoked the fire.

"Well, now that's a fine-lookin' book you have there, Jack," Duel said. Jack turned and saw that he was eyeing the book that'd fallen out of his satchel. He'd forgotten he'd even had it, he thought, smiling a bit as he picked it up and handed it to his friend.

"My mama's Bible," Jack supplied. "My sister Callie sent it to me some time back. Guess she figured I needed it more'n she did." He laughed then, a forced kind of laugh, and Duel looked up from the book, his dark eyes questioning.

"My Celie had a Bible, read it to me some nights," he said after awhile, "never did know what happened to it."

Jack looked up sharply, the big man's voice sounding so different. Wistful, almost.

"You take it, Duel," he said on impulse and when he saw the surprise and pleasure on Duel's face, he couldn't help smiling. "I reckon you'd make better use of it than me."

Duel glanced up from the tattered leather cover he'd been looking at like it was some kind of treasure. His expression seemed to turn thoughtful for a moment.

"I'll take good care of it, Jack," he said with great seriousness. "In case you ever want it back, it bein' your ma's and all."

Later, after they'd bedded down by the fire, Jack watched through slitted eyes as Duel leaned close to the crackling flames, carefully turning over each page of the old Bible. He started a bit when he realized Duel wasn't *really* reading the words—maybe couldn't read them. Instead, he just ran his calloused hands over page after page, smiling a strange kind of smile like he was remembering something fine.

Why in the world would he want something he couldn't even read? Jack wondered briefly. The odd memory of his pa's face the day he died came to Jack, and he remembered the smile when his pa had called out his mama's name that last time. It suddenly occurred to him how Duel had looked much the same. For just a moment, he allowed himself to wonder what it would be like to care that much—to be *cared for* so much that even the memories left made a difference. No sooner had he brushed the thought away than the rusty feeling of *need* filled him.

Duel finally nodded off, holding the Bible to his chest. Unable to find sleep himself and not sure what the morning would bring, Jack pulled some paper from the side of his saddle, hunkered down near the dwindling fire, and began to write.

Montana Territory
May 30, 1864

Mrs. Callie McGregor
Plumas City, California

Dear Callie,

It's a cold one out here tonight. I never thought I'd miss that cramped little room at the Pair-O-Dice, but I do. Funny ain't it? I mean how you can think things could be better, when really they ain't that bad? I ain't left Virginia City yet, not exactly. I just got invited along on this little outing with these fellows who call themselves vigilantes. They are more or less the law in these parts—they hung their sheriff a few months back. He was a thief and a killer. But they all agree his Thanksgiving dinner was first rate.

Something to keep in mind, I guess.

Do you recall little Nell I wrote about? Well, it's turned out that her pa might have met a foul end. The fellows the men suspect are a rough bunch of road agents. Duel says they would steal half-dollars from their dead mothers' eyes for gain. One of the miners told me they shot a fellow not two weeks back on the road outside town for a five-dollar treasury note. He says its a bad sign of the times—I told him it sure ain't Sunday School. I know one thing, these vigilantes mean business. They are through playing games. Most of them have families, too. I wonder if them road agents thought of that—that the fellow might be a pa or something?

I don't know why I'm writing all this. I didn't aim to worry you. I guess I just got to thinking of family. I best quit this letter anyway; we're due to ride out in a couple hours. I sure hope Duel and them are wrong about all this; that kid could use some good news for a change. But Sis, even I won't bet on that hand.

Jack

P.S. I think Ely was right about trouble finding you—even if he was drunk when he said it.

Six

The men reined in a mile short of the wakiup just before day-break. They dismounted quietly, holding their bridles as the horses huffed steam in the thin cold air and waited for the sun to rise. It was just peaking through when Jack started making out the shapes around the hut.

"Well, there's the mules," he said grimly.

"I don't see nothin'," one of the miners complained, but Jack and Duel had already mounted and were riding for the wakiup by the time the rest of the group followed. A small mongrel of a dog started yapping in the yard as they pulled up, bringing Ned Wayne stumbling from the hut dressed in a pair of soiled long johns.

"I tolt ye I would kick ye to pieces if ye yapped again," Ned said, rearing a scrawny leg back to kick the mutt. He pitched forward, nearly losing his balance as he spied Jack and Duel watching him from their horses. His eyes grew wide as he saw the rest of the vigilantes filing into the yard behind them.

"Where's the party?" he asked, licking his lips. Jack saw his eyes dart nervously to where the span of mules were.

"I guess you know why we're here," Duel said. "That there's Nick Kelly's mules. Now, we'd be obliged if you'd tell us where he is."

"If yer so smart, *nigger,* ye can figure that out yerself," Ned said and Jack pulled the hammer back on his pistol.

"Move away from the hut," Jack ordered, dismounting. He shoved Ned to the ground roughly, tying his hands behind his back. Duel and the other men kept their guns trained on the door of the wakiup.

"Anyone else in there better come out now," Duel called. A young, red-headed fellow with a dirt-streaked face stumbled out with his hands in the air. He looked at the men in the yard, then to Ned with disgust.

"I told my brother we shouldn't've joined up with you all," was all he said. He sat down on the ground next to Ned with a sigh, allowing Duel to tie his hands.

Ned's laughter jolted Jack. "I guess you ought to know he had two girls, one twelve and a baby," he said, attempting to find some remorse in the man.

"More's the pity the older one wasn't with him," Ned said, with an ugly leer.

"By God, I hope someone shoots me if I get as rough as you, Ned," Jack said.

"Untie me, Wade, and I'll oblige ye," Ned taunted and this time Jack laughed.

"And end your misery?" Jack asked softly, remembering Nell's face. "I think I'd rather see you swing."

While the vigilantes put the prisoners on horseback, Jack and Duel scoured the area for signs of Nick Kelly. Jack was the first to reach the body. In the brush not too far away from the house, he found the man he figured to be little Nell's pa, his neck scarred by rope tracks, his hands still death-gripped on the sagebrush he'd pulled up while being dragged to his end.

"Men that'd do that are too small to look a snake in the eye," Duel said quietly as he came up behind him.

With unsteady hands, Jack closed the man's eyes—eyes that reminded him so much of little Nell. He felt an anger roll over him in great waves. By the time he mounted his horse, he just felt weary. *How am I going to tell that little girl, tell Lillie?* he wondered over and over again as he felt his past rise up like the bile in his throat.

Of all the memories, there was one that stayed with him, stayed under his skin even in his waking hours. It was the day he'd paced up and down that street in Salt Lake, not knowing what else to do as his sister Rose lay dying in a rented room of the boardinghouse. He'd walked and walked until Callie had come and told him Rose was gone. Then he'd felt the stabbing regret that he'd done nothing to try to stop it. *He'd never even told her good-bye.* The guilt of it nearly drove him crazy for awhile; now it just lingered, taunting when it could. Like now.

Jack looked at the lifeless eyes that stared upwards, then glanced at Duel, who seemed to understand.

"We done what we could," he said somberly. "Guess we ought to take the poor fella back for a proper buryin'. That gal's gonna want to say good-bye to her daddy."

Jack merely nodded. He knew no matter how dirty the job, it had to be done. He was learning that closing his eyes to it wouldn't make it go away, no matter how hard he wished it would.

But as they finally mounted up for the ride back to Virginia City, Jack couldn't help thinking there was so much that he wished to God he'd never had to see.

Virginia City,
Montana Territory
June 2, 1864

Mrs. Callie McGregor
Plumas City, California

Dear Callie,
    Duel was right as rain about them road agents. We only caught but two of them but they had the goods: the mules and that little girl's

dead pa. I tell you, I hope to God I never have to see such a sight again.

Oh, I've seen my share in my travels. Even in town, there ain't a day that goes by that someone ain't threatening to shoot someone or cut off a body part, but mostly it's just liquor talking. Callie, these men are plain cold-blooded killers who don't care to take a life for money.

I remember Pa saying once that good men sometimes do bad deeds, but I think you could look till Kingdom Come and not find any good in these fellows. I told Lillie as much, but she marched right up to them and asked them why they did it anyway. They just laughed at her. I never felt like killing anyone until then. Lillie just looked at me and said, "How do you explain that to a kid?"

Funny how you think you have the answers until someone asks a question like that.

It'll all be over soon anyway. They aim to hang them come morning.

Jack

The sound of the horses and the shuffling, dragging feet of the prisoners made a low echo along Wallace Street as the vigilantes pushed the two men on towards the makeshift scaffold. People began gathering on either side to watch. Merchants came from their stores, children played rowdily in the muddy street, running and laughing behind them like it was a parade. Jack glanced over to where Nell stood on the other side of Lillie. Her face was set, stoic as an Indian as they led the murderers past her, but her eyes showed the haunted look of a hurt animal. He saw the prisoners glance over at her; the red-headed fellow who was called Hop looked away, but Ned Wayne grinned meanly.

"Why, lookit Hop, she's got her daddy's eyes," he said, smiling a cold smile.

Jack lunged for him, but Duel's large hand caught him on the shoulder.

"He'll get his soon enough," Duel said softly.

Jack held himself back and watched as they led Ned up the stairs of the scaffold. He felt Lillie shake a bit next to him and took her hand as she looked up at him with a sad smile. For some reason the smile caused his heart to catch, and he turned his eyes back to the scaffold.

Ned showed little emotion until they faced him to the crowd, then Jack saw his eyes squint past them briefly and he grinned coldly, looking down at Jack as they set the noose about his neck.

"Frank ain't going to like this," he said, still smiling. Jack felt Lillie go stiff beside him. "See you in Hell, Wade."

"I doubt it," Jack said evenly. "But don't you forget who sent you."

Frank Monroe and his men sat on their horses just out of view of the town and watched silently as Ned danced his death at the end of the vigilante's rope. Frank watched, only half interested. Hangings were hangings. If one of his bunch got strung up, there was always a fresh one to replace him, after all. What held his attention at the moment was Lillie Lee draped on the arm of the tall stranger.

"Shoot the rope, Mr. Monroe," the youngest of the bunch blurted loudly, distracting him. Frank gave the boy a cold look.

"Shut your trap," he snapped, turning back to watch Lillie. He'd thought the whore would be too scared to move on so soon but there she was, sidled up to some newcomer with the kind of young handsomeness that had long since faded on Frank.

"It's my *pa* they got swingin'," the kid cried, no longer caring what the others thought. Frank suddenly drew his revolver, aimed at the kid's head, and fired. The ball only took a good piece of hat and grazed the kid's scalp enough to bleed a fair amount. The kid looked like he might get sick, but none of the men made a move to help. Frank had already turned his attention back to the crowded street in town.

"Looks like Lillie's got herself a regular beau," he commented, leaning on his pommel, but his casual air didn't fool the men. Frank never let go of much, be it a grudge or a woman.

"Gambler named of Jack Wade. He cheated me and Pa of our poke," the boy said dully, touching his scalp as he stared at the figure of his pa swinging.

"*Jack Wade*, you say?" Frank sat back and smiled a mean smile. Life was something, he thought, then signaled for the group to head out. "Well, ain't this cozy," he said almost to himself.

"Yessir," the boy said calmly—dead sounding almost. As they started to trot off, Frank suddenly had the thought that with a bit more molding the kid might just make a first-rate outlaw.

"I guess that hat's sturdier'n it looks," he chuckled, sidling his horse next to the boy's as the rest of the bunch rode ahead. The hat was ruined, but the kid didn't pay much mind to it or to the trickle of blood that ran through the matted blond hair and down his cheek. His face was blank.

"I see the boys set you up with a fine mount," Frank commented, watching the kid's eyes dart up in fear. He smiled inwardly. "Must mean you're a top hand. Only my top hands get horseflesh like that."

Frank could use a kid like him. He glanced back once to where Lillie stood with the thieving gambler who had eluded him, saw the caring way she looked up at him, and he felt a white anger go low in his belly. He could use the kid, alright.

"Ever heard the sayin' about killing two birds with one stone, Riley Wayne?" Frank added, using his name for the first time ever. When the boy looked at him curiously, he just laughed.

Jack purely hated graveyards, more than anything he could think of. They kept death alive, if that made any sense, and for that reason alone, he figured to stay clear of them. *Here I am anyway,*

he thought, *riding up to Duel's fire, built close enough to Boot Hill for me to see nothing but those damned mounds of upturned dirt.* Still, he probably would've faced just about anything than the sight of little Nell sitting on Lillie's bed with that baby in her arms.

How did I ever let myself get in this deep? Jack wondered as he dismounted. In spite of his balking, somewhere along the way he'd let them in: Lillie, Duel, even ol' Ely. Hell, if he were honest about it, he'd let the whole derned town in. He thought of Lillie and how he'd felt the night he'd ridden back in with the vigilantes. She had come running to the corral where he stabled Big Black, flushed and worried and looking better than any woman had a right to. When he had pulled her into his arms, he had felt the strong yearnings to kiss her, to have her beneath him. But more, too; like all of the stiffness had rushed out of him like a sigh. The only other time he'd ever felt such relief was in his dreams: He would ride up to the old farm in Missouri and see his ma and pa standing on the porch like they always had when they were alive and Callie and Rose would be there, arguing with him about what chores he'd shirked, but loving him anyway. . . .

Jack dismounted and pulled the jug of rot-gut he'd bought off Ely from his saddle and sauntered over to where Duel sat.

"I know you ain't much of a drinker, but I figured you might want a nip. I know I do. You picked one heck of a spot to parlay, my friend."

"Mostly it picked me," Duel said. Jack heard the smile in his voice, but as he neared he saw Duel looked thoughtful. "Got to lookin' at them graves and thinkin' them fellows died same as they lived—apart from everyone else."

Buryin' ground for the lawless, Jack thought, gazing over the sparse ground of Boot Hill as a chill wind blew down over the valley of the gulch. In a way, he'd lived his life much the same as the outlaws, keeping himself separated from folks. He lit his smoke and hunkered down next to the fire, watching Duel through the sparks that shot up into the night as he took a modest swallow from the jug.

"At least that little gal saw some justice," Duel said, handing the jug back to Jack.

"Justice? That kid needed her *pa,* not a hanging," Jack said, suddenly riled. "It ain't enough." But even in the heat of his anger he wondered a little guiltily if he hadn't been thinking of the deaths in his own life—of the fear of taking another chance in a world where there were no guarantees.

"Sometimes it's got to be enough," Duel said quietly. "More than nothin' 'tall."

Jack glanced over at Duel. It was clear he was a deep thinker, putting him to mind a little of his old friend, Stem.

"I thought like you once, when my Celie died," Duel said out of the blue. "Ended up sending my boy back east to Kansas. Figured he'd be better off with Celie's sister than with a pa that was half out of his mind." He shrugged his big shoulders then, as if to lighten the burden. "Thing is, I found no one to blame for me losing her. She just up and took sick with what folks call the summer complaint. Fellow I knew told me later it was carried by the wind. Can you imagine that?" Jack watched Duel stare hard into the night, as if he was trying to find some invisible enemy.

After awhile, Duel rose and as was his habit, started back home, not bothering to say goodnight. This time, however, he surprised Jack by turning around. When their gazes met, Jack saw something in Duel's eyes as if he'd seen too much, and a deep understanding passed between the two men.

"Ever try to curse the wind, Jack?" Duel asked but walked away before Jack could think of an answer.

Virginia City,
Montana Territory
June 3, 1864

Mrs. Callie McGregor
Plumas City, California

Dear Callie,

They hung the men who killed Nell's pa. It wasn't what I expected. But then what do folks expect? I guess I thought I'd feel better, that I'd done something that made a difference—a good one, that is. But mostly all I felt was angry.

I stood there and watched two men die at the end of a rope and all I could think of was it wasn't enough. I felt nothing, though the one fellow called for his mother up to the very end. I might have felt sorry for him, but my mind kept thinking of that girl's pa laid out at Ely's on a board held up by two butter tubs. Where is the justice in that?

Duel says even the little bits of justice have got to be enough, that sometimes there ain't no one to blame at all.

He may be right about that but you know, Callie, for some reason I can't find it in me to accept it.

Jack

Virginia City,
Montana Territory
June 6, 1864

Mrs. Callie McGregor
Plumas City, California

Dear Callie,

More bad news. Nell has left town.

Duel came in, looking bad, and said that he'd gone to check on her and she told him the baby had died and she was going. By the time Lillie and I got to her wagon, she was pulling out. She didn't stop neither when she saw us, just hawed that team like we weren't there. I yelled to her and told her she didn't have a chance out there alone. She said to me, "Mister, it's the only chance I got." She looked at Lillie, then to me and for a moment, Callie, it was shock seeing her like that. She looked old.

It doesn't seem right, does it, for a kid to have to get grown so fast. I don't know much about the Good Book, but don't it say somewhere in there that God ain't got wrath for the innocent?

Jack

P.S. I can't shake the thought that if I hadn't been so dern worried about getting too close to Nell, so worried that I might end up feeling as helpless as I did with Rose, that I might've been able to help that kid better, Sis. Why is it that we only see things when it's too late? I feel old myself tonight. Like life's tricked me and I can't figure how to fight back.

Seven

Rain punished the gulch over the next few days with such wrath that Lillie wondered if it wasn't God's way of showing his anger at the senseless loss of lives; four graves in less than a week. It had to be some kind of record, she thought, even for Virginia City. She shrugged at the ache in her shoulders. It had been a long day of dealing with the miners being washed out of their diggings, but at least it was almost over.

She glanced around the room as she drew winners and losers from her case box to the lone miner who stood at her faro table. With dawn coming, the saloon was nearly empty save for the few regulars who leaned against the bar jawing with Ely and Mabel. Her eyes finally rested on Jack. She had been so scared that Frank would show up and ruin everything, that either he or Jack would wind up killing the other, but nothing had happened. Well, that wasn't true, either.

Jack had hardly slept since the hanging. He just stayed at the tables, drinking and betting, and the constant pace was beginning to show. Only tonight she had noticed the dark circles beneath his eyes. Lillie glanced at the empty table where Jack sat; the fellow he had been playing had folded and left awhile back, but Jack continued to sit there, smoking and flipping over cards as if he hadn't a care in the world. But she knew better.

Oh, he still came to her room at night, needing to hold her next to him until he fell off to sleep. But there was something lost in him. *If only we could talk like our hearts do,* she thought with a kind of restless ache. Something had to give, she figured. And soon.

She pulled a jack and a seven, then glanced to the coppered seven on the table. "Well, Harm, looks like you stayed away long enough, huh?" she said, smiling softly. The miner laughed and slapped his thigh.

"I guess you're right about that, Miss Lillie," he said, his eyes going soft on her as he collected his chips from the green felt. "Well, might as well go before the luck runs out." Lillie capped her box and made her way to the bar, catching the snatch of conversation here and there. The rain had cast a gloom over the miners as well. If they weren't talking about the hanging, they were talking about little Nell striking out on her own and the various horrors that could befall her.

"Well, she didn't have no call to go off like that," Ely said, warming up to the discussion.

"Why shouldn't she?" Lillie said abruptly, stopping at the bar. "She ain't got no one here."

"Well, maybe I could've helped her," Ely offered and Lillie looked at him incredulously. "Well, you ain't done so bad, have you?" he asked, looking hurt.

"Oh, it's been a party, Ely," Lillie snapped and Mabel snorted, unladylike, in spite of her recent efforts to improve. Lillie saw Ely give her a warning look, as if they were an old couple, and she wondered at it.

"By God, you'd think this was an orphanage, not a saloon, the way you all carry on," Jack said with a rough sound to his voice. Lillie turned and saw him take the last draw of the whiskey in his glass before he slid the chair back and made his way through the batwings of the saloon. She hesitated, then followed him out into the street.

"Jack!"

Jack stopped, standing stock-still in the muddied ruts of the street. When he turned back to her, Lillie was surprised to see that his face didn't really look angry, just weary. Like he had tortured himself for answers that he couldn't find.

Lillie wanted Jack to say something, but he kept quiet, his eyes blank and far away, so she moved next to him and just put her hand on his arm. It was in that small touch that she felt something in Jack finally give and break free.

"I had another sister besides Callie," he said after awhile, still staring off past her. Lillie kept quiet, fearing if she spoke he wouldn't finish. "She was the baby of the family, 'tho she'd never let you know it." He smiled then, but it was a smile of pain. "We all knew she was bad off when we signed on with the wagon train in Missouri, but Pa'd heard the air out west could clear bad lungs. When we buried Pa along the trail, I figured to get her there, come hell or high water. She almost made it, too. Almost made it."

Thunder rumbled far off, and Jack reached down and tucked a long curl behind her ear.

"I could've done more for Nell," he said. The regret on his face was so harsh she almost wanted to shy from it. The fight in him seemed to have gone too, and she felt helpless, not knowing how to get it back. "She was just a kid, Lillie. It wasn't her fault she looked like Rose." Jack stared down at her, and in the dismal morning light she saw a different look in his eyes and she realized he had been scared of making another mistake. *He's fighting himself,* she thought. *Fighting against the man he could be—wanted to be.*

It doesn't matter, Jack, she was just some kid we barely knew, she wanted to tell him, fearing the running look in his eyes. *It doesn't matter.* But that would have been a lie and lying was for cowards.

Jack looked at her a moment, like he was half expecting her to say something. Like he was *wanting* her to lie. But then he caught the war going on inside of her and he smiled bitterly.

Thunder rumbled again from the mountains in the distance, and Lillie caught the scent of rain as it once again weighted the air around them. She thought she heard Jack say something like death stalking him in between the claps of thunder that came closer and closer but she wasn't sure. By the time the first heavy drops began to fall, Jack was gone, and Lillie, as she walked the lonely stretch of boardwalk back to the Pair-O-Dice, couldn't help wishing she'd just lied.

Frank Monroe stood on the other side of the street with some of his men and watched Lillie stroll the muddied plank walk toward the saloon as the heavy drops of rain splashed over the brim of his hat. He smiled, taking his hat off and shaking the water from it as he raked his hands through his crop of long black hair.

Trouble seemed to be brewing between the love birds, he thought with some satisfaction, then his smile dimmed. But it wasn't enough.

He could've done it easy, he figured. He and his boys could have followed Wade and waylaid him, but that was too simple and he hadn't gotten where he was by being a man of simple nature. And of course, that wouldn't have taken care of Lillie and the little nest egg he knew she was building.

He waited until he saw the light go on in her room above the saloon, like he knew it would. He was caught a little off guard, seeing the shadow of her figure come to the window and peek out, but he was quick to realize she hadn't been looking for him. Frank's face turned dark and he glanced back at his men standing at the edge of the boardwalk. Most of them were three sheets to the wind from drinking and carousing all night, but he wouldn't need them for much tonight. Frank took a last glance down the street, then made his way toward the Pair-O-Dice.

The Pair-O-Dice smelled rank. After a boom night it always smelled worse, stale beer and smoke clinging to the barroom in spite of burning all the sweetgrass he could find, but it was still Ely's favorite time.

The last of the crowd had gone except for the few stragglers, lifeless humps curled up on the bed-straw in the corner of the room until they struggled awake for an eye-opener to get them going, but they weren't moving for now and that made it the best time to sweep. Sweepings could sometimes pan out from fifty to a hundred in spilled dust, and Ely often thought the thrill of finding it must be close to having his own claim. He'd collected a fine pile by the time he heard heavy boots hitting his floor and looked up to see Frank Monroe.

He and Lillie had both breathed a sigh of relief when they heard Frank had gone off to Colorado, looking for his brother, Jude. Now he was back and that could only mean trouble.

Frank walked into the room easily, as if he owned it himself. Ely glanced to Mabel worriedly, but she was the picture of manners and she had the good sense to be quiet when he'd come in.

"Got a proposition for you, Ely," Frank announced abruptly and Ely tried not to appear puzzled. Frank had a way of doing that to him, making him so nervous he felt confused.

"Well, I don't know, Frank. I ain't sure I could afford this proposition of yours. Where would I put it?" Ely asked finally and one of Frank's men sniggered.

"A business deal, Ely. I figure you know what that means." Ely watched the outlaw reach behind his bar for a bottle. He poured himself and drink and sighed. "You see, I've been watching you and I figure you need a chance to catch up with the other fellows in town. Hell, Ely, they're making money hand over fist."

"Well, what do I have to do?" Ely asked, knowing whatever it was, he would have to do it, anyway.

"Got a few friends coming into town who fancy a big game," Frank answered, keeping his voice low. "High stakes. But they want an out-of-the-way place, if you know what I mean. They're willing to pay for it, too. You wouldn't have to do a thing, just let the business roll in." He smiled friendly at Ely. "Couldn't ask for more than that, could you?" .

"Well, it sounds good, Frank," Ely said slowly. His mind was racing ahead. He could maybe even get Jack in on the game, help him with the ante. Jack was a sure thing with cards, he thought prudently.

Frank ground his cigar down on the table, which annoyed Ely to no end, but he chose not to say anything. When he looked up from the smoldering butt, Frank smiled thinly.

"Good doin' business with ya, Ely," he said, heading for the door. "I always told Lillie you were a sharp fellow." A few of the men laughed outright on the way out and Frank turned back and grinned. "You be sure and tell that gal I send my best."

Your best is most folks' worst, Ely thought grimly, but he nodded and waved back friendly. He'd learned long ago that it was best not to rile Frank Monroe, even if he didn't plan on giving Lillie the message. Things were dicey enough. If Lillie knew Frank was in on a deal, there'd be no chance of peace at all. Of course, he couldn't fault her. Everyone and their brother knew Frank Monroe was bad news.

His worry must have showed because Mabel picked up the broom he laid on the floor and sauntered over.

"This might be just the thing to put you in with the likes of The Mammoth," she said. When he looked doubtful, she frowned and put her hands on her hips. "How do you think them other fellows got going? Ain't from crocheting with their grannies, that's for sure. Careful is just another word for coward, Ely."

"Maybe you're right," Ely said slowly and Mabel looked as

pleased as he had ever seen her. She had a forceful turn to her, but at least she wasn't spiteful. Not like his first wife, who would just as soon see him fail for the spite of it.

"I guess we ought to toast the occasion," he announced and went to the bar and poured them each out a shot of whiskey. Mabel smiled big, but she took only a small swallow, then set the glass down primly to show him she didn't really need it.

Ely ran his hand over the carved, dark wood counter of the bar and remembered back to the time when he'd set up the drinks on pine planks and sacks of flour. Business *had* grown. But he supposed it could be better. *Likes of The Mammoth,* Mabel had said, and he thought of all of the finery he'd seen in the big game house.

Still, an uneasiness crept over him that he couldn't explain. *Dance with the devil and you'll end up paying the band,* the old saying went. Ely picked up the bar rag and went to work once again, scrubbing over the burn hole in the table.

He had come back. He had walked and walked—much like he did that day in Salt Lake—not really knowing where he was going but needing to work out the tension that coiled through him like a snake. After awhile, he had just stood, letting the rain soak him, and thought of leaving. But this time he didn't.

Jack rolled over and pulled Lillie to him, breathing in the sweet familiar smell of her hair. Somewhere along noon the sun had come out and a hazy light slanted through the window, and he could hear the clatter of wagons and distant blasts of mining as the gulch got back to business. But he and Lillie had stayed holed up in the room together; holding each other, kissing, and laughing like they never had before. As strong as their body cravings were for each other, they had pushed those yearnings aside, and in doing that it seemed their hearts had been allowed to stretch and grow together, Jack thought with something akin to awe. It was as if their needing each other went far beyond passion or words but deeper, to touch the places that made you glad to be human so you could feel it.

Even if you couldn't quite understand it.

How did he let her get under his skin? Jack wondered, listening to the sounds of life on the street below. He had gone as far as saddling up Big Black when he realized he couldn't leave Lillie. Telling her about his life, about his family, had opened a door he couldn't shut again. And when he had walked back into her room and saw those wide blue eyes of hers look at him with such care, he knew he had done right. She made him feel things he hadn't ever felt. Feeling her small, warm body in his arms seemed to put back the missing pieces of him that had been taken by his grief and his loneliness. It didn't matter if they were in a cramped little room above a saloon. Crazy as it sounded, he felt for the first time in a long, long while that he had allowed himself to feel. And it felt like home.

Lillie looked up at him. "Got some good news," Lillie said as she set the plate of food between them. They were both sitting Indian-style on the bed like two kids playing picnic. Jack picked up a biscuit and watched Lillie grin like the cat that ate the canary. The smile caused the dimple in her cheek to come out and Jack couldn't help chuckling.

"I'm almost afraid to ask," he said. As he brushed the hair back from her forehead, Lillie felt a warm contentment spread through her. She could hardly believe he was there with her. Underneath her hope had been the needle that pricked her with the constant thought that most good things didn't last. But he had come back— and different, too. Something in him had softened, she thought, studying the handsome, lean face.

"Ely's setting up a big game, high stakes, too," she told him, watching the flicker of interest light in his eyes as he traced a finger along her jaw.

"How high?"

"Ten thousand to sit down."

Jack let out a whistle. "Ten thousand? How'd Ely manage to set up something like that?"

Lillie had pondered the same question when Ely gave her the news, but as she watched Jack sit up in bed, the wheels already turning in his head, she couldn't help smiling. It made her feel good to see him so excited again.

"Well, I have about six now," Jack said almost to himself.

"I could maybe spot you the rest," Lillie said, thinking of her stash. She knew she had made herself promise never to gamble away her hope, but Jack was a sure bet. Surer than anything she'd ever known. Maybe more than she had dreamed. She saw the look of surprise in his eyes, and it made her feel like the decision was a good one. "Of course, I get a cut of the pot. That is, if you think you can manage to win."

"*Manage* to win?" He gave her a dangerous grin. "And what makes you think I'd want to go in on it with you?"

"Only place around that'll guarantee you a square deal." She laughed and Jack pushed her back down on the bed, holding her arms down as he kissed her. For some reason, Lillie couldn't help wishing she could freeze the moment in time, that it could be the way it was right then forever. But then, what right did someone like her have to wish for something like that?

Wishes are for fools, the hurt kid part of her warned. But when she looked up into Jack's handsome face and saw the tenderness in those green eyes, she felt her heart swell, and a yearning to hope came from deep inside of her.

That was, unless those wishes were to come true. . . .

"I recall you saying we were going to have a picnic, but I don't remember anything being said about wading."

Jack chuckled, glancing back over his shoulder at Lillie, who stood at the edge of Alder Creek, holding onto her shoes and stockings. There were still a few wet spots along the bank from the rain, but at least they had chosen to picnic a ways from the heaps of mud left behind from the diggings.

"Well, wading's part of it. Back where I come from, folks would think it unnatural not to do a little wading at a picnic. It stirs the appetite."

"We already ate," Lillie pointed out. She was sticking her bare toe in and out of the water like a turtle peeking out of its shell, and when she looked at him Jack thought her eyes matched the blue of the sky.

"Ain't you ever heard of dessert?" he asked with a grin, sitting down next to her. "Work's the meat of life, pleasure the dessert, my Pa always liked to say. 'Course, I always tended to want my dessert first."

Lillie laughed. "Why doesn't that surprise me? I bet you were a *handful.*"

"Guess I was. 'Specially when my pa went out of town; not yet eleven and I'd be sneakin' in taverns to play cards. It'd get my ma so riled she'd call strangers off the street to give me a lickin'." Jack smiled at the memory, shaking his head. "But I think that was mostly because she never had the heart to do it herself."

"What else do you remember?" Lillie asked as Jack lit his smoke. He glanced sideways at her; her voice sounded almost needy.

"Well, I remember they were decent and good. A sight better than me I guess," he laughed and felt Lillie lay her hand over his as she looked across the creek with a soft smile on her face, as if she was trying to imagine his family. "You remember much about your folks?"

Lillie pulled her hand away, and he saw her clasp both hands together tight as she looked down. "I can't recall much about them, Jack," she said without much emotion, which jarred him. *What kind of family did she have that she couldn't speak of?* he wondered. It would be her choice to tell, he figured, if she ever did. Jack lifted his hand and brushed back her hair, making Lillie flinch.

"I might've done a lot I ain't proud of, Lillie, but I ain't ever hurt a woman," he said with puzzlement in his voice, and Lillie looked up at him. She hadn't meant to flinch—it was just an old habit she'd earned from Frank—but her mind had been on family and the poor memories she had of hers compared with Jack's. As she looked at him and felt her heart give, it made her suddenly want to tell him about her life.

"I know you wouldn't hurt me, Jack," she said with childlike trust. "My family wasn't much to speak of—not like yours, at least. My mama ran off with some miner not long after my pa staked a claim in Colorado. 'Course he wasn't the best husband—used his fist more than not." Lillie took a deep breath. "He kind of lost his senses . . . we pulled up stakes and ended up here with nothing but a bad case of mountain fever to show for all the miles we came. Then he died and Ely was the only one willing to take me in." Lillie looked up at him cautiously and was heartened by the compassion in Jack's eyes. But she couldn't dredge up enough courage to tell him about Frank—not yet. Not now, when things had just gotten better.

"Well, I swear, Lillie you've been through enough, haven't you?" he asked softly. "My sister Callie always said that sometimes God can take something bad and turn it to good. Maybe us meeting will be the good, you think?"

Lillie wanted to cry at the tender words and the hopeful, almost shy way Jack said them. "I think she might be right at that, Jack," she said softly, then smiled to break the mood. She hadn't met a man yet whose thoughts couldn't be changed by a smile, and Jack himself appeared relieved.

"So, what are you going to do with your share of the winnings?" he asked finally. She thought for a moment, trying to decide if she could tell him or not. Mostly her dreams were of having a fine house, one built smooth with milled lumber—not the rough green stuff they carted down from the mountains, either—a clapboard with colored glass panes and a gingerbread-trimmed porch. But it wouldn't do for him to know everything, so she made it simple.

"I figure I'll get me a home," she answered finally. "One that's mine so no one can make me leave it." Lillie snuck a glance at him to see if he'd poke fun, but his eyes had nothing but kindness in them and she recovered some of her ginger. "And what about you, Mr. Big Time, what are you gonna do with your share?"

Jack laughed but he looked put out, as if a thought had suddenly occurred to him. "Truth is, I've never thought that far," he said slowly. "The past few years have always been another town and another game—I don't guess I've ever sat still long enough to think about what could come next." Lillie watched the emotions wash over his face as he realized he had been so busy running from his past that he had forgotten his dreams.

"Maybe I'll stick around here long enough to find out this time," he said again with such hopefulness to his voice she felt it go to her heart. They both glanced upwards as a hawk appeared, soaring high above them, his wings spread wide.

"Days like this back home, I'd sneak off from the farm and go out to the meadows where I'd lie down in the grass and watch the sky, just watch it. Sometimes for so long I forgot about the time till the folks sent Callie or Rose after me." Jack smiled a different smile than she'd ever seen before, and she thought maybe it was the smile of the boy he used to be. He then pushed her back against the grass and lay next to her close, like they were two kids sharing a secret.

"Look up," he said. When she did, she saw the hawk was gone but the sky above them was wide and open. It seemed to have taken over everything, as if everything she had known had been wiped clean by the blue. Of all the time she had lived in the gulch, she couldn't remember the sky ever looking like that. Living there made her a part of it, she figured, and the thought made her feel small and big at the same time—like a kid holding a toy she couldn't believe she had. Lillie smiled and turned her head to see Jack watching her closely.

"What did you feel?" he asked.

"Like the world could be anything I imagined," she said, trying to find the right words. "Like I was free to hope."

Jack looked as pleased as she had ever seen, and they both looked back up to the blue above them once more. In that moment, Lillie felt as if they finally understood each other. Not so much with words or touches . . . but with their hearts.

> *Virginia City,*
> *Montana Territory*
> *June 10, 1864*

Mrs. Callie McGregor
Plumas City, California

Dear Callie,

Just reading your letter has made me feel like a real horse's behind for worrying you. I was down in the mouth is all, after what went on. Nearly left Virginia City, too, but this time I've chosen to stay instead of run. I guess I was a fool to try to run from my problems—it's like trying to run from yourself. Now, for the first time in a long while, I feel like I belong, Sis. I guess if ever there were a place for someone like me to belong, it would be here. I'm happy to say things are looking up at the tables as well, so I can't come for a visit just yet. There's some fellows coming to town for a big game Ely's set up and I ain't about to miss it.

Lady Luck is a sight for these sore eyes, even if she is a fickle wench.

I told Lillie as much and she laughed and said that as much as we gripe about Lady Luck, none of us would want to play if it was easy. She says she's seen a rumor stir fellows more than holding papers to the mother lode—that it's the thrill of getting there.

Which brings me to mind of a joke Lillie tells around here: This old miner makes it to Heaven only to find Saint Peter standing at the Pearly Gates with a sour look on his face. "What's ailing you, Saint Pete?" the old fellow asks. "It's them friends of yours," Saint Peter says. "They're digging up our streets of gold." The old miner, eager to help such a man of God, got an idea. He spread a rumor to the others about a huge strike below, of nuggets so big you could trip over them, and soon every last one of those miners were running out the Pearly Gates—including the old fellow who spread the tale. "Where are you going?" Saint Peter asked, shocked to see the little man gather up his pan and follow. "Might be something to that rumor!" the miner cried.

Lillie may be right about the thrill, but I tell you, I win this one, Sis, and you and Quinn won't have to wait so long for them dreams of yours. Might be, too, that I'll finally have the chance to figure out what mine are.

Jack

Eight

"Miss Lillie, you get any shinier and I'll have to move my claim to the Pair-O-Dice," a young, beet-faced miner declared as he slid a chip to the queen.

"And break poor Sarah Foster's heart?" Lillie asked in mock seriousness. "Why, Billy, ain't you learned the first rule of courting in the gulch? Many's the men that've lost an eye by letting it rove." The men around the table roared and Lillie smiled good-naturedly; truth was, she *felt* shiny. The last few days she and Jack had been like two kids waiting on an overdue Christmas, what with the big game just around the corner. Lillie looked down with pleasure at the new, cream-colored dress Jack gave her before riding off with Duel. There was another upstairs, too; a blue velveteen that he'd picked out just for the game. But it wasn't just the dresses; life itself looked new.

Lillie pulled the next two cards from the case box, calling winner and loser, and as she did she noticed some of the men casting looks toward the front of the saloon. She raised her head and saw Frank Monroe standing in the door. She thought it felt a bit like holding a rose and suddenly getting pricked by the thorn. A reminder, she supposed, that life could be good—just not perfect.

Laughter fell off and the men who had been playing at her table edged away, one by one, until she was left standing alone, shuffling her cards with an air that was meant to be casual; Frank fed off fear. But then, most bullies did.

While she figured she was pretty much over being surprised by much that happened, she never dreamed she'd see him standing in the Pair-O-Dice again, looking at her like he owned her. It was the look that rankled her. *You're in for a surprise, Frank,* she thought pertly. She wasn't the same person who wilted inside at the thought of trouble. It had taken her awhile to climb out of the hole, so she wasn't about to crawl back in for anyone. *Trouble, let 'er buck,* she figured.

Frank smiled widely as he strolled over to her table. Maybe it was meant to be cordial but Lillie doubted it. It was strange to her how she could have ever been fooled by the man. What she'd thought was charm had been nothing more than shined-up lies. Once he got his way, the effort to be appealing disappeared, which was when folks saw the real Frank—and all of his ugliness. Lillie suddenly felt cornered and was obliged to end it.

"What are you doing here, Frank?" she asked abruptly.

"Bad day, Lillie?" he asked personally, like they had never been apart. She narrowed her eyes.

"No, just bad company."

Frank chuckled. "Well, now, Lillie, is that a way to talk? Here I ride all the way into town to see how you've been farin' since I've been gone and this is how you treat me." His eyes raked over her. "You look good. I guess the rumors are true, then?"

"What rumors would those be?" she asked finally. He smiled but there was a chill in his eyes that she couldn't miss, and she felt a cold fear start in her belly.

"Why, that you're doin' so well you might just start up your own place," he said. She knew he was lying as soon as he said it.

"First I ever heard of it," she said, trying to read the look in his eyes. "But then, you never know, do you?"

"Ain't that the truth," he said softly. When she remained silent, he just stood there, looking at her until she thought she might scream. Finally, he glanced to his men and they pushed away from the bar, trailing behind him as he made his way through the crowd.

"Good luck, Lillie," he called for all to hear, but there was nothing friendly in his tone. Lillie stared at the door long after Frank and his men had disappeared into the street, trying to figure out what he had meant by the odd visit. Surely Ely hadn't been fool enough to let Frank in on the game, she thought, cold fear suddenly gripping her insides. And why hadn't the thought occurred to her before now? She considered telling Jack about Frank but with the game only a day away, it might queer his luck. Lillie shook her uneasiness off. She was just thinking too much, is all. There was so much to look forward to now, she had no intentions of letting a little run-in with Frank Monroe spoil it.

"You ever wonder about the folks you throw in with, Duel? I mean, why it is that you might not even mean to get close to certain people, but it just happens?" Jack asked out of the blue. They had ridden for nearly an hour, steadily making their way upwards through mountain country, skirting ledges and dipping into shaded coulees. The peaceful scenery lulled Jack, and he had turned to thinking of the recent turn his life had taken.

"I reckon I might've wondered once," Duel said after a pause. "Don't no more." He looked over his shoulder at Jack for a moment, then turned back to face the trail ahead. "Way I got it figured, life's our road. Folks we meet are like these here stones we're riding over. Some's big, some's so small you don't notice, some you reckon to kick out of the way." A small twitch that might've been a smile touched Duel's lips. "Others, well, you can't help take notice of and throw in with them, like you say. Those are the ones—if you're lucky—you get to hold real long, the ones you keep in your pocket until it gets too heavy and you have to set 'em back on the road."

While Jack pondered what his friend had said, Duel squinted against the glare of sun that touched off the walls of the canyon and abruptly reined in.

"Well, here she is," he announced with soft pride. "The Celie Mae." He dismounted and Jack followed, watching as Duel pulled his knife from his belt and began to work a piece of rock from inside a half-dug hole on the hillside. "Now, this here is another kind of rock," he said, putting it in Jack's hand.

Jack weighed the jagged piece in his hand; it didn't look like much but quartz, he thought. But then, he was no miner. He peered thoughtfully into the hole and saw what looked to be an old pick and shovel propped against the wall of rock. There were cobwebs on them and a thick layer of dust, like ghosts of a dream.

"Ever come up with anything?" he asked, handing the rock back to Duel.

"Oh, she's showed color—enough to tide me over for a time," Duel said. "Got a feeling there's more up there for the taking, too."

"Hell, why don't you work it?" Jack asked, puzzled.

"Don't seem as important as it used to be. Lost the fever, I guess," Duel said with a shrug. Jack wondered if it was losing his wife that caused Duel to quit.

"Well, we're a pair; you don't want nothin' and I can't seem to get enough," Jack laughed awkwardly.

"That's why I brought you here. Anything ever happens to me, Jack, and she's half yours—the other half is my son Coy's, if he ever decides to come back."

Duel found himself a seat on an outcropping of rock and chewed thoughtfully on a piece of jerky he'd pulled from the side of his saddle, looking down at the stream that ran below them. Jack felt uncomfortable just standing there, so he joined him, accepting the piece of jerky Duel offered him as he sat down.

The hurried feeling he had within him most of the time always slowed when he was with Duel. Jack took a thoughtful swig of water from his canteen and glanced over at his friend. There was something different about Duel, not because of what he'd said but more of a feeling Jack couldn't place.

"You ain't sick or nothin' are you?" he asked finally as Duel gave him a tolerant look.

"No, I ain't sick. I just got to thinkin' it'd be a waste to keep Celie Mae a secret. You and my boy, Coy, seem to have a powerful lot of *wantin'*, I figured to give it to you two. Only thing I ask of the good Lord is some better fishin' weather." Duel took another bite of his jerky. " 'Bout the only other thing I'd fancy'd be a giant of a marker when I go, like one of them angels or such," he added.

"I don't guess you're going anywhere, yet," Jack said, grinning to hide his discomfort. He hated talk of death—especially Duel's. Besides, he figured them to be near enough in age and he had no plans of dying anytime soon. Jack suddenly felt annoyed; he hadn't come to discuss death or tombstones. He had come to see Duel's claim and maybe talk a little of the big game. "You sure have an odd way of lookin' at things," he said after a lengthy pause.

"Life's odd, Jack. I thought you knew that," Duel said, looking amused. He took a modest swig from his own canteen and wiped his face with his sleeve.

"And getting odder by the minute," Jack said. "What say we play a little game of cards before you kick off—that's if you think you have time."

Duel laughed. "Oh, I always got time for a game, Jack."

Duel stared up at the clear, starlit sky from his bedroll and thought of the conversation he had had with Jack up at his claim. He knew he'd put Jack off with all of his talk of death and angel headstones, but it had been a constant thing on his mind as of late. Especially since the hangings. Funny thing was, he didn't fear death for some reason as much as he feared a poor burial.

It *was* an odd train of thought to have, he thought, and considered the possibility that being alone for so long had caused him to be touched in the head a bit.

He sat up in his bedroll and reached for the side pouch in his saddle, extracting the large piece of quartz he had brought back from the Celie Mae. He hadn't missed the doubt on Jack's face when his friend had studied the rock. Duel could've told him it wouldn't look like much in its pure form, that the quartz ledges were the stuff of every miner's dream, for they held the richest gold before it got washed downstream, but a silence had come over him before he could explain. There was a lot more he could teach Jack, he knew, but he had sensed a *searching* in him. In spite of what his friend thought, Duel knew that until Jack made peace with that, his journey would be far from over. It made Duel wonder if his urge for silence wasn't the good Lord's way of telling him Jack would have to learn his lessons for himself.

The gambler's road wouldn't be without its own kind of stones, that was for sure.

Duel sighed, dropped the rock back into the satchel, and pulled his blanket up over him, thinking of the strange ways of fate, and willed himself back to sleep.

The day of the game dawned like any other day. What made it different, Lillie figured, was the fever pitch she and Jack had been in since they had risen. Jack at least had gotten himself ready while she sat on the bed, hair still loose down her back, hugging her knees, and trying to decide what to do first.

"I ain't worn clothes like this in awhile. Might take some gettin' used to," Jack said, turning to her with a boyish grin as he slipped the brocaded waistcoat on over the new white shirt and string tie. In spite of what he believed, he looked just as at ease in the gambler's dress as he did in trail clothes—and just as handsome, she thought with a pleasant twinge to her heart. He sat down next to her on the bed and pulled his boots on, stamping them on the floor with the impatience to get going. She saw the impatience in his face, too, but his expression softened when he looked at her. He leaned over and kissed her slowly then, leaving his warmth on her lips.

"This is *our* chance, Lillie," he said as he finally pulled away. "Stick with me and we'll see to all of those dreams and then some." Lillie smiled up at him; he had been saying *our* and *we* a lot lately and it gave her a heady feeling.

"I guess you'll do," she sniffed. A laugh burst out of Jack, wild and reckless, matching the anticipation bubbling up in her for what was to come.

"You're one of a kind," he said as she handed him his overcoat. They grinned at each other like two kids. Noises from below intruded: hearty male laughter, heavy boots, and fiddle music. The fiddle music was good, being that Ely bribed old J.T. to stay sober for as long as he played.

"Sounds like Ely's got half the town down there already," she said. "You best go on and warm your hand. I'll be down in no time."

Jack turned his back to her and as he shrugged into the jacket, she thought she noticed an odd quirk of movement, like a shiver running over his broad shoulders, down the muscles of his back. She could only see the side of his face, but it looked tense.

"Jack?" she said, moving towards him, but when he glanced over his shoulder the easy smile was back.

"Goose-walked over my grave is all," Jack chuckled, opening the door. "Best hurry on down—I might need you to help me warm up."

Lillie shook her head, laughing as the door closed behind her, and plucked her new dress off the nail in the wall that served as her closet. Jack was one of a kind, himself, she thought, slipping on the blue velveteen. All those dreams she'd felt so far from her reach, and he made it seem he was tall enough to snatch them all down for her. She pulled the little combs—the only thing she had left of her mama—from the slip of paper in the bottom of her drawer and tucked them in her thick hair. When she glanced at herself in the mirror on the wall, she couldn't help but smile. Hope bloomed outright on her face for the first time in a long, long while. *That money I saved wasn't my hope, Jack. You are,* she thought. *So, you pull this off, I might just call it even. Might be we'll both be able to start fresh together.*

Jack surveyed the crowd that had jammed themselves into the one room of the Pair-O-Dice and felt his blood quicken. It appeared that more than half of the town showed up to witness the game: miners and cowboys, muleskinners and businessmen, some he couldn't even put a name to. They pressed around him, clapping him on the back with good cheer and advice, offering him drinks as they began to spin wild yarns of his gambling talents. Jack grinned and took it as all part of the show, but when he glanced back at the stairs and saw Lillie standing at the bottom of them, looking prettier than he had ever seen, he decided to take his leave. "Well, boys, as my pa always said, 'You keep listenin' to them tall tales long enough and one day you'll believe 'em,' " he called over his shoulder and the men all laughed.

Lillie smiled as she drew close to him. He let out a whistle, then leaned over and whispered, "You ain't part of the take, are you?"

"If you're the winner, I am," she said with a saucy grin. He laughed outright as he steered them through the crowd to the table where he was to play. The two men who were already seated stood and shook his hand, their expressions tighter than he was used to seeing on gaming men. Jack had no more gotten seated when he heard a murmur go through the crowd and a few men stepped out of the way, giving way to the man who moved past them with a jaunty gait. Duel, who had been standing off to one side, moved nearer to the table, his dark eyes meeting Jack's with a look of warning.

"I'm not late for the dance, am I?" the man asked as he sat down. The other men at the table laughed as if they knew him. Jack studied him closely. There was something familiar about him. He judged them to be of about the same height, although the fellow had at least ten years on him, time and weather digging into his sharp features, giving him a rough look despite the fancy clothes he wore. When he smiled, Jack felt the hackles on his neck rise, and he wondered at it as the stranger introduced himself, holding a hand out to Jack.

"Name's Frank," he said, his dark eyes flicking up to where Lillie stood behind him. Jack thought he read something proprietary in the look, and he felt Lillie's hand press into his shoulder, but then Frank leaned back in his chair and smiled amiably as Jack opened the new deck.

"I guess you ought to commence dealing, son," he said, still smiling, but his tone sounded insolent.

"Well, I didn't open this deck for the exercise," he replied, his tone just as insolent but he covered it with a wide, easy grin as he cut the cards. Jack forced his attention to the game as he dealt, feeling a rush like he'd never felt before build in him. A pot of forty thousand wasn't nothing to sneeze at, and this time it wasn't just his money on the line. He glanced over his shoulder at Lillie and winked.

The first two hands, he laid back on, studying each man for their tells and once he felt comfortable he began in earnest. Both he and Frank raised several times until the other players were driven out of the hand.

"I'll call," Frank said finally.

"I got two pairs," Jack said, appearing disheartened.

"Well, *three* jacks just did you in, boy," Frank laughed, reaching for the pot as a disappointed sigh went through the crowd until Jack spread his hand across the felt.

"Not when both my pairs are kings," Jack said, grinning. One of the miners who had been taking side bets hooted.

"Hell, Wade just beat him out," the old miner declared. As he did, Jack saw Frank draw his chips back, a wide smile of anticipation on his face.

"Jack Wade, you say?" he said, sounding surprised. "Well, don't that beat all. I guess you know my brother, Jude Monroe?"

Jack's hands paused above the stack of chips in the center of the table and his eyes raised to Frank's face: narrow jaw, high forehead, small dark eyes. He felt like God's own fool that he hadn't noticed the man's resemblance to Jude. He wondered how long Frank had known he was in town. Long enough to set him up, that was plain, he thought, taking in the other players' expressions of contempt. There was no doubt left in Jack's mind the men were a part of Frank's plan. He held his temper down as best he could as he glanced first to Ely, then Lillie, but their faces were set in shock and worry. He tried to find Duel, but he was gone from the spot where he'd been standing.

Jack wondered why it surprised him, the way fate worked; never slow or subtle, but falling on him fast, like a damned bear trap that's jaws snap closed before he could pull free.

"Didn't know Jude as good as I thought," Jack said with great control, "or else he might've shared the fact he was on the run with money that wasn't his."

"Well, to hear the law tell it, you're the one with the money. *My* money, I should say." A fair-haired fellow stepped forward from behind Frank, and Jack recognized him as the kid he'd buffaloed back on the first day he and Duel met. He looked the same except for his eyes. They looked dead.

"Let's see you get out of this one, Mr. Big Time," he said, but when Jack's eyes stayed on him, he turned away and pretended to spit tobacco in the direction of the spittoon.

"Listen, Monroe, I ain't got the money—your brother does. As far as what's on this table, I won that fair. You and your boys try to kick that and I'll fight you," Jack said. There was a moment when all was quiet in the saloon.

The moment was just that, though; somewhere down deep Jack had expected the day to come.

"No, Frank!" Lillie shouted as he went for his gun and people scrambled for cover. Those who didn't make it out the door fell to the floor, covering their heads, but Jack's shot hit first, ripping the gun from Frank's hand, and he fell to the floor howling as he tried to staunch the blood that pumped from his two missing fingers.

"You're dead, Wade," Frank rasped. The words set the other men at the table in motion. They lunged at Jack, two pinning him while the other struck blow after blow between his shoulder blades until Jack dropped to his knees in pain, then they took turns kicking him in the ribs. Somewhere in the haze of pain, he thought he heard Lillie scream and he fought to stay conscious.

"Finish him," Frank ordered as some of his men helped him to his feet and he turned to the boy. "Riley, you get the money." The towhead held his gun on Ely and grabbed the bag of money behind the bar.

Another shot roared, shattering the bottles above Ely's head. Ely swiped at the whiskey running down his face and came away with blood on his hand. Not realizing he'd only suffered a minor cut from flying glass, his face went white with anxiety. "I ain't ever goin' to wish for more again, Mabel," he said tersely and passed out. Those left in the saloon turned and saw Duel standing just inside the door, guns trained on Frank and his men—and theirs on him.

"Riders coming," one of Frank's men shouted. "I bet that nigger fetched 'em." The men holding Jack dumped him on the floor and grabbed their guns as they quickly headed for the door behind the men who supported Frank. Riley Wayne paused for a moment, turning back to Duel.

"I ain't forgot you," he said with naked hatred in his eyes.

"You said that before," Duel said evenly and the kid just smiled.

"I don't want *you* to forget," he said, spitting on the floor as he walked out.

Duel walked over to where Jack sat kneeling on the floor, trying to catch his wind as Lillie blotted the blood seeping from the corner of his lips. Lillie raised her head and when their eyes met, the emotions that showed were like a mirror image; worry and love for the stubborn, reckless man who sat between them, his green eyes filled with pain as he tried to figure out what to do next. But they already knew.

Most of the time a man wounded at the table in Virginia City wasn't much of a big to-do, especially if the wound wasn't mortal. Frank Monroe was another story, though. Lillie and Duel both knew Jack would've been better off killing Frank—for his sake as well as theirs.

"What do you think, Duel?" Jack asked, wincing a bit as he turned to his friend who had remained silent after all the commotion had died down. Lillie had already gone to Jack's room to pack his things, and he felt like the decision had been taken out of his hands.

"Never trust a wolf for dead till he's been skun," Duel speculated. He turned and caught Jack's eye. "You may be a gambler, but you ain't no killer, Jack. That's what you'd have to be to stay."

Jack digested the information somberly. Duel was never one to mince words, and Jack felt the truth of what he said weigh him down. Why he *didn't* kill Frank was still a mystery. He could've easily, but there had been that last second of doubt.

"I could stand and fight," Jack said almost to himself. "I could take him, Duel."

"Frank's got the edge," Duel said, shaking his head. "You bein' wanted gave him that. Oh, he might pretend he's goin' to turn you into the law, but I'd lay odds you'd never make it there alive. Best thing you can do is head for north country. Deer Lodge ain't too awful far. Might buy you some time to sort it out."

Jack stood tight-lipped, wanting to argue, but he knew it was pointless. He suddenly saw his days ahead, riding for nowhere again, and the loneliness of it loomed large before him. When he glanced at Duel, he saw the worry in his friend's eyes and he tried to smile. Duel had become family to him.

"I couldn't've asked for a better man to back me today," Jack said, looking at him earnestly. "You've been there when most men wouldn't."

"Don't believe I would've missed it," Duel said with that smile of his. "No, sir. 'Tho I do think I'll be more careful next time I wish for some excitement in my life." Both men chuckled, then fell quiet for a time. It was Duel who finally broke the silence.

"It sure has been somethin', ain't it?" he asked and the look on his face startled Jack, as if they wouldn't be seeing each other again.

"Oh, you ain't gettin' rid of me that easy." Jack looked at Duel, trying to find the right words. "I'll be back, you wait and see," he said finally, then grinned. "If my memory serves me, you still owe me a game."

"Always be another game, Jack," Duel said.

Jack grasped his hand hard, a brother-like grip that said more than words ever could. In spite of that, a sudden urge came over Jack to tell Duel what his friendship meant to him, but it was quick to pass, as those types of urges in men do.

"Well, Duel says I should leave town, too," Jack said, closing the door behind him. Lillie looked up from the clothes she had placed into a neat bedroll, then finished tying it off tight. "I might've shied from some things in my life, Lillie, but a fight ain't one of them."

He sounded more weary than angry and Lillie straightened up from the chore, bracing herself. She felt as if she could burst into tears at any moment. *Was it only this morning that we were laughing?* she thought, and she wanted with all her might to curse at somebody or spit on them she was so mad. But she knew if she was going to blame anyone it would be herself; she had pretended is all. She had made herself believe that the world couldn't touch them. Thing was, she had lived long enough to know better. "You got to know when to pick your battles, Jack," she said. "Frank makes his own laws out here—or his money does. Now he's got ours, too, and that doesn't leave you with much of a choice."

"Cowards run."

"Well," Lillie snapped, more out of fear than anything else. "I think I'd rather say, 'Here's where he ran' than 'Here's where he died.' "

Jack let out a long breath as if giving in to his fate, and he saw Lillie's eyes mist a little but she nodded, her chin jutted out strong.

He searched her face. "I'll be back," he said finally, surprised to see the expression on her face, as if she knew better. In her eyes he saw clearly the image of his past: riding away from Salt Lake, Callie standing in the middle of the dusty road, waving as the tears streamed down her face.

His mind sifted through memories of him and Lillie, laughing together at the races, the picnic . . . all their plans. Such big plans. They were different and alike, the two of them. Lillie always trying to find life and he always trying to run away from it. But there was always an understanding between them, a bond, for in spite of it all, they had both learned to survive.

And that, maybe more than even blood, would always bind them.

Maybe that was why Lillie had always given so much, never asking for anything except for him to care, he thought. *And he did.*

That occurring to him, Jack wondered with dread if he would always be cursed with realizing what he'd lost after it was too late to change it.

When he finally forced himself to move closer, he felt something in him tear as he looked down at her.

"I love you, Lillie," he said softly, glad for only a moment that he had spoken the words. Lillie looked as if he had struck her and he realized speaking the words so late, with him leaving, had maybe hurt her worse than if he had never said them at all.

Jack moved to touch her face, but she stopped him short, placing a wad of greenbacks in his open hand, then closing it with her own. Jack started to protest but she shook her head.

"Take the money, Jack. I can get more," she said a bit surer than she felt.

"Got a heart of gold, Lillie," Jack said softly. She laughed bitterly to drown out the hurt.

"A heart of gold?" Lillie repeated, but when she looked up at Jack's face, she saw his eyes were unreadable—gambler's eyes. The expression on his face was that of a man on the run . . . and once again alone. Lillie steeled herself against the pain of his leaving then . . . against caring. "You don't know me at all, Jack. If I'd had a heart of gold, I'd have sold it long ago."

Jack was unaware of Lillie's vigil by the window as she watched him ride out of town, of the hopelessness that returned like an old enemy resurrected, or the way she'd crossed her arms tight over her chest as if to shield her heart. *Should've been used to losing by now,* she thought with a stubborn jut of her chin.

She saw Jack turn back and wave and was thankful that he was too far away to see the tears that streamed down her face as she pulled the tattered old curtain closed on the night and on the dream of a life different from what she'd been dealt.

Along the Beaverhead River,
Montana Territory
June, 1864

Mrs. Callie McGregor
Plumas City, California

Dear Callie,

I guess you won't be too surprised to hear I got myself in another pinch. I wouldn't waste the ink to explain, but I figure I might as well write a finish to it. I do want you to know that in spite of what folks might say, or whatever may come of me, it wasn't my doing.

Do you recall that gambler I wrote about named Jude? Well, his brother showed up during the big poker game, claiming I had his money and wasn't taking no for an answer. I ended up having to wing him— but didn't kill him. I'm hoping I won't regret the latter—Frank Monroe would just as soon cut your gizzard out for the fun.

The kick of all of this is that he was the ringleader in that bunch of roughs who killed Nell's pa. Seems like Frank's been looking for me for awhile. He only got wind of me because of the hanging. How's that for life stabbing you in the back? That card game was nothing but a setup and he's not finished yet. I thought to stay for the fun but Duel and Lillie are sure that I will be killed if I do. So, I've left Virginia City for the time being.

Seems like my life has been filled with me escaping from one thing or another. Funny thing is, I was willing to stay put this time. It was the first time since leaving Salt Lake that I'd put down some roots, you know, made a name for myself.

Lillie always did say the only way most fellows get a name out here is on a tombstone. I guess I ain't ready to oblige them just yet.

Jack

Montana Territory
June, 1864

Mrs. Callie McGregor
Plumas City, California

Dear Callie,

Things ain't going too great. I have been hiding out for the past two nights after I was forced to leave Helena. I was playing a game of cards with some miners there when I overheard some fellows asking the bartender if he'd heard of a man named Jack Wade so I lit out of there. They just missed my camp last night, riding right past it. It was pure luck that I camped near such thick brush. That and they ain't the sharpest of fellows. But there are more of them than me.

None of this seems real. How can it be that only a few days ago everything was looking up? I best quit this letter, it's getting dark again and I have to find cover in case those stinking cutthroats of Frank's are lurking around here.

The only shelter I've been able to spot is an old outhouse standing alone in the middle of the valley here, so I guess that's where I'll be staying.

Fitting, ain't it?

Jack

Nine

Lillie sat on her stool with her back to the window, studying the crack in the wall as a fat brown bug crawled along the seam. *Is this all there is?* she wondered and the thought startled her some. She'd never really had such hopeless thoughts before. Truth was, she saw things differently since Jack's leaving; clearer, maybe. The bit of fixing up she'd done on her room before the game hadn't changed things as much as she'd once thought. It was still bare looking; no amount of wildflowers or old doilies would change that. As trapped feeling as she was, she couldn't help thinking of it as Hell. Or at least purgatory.

Downstairs wasn't much better. The men, so put off by her sudden silences, had tried every way to get her back to her old self but failed. It had aggravated Ely so, seeing her that way, that he'd taken to his bed again. Which was just as well as far as Lillie was concerned. His looks of pity annoyed her.

Getting your hopes up and then having them taken away was hard enough to swallow, she thought. Someone else's pity could choke you to death.

What surprised her was how quick it was that she'd been brought down to such a mood. The hurt in Jack's leaving seemed to stay with her all of the time, like a bad toothache. One week was all he'd been gone, after all. What was a week? Trying not to dwell on it too much, Lillie forced herself to look out the window and watch as life in the gulch hurried on without her and she felt her cheeks flush with anger.

She wondered for the hundredth time why Jack hadn't told her of Jude Monroe. Not that he had ever told her much of anything. But she hadn't told him of Frank, either.

There was so much left undone, unfinished between them.

I love you . . . Jack's words haunted her again and again and she fought the tears that sprang to her eyes.

It isn't fair, she thought childishly.

To make matters worse, Frank Monroe appeared in her line of sight on the street with some of his men, puffed up like a banty rooster, strutting and laughing easily, as if the bandage on his hand was no trouble at all. The mean thought of wishing the wound had been fatal came to Lillie, and she dropped the curtains back, frustrated.

The rumors hadn't helped: whispers of Frank sending a party out to hunt Jack down. For all she knew Jack could already be lying somewhere hurt. The image of Nell's pa's lifeless body being carried in on a buckboard filled her mind and she shuddered. Jack wouldn't give up without a fight, of course. But then, she thought, Frank never fought fair in his life.

What was needed was someone to even the odds; someone who knew the country well enough to get to Jack first and warn him. Worrying filled her with such tension, she felt she might snap like a dry twig if something didn't give. Lillie tortured her brain for an answer as to what to do. When the image of Duel came to her suddenly and clearly, Lillie stood up, beginning to recover some of her ginger. *Duel* knew the Territory. And he was someone Jack trusted. Lillie quickly gathered her things for the ride out to Duel's shanty. It felt good to be doing something, she thought, as a rueful smile crossed her lips. Feeling sorry for yourself was alright, but sitting on that stool as long as she did had started to give her a cramp.

Making her way down the stairs, Lillie smiled her best smile, waving to some of Frank's men as she passed.

"You boys ready for a game?" she called. The men in the room cheered, glad to see the old Lillie back in business. Frank's men seemed to relax at this, and she felt a sense of satisfaction. There was more than one way to play poker, she thought smugly.

"Never show your hand too soon," Jack had told her once. *"Keep the sonsabitches guessing so hard, Lillie, they'll soon forget all about what they're holding."*

It hadn't been hard to find Duel, of course. As she dismounted near the little log cabin where he lived, Lillie caught a glimpse of him standing over a makeshift forge, tinkering on something she couldn't quite see with that quiet way he had in going about whatever needed to be done. He'd backed up Jack that first day in much the same way, she thought. Funny thing was, he'd been at least as fast as Jack on the draw, yet she could never remember seeing Duel with a gun until that day.

"Got another game going, Miss Lillie?" Duel called, looking up.

"You might say that," she answered grimly. As she moved closer, she saw the remnants of an old fire and a bedroll tucked neatly beneath an open lean-to. Lillie recalled Jack telling her that Duel didn't live in his house and she had thought it odd at the time. *Funny how life changes the way we see things,* Lillie thought. Somewhere along the line, Duel had come to feel he didn't fit to that life anymore and Lillie understood it. Duel no more belonged in that cabin than she belonged at Ely's. Lillie saw Duel watching her curiously, and she smiled as she wondered to herself how she was going to approach him with everything.

What she did know was that she needed him—that *Jack* needed him.

"I think Jack's in more trouble than he can handle, Duel," she said. She saw a flicker of interest in his dark eyes and rushed on. "There's talk of Frank sending some men after him to hunt him down. I can't say as I doubt it, knowing Frank."

Duel nodded. "He's a hard customer, that's for sure." He set his tools aside and began to wipe the grime from his work-worn hands.

"I know Jack was figuring on heading north and I heard you know your way around. I wouldn't ask but . . ."

"Ain't nothin' I wouldn't do for Jack," Duel interrupted and went about packing up the little bit of tools he owned. But it wasn't until he'd slipped his carbine in its sheath on the side of the saddle that she realized he was going to find Jack. That was it. No hesitation, no questions asked. She felt a surge of admiration and gratitude for the colored man. Few men would act so unselfishly.

"Think he'll get out of this one?" Lillie asked and Duel glanced back at her.

"I imagine Jack'll find a way, Miss Lillie," he said, the respect in his voice tinged with a note of humor. "Either that or he'll *make* one. Best thing for me to do is to back him in whatever he decides." For a moment, Duel turned and stared at the little house he'd built, then picked up an old leather-bound Bible he had lying next to his bedroll and tucked it carefully into his saddlebag. He nodded, almost to himself, and grabbed the reins of his horse.

"You're a good man, Duel Harper," Lillie blurted out. At first she resisted the sudden peculiar notion to embrace him—and embarrass them both. In spite of the thought, she reached up on her tiptoes and wrapped her arms around his thick neck, hugging him quickly and for all she was worth.

As she stepped back, a rare kind of smile crossed Duel's face as if he understood. For a time after he'd ridden off, Lillie just stood there, watching his shape fade farther and farther away, and she couldn't help wonder if Jack would ever realize just how much of a friend he had in Duel.

Duel felt the tension in his body unwind as he rode away from Virginia City. Truth be known, he was glad to put some miles behind him and the cabin he'd once considered his refuge. The irksome dreams he'd been having for three nights straight had made him wary of even stepping foot inside his cabin. Restless. The first dream had been of snakes. His mother had always told him dreams of snakes meant enemies. If that was the case, he had a pack of them. The thought occurred to him then that maybe Jack's trouble tied in to his dreams somehow and he felt a surge of worry for his friend.

Deer Lodge seemed the best place to start and the easiest for Jack to find, heading north as he was. Thinking of the little settlement perked up Duel's spirits some. It'd been awhile since he'd ridden up that way, but he never regretted it once he was there. There were good people there. And the valley always seemed to have a way of healing his mind troubles.

Riding along, Duel tried not to think of his last dream; a strange dream of him trying to clean his cabin but never being able to finish the chore. His wife Celie had appeared in the doorway and laughed when he started at seeing her. *"Quit your fretting, man,"* she'd said. *"I got us a room all fixed. You just come along with me."* He'd tried to follow but when he got out the door, she'd disappeared. When he woke up, he could have sworn her scent lingered and he'd sat up in his bedroll uneasily and held tight to the Bible Jack had given him until morning had peaked over the mountains again.

He had paged through some of the book that morning, his large hands feeling clumsy as he moved his fingers down the writing, trying to spot the few words Celie had taught him. He had found a few, such as *Lord, rock,* and *sword,* and the words had made him feel as though he should be ready for something—but peaceful, too. Then Miss Lillie had come.

Duel knew better than most that things happen for a reason. His befriending Jack and Lillie coming to him was all meant to be. And although he couldn't explain it, he knew it was meant for him to be the one to find Jack and warn him, too.

"Reasons for everything, Duel," Celie liked to say.

As he spurred on his horse, Duel's face was set grimly against the endless bursts of wind that rode the land. He shivered unexpectedly and fought the sudden peculiar urge to look back over his shoulder. Yessir, he thought, might be I can talk Jack into staying on in Deer Lodge for awhile. Winter coming, the valley would be a better resting place than most. More peaceful than Virginia City and not much wind to speak of at all.

And Duel of all people knew just how hateful the wind could be.

The Indian woman was about as sturdy as they come, Duel thought as he sat astride his horse watching her wade the stream. He recalled some of the trappers' wives he had met last time he had come into Deer Lodge, but this one didn't look familiar. As if she sensed someone near, he saw her glance around, and he waved a couple of times to get her attention. When she finally did see him, a startled look crossed her face and she turned and scrambled up the bank on the other side of the creek and took off running wild through the woods. Duel saw her trip once but she was on her feet again in no time, in spite of her large size.

"Ain't no need to run, woman," he called out friendly but the sound of a single rifle shot cut off anything else he would have said. Duel felt the jolt of the bullet tear into him, throwing him forward with a blinding pain that seared through him. He groaned, trying to grasp the pommel to keep from falling.

We ain't never goin' to get to play that game, Jack, he thought sorrowfully, feeling himself slump over the neck of his horse. Another pain stabbed him from his belly to his groin, and he slid off the horse and fell hard to the ground as a thick curtain of black filled his vision. He heard his killer ride up and dismount, heard the steady crunch of steps until they stopped next to him, then he felt the boot slam into his ribs.

"Told you I wouldn't forget you, nigger," the voice sneered.

With the air knocked out of him, Duel couldn't find his voice, but he felt his blood run cold. *It was the kid.* Lillie had been right about it all, he thought, and the knowledge that he'd never make it to Jack to warn him put a pain in him worse than the one that was taking his life. The kid must have realized he was dying because he soon lost interest in kicking him and Duel heard him finally ride away. When it got quiet again, Duel began to drift in and out, memories of little things filling his head. Some he was surprised his mind even bothered to recall; a handshake, a smile, putting an arm around some grieved stranger whose name he couldn't remember. He saw bigger moments, too, of family and friends, the choices he had made, some good, some not so good. *So, this is death,* he thought, wondering in a detached kind of way as he floated along what would come next. World sounds came to him suddenly, pulling him from his stupor, and the familiar noise of a horse huffing filled his ears, then footsteps coming close.

Duel blinked away the haze that filled his vision with great effort and saw a scrawny-looking old white man with a gray beard that hung down past his chest standing over him.

"Little Woman said there was a dark feller out here bein' kilt but I thought she was jes' tryin' ter get me out of my chair," he said, peering down at Duel. "Good thing for you she's got a temper. Many men's the fool that don't fear a woman's temper but I ain't in their number."

"Thought I was dead," Duel whispered as another pain racked his body, and the old man looked somber.

"Well, ye ain't yet, feller. But ye soon will be, I hate t'say," he speculated. Duel nodded and tried to gather what strength he had left to speak.

"Tell Jack it ain't his fault . . . it was the kid," Duel rasped. "Tell him . . . I'd be obliged if he'd plant me decent. . . ."

Duel was surprised to see tears in the sorry brown eyes that studied his face. The old man sat down hard next to him in the dirt. "It don't ever git easy seein' death," he sighed. "I reckon t've seen enough of it, too."

It felt good, the way the old-timer propped him up, patting his hand as though he cared, Duel thought wearily as he felt himself fading. His Celie used to do for him like that. Duel was suddenly startled from the pleasantness of the thought as a blinding shaft of sunlight hit his eyes and he tried to raise his arm to shield them, but his arms didn't work anymore so he tried to speak.

"What's it you say?" the old man asked, leaning his ear to Duel's lips, but the big man realized it didn't matter anymore. His Celie was there.

The nightmare startled Jack awake and he laid still in his bedroll, taking deep gulps of air in an effort to steady his nerves. He couldn't remember much but the running and the feeling of terror. He sat up and lit the last cigar he'd won off a miner he had played in Helena and looked around at the empty countryside as daylight began to break over the horizon. The realization that he should've taken Duel's advice on going straight to Deer Lodge had seeped in days ago, but the urge he felt at the moment to get going was stronger than he ever felt before. He packed up the little he had and mounted, putting Big Black into a steady pace as he fought down the urge to look over his shoulder.

Along noon, Jack felt his spirits rise. It had turned out to be a fine day, sunny and a bit cool, but with hardly any wind, it made for perfect riding weather. He found himself even smiling as he rode across the high-grass bottoms of the broad mountain valley, pushing Big Black to a quick lope as he spotted the beginnings of civilization.

Not long after he'd passed the few huts and cabins, he came across a rather large squaw and what looked to be three half-breed children playing along the banks of a creek. The squaw squinted at him briefly as he passed, not saying anything. But when he glanced back, he caught her looking at him queerly before she stooped back over her fire and he felt an odd tingle go up his neck. *Something's wrong,* Jack thought, pushing his horse on. The hair on his neck was still standing by the time he reached the good-size log house farther down the stream. Jack pulled the horse down to a walk as he scanned the yard, spotting a man of indeterminate age sitting on the front porch of the house.

He had one elbow on his knee and was snoring heavily until something in his sleep jerked him awake and he rolled his eyes toward Jack. He woke quickly and leaned forward in his chair, apparently eager for the company. "Well, I was only thinkin' this mornin' it'd be nice to have some comp'ny fer a change. Yer welcome ta stay the night if ye can put up with the fare that's offered," he said, struggling to stand as Jack dismounted.

Before Jack could reply, the man motioned for an Indian boy who exited one of the tepees in the yard and instructed him to unsaddle Big Black and turn him out to grass. The boy narrowed his eyes and spoke under his breath, but when the old guy chuckled, so did the boy, producing a kind of cheerful animosity between the two. Amused, Jack followed the talkative fellow around the side of the house to wash up, then he froze in midstride. Not because of the man's words but because of the crude coffin standing on end against the house, Duel's face set in an oddly stoic look of death.

The old-timer followed Jack's unbelieving gaze and quieted suddenly, a knowing look coming across the old face, lined and cracked like dry earth.

"Found 'im yest'day jes' before sundown, holdin' on to his last breath," he supplied. Said, 'Tell Jack it weren't his fault, it was the kid,' then he looked past me and smiled, like he weren't seein' me no more. Never saw a smile like that." The old man shook his head. "Had this with him," he added. Jack saw the old man pull his mama's Bible from under his lap robe. *Book of Promises,* he recalled his mama saying, and he felt a sudden bitterness sweep over him and he glanced away.

"The wives said I should've buried him already. But I figured to wait." He watched Jack closely. "I guess I'm getting soft, but I figured he got shot in the back for his trouble and this friend ought to know. Little Woman says the feller that shot him was a young, white-headed scamp. Said his eyes looked like death, whatever that means. . . ," he finished, letting his words trail off for a moment. "Gone now, near as I can figger. Anyway, there's the story."

Open your eyes, Duel. Damnit, open your eyes, Jack's mind shouted, then begged. But Duel never moved. For a brief moment, Jack wanted to touch him, touch his hand, his face, but he resisted the urge.

One day too late. Jack wanted to set down in the dirt, his legs felt so weak. Instead, all of the pent up rage and despair he'd worked so hard to hide began to build within him as he stood there staring at Duel, hemmed in by four old pieces of plank board. *If I had one man to call friend on this sorry earth,* he thought, *it would've been you.* Jack felt a sudden pang of sickness as his eyes focused on the hastily scrawled note tacked to Duel's shirt saying, *Know this feller?*

How much is enough, God? Jack wondered bitterly. He then grabbed the soiled piece of paper with such force, the old fellow stepped back some and watched with wide eyes as he tore the paper into shreds. Jack pulled out most of the money Lillie had given him and offered it to the man, his mouth setting down in a hard line of sorrow and regret.

"There are people in Virginia City that'll see that he has a proper burial," Jack said, remembering his promise to Duel. "That should be enough money for you to see that he gets there. I'd do it myself, but I have something to take care of." He pulled out a scrap of paper and penned a quick note to Lillie: *Duel was shot in the back,* he wrote. *I intend to find Riley Wayne and make him pay to hell. I don't know how long it'll be before I can come back, but I know you'll see Duel gets buried right.* He wrote what little he knew of Duel Harper . . . Jack tried to recall if Duel had ever told him where he'd come from, but couldn't. . . . *And a big marker, Lillie. The biggest angel you can find. . . .* Jack handed the slip of paper to the old man. "He ain't no pauper, old-timer. Get him to Virginia City and the lady I wrote to will see to your trouble. I'll be back."

Jack could see the old fellow understood his meaning. "Ain't no call for threats, mister," he said, pulling himself up. "I reckon I have only a few good years left and I figure to keep 'em."

"I'm obliged," Jack said softly. The old guy waved a gnarled hand at him as Jack turned to walk away, his wide shoulders drawn down with his burden.

"Glad to help ye," he called but Jack just walked on without looking back, not having the strength to turn around again and tell the man his thanks was meant for Duel.

It was just nearing dusk by the time Jack hit open country, gigging Big Black up and down hill after hill, snaking around the scrub pine, spruce, and cedar scattered in the purple shadowed coulees. Even though nearly a full day had passed, it hadn't taken long for him to pick the gunman's trail out of Deer Lodge and with each mile gained, he felt his rage mount. The murderer stood for all that had been taken from him—the deaths: his pa's, Rose's, Duel's, even his own life in a way. Whatever was left of the old Jack who had started to come alive again in Virginia City was rubbed out when he'd stood gazing at the death mask of his friend. He'd never thought of himself as a shooter—until he'd seen Duel.

"Don't use a gun if 'n ye don't have ter, Jack," his old friend Stem had once told him. *"But if 'n ye do, don't miss."* And he didn't intend to miss.

Jack felt an unnatural calm take over as he realized he was closing in on his quarry; the snapped twigs and churned up ground was still fresh and he could almost smell the man's fear. As he entered a wash, a shot sang overhead and Jack spurred his horse into the stand of trees where he figured the shot came from.

"Who sent you?" he called out and was gifted with another shot, this time way off its mark. The shooter was a poor one, whoever sent him, Jack thought.

"I figure you know," came the malignant voice. The final shot was lucky and Jack grunted as he felt a burning pain shoot from his shoulder down to his fingers. "That was for my pa," the voice cackled with triumph. Jack recognized it was Riley Wayne, the kid that Duel had buffaloed in the Pair-O-Dice.

With reflexes that didn't seem his own, Jack moved in and returned the fire, ignoring the pain in his arm, and was gratified with a loud groan that grew as he entered the stand of trees.

"You winged me you son of a bitch," the kid hollered, his voice cracking.

"Why Duel?" Jack asked quietly as he dismounted and pulled his rifle from his saddle.

The boy shrugged, then winced. "I can't recall, exactly," he said with an evil grin. "He weren't nothing but a nigger, anyway. Nosy one at that, putting his nose in my business, in *Frank's*. You ain't figuring on finishing me, are you? I'm down." He knew the tone was meant to be friendly, but Jack didn't miss the glance to his gun that lay a short distance away, judging his odds. The boy's eyes widened though as he watched Jack move forward and raise the barrel of his gun.

"I knew you was a cheat and Frank said you was a thief," he taunted, bloodlust in his eyes. "Didn't know you was a murderin' coward, too."

"Son, you shot a man in the back you didn't know for reasons you can't even figure. That's murder," Jack said. "*This* is justice."

Jack pulled the trigger as the boy made for his gun and the force of the shot blew his body back into a pile of brush. For what seemed an eternity afterwards, Jack stood there, staring at the dead young man, feeling the blood from the wound in his own arm peck the ground.

In the lonely silence, Jack discovered that the satisfaction of avenging Duel's murder didn't last nearly long enough. He felt an emptiness return as he stared down at the boy, watching the last of his life seep through his dirty shirt, one lifeless hand lying across an old belt, the initials R.W. childishly etched into the leather. For some reason it bothered him that Duel's murderer had been so young. Jack couldn't help wondering if the boy had come west for a different life, land, or fortunes, or if he'd just always been bad.

Young ain't always innocent, he remembered Duel saying not so long ago, and recalling the bloodlust he'd seen not minutes ago in the kid's eyes, Jack figured Duel had been right. Just like he had so many other times. . . .

Memories of Duel swept through Jack: Duel smiling as he touched the tall blades of grass . . . the two of them laughing together . . . remembering the tears that fell down his face, taking that little girl's pain like it was his own. . . . *Are we all fools, Duel?* Jack thought. *Are we just here to play out some game that's end is already figured?*

For only a moment, Jack had the oddest feeling that Duel stood somewhere behind him, his spirit lingering, longing to tell him answers he wasn't able to hear.

Riley Wayne's horse snorted, shaking him from his thoughts, and Jack noticed Frank Monroe's brand on its back haunch. It was a fine-looking horse. Jack picked up his gun and shot it. It was too risky keeping something with the Monroe name—even if he could've stomached it.

Wounded and without anything to dig with, Jack turned and began to bury his enemy rock by rock until all that showed was a jagged mound of stone. The inscription he carved on an old weathered piece of wood was simple:

Here lies Riley Wayne
Bound for Hell. . . .

Montana Territory
June, 1864

Mrs. Callie McGregor
Plumas City, California

Dear Callie,

I ought to have just stayed in Virginia City and faced the music. Duel's dead, Callie, killed by one of Frank Monroe's pack of dogs. I guess he'd come to warn me.

So now two men have breathed their last because of me. One for being my friend, the other, well, it was part revenge, part self-defense, for he was gunning after me. I'm wounded but not badly. I guess he would've killed me if he'd had the chance. In spite of that, I ain't proud of having to shoot him, but then I didn't exactly have any choice in the matter, Sis.

I tell you, though, self-defense or not, it does something to you to see a person go on because of you. I've gotten in scrapes before—winged a few men in my time. But I guess I'll take to my own grave the look on that fella's face as he died.

It's true that it's almost as bad to kill as it is to be killed. Vengeance is a funny thing, Sis—the price of it, I mean. It does something to you I can't exactly explain. Taking a life—even in the name of justice—well, it's stolen a part of me I don't think I'll ever be able to get back.

I keep thinking how foolish I've been, acting like my life was some kind of dern dime novel to live out. More I live, the more I figure them stories of western adventure I used to read weren't just stories.

They were a damned pack of lies.

Jack

P.S. If I ever get out of this mess, I aim to find that place where we buried Pa. I aim to get him a headstone.

Ten

～

There were few mourners for Duel. Some of his miner friends had showed, a few townspeople—those sharp enough to know what a good man he was, Lillie thought, standing next to Ely as tears streamed down his thin face. Mabel stood on the other side, patting his arm like a child. She'd heard somewhere that Mabel had threatened to burn his bed if he went to it. Lillie glanced at the sport, standing like some pious pillar of the community next to Ely. She knew some would think that the likes of women like her and Mabel could never change or make a difference, but Lillie knew better. That she'd gotten Ely out of bed long enough to pay his respects to Duel said something. Sometimes life worked out in its own odd way.

Just not for the likes of us, Duel, she thought, holding his old leather Bible to her chest. The old man who had brought Duel in had given it to her, saying Jack thought it should go with his friend, and for some reason she hadn't been able to part with it, even when Ely suggested she bury it with Duel. She hadn't been raised religious, but there was a fuzzy memory from her childhood of her grandma and the Bible she'd carried with her everywhere like a comfort. And she figured she could use all the comfort she could get.

Lillie glanced up at the white angel that stood over his grave. *That statue appears more vengeful than sweet,* she reflected, then smiled. Jack would've thought it fitting.

Pulling her shawl tight, she looked out across the landscape for what seemed the hundredth time and stared hard at every nook and cranny along the mountainside. The peaks were already weighted down with snow, a sure sign winter would be coming early to the Territory. Still, she searched for the lone rider that she kept expecting to appear, kept *hoping* to appear.

But of course, he never did.

Montana Territory
June, 1864

Mrs. Callie McGregor
Plumas City, California

Dear Callie,

I have no way of knowing if this letter will ever reach you. If it ends up serving as my last words on this sorry earth, so be it.

Callie, I'm lost. Even staring at the words on this page I still can't believe it. But it's true. Chalk it up to carelessness, to running blind, to whatever. All I know is I'm lost.

I haven't slept for days. My arm is giving me trouble. Even so, I try to keep my guns in easy reach. I don't imagine I'll need them out in the middle of nowhere, but then, I didn't figure I'd need them in Virginia City, either.

I did manage to light a fire, probably the last for awhile. I used some leaves I scrounged for kindling as I couldn't part with the paper I use to write you. I can't help thinking, watching the smoke go up into nothing, that that is just how my life has turned out.

I saw my face in a pool of water today and I could've sworn I was seeing a stranger. Most of the time it's hard to remember the way I was before, but sometimes, just before I drift off, I can see us both at the old farm, lying on our backs in the grass, talking about our dreams. Laughing. It's been so long since I heard your laugh.

Life's funny, ain't it, Sis? In the good times you're always looking for something better. In the bad times, you're wishing for the past.

Say a prayer for me, will you? I have a hunch your words have a better chance at being heard by Him than mine. I haven't prayed much since Pa and Rose died.

Jack

Montana Territory
June, 1864

Mrs. Callie McGregor
Plumas City, California

Dear Callie,

I'm in bad shape. I've gone maybe four miles since I last wrote. The wound in my arm has given me the fever and I've gotten too weak to clean it, much less get around for food or water. I haven't seen Big Black all day. Can't say I blame him. I'd leave, too.

I think I'm going mad. I lay here helpless all morning and got so aggravated I screamed until I was hoarse. After all the years of trying to hold my rage in, it seems pointless now. I've been thinking a lot about Pa and Rose . . . Duel . . . even of Ma. . . .

I see life everywhere, most not worthy of the gift. Like this stinking ant crawling over my arm, alive when they're not, when I'm not, by much.

This is a poor letter, Sis. But it's hard not to be bitter out here. If the world was considered a mule, this place would be the ass end.

Jack

Eleven

Jack watched the sunrise just as he had the four days before—with dread. The beauty was all but lost on him. But in spite of his feelings, the light once again shot slowly across the wide Montana sky in a blue wash of color that seeped between the gaps of the mountains, then off in the distance. He could hear the birds begin to holler and by the time the sun edged over the highest peak, Jack came to the conclusion he was going to die.

He drifted in and out of sleep—or maybe it was slow death. At one point he woke up to find a big buck standing a short distance away and he glanced at his gun that lay only an arm's length away. But then the buck's head snapped up from the grass and Jack's senses went on alert. He saw the deer's ears flick and then it shot off into the trees, and Jack forced his eyes to stay open on the glade only by sheer will.

He was rewarded finally by the startling sight of an elderly Indian stepping out from the glade. Through slitted eyes, Jack saw the leather leggings move closer, then the faded calico shirt, missing its buttons, flapping open as the Indian bent over him, easy as you please, and peered down at him. Getting no response, the Indian scooped up some loose dirt and let it sift through his fingers and onto Jack's face.

The shock of it caused Jack to jolt up shakily from his bedroll and he locked eyes with the old man, no longer caring what might happen to him. "Go ahead and kill me, you old son of a bitch," he rasped, then laughed hoarsely. "It'd serve them all right if I died by the hands of an old half-naked Indian."

A grin peeked out from the face painted with reddish-brown ochre, displaying strong white teeth that were at odds with his feeble appearance. He stood for a moment and stared. He grunted, sounding pleased, then to Jack's surprise, he walked away.

It was this time that the darkness chose to pull at Jack's eyes again and he tried to fight it, to push it back and get up, but he lost. Just before he went out altogether, he thought he saw Lillie smiling down at him, with the saucy dimple in her cheek.

Jack smiled back and the blackness took advantage of the moment, finally putting an end to his struggle.

Montana Territory
June, 1864

Mrs. Callie McGregor
Plumas City, California

Dear Callie,

Just woke up and I'm not sure how much time I have to write. There's an old Indian sitting across the fire from me and from the looks of it, we've been camped here a few days. I think the old fellow has been nursing me. Why, I ain't figured out yet. I must've looked pretty rough when he found me, though. He acted like he was weighing just burying me to save the trouble. I do feel a sight better, though—even if I am a little uneasy. I just hope I can buy enough time to get my wind back so's to deal with whatever comes.

Lillie once told me it takes a lot of strength for a person to live, but I think she might've been wrong. I think it takes a hell of a lot more courage to die.

In spite of this new predicament, I want you to know that I ain't that courageous. I intend to fight till the end, Sis . . . for however long that is. . . .

Jack

P.S. I want you to know that I love you, Sis. I expect you've known this, but I thought to tell you again. I guess that's it for now.

Later—I am placing this letter in my shirt for safekeeping in case I don't get to mail it myself. I thought about my boots, but I figure they're the first to go if I don't make it—the old Indian has been inspecting them closely. Can't blame him. They are good boots.

Part Two

∽

"Most of us don't put our best foot forward
till the other is in hot water."

—*Jack Wade*

Twelve

The searing pain in his arm startled Jack awake. He saw only shadows at first, shifting and moving around him, and he wondered if he must have died. Jack blinked a couple more times to check his theory but just as his vision cleared, a puff of pungent smoke was blown into his face, causing him to cough. It wasn't until the smoke cleared that Jack saw the pair of dark eyes peering down at him. The old Indian grinned at him, then straightened up, making a grunting sound of satisfaction as he threw a handful of something on the fire that hissed and filled the room once more with smoke. As he lifted his arms upwards, in what looked to be thanks, Jack shifted his gaze and quickly began to search the murky room for any other Indians.

It was a bit dark but he could still make out the hide walls, stretched around the living area, and he saw what looked to be a couch of sorts and backrests with fur rugs and blankets. The odd thought came to him that it was almost homey. *Well, they don't take you into their home to kill you,* Jack thought hopefully, but the thought was followed by the memory of Duel telling him about the Apaches and how they'd take whites back to their camps just to peel the skin off of them.

Jack felt his neck begin to cramp from keeping his head up for so long, and in spite of the unnerving thought of having his skin peeled, he gave in to the cramp and lay his head back against the thick pile of buffalo robes. He stared at the strange utensils and pouches hanging from the poles that jutted upwards. Peering at the blue circle of sky above in the ceiling, he thought of the days he had lain helpless, staring up at the sky waiting to die and how Duel's face would come to him, and he shut his eyes suddenly against the pain of his grief.

Could sure use a hand up along now, Duel, Jack thought, his weakened body making the grief all the more acute. He had never had a problem facing a fight but it was situations like the one he was in that Duel was better at figuring. *If you can't fight with your fists, use your mind, Duel had told him once. Ain't no man that can kill a good idea.*

The only problem was he didn't have any ideas—good or otherwise.

Feeling hopeless, he closed his eyes. As he did, an odor of a different kind of smoke fill the room; a musky smell of wild game and something else. In spite of his predicament he felt his mouth begin to water. When he forced his eyes to open again, a movement in the shadows of the lodge caught his attention and he saw a pretty young Indian woman dressed in a soft-skin dress and leggings draw closer to the fire as she inspected the boiling pot.

Jack studied her as she leaned forward, her long waist-length hair brushing over her arm, and he couldn't help staring at the bronze skin of her arm. When she looked up, he noticed that she didn't shy away from his stares but returned them with dark eyes that were intelligent and kind.

Jack suddenly fidgeted beneath the skins that covered him and as he did, it occurred to him he was naked. He felt a flush of embarrassment rush over him.

"Where are my clothes, old man?" he asked, trying to sound more in control than he felt, but the Indian appeared not to understand.

He tried to hide his embarrassment by giving the old man a surly look as he pushed himself up on the thick pile of buffalo robes and felt his arm. The pain had died down to a low throb, and he saw that someone had spread a paste of some kind over the wound, wondering if it was the woman.

"My clothes," he said again, but the old Indian appeared unconcerned. He grinned at Jack, then turned and motioned to the woman, saying something to her in a strange tongue that made Jack forget his anger. Suddenly he felt uneasy again. And foolish. He wasn't in Virginia City anymore, he reminded himself. He was in an Indian camp. A white man in an Indian camp.

The woman came forward with a bowl of what appeared to be stew and handed it to Jack, then stepped back while both she and the man watched him expectantly. When he started to eat, they smiled, then broke into laughter, making comments to each other as he scooped spoonful after spoonful into his mouth, barely taking the time to swallow. It wasn't until Jack looked up from the empty bowl that he realized the man was preparing to leave. Jack felt his stomach begin to churn at the same moment, and the fear suddenly took him that maybe they had poisoned him.

Then the thought occurred to him: *Well, what if I do die?* After all, he didn't exactly have much left; no friends left, no wife or kids to grieve for him. He had Callie, but she had her own family and he felt she would fare all right after awhile. As his mind settled the matter, Jack felt a sharp cramp hit his stomach. He tried to stifle a groan but the old Indian heard it and turned around at the open flaps of the entrance. He looked at Jack, then glanced to the young woman who was back to tending the fire.

"His stomach is still poor," he announced knowingly, his English shocking Jack so that he forgot that he was supposed to be dying. "Give him only a little food next time so he will keep it down." The old man smiled a wide, healthy tooth smile. "He doesn't look like much, but fattened up, he might be worth something."

The flap closed and when the woman's eyes met Jack's again, this time they were alight with humor and Jack knew she'd understood the old man's words.

Blackfoot Encampment
Montana Territory
1864

Mrs. Callie McGregor
Plumas City, California

Dear Callie,

I'm not sure what day it is, but I'm still alive and as near as I can figure these Indians don't plan to do anything to me just yet. Weak as I am, I don't guess I could do much to stop them anyway. Even the old fellow who found me could probably do the job. Medicine Weasel (that's his name) is a bit wrinkly to look at but is wiry. I guess he'd have to be to cart my dead weight all the way back here. When I asked him how he managed, he just shrugged and told me I was pretty played out and slept most of the time and when I didn't sleep I talked out of my head to someone he couldn't see. The last part seemed to make him nervous. I can tell you I was nervous myself to wake up in an Indian hut. Another shock was to find out that some even know how to speak English. I guess whoever wrote them dime novels I read didn't know squat about Indians either.

I haven't seen the village yet, but my hope is the rest of them are like Medicine Weasel or his daughter, Raven. They are good people. The old man treats me pretty fair and the daughter is good to me, too. I think Medicine Weasel figures I'm homesick. He told me today that the traders will be coming soon before winter sets in. He said that they sometimes make trips to the "Many Houses" Fort and I could go back with them if I want. The kick of it was I didn't know what to say when he told me that. All I could think was, "Back where?" I guess my being quiet puz-

zled the old man. He looked at me for a long time, then left the tepee. I just didn't know how to tell him I ain't up to making a choice just yet.

I can't go back to Virginia City, Sis—at least not yet—not until I'm strong again. Strong enough to make the right choice. Seems like all the choices I've made have been bad. It's like this: I chose to care for Lillie and had to leave her, I chose to be a friend to Duel and got him killed. What could you call it besides bad?

Lillie once told me that I had to choose my battles and she was right about that. But even if I have to wait, I can tell you, Callie, there will be a battle. Until then, I figure the best thing is stay here until I'm able enough to stand against Frank Monroe and his bunch. If there is any justice on this sorry ball of dust, I will see them again and make them pay for all they took from me.

I got to quit this letter now, Sis—tuck it away with the others until I can get them mailed. There's a bunch of fellows that just come in. The old man's been getting visitors all day long and though they don't say much to me, I think they've come to gawk. I guess I'd gawk too. I can't imagine what they think of a white man living in their camp.

Jack

Raven unrolled the blackhorn hide and set about pounding the stakes down with her stone hammer. It felt good to be outside working, the moon of the falling leaves being her favorite time. But the main reason for her work this day was to watch the lodge of Many Horses. A council meeting had been called about the white man, and she knew a decision was going to be made if he should be allowed to stay, now that he was better.

Lone Elk might be a problem, she thought, a furrow between her brows as she worked her fleshing knife, scraping away the dark meat. She had watched him earlier, strutting into Many Horse's lodge with his group of followers. Lone Elk was young but wealthy, with his many horses and wives. He was also respected as a warrior and people listened when he spoke. Lone Elk didn't care for the *Napikwan*. But Medicine Weasel was well respected—maybe more—and she knew they would listen to what her father had to say.

Her father felt JackWade should be allowed to stay; he had told her it would be good to learn more of the ways of the *Napikwan* and he was right, although she wondered if her father also felt a comfort by having JackWade in their lodge. Even though he was white, he was of about the same age as her brother.

Raven thought her reasons were the same but different.

JackWade had seen death—she had seen it in his green eyes and she knew the look of grief, for she had carried the same in her heart the past two winters.

Her mother and brother were the first to go, then her young husband of only one winter. Last had been her baby. They had all thought it a rash at first; small red sores that crept from the arms to the belly like a snake. Her father had made a paste that she had smoothed on the sickness while he performed the curing ceremony, but in the end, they had watched all three go on to the Shadowlands. When her baby had come, she and her father had been happy to have the new life in their home. Raven felt the sharp pang of memory of the baby at her breast, then the morning her father had seen the first sore on her little one's head.

She was ashamed of the memory of her fighting her father like a she-devil when he tried to take the lifeless boy from her. In her mind, if she held him, he wouldn't be gone and she wouldn't have failed him.

Medicine Weasel had been gentle with her, waiting until she fell into an exhausted sleep before he dressed his grandson and fit him with the little moccasins to prepare him for his journey to the Sand Hills.

With her father's love she had healed, but not yet enough to take another husband or to think of holding another child in her arms because deep down she knew she hadn't shed all of her hate. If the sickness had been a human being, she would've murdered it, she thought fiercely, but it was white scabs, the sickness the *Napikwans* called smallpox.

Raven heard a stirring in the lodge and she knew Jack Wade was restless again. He would be grumbling under his breath, she was sure. He had asked about his horse several times: *Had her father seen it? Could he look for it? Where are my guns?* Then, *How long till this arm heals?* After those questions, he would usually grow quiet and stare into the fire, his eyes full of hate for something he hadn't yet put a name to.

Raven saw the shadow fall across her work and raised her head to see her father standing over her. "Jack Wade can stay," he announced with a smile. She smiled, too, then bent back over her work so he couldn't see her emotions. "You work too hard," Medicine Weasel said after awhile and she glanced back up at him.

"Would you rather me be fat and lazy and gossip all day?"

"I doubt you would get fat or lazy," he said with a teasing look in his eyes. Raven laughed as he walked away.

It was a good thing, letting Jack Wade stay, she thought, smiling as she unrolled another hide. The council's decision made her think her feelings had been the right ones. And just as her father helped her, she knew she was supposed to help the white man.

Jack watched the dancers with a kind of detached feeling. He had gotten past fearing the Blackfoot, but the little social they had organized was still of no interest to him. Instead, his mind kept straying to the mess his life had become and wishing he could somehow turn back time.

At least he was comfortable in his troubles. The weather had turned cooler, making him think it was close to fall, but the fires had been built large, shooting sparks into the huge dark bowl of sky as the men and women danced about, bending knees and stomping feet as their bodies swayed to the drumbeats. As he raised his hands toward the fire to warm them, Jack listened to the snatches of laughter, the sounds of kids roughhousing with each other, and camp dogs barking for scraps, and the thought came to him if he closed his eyes just right, he could just as easily pretend he was back in Virginia City. But in life's usual fashion, he was shaken from the thought as his eyes met the sullen glare from across the fire.

The fierce-looking fellow they called Lone Elk had wasted no time in letting Jack know his feelings about him being in camp. The few times he had visited Medicine Weasel's lodge, he had watched Jack with open hostility, and even though he was a bit smaller, Jack judged him as a formidable opponent. He was built thicker across the chest and arms than most of the other braves and moved like a bobcat stalking its prey. A man who seemed to draw attention without even trying. A man who didn't so much demand to lead, Jack thought with a kind of grudging respect, but was born to. Jack watched him speaking with the other braves, trying to judge if they meant him harm, but Lone Elk finally moved on to his family. As Jack allowed his gaze to wander again, his eyes stopped on Raven in the crowd of dancers.

He couldn't help notice her, being nearly a head taller than most of the women, her long, lithe body graceful in motion as she danced. She was clothed in a fine dress of antelope skin with broad bands of beadwork and elk teeth. There was something almost regal about her, Jack thought. Their eyes had met as well, but hers had been the only ones that had lingered long enough to make him uncomfortable. There was something in her look that made him feel as though she could see right through the stony face he had put on. Jack heard her laugh suddenly and he couldn't help smiling. As he did, he felt Medicine Weasel shift his body next to him.

"Why don't you join them?" the old man asked, his lined face glowing by the light of the fire. "You know you are welcome."

"I ain't much for dancin'," Jack said, trying to find the right words to explain to the medicine man but since he could find none, he lit the cheroot he'd rolled instead. He smiled apologetically as the old man's small, dark eyes studied him. Jack squirmed a bit—he had grown to like Medicine Weasel and didn't want to offend him if he could help it. In the few weeks that he'd been there they *had* tried their best to make him feel welcome, feeding him choice meats and soups, and he had felt his strength quickly return. His arm had healed well, too, but his mind had stayed in Virginia City, going over and over what had happened like a bad tooth that he couldn't pull.

He was well enough to travel but he had no horse, no guns, no way of knowing how to get back until the traders came, so he had kept the events alive in his mind and his hatred for Frank Monroe grew. The only upshot of it was that it helped him to block out missing Lillie. Every once in a while though, her face would appear before him and he would feel his heart give a lurch.

Jack's eyes traveled from the dancers to the copper faces of the men and women sitting around the fires. He suddenly felt like a kid lost in a crowd of strangers—like he was in another world—and a fear came over him that he might not ever get back to what he'd had. He threw the butt of the cheroot in the fire and stood, feeling frustrated at his predicament.

The frustration only grew as he started off, his weakness making the short walk through the rows of lodges an effort. A camp dog trotted up to him, sniffed the air, then cast a wise look at him before trotting off, and Jack half wondered what the dog had sensed. He watched the dog for a moment, winding its way through the maze of lodges before coming to rest in front of its owner's doorway, a small fire splashing light on its mottled coat as it yapped its arrival. Jack shook his head and started again toward the lodge marked with a large weasel. He was so intent on getting where he was going that he didn't notice Raven standing in the shadows until he nearly ran her over.

"You are leaving the dance," she said, more a statement than a question. Jack felt the same uncomfortableness come over him as it had at the dance. It was a different feeling than he'd had for her in the lodge, as if seeing her dance had made her into something other than his caretaker. She was a woman—a pretty one, too—and she appeared to have an opinion on something. All he could think was to mumble quickly and go before she shared it.

"I ain't much for dancin'," he repeated, feeling foolish even though he was sure that she hadn't heard him the first time. He was sorry, too, he thought as he started to walk off. Sorry that he didn't have it in him to say any more than that. He had the suspicion he would've liked her conversation.

"I have had grief," she offered hesitantly as he stopped and looked over his shoulder. Her eyes were large and serious and Jack noticed she had touched her hand to her heart as if the grief was still in there somewhere. But instead of answering, he merely turned and looked out into the night, listening to the far off sound of drums beating and feeling like he didn't have the patience to listen. He preferred keeping his mind on his enemy. His body wasn't yet up to the fight but at least his mind was. Already, his mind had played out several different acts of revenge that had suited him pretty well.

"Anger, too," Raven added as if reading his thoughts. She tilted her head and pursed her lips, as if she were trying to find the right words to get her point across. "If your anger has nowhere to go it will eat up your insides, JackWade."

Jack bristled. "Oh, it has somewhere to go. I just ain't strong enough to take it there yet."

"Your anger will keep you weak," Raven suggested. She appeared calm, but Jack had seen the flash of irritation in her eyes and he felt a tug of interest in spite of himself.

"Maybe not. Maybe it's just the thing that'll get me goin'. Get me strong again," Jack countered but a bit more quietly. Already he could feel the swell of anger fade, having nowhere to go, and be replaced by the dull, hard feeling that had become his constant companion when trouble came over the years. He glanced once toward the lodge, then back to Raven, but she was already gone.

Jack thought it was probably just as well. Besides his anger, he felt he was used up. Sometimes it was all too much, he thought, heading for the lodge.

Just as he seated himself against the willow backrest, Medicine Weasel entered the lodge.

Jack sensed the old man had something he wanted to say but as was his way, he worked around it, checking his medicine bundle, opening a parfleche of dried meat. He glanced up once at Jack, then mumbled something in Blackfoot Jack had yet to learn.

Medicine Weasel felt his rummaging was foolish, but he was trying to form in his mind what he could say to JackWade. Whether Raven realized it or not, he saw that his daughter had started to have feelings for the white man. He liked him himself, but he didn't want his daughter to pine for a man who was disturbed. He chanced a glance at the white man who sat across the lodge from him.

Raven had told him JackWade's wounds had healed, but he suspected there were deeper wounds. Wounds of the spirit, possibly; he had eyes of a man who was hunted, eyes that were sometimes even dead looking. He frowned. The *Napikwans* were a strange people. When he was younger, he wondered if they were even human beings but he had seen them doing things of intelligence at times. Then later during the treaty talks, he'd learned their words and had even made good friends with some of the men.

Medicine Weasel studied Jack from time to time for a bit, chewing thoughtfully on a piece of dried buffalo meat he'd pulled from a parfleche. He made an attempt to appear busy as he watched him, stoking the fire with a stick, but when he finally could take no more of the sometimes sullen, sometimes blank expression the white man wore, he threw the stick in the fire.

"What was it that killed you, JackWade?" he asked a bit impolitely. He saw a startled look come to the green eyes.

"I ain't dead."

"You are breathing, that's true," Medicine Weasel said finally, hoping to shed some light on the problem. "But your spirit has left you."

Blackfoot Encampment,
Montana Territory
1864

Mrs. Callie McGregor
Plumas City, California

Dear Callie,

At least I know where I am now. Medicine Weasel told me today that this river they've set their lodges up along is the Bear River (he says it's called the Marias by traders from the "Many Houses" Fort, which I figure is Fort Benton) and that they winter here. He says even more Blackfoot will come. I've only been out of the tepee once for a dance they had, and even though it was dark it seemed there were a lot of folks here already. I guess it should make me feel edgy, the only white fellow in a camp of Indians, but mostly the ones I met appear just as friendly as the old man and his daughter.

The dance was a sight to behold, though. And the laughter, too. I don't know why, but hearing Indians laughing was a shock.

The Blackfoot sure like their fun. I guess that surprised me too, as I'd always heard they were a nasty bunch to tangle with. Way I heard it back in Virginia City was they liked to kill for the plain fun of it. I'm not sure if that's true, but I'll allow I wouldn't want to be on their bad side. Medicine Weasel has a few hunks of hair hanging in here that unnerved me, so I finally asked him about them. He smiled funny and said it was a bad habit the French had taught them but he didn't think the warriors were going to quit it anytime soon. Death doesn't seem to scare them, either. Hearing Medicine Weasel talk, I'd wager they know a lot more about it than we do—but I think they also know a lot more about living life than we do, Sis. They are just happy to be with each other. I think they enjoy a good story, too.

The few times I've told them about back home, Medicine Weasel and his daughter both have dropped whatever they were doing and come set next to me at the fire. Medicine Weasel is mostly interested in hearing how I came west. He told me later that they don't worry about rushing to get something done if there's a story, that they know their work will be there tomorrow and that the story might not. Makes me wonder if we couldn't learn a thing or two from them, Callie. I probably could myself, but sometimes I think my anger has dried up whatever good I'd started to feel back in Virginia City. I know Medicine Weasel senses something happened and has pressed me to tell him in a way. He says the darndest things, too. Just the other night he asked what killed me. . . .

Anyway, I best quit this letter; I can see I'm starting to ramble. Rambling seems to be the thing to do when you can't get around. I can hoof it pretty well around this tepee now but going outside is a problem being that I ain't got my boots no more—I woke this morning with them gone. None of them have spoken of the boots. My guess is Medicine Weasel decided to take them in trade for his doctoring.

Jack

Blackfoot Encampment,
Montana Territory
1864

Mrs. Callie McGregor
Plumas City, California

Dear Callie,

They gave me some shoes today. Well, not shoes—they're moccasins—but they do the job and are fairly comfortable. Medicine Weasel's daughter, Raven, made them for me. I admit I was a bit put off when I first saw them, as one was tanned white and the other a kind of blue, but I put them on anyway—mismatched or not I was itching to go for a walk. A good thing I kept quiet, too, because when I got outside I noticed several of the fellows with the same situation.

Callie, if I thought I'd seen something before I will tell you it was nothing compared with today. There are even more Indians camped here, now—mainly for the trading that'll commence soon as the fellows from Ft. Benton show—and just the sight of it all kept me standing in one place for awhile. You know, I've sat here, trying to find easy words to explain the feeling that came over me, but there ain't no easy words. Maybe a bit like stepping off into another world. There are tepees as far as you can see planted along these valley bottoms, fires going, dogs barking, some of the biggest horse herds I've seen, splitting to let riders in or out of camp . . . and all that kept coming to my mind was how strange it was that I was standing in the midst of it—that the odds would be just as likely to find me in the middle of Heaven itself. I thought of the fellows back in Virginia City, too, and how their hair would stand on end at seeing so many Indians in one place. Odd thing is, Sis, I never felt that fear. Oh, I got some unfriendly stares from a few of the braves, but for the most part once they saw me standing there, everyone got pretty curious and came over and chatted with me even though I didn't understand most of what they were saying. The kids were a kick; checking my pockets and tugging on my beard before they'd laugh and run off. Thing is, as the crowd started to trail away and I watched the kids run down toward the river, the women go back to their chatter as they stretched their skins, and the braves mount horses and ride off to hunt, I had the oddest feeling of loneliness come over me.

It wasn't long after that I walked down toward the river and I happened on this Indian fellow who looked like he could be Methuselah's granddad, painting on a huge lodge cover that was spread out on the ground. He startled me some, greeting me in English without turning around. I still don't know why but I sat with him for a long while, asking him questions and him answering as he hunched over the skin, painting his pictures with a whittled-down old hipbone off a buffalo. He told me his name was Lodge Skins and that most everyone had heard I had come and he thought it was a good thing. For me, he added. We both got quiet then, but after a time, he finally turned to me and that's when I got a shock. He was blind. I guess he sensed my shock because he chuckled and went on to tell me that he could only see a bit of light from time to time, but when he got that light he worked as hard as he could.

"My paintings aren't like they used to be. Not like before," he told me, then tapped his forehead with his leathered old claw and grinned. "But, if you could see what I paint up here."

He gathered up his bones and paints shortly after that and left without so much as a so-long but the funny thing is, Sis, I couldn't bring myself to leave. I found myself sitting there for the longest time thinking of that old fellow and wishing with all my might I could have a glimpse of what he painted in his head.

Jack

Thirteen

~

Medicine Weasel shifted uncomfortably in his spot, wiggling his cramped feet as he watched JackWade and his nephew with concern from across the fire while everyone gathered in the lodge for the feast. JackWade's boots pinching his big toes was an irritation but his nephew was even more of an irritation, the old man thought. He could accept his sore toes with good grace since he had always wanted a pair of the white-man's shoes, but Lone Elk's bad manners he did not have to accept.

The medicine man sighed heavily. If it weren't for Lone Elk, he could've counted the day as a good one. His buffalo-charming song had made the hunt successful and the men had paid him well with the best cuts from their own kills. A good thing, since his son-in-law—the hunter of the family—was no more. But now his nephew had come and cast a cloud over it all by behaving rudely to his guest at every opportunity. JackWade appeared ignorant, but his eyes said he knew and that was enough to cause concern. Enough of a concern to make Medicine Weasel wonder if he had made a bad decision bringing the white man back with him.

What good can come of this, now? he wondered. The urge to save JackWade had been a strong one, so strong he felt he couldn't have made any other choice. The only other time he could recall such a feeling was when he had been young and had sweated and prayed to the Above Ones for a wife. Many Elk's daughter had walked by not long after that, and the urge that came over him was so powerful he knew he couldn't deny Red Paint. So, he didn't deny it in JackWade's case either. Although there had been many times such as tonight when he would find himself looking at JackWade, thinking: *Who are you to me, white man? Who am I to you?*

Medicine Weasel bit into the cooked buffalo rib, chewing carefully as he pondered the situation. He *had* seen the yearning to belong in JackWade's eyes lately, but all of his attempts to bring him into *living* again had failed. It was as if JackWade was being handed a solution but wouldn't let go of the problem. As he glanced once more to his nephew's sullen face, it convinced him that Lone Elk's bad manners could set the whole thing back even further.

"He has smooth hands. Maybe he is a near-woman," Lone Elk speculated loudly in Blackfoot, glaring at Jack, and a few of the braves laughed.

"You are a child," Medicine Weasel said quietly but his tone silenced them all. He saw Lone Elk's eyes were still mean though, and he frowned and set his rib down as he felt a bit of burning start in his stomach. The old ones preferred calf intestines because it was easy on their stomachs as well as their teeth but he was sure he was not that old yet. The indigestion he felt coming was most likely caused by his nephew.

Medicine Weasel glanced across the lodge as trails of laughter nipped into his thoughts. He saw Raven laughing as she moved from man to man serving the dessert, and it made him smile in spite of his worries. When she paused behind JackWade, he grew alert, then thoughtful as he saw her hand rest on the white man's shoulder; he had sensed that the two of them had come to an understanding of each other and this just confirmed it. The odd thing was how calmly he accepted it. In his younger days he might have tried to prevent the friendship, but he had lived long enough to realize what was to be would be. For whatever reason, Medicine Weasel felt Jack Wade's destiny was linked to his and Raven's. The old man suddenly sensed that Lone Elk had seen the exchange, too, and as he glanced to his left he saw that his nephew's face had gone dark with anger.

"*Napikwans* try to take what is not theirs," Lone Elk spoke between gritted teeth. "That is their way."

"He has taken nothing," Medicine Weasel answered just as Raven leaned forward to serve him. His daughter's long, glossy hair hid her fearful expression from the others but he saw it and gave her a gentle look before she moved to the next man.

"He will," Lone Elk continued angrily. "He is *white*—just like the traders who come and smile and say good things while they pour bad whiskey down our throats and heap our furs and skins into their wagons. You once said the enemy cannot come to your home if you don't open the door. I tell you, Uncle, close the door or one day they will take everything from us."

Before he could say any more, Medicine Weasel motioned for him to be silent; Lone Elk generally spoke more than he listened when angry and the subject of whites always made him angry. Lone Elk felt whites were to blame for all that was bad, including the dream that plagued him over the past few months. Medicine Weasel knew the dream spooked his nephew but he felt Lone Elk dwelled on it and his anger too much. It was a shame he disliked whites for he and Jack Wade had much in common, Medicine Weasel thought, and as soon as the thought surfaced he became amused, so amused at the two men having anything in common that he chuckled out loud.

Lone Elk looked injured by his uncle's laughter and his gaze moved sharply to the white man again. Jack, looking up from his bowl of buffalo fat and berries at the same moment, felt the sudden uneasy feeling of an uninvited guest and with that feeling, his spirits sank low.

Jack set his bowl down slowly and looked from Medicine Weasel to the brave named Lone Elk. The medicine man appeared amused but Lone Elk's face seemed set in a hard mask of anger. Jack had sensed the brave's dislike from the moment he had walked in but chose to ignore it. He was, after all, outnumbered and he figured no matter how much the old man and his daughter had taken a liking to him they were still part of the tribe. The trouble was he wanted to be a part of it, too—more than he'd wanted to be a part of anything in a long time. He had known it from the moment he'd sat with the old blind man when he had felt the wonder of something in his spirit coming alive again. In spite of this, Jack couldn't make himself back down completely. Like an animal that had been cornered once too often, he met Lone Elk's stare unblinking.

Lone Elk hesitated, as if surprised by this unexpected turn, then his dark eyes narrowed and Jack watched him slowly stand. His size alone could command attention, but there was a fierce kind of loyalty in his eyes that Jack saw, too, and as he looked around the room at the others, he realized it was that that held their attention. All eyes were fixed on Lone Elk as he began to speak, the room becoming silent as a tomb as the brave finally ended his speech with a blow of his fist to his hand and a word that sounded something like *napkin* as he turned to glare at Jack. Jack wasn't sure what the word meant, but he knew it couldn't be good, especially if the old medicine man was choosing not to translate it. That and the fact most everyone in the room had averted their eyes from him, Jack thought.

"We will smoke," Medicine Weasel said finally as if settling the matter. He packed his pipe with a kind of deliberate slowness that said he expected the men to wait until he was good and ready. Just when Jack thought he couldn't take anymore of the thick silence, the old man passed the pipe and began to speak. Like a seasoned politician, he immediately turned the talk to traders who were coming, as if the ruckus between Lone Elk and Jack had never happened.

Lone Elk, however, went for the topic like he was grabbing a new weapon. As heated as his tone was, he paused many times to make sure his uncle translated his objections against trading any of their robes or furs for the liquor the white traders would offer, making a point of glaring at Jack as he spoke.

"Fools Crow nearly died because of the sneaking drink givers," Lone Elk said. "When I smelled the white man's water he had, its odor was of death."

When Medicine Weasel translated, *sneaking drink givers,* Jack almost laughed but was quick to catch himself. There was still an odd kind of tension in the room, as if they were all expecting something to happen and he knew if he didn't turn things, what happened wouldn't be good. Like any good poker player, Jack quickly moved the attention from himself.

"Well, it ain't pure," he offered suddenly and a row of startled dark eyes moved to him. "The stuff they give you all is tainted." He saw their confusion and looked to Medicine Weasel for help. "I've heard that they add things to it to make it go further, and not good things, either; black tobacco, pepper, molasses, 'bout anything they can lay their hands on. I'd be doin' wrong not to tell you the stuff's poison. Lone Elk's right—best thing is not to trade for liquor. I imagine they want those hides enough so as to agree. Besides," Jack finished, smiling, "been my experience that even good liquor can make a fellow feel bad."

The tightness on Medicine Weasel's face eased and he gave Jack a slight smile. As the old man finished translating, Lone Elk's eyes met Jack's across the fire once more, and although they appeared just as hard, Jack thought he saw a considering look in them, too. Jack was as surprised as everyone else when the fierce-looking brave abruptly sat back down at the fire and leaned forward as he began to speak.

"When I was a bit younger and foolish," Lone Elk began and there was a release of tension that swept through the room, followed by a few chuckles as the crowd anticipated the story to come. "I would drink the white-man's water sometimes. When I did this I would often steal my wives' fancy beadwork and give it to other women. My wives would get together and try to overtake me and bring me back to the lodge until I came to my senses, but on this day they couldn't catch me; they chased me through camp, out to the hills, to the river, and back to camp and still couldn't catch me. By this time, many people had gathered to watch and laugh and I climbed to the top of my lodge by a travois that was propped against it, sitting over the hole where the poles crossed. I then shouted down insults of what puny runners my wives were and they soon gathered in a little group, whispering. I saw Laughs-A-Lot disappear but didn't pay it much mind and began to sing my drinking song. It went something like, 'Bear chief he gave me a drink, Bear chief—' but I got no further than that because Laughs-A-Lot had thrown an armful of rye grass from her couch onto the fire in our lodge and it made a great roar. The flames leapt up and struck me in my tender area, and I fell to the ground where they tied me until I became myself again."

Several men, who obviously had been there, began making comments about him screaming like a woman about his pain. Jack was surprised to see Lone Elk take his ribbing so well. Lone Elk waited until the voices had died down and like any born storyteller, he finished with a flourish.

"Whenever I think of drinking the white man's water again, I think of days of walking like I had a pony between my legs and I don't drink."

The circle of friends and family roared with laughter. It reminded Jack so much of the gatherings back home, he felt he had found his chance to join in.

"Back home, sometimes I would slip off to the little tavern in town and sneak a few drinks without my folks knowing," he began, surprising even himself. All heads turned toward him, looking first startled, then pleased, and the warmth of their smiles pushed him on. Medicine Weasel's smile widened and he quickly caught up the ones who didn't understand English.

"They didn't approve much of the *white man's water* as you call it—and mostly they were right about it—but I was young and foolish." Jack grinned and the crowd chuckled. "My sister, she didn't approve of the liquor either, but she'd wait up for me anyway, mostly to make sure I made it home without falling into a puddle or something. This one night I guess I was later than usual and so she came to town herself and waited outside the tavern for me. She'd put up with several drunk fellows approaching her by the time I came stumbling out, and she let me have it with her tongue. 'So, you think you're a big man drinking and gambling,' she says, hands on her hips, and I say, 'I know I am,' puffing my chest out."

The women, sitting near the entrance of the lodge laughed heartily and Jack grinned sheepishly before going on. " 'What big man do you know who lets his sister get insulted?' she asks and I got mad. 'Who insulted you?' I roar. 'Let me at 'em!' I spy a big branch of a tree that had fallen near the side of the tavern and start to hoist it up, hollering what I am going to do to these men but as hard as I try, I can't lift it. I go from one end to the other and still can't lift it. Finally I have to sit down and rest. By this time, sweat is dripping down the sides of my face and I feel a bit sick to my stomach and my sister Callie, she starts to laugh. 'All right, Mr. Big Man,' she says, 'it's time you got home.' Then she walks over to where the huge branch lay and picks it up and tosses it out of her way."

"Was this sister of yours a big woman?" Medicine Weasel interrupted. Jack could see the old man sizing him up with his dark eyes, as if trying to imagine the size of the sister who had bested him.

"No, as a matter of fact, she's pretty small," Jack answered wryly. "It wasn't until the next day she told me I'd been standing on that dern branch the whole time I tried to lift it." There was a moment of silence in the room, then everyone began to laugh. As they did,

Lone Elk's eyes met Jack's across the fire and Jack saw a grudging kind of amusement on the brave's face and he felt something give between the two of them.

Temporary truce, Jack thought, noticing the way Lone Elk studied him a bit more, as if forming his next move in his mind. When the warrior's eyes met Jack's again, he appeared to catch himself and he gave Jack a sudden ghost of a grin.

"Blackfoot and white women are alike," he said then, attempting to sound friendly. "They both try to make their men look foolish."

"It is easy work," came Raven's voice from somewhere behind them. They both turned and she shot a pointed look toward her cousin, then to Jack. Laughter filled the lodge once more, and as Jack glanced around at all of the smiling faces, the happiness in Raven's eyes, the contented look on Medicine Weasel's leathered face, he felt an odd sensation come over him, lulling him with a feeling that he hadn't felt in so long it was hard for him to put a name to, even though his mind searched and searched for it. Like a whisper he strained to hear long after it was gone. Only this time, the feeling had remained.

It wasn't until an hour or so later as he was drifting off to sleep that Jack realized that it was peace.

Blackfoot Encampment,
Montana Territory
1864

Mrs. Callie McGregor
Plumas City, California

Dear Callie,
    I guess it won't surprise you to hear that I came near to becoming a hank of hair hanging off one of these fellows' lances. What might sur-

prise you is that it was one of my stories that saved my hide. Who says talk is cheap?

Lone Elk (the warrior who would've been doing the scalp lifting) is a pretty interesting fellow, in spite of our rocky start. He is about the fiercest-looking Indian I've ever come across, and judging from the way he's treated around here I don't imagine it's all bluff. But like Stem always said, "All great men have a downfall," and I'd wager Lone Elk's is his wives. He has four of them and when they get together on something, Lone Elk always ends up the loser. I had Medicine Weasel tell him white men must have figured out early on this was a losing battle and that's why they only took one woman and he laughed. "What makes you think one is any easier?" he asked and I admit I was stumped for an answer. Lone Elk slapped his leg and laughed hard at seeing me stumped. That is nothing compared with his all-out glee when I try to use a bow. (I have a hunch his burn on whites ain't as dead as he'd like me to think). But he has been in a high humor the past couple of days, anyway. All the braves have. Seems they've got word some scouts of theirs will be returning to camp in the next day or so. I sure hope the news they're expecting is good.

Jack

Blackfoot Encampment,
Montana Territory
1864

Mrs. Callie McGregor
Plumas City, California

Dear Callie,

It's a somber affair here today. Camp scouts brought in three of their own that'd been found dead on the other side of the river this morning. Medicine Weasel says it's the work of the Crows. Whoever they are, *they're a bad bunch. The only fellow who lived had his fingers cut clean off as well as a few other body parts and has been hollering and begging anyone to kill him and put him out of his misery. Lone Elk is in a lather since the man is his brother-in-law.*

I ain't sure what they figure to do to get even, but whatever it is, it's big. This place is busy as a hive. Old Medicine Weasel's been gone since it happened, and Raven and her women friends are all the time so deep in talk, they rarely notice I'm around.

Strange as this might sound, I feel left out. It might be that they don't figure I care. I'm tempted to go and tell them how I feel, but I ain't sure how Lone Elk would take it. I have a hunch his tolerating me has been marked for a near miracle amongst the tribe. Pushing it might just queer my luck.

Jack

The heavy pound of drums began to beat through the stillness of the encampment as Jack took the stone pipe Medicine Weasel offered him, pulling the strong tobacco into his lungs as he watched daylight fade from the opening at the top of the lodge. It was a strange turn his life had taken, Jack thought, listening to the distant drumbeats mingling with Raven humming, cooking over the fire. *Indian sounds,* yet they were familiar to him now, as familiar as hearing the low of a cow or the steady chink of chips hitting a table. *How* it came to be like that he still wasn't sure—or maybe he didn't care to figure it. He didn't know if it was that he was too weary or if he'd just grown tired of asking why, but he had stopped asking shortly after the night of the feast.

Jack glanced over at Raven then, with her shiny black hair almost hiding her face as she leaned over the pot—but not so much that he couldn't see the slight smile on her mouth. He found himself wondering things about her as he had been for the past few days, odd wonderings, like what kinds of things made her smile or frown, what did she think about while she worked, what it was her friends said to make her laugh so hard. Part of his curiosity, he figured, was because she had been good to him. They had fallen into a kind of morning habit lately, taking walks, Raven trying to teach him Blackfoot words and Jack trying to describe white ways. Some things she liked hearing about; women things, like quilting bees and dances and cooking, for she had similar ways. Other things she fiercely disapproved of, like thinking you could own the land. But even in her fierceness there was something so innocent about her, so untarnished that he sometimes envied what she *didn't* know about the world beyond the Blackfoot.

As if sensing his eyes on her, Raven looked up. He saw her smile widen and with it was the odd hope that he had been the cause of it.

Trying to shake the thought, he passed the pipe back to Medicine Weasel and was jolted by the eerie howl of a wolf, followed by a chorus of yips and cries of other wolves. Jack glanced at the old man questioningly. He saw a wistful look cross the old man's leathered features before he drew on the pipe, nodding almost to himself. After a moment, Medicine Weasel turned to Jack and smiled.

"They sing the song of the wolf," he explained. "The men go on a raid against the Crows in the morning."

"Sounds like they plan to pick off a mess of them," Jack said, feeling every bit the outsider. He had wanted to ask if he could go along, but the days had gone by and so had his chance.

"Killing your enemy is easy," Medicine Weasel said with a tinge of scorn in his voice, but his eyes held the tolerant look of a teacher as he studied Jack. "More honor is gained by shaming him."

"Why not just kill 'em and be done with them?" Jack asked with as much respect as he could muster. Talking of enemies brought Frank Monroe to mind, and as much as Jack liked the old medicine man he couldn't see the wisdom in just shaming Frank.

Medicine Weasel simply shrugged. "Death is quick," he answered solemnly, "but a poor life is long." In the sardonic smile that followed, Jack saw the warrior that the old man had once been, full of cunning and patience, and he remembered Lone Elk's finger- less brother-in-law. No longer able to draw a bow or shoot, he was marked for a poor life. The Indians had a point, all right. It made him think, too, of the loss the whites would have on their hands if it weren't for their numbers.

As he accepted the pipe again, he heard the drumming become louder still, followed by sharp barks and howls that seemed to come from right outside the entrance of the lodge. He saw Raven quickly leave her cooking and peer out of the doorway. The howls had stopped abruptly as someone began to shout in Blackfoot.

Jack saw Medicine Weasel look up, appearing a bit startled at the words, then struggle to his feet. Jack rose as well and followed him to the entrance of the lodge as Raven was attempting to speak to the visitor, but was halted by another torrent of Blackfoot too fast for Jack to decipher.

"It is Lone Elk," Raven announced finally, her voice tinged with agitation. She turned to Jack with high color flooding her tawny cheeks. "He says after many smokes they decided to invite you along just as they would a poor relative they have taken pity on. He says now that you are walking well you would be good for holding their horses."

"That so?" Jack said, stepping outside to face the group of braves. Lone Elk was standing in front of the smirking group of men with a haughty look on his proud features. His face paint was simple; a blue streak running from his forehead to his nose but the buffalo headdress he wore seemed to make him look bigger than Jack remembered, more fierce. Jack sensed Lone Elk taking stock of him as well, and knowing in spite of his recent sickness that the broad shoulders and thick arms he'd inherited from his pa filled out the deer hide shirt Raven made him in a way that men were quick to judge when gearing up for a fight. An odd light came to the warrior's eyes as he crossed his arms over his chest, and it came to Jack that this was to be a test of sorts. Jack could feel the apprehension in Medicine Weasel—Raven, too—and he bit back the acid reply on the tip of his tongue. He had a feeling he had better weigh what he said next, not only to keep his honor but theirs as well.

"Tell him that I agree to go along if they scare up a horse for me," he told Raven. " 'Sides that, any other horses I choose to hold, I keep."

At Raven's words, Lone Elk grunted and quickly motioned for one of his braves at the back of the group. A boy came trotting forward, wearing a sheepish grin on his face as he led Big Black into the clearing. His face was painted as well, but Jack couldn't help noticing that the paint failed to hide his reluctance at having to give up Big Black.

"Well, I'll be," Jack whispered softly after the boy finally turned the animal loose. He held his hand out and his horse snorted and nuzzled his palm, just as he had so many times over the years, and for a moment Jack forgot all that was around him. He could have never admitted it aloud, but Big Black was the only tie he had left to his pa, to his memories. How many nights had he brushed him down thinking of his pa's own hands being in the very same place and deep down wishing some of the man's goodness would seep into himself? Realizing how quiet it had become, Jack glanced up and saw Lone Elk watching him closely and he stiffened a bit.

"I thank you," Jack said. "He's getting on in years but he's a fine horse."

With no one translating, Lone Elk merely shrugged but his eyes were solemn, as if in some way he understood. He turned to Raven and after another flurry of Blackfoot, he and his band were gone, weaving down the rows between the lodges.

"What did he say?" Jack asked, turning to Raven. He was struck by the different way she was looking at him, as if he was all of a sudden Blackfoot, not white. That for a moment, she had expected him to understand what the warrior had said.

"Lone Elk said that you are to meet them at the edge of camp just before SunChief rises in the sky," she replied, quickly regaining her composure. "He said something else." When she looked at him again, there was a hint of a smile that played on her lips, and Jack was struck again by her beauty. There wasn't any of the aching want like he had with Lillie, none of the passion . . . just the odd yearning to want to sit next to her. To smile with her.

"Well, let's have it," he said in mock seriousness.

"He said you will never have many horses if you keep losing them."

In spite of the sally, Jack laughed and Raven, who had been trying her best not to, joined in.

Medicine Weasel, who had gone to retrieve something from the lodge, was now walking gingerly toward them. Jack hid his smile, knowing the old man's careful steps were due to the poor fit of his boots. Seemingly unconcerned about his discomfort, Medicine Weasel's own grin was wide as he neared, looking from Jack to Raven.

"It is a good day," he announced a bit breathlessly, but when his gaze met Jack's something in his demeanor changed. He appeared to be weighing the words he was about to say. "Sometimes an invitation is not made by a pure heart. But what you do with the invitation, JackWade, is what will be remembered."

Jack simply nodded. The thought that Lone Elk's sudden change of heart might be just an act had already occurred to him as well as a few other concerns. But his worries weren't as strong as his urge to go. Already, Jack could feel the swirl of adrenaline begin in him and it appeared Medicine Weasel understood.

With an air of great ceremony, the old man gingerly pulled a necklace that bore the figure of a running horse stamped out of brass from his medicine pouch and placed it around Jack's neck, then stood back. Jack noticed the medicine man looked thinner to him with a bit of a gray cast to his skin, and it dawned on him where he had been the past few days. What little he knew of such things, he knew the Blackfoot only passed their medicine on after much sweating and praying, and it hit him deep down to know Medicine Weasel had gone to such trouble for *him.*

"When a warrior gets on in years, he passes his strong war medicine on. The horse charm is for swiftness," Medicine Weasel said simply, but Jack had heard the gruffness in his voice and he had the sudden feeling it wasn't so simple for him to give such a gift. He knew Medicine Weasel had meant to pass his medicine on to his son.

Jack touched the necklace reverently and smiled his thanks to Medicine Weasel as the Indian stood still as a grave, his long hair whipping about him while a cold wind bore down across the valley. Jack couldn't shake the feeling how suddenly *lonely* the medicine man appeared, standing there like that. When he looked over at Raven, he saw the sorrow of her father's loss was mirrored in her own eyes. But he saw something else there, like a yearning for something new, and he felt heartened by it. Grateful, too, and he was filled with the desire to make them both proud.

"I won't let you down," he told them, trying to swallow back the emotion in his voice. In the distance, Jack could hear the war cries and he saw puffs of smoke fill the wide, clear fall sky as the braves shot off their weapons. He felt Raven shyly take his hand, filling him with the warmth of companionship, a feeling that he hadn't realized he needed so badly until now. Raven felt it, too.

How long had it been since she had felt the touch of a man other than her father? she wondered. She glanced up at the white man who stood beside her and felt a calm warmth go through her. JackWade *was* a good man, she decided. A handsome man, too, with his strong face and eyes the color of spring grass. She had seen much in those eyes: sorrow, anger, curiosity, all teaching her of the man behind them. Now she saw hope and it made her feel like something great had happened—a thing more important than the raid against the Crow—and the urge to tell him was strong.

Raven started to whisper it to JackWade and it seemed he even leaned in a bit, as if he might have something to say as well, but her father, with his seemingly casual eye on them, rustled somewhere behind them and they both fell silent.

When Raven glanced back at her father, his head was turned away as he appeared to be watching yet another group of braves race by, shouting insults and singing war songs, but she knew better. "Let us smoke, JackWade," he announced, grimacing a bit as he started walking toward his lodge. But there was a glint of *knowing* in his dark eyes as he glanced over his shoulder at her. "We must pray to the Above Ones for your safe return."

Blackfoot Encampment,
Montana Territory
1864

Mrs. Callie McGregor
Plumas City, California

Dear Callie,
Lone Elk has invited me to go along with him and his warriors on the raid come morning. I'll wager the invite ain't just out of the goodness of his heart, either, but I figure on going just the same. I ain't never chose to "lose face" and I don't plan to this time. Honor is a big thing here. I guess it should be anywhere but it's more important this time, Sis. They don't come right out and say it, but I know Medicine Weasel and Raven are counting on me because of them taking me in against the tribe's advice and I don't aim to let them down. The old man gave me a neck-lace from his medicine pouch for my journey. It's a figure of a running horse. He sprinkled some stuff on it tonight and said some kind of prayer

over it for swiftness. I ain't sure about all that but I figure it can't hurt. Raven told me tonight her father has "big faith" in me. She gave me a fine gift of an elkskin shirt to wear on the raid, too. I wonder if you'd even recognize your ol' bro' with this long hair and Indian garb. I feel a bit like a kid getting slicked up for Sunday. Medicine Weasel and Raven are all smiles but I think they're worried, too. Can't say I blame them. I liken it to putting all your money on a puny horse you've nursed and hoping it'll win so you're not laughed out of town.

Speaking of horses, I got Big Black back in the deal, too. Guess I feel a bit the fool not to have noticed my own horse here in this camp. But then, these Blackfeet can be a crafty bunch. I can't help liking them—in spite of their craftiness. Or maybe because of it, I ain't sure. What I do know is there's something about them that makes me want to stay for awhile and be a part of it. Truth is, when they gave me Big Black and my guns, I could have just ridden on out but I didn't. I did think hard on it but when I tried to picture going back to Virginia City, to Lillie, Frank Monroe came with the picture. Callie, I'd only tell you this: I've lost something in me. I can't explain it any better than that but I think it left me when I found Duel like I did. Medicine Weasel says it's my spirit. All I know is I've started to get it back and I don't want to leave until I am right again. Because when I do face Frank and his bunch again, it's to win. I owe Duel that.

I guess that's all I'll write for now. I'm feeling a bit on the edgy side tonight waiting for morning to come. Remember what it was like when we were kids, waiting for time to go play? It's like that. At least the braves are restless, too. They have been riding through and all around camp for hours, hollering, shooting off guns. Lone Elk ain't been back, though. If I know him like I think I do, he's going to wait and see if I measure up.

I might say the same for myself.

Jack

Fourteen

Jack felt like the whole world had turned Indian as he reined in Big Black and watched the massive war party that he followed leave the bluffs and spill out onto the plain. No book, no words he'd ever read could do the scene justice; line after line of Blackfoot warriors with horses that bore war paint on their shoulders and haunches moving across the wide swatch of land, black hair gleaming in the sun, painted faces and fringed finery stitched with scalp locks, teeth, or claws, their plumed lances waving in the wind. Some had shields and most had guns, but it wasn't the weapons, he thought, it was the *power* of the scene, of viewing so many together—and knowing few whites had—that made him feel as if he could only be dreaming it all.

But it wasn't a dream. He was riding *with* them and the very thought made him feel big and small at the same time. Out of the corner of his eye, Jack caught a lone rider pull away from the group and come riding toward him. He nudged Big Black into a trot to meet him. Even from a distance, he knew the rider was Lone Elk. The haughty grin was hard to miss in spite of the broad slashes of paint on the warrior's face.

"Haiya!" Lone Elk called in greeting. "My young men, they

worry you will not keep up." Just as the translator finished, his grin widened. "I told them you are not as puny as you look."

So, it was starting already, Jack thought grimly. Medicine Weasel had warned him the warriors would not go easy on him. He had no doubt this was only the beginning, but he smiled anyway. As he knew, there was always more than one way to play poker.

"Tell him the puny one will keep up," Jack told the translator with unconcealed sarcasm. "Tell him the Above Ones take pity on me today."

As he finished, Jack saw a flicker of surprise, then respect enter the warrior's eyes beneath the shadow of his buffalo headdress.

"It is good they do," Lone Elk said, ending with a dismissive motion to show he was through. But Jack didn't miss the eagerness in the Blackfoot's eyes for what was to come, and as the warrior headed back to his men, Jack felt his own blood run swift with the promise of it as well. *You've thrown down the challenge, now let's just see if I don't meet it,* Jack thought with a fierce kind of resolve.

Jack briefly touched the necklace Medicine Weasel gave him then spurred Big Black on to catch up with Lone Elk and the rest of the party. Medicine Weasel had told him it gave the wearer *strong medicine,* that no brave took the war trail without good medicine for fear he would lose his courage. He had no thoughts of losing his courage, but he rubbed the brass horse in between his fingers once more just the same.

After all, a good gambler never shunned any extra edge he was given.

Jack checked the worn soles of yet another pair of moccasins by the dim light of the moon, wondering if they would last the night. Their trek to Crow land seemed endless but the last four days had been the hardest, traveling only at night as they felt their way across the plains, fording icy waters and making cold camps. But even as his body ached from the strain, he felt his senses sharpen—as if the strain along with eating light had cleared his head somehow. Like the others, he'd become familiar with the night sounds and smells, with feeling instead of seeing the moods of the men, and now he could feel them collectively ticking off what they would need for the raid. None of them had much sleep in spite of Lone Elk's urgings. They had strung bows, shaped feathers for their arrows, checked their medicine bags, painted their faces and his, and changed into their war shirts so quietly he could've sworn he was in church instead of out on the rocky outcropping they huddled beneath, waiting for the scouts to return and give Lone Elk the go ahead.

Just when they felt like they couldn't wait any longer, Lone Elk appeared. As he crouched down to whisper, Jack saw the left half of his face was painted white with blue spots, giving him a fierce, ghostly look. "We go now," he instructed. "Wolf Runner has come back with good news. He says there are *two* horse herds. Enough to make us all wealthy." As the men scrambled for their packs, Lone Elk glanced over his shoulder at Jack and grinned. "Maybe you will even find a Crow woman, JackWade. One that can make many moccasins."

"And maybe you will find one that will listen to you," Jack countered. He heard more than a few of the men try to stifle their laughter as they clambered up out of the draw.

The Blackfoot made their way quickly through Crow country, keeping to the swales and washes as they snaked around the clumps of greasewood and sage that brought them closer to the enemy's camp. As Jack kept pace with the group to the right, he felt their weariness fade and he knew the lure of the large horse herds had lightened their steps. As they crept forward, some whispered excitedly of the good fortune that gave them the cold wind blowing against them so the Crows' dogs could not smell them, some spoke of the thin slide of clouds that blocked enough of the moon so they couldn't be seen as well, but eventually they all fell silent, sensing they were close to the camp. In the silence, Jack's mind wandered again, as it had over the past few nights, taking him back to the morning he had ridden out with the war party. He had lost count of how many times Raven's image, just as he had found her that morning, had come to him.

He hadn't expected to encounter anyone as he walked down by the river but there Raven had been, bathing, her bare back to him with the sun just starting to peek through the trees. He had felt like a kid, not knowing whether to go or stay. So he had stayed, taking in her honey-colored skin, the soft curve of her hips, the way her damp hair stuck to the small of her back, and he was stuck by the natural beauty of what he saw. Raven had picked that moment to turn and look over her shoulder, as if she sensed him standing there. As their eyes met, Jack saw a flush creep over her cheeks and she had quickly turned her back to him, as if to save them both the embarrassment. But the truth was, Jack knew the damage was already done.

Seeing Raven like that changed things. A flood of confusing thoughts and wants invaded his mind. When he had turned to go back to the lodge, he was startled to find old Lodge Skins standing before him.

"It is a good morning," the old man said casually, but the way he had smiled and cocked his head to one side made Jack think for a moment that Lodge Skins had actually *seen* what had taken place. Jack had mumbled some sort of greeting and hurried back to camp. When he had ridden off, only Medicine Weasel was there to say good-bye but Raven's image never left him.

Jack felt a sharp tug at his shirt and was suddenly embarrassed to see the young brave they called One Shot looking at him strangely. One Shot motioned for him to get on the ground, then pointed up the hill to the mass of warriors crawling along on their bellies. Suddenly all of his thoughts were brushed aside as his mind went to the fight ahead. He dropped down on all fours and followed along next to One Shot. When he finally reached the brow, he fell to his belly and surveyed the large Crow camp, his eyes following Lone Elk's hand as he pointed out what lay below. Jack saw the lodges first, looming white beneath the moon with low fires burning down. A few dogs were picking around the edges of the fires for scraps, but besides that it appeared the Crows had bedded down for the night. His eyes moved down past the camp and that's when he saw the huge horse herds, too many to count, flanking each side of the river, and he felt a heady rush of excitement. Lone Elk nudged him and pointed away from the herds. Jack had to squint to make out what he was looking at and then he realized what it was.

White men's tents.

Jack felt the blood rush out of him and he glanced over at Lone Elk, but the warrior didn't appear disturbed at all by what he saw.

"It is good they are there," Lone Elk whispered as if reading Jack's thoughts. "Wolf Runner says the Crow have filled their bellies with the white man's water all night. While we take their horses, the Crow will be sleeping like babies."

Jack wanted to ask what they planned to do to the white men but Lone Elk was already directing the men. Most were sent to round up the herds, but some of the more seasoned warriors were planning to take the best of the lot: the buffalo runners the Crow kept carefully staked to their lodges.

Lone Elk pointed out a blue buffalo tepee that seemed to stand out from the rest. "The one who tortured my wife's brother will wake in the morning to find his best horse gone as well as the herd and he will be like a poor man," the warrior declared with venom in his voice. "Then he will think twice about coming to our land and killing our men."

"I'm going, too," Jack whispered, ready to argue if need be. He had already spotted a runner he wanted for himself. Besides, if he stayed close enough to Lone Elk and the others, he could keep an eye on the traders' tents.

Lone Elk shrugged. "If you wish," he said and the group quickly made their way down toward the outskirts of the camp.

Jack watched as three of the warriors moved soundlessly toward the left side of the camp, then he turned and followed Lone Elk toward the blue buffalo tepee. To the right of that tepee sat another with the horse Jack had been eyeing and just beyond the tepees were the traders' tents. As they crept toward the tepees, Jack felt every nerve in his body flame up. Every one of his senses went on alert; he heard a sigh come from inside the tepee and he froze for a moment until it appeared sleep had returned and he continued on. The horse snorted softly as he reached out to release it from the lodgepole it was tethered to, but it calmed and went with him willingly and he felt a sharp urge to laugh at his good fortune. When he looked back for Lone Elk, the warrior had fashioned a bridle from his lariat and was getting ready to mount his own horse when Jack saw something move in behind him. He saw a man's arm rise in a wide arc and the flash of steel and then heard a guttural cry that sounded nothing like Blackfoot.

"Lone Elk!" Jack uttered hoarsely as rage filled him. Suddenly, the Crow wasn't a Crow; he was Frank Monroe and without thinking, Jack drew his pistols and fired at the man whose knife was only inches from Lone Elk's back, causing the entire Crow camp to startle awake. The dead Crow fell face forward in the dirt and without missing a beat, Lone Elk kneeled next to him, ignoring the Crow who begun scrambling from their lodges. The Blackfoot warrior pulled the Crow's head back by his hair, and with one swipe of a knife, he cut around the dead man's crown and jerked the hair free. When Lone Elk looked up, Jack was surprised to see his face wasn't set in savage glee as he expected, just more resolved to finish with his deed.

"We go now," Lone Elk said as he mounted the sleek buffalo runner. As Jack turned to find his own, he came face to face with one of the white traders. The man looked as if he had just roused out of a sleep, hair all askew, his face confused as he glanced from Lone Elk to Jack. The whiteness of his skin shocked Jack.

" 'The Hell," was all the man got out when he realized he had a pistol aimed at his forehead. Jack knocked the limply held gun out from under the man's arm.

"Get back to your tent," Jack growled and shoved the trader for all he was worth through the tent door. The man tumbled backwards, grabbing on to Jack's shirt, pulling him into the opening of the tent where the stench of whiskey hung in the air. Another man already cowering inside took one look at Jack's crimson-painted face and gurgled a strange high-pitched sound as Jack shoved the trader down beside his friend. For a split second, the trader just gaped at him and their eyes met under the flickering light of the lantern.

"Yer *white,*" he blurted out, but Jack had already moved back out into the darkness where he found Lone Elk waiting with their horses. The Crow camp was quickly stirring to life; Crow braves stumbled from their tepees, calling to one another as they grabbed their weapons. Lone Elk pitched the bridle to him, and Jack swung up on the sleek black horse he had taken, feeling his fear mount to near hysteria.

"Their drinking has slowed them some, but that will not last," Lone Elk said breathlessly. They both kicked their horses into a run as they headed for the river. Lone Elk was the first to reach the Blackfoot warriors and tell them what happened.

There was no time to laugh or tell stories of the raid as the Crow were fast on their heels but there was a euphoria amongst the men. They were all accounted for and had with them the largest herd ever to be taken from an enemy—and they planned to keep them. The warriors quickly split up and began to move the herd away from the river, swatting the horses' rumps with urgency. The animals broke into a trot, filling Jack's ears with the drumming sounds of hundreds of hooves.

Once the horses began to climb up out of the draw and fill the plains, Lone Elk sidled his horse next to Jack's and handed him the lance that carried the Crow's scalp at its tip.

"The scalp is yours," Lone Elk said with a generous smile. As Lone Elk rode forward, Jack saw him tip his head back and give a loud triumphant cry that the others began to echo, and the whole of them broke into a run, pushing the herd faster and faster.

Listening to their cries, Jack suddenly felt the empty part in him being filled up again. . . . *Like being set free,* he thought. As if all of the pent-up anger, the urge to just go mad and break free of what was expected of him was opened up and all the ugliness life dealt him began to drain out. His eyes went to the riders ahead as he rode on in a thunder of hooves, and he took it all in: the shadow bodies and horses, looking and moving as if they were one in a dark blur of hide and feathers and flying hair. The wildness of it all took hold of his past and threw it over his shoulder, and he felt new as a babe that had just been put in its mama's arms for the first time. He saw Lone Elk glance over his shoulder and grin wide as if to let him know he understood. In that moment Jack felt a bond between them as strong as he ever had with Duel.

When Lone Elk let out another whoop, Jack echoed it with one of his own as the horses rushed over the dark plains.

Lone Elk leaned against the backrest he had made from sticks and pine boughs, grunting contentedly. His stomach was full after eating several roasted chunks of the yearling Wolf-Runner had killed, and he felt lulled by the first real fire they had had in days. It was a good day, he silently declared. As his eyes roved happily over the herd once again, he felt a swell of pride. One hundred seventy horses, surely the largest herd to be taken. There would be much celebrating when they returned. Lone Elk imagined the happy smiles of his wives, the looks of envy from the men who had stayed behind, and he wished to be on the trail again, to be *home* to taste his success. He heard bits of talking from the group of warriors around the fire, their stories becoming bigger, their laughter loud, and he knew they were eager to show their new wealth, too. His eyes found JackWade. He was doing his white man's scratching on paper again—something the warrior considered a waste of time. Still, JackWade had proven himself well in the raid, in spite of Lone Elk thinking he wouldn't. But one act of bravery had never changed his feelings before, the warrior thought. It was odd his feelings had been changed about the white man, like something had turned his thinking on purpose.

A bit superstitious by nature, he glanced to the sky briefly in case there might be some sort of sign from the Above Ones, then he looked at the white man again. The feeling he got was the same feeling he had out on the plains when he had squinted his eyes while looking at JackWade and thought that he didn't look white, but almost *Blackfoot.*

Almost, a voice reminded him pointedly, as he felt a bit of his old self return. Only time could prove what this man was made of, he thought with a self-satisfied air. Time and tests. Lone Elk smiled to himself as he rose from the fire. He was good at testing a man. Without a word to the others, he grabbed his medicine pouch and strolled to the other side of the fire.

As if sensing his presence, the green eyes peered up from the paper, tired but curious.

"Lone Elk," JackWade greeted in passable Blackfoot. "How long before we move on?"

"Not long," he replied in English. He had stopped pretending that he couldn't speak the white language only because the game was more troublesome than it was worth. He saw a flicker of surprise in the green eyes.

"We ride again tonight after we have rested some," Lone Elk added, noting the tired droop of shoulders but seeing that the white man's face was set hard and ready to endure. He felt his grudging respect grow; JackWade *had* held up well so far. Lone Elk abruptly crouched before he could change his mind, and he took a pinch of herbs from his medicine pouch, then added them to a gourd of warm water.

"We must sleep light. The Crow are crafty and will try to find a way to steal back their horses before we reach our camp," he whispered conspiratorially as he stirred the drink. When he was finished, he handed the drink to Jack Wade but avoided the intense green stare.

"Drink this, it will strengthen you," he urged somberly, then turned and walked off before the white man could see the twitch that threatened his mouth with a smile.

Montana Territory
1864

Mrs. Callie McGregor
Plumas City, California

Dear Callie,

I don't think I've been so tired in all my life but there's no way to sleep until I tell you a little of what happened tonight. We raided the Crow, Sis, and if I live to be a hundred I don't think I'll ever forget all I saw. I know it's hard for you to imagine your bro' riding with one set of Indians against another—with any Indians for that matter—and truth is, I can hardly believe it myself. Seeing this sizable herd of Crow horseflesh milling around us tends to make me a believer, though. They are a sight, all painted up with brands from each of us who claimed them. I've claimed twenty for myself, including a prized "buffalo runner." Several of the fellows keep walking over and checking on them like they expect them to disappear. The funniest thing is hearing them try to top each other's stories. If I closed my eyes, I'd swear I was back in Virginia City, the way they are carrying on. Horses are the Blackfoot's idea of wealth, so you could liken tonight to a bunch of miners celebrating after finding the mother lode.

I will say, sneaking that many horses out of that Crow camp was touch and go, but we did it and with almost no loss of life. I was forced to kill a Crow ready to stab Lone Elk in the back. I ain't proud of it, but I am glad it was him and not Lone Elk. Lone Elk lost no time scalping the fellow. But he ended up giving me the scalp. Way I understand it, since the Crow wasn't his kill, the generous thing to do was to turn it over to me. I say I wish he wasn't so generous.

I—

Well, Lone Elk was just here and told me to get some rest as we will be moving again come nightfall. He says the Crow won't quit us until we get back to our own camp.

I guess he doesn't have to tell me twice. I feel like I can barely keep my eyes open to finish this. I know this ain't exactly the kind of letter a brother should send his sister but then, I ain't always been known for watching what I say, have I?

Jack

P.S. There were some white traders in that Crow camp. I think they recognized me as white, too. I wonder if that's what's making Lone Elk act out of sorts. Heck, even if they did recognize me, I can't imagine anything coming of it.

Jack startled awake, sensing something was wrong. The sun was heavy on his face in spite of the cold wind, and as he blinked the last of his sleep away he sensed something else. It was too quiet. He bolted upright, throwing back the robe that covered him, and looked around. The camp was deserted, except for the lone buzzard pecking at scraps around a cold fire.

As he stood, something brushed his head and he looked up to see a pair of grimy, hole-eaten moccasins dangling from a low branch of the tree he had bedded down under, mocking him. He tore them from the branch, looking at them as if he expected them to give him his answers. They weren't Crow, the design alone marked them as Blackfoot. *What the hell was going on?* he wondered with rage-filled confusion.

Maybe the Crow had taken Lone Elk and the others by surprise and that in their hurry to escape, they had forgotten him, he thought. Jack frowned as he trudged along. That didn't make any sense, either. If there was a ruckus, he surely would have heard it—not in all of his years had he ever been known to sleep through noise like that. He tried to sort through it all but his mind turned slower than normal, like a wheel in bad need of oiling. It was only after he had gathered up his gear and pulled his pack over his shoulder that the thought finally came to him that Lone Elk's brew might have been what did him in. *Drink this, it will strengthen you,* he remembered Lone Elk saying, and he didn't recall much else after that. He felt something wet hit his nose and looked up to see the first snow begin to fall.

Jack readjusted the makeshift pack with a grimace and began to climb the slope, searching for signs of which way they might have gone. There wasn't time for figuring out how it had all happened.

As he reached the crest of a hill, he felt a chill of fear looking out over the empty miles that were shrouded by the huge splash of sky choked gray with snow. The snow was beginning to fall heavier on the plains, but when he looked at the ground, he felt his hope rise in spite of the weather. The snow hadn't started sticking, but it had kept the ground damp—enough so as to see the trail of hundreds of hoofprints.

Jack grinned for the first time that morning and quickly stuffed the old pair of moccasins in his pocket as he headed off in a quick jog.

It was an odd thing to walk along on feet you couldn't even feel any-more. Jack glanced down at the worn-through moccasins, noticing with a kind of detached alarm how blue his toes had become. He had thought the first day of hoofing it over the rockiest country he had ever seen was bad, but he had been wrong. The second day was the worst. The snow had hidden every hole and rock just enough to tor-ture his feet, and every body part that ached from the day before now screamed. He had considered from time to time that he ought to just sit down and give in to the screams, but his mind wouldn't allow it. The mind was funny like that; you could try to let it just go blank, but there was still the sound. Head chatter, Duel called it. The kind of nagging you might get from your ma or pa or maybe a wife if you had one that kept you going even when you didn't feel like it.

Jack glanced at his blue toes again and shocked himself by the hoarse chuckle that came from his throat, and he wondered if he was going crazy. *Maybe I ought to just go crazy,* he thought defiantly. *Then I won't care anymore if I find that derned bunch or not.* He laughed again, stumbling as he clawed his way up a frozen embankment, but the laughter died in his throat when he finally reached the top and looked below.

The sun was just beginning to set but he could still see the massive herd of horses spread out along the icy stream, nosing through the snow for bits of grass and lulling about, as if they had been there forever. Just beyond the herd, he saw the band of warriors that he had come to know so well. From the looks of it, they were in deep discussion; buffalo-capped heads bowed as the tallest of the bunch puffed streams of smoke from his lips as he spoke. Jack would've recognized Lone Elk anywhere in spite of the heavy winter garb he wore as the warrior punctuated his plan with an occasional slap of a fist to his palm.

Forgetting about his feet, Jack part-scrambled, part-slid down the embankment, making his way toward the camp with a determined stride that hid his pain. Lone Elk glanced up from his speech and his eyes widened a bit, then he grinned broadly.

"Jack Wade!" he called cheerily, breaking through the group that surrounded him. His eyes briefly flicked over Jack's shoddy appearance down to his feet, then back to the green eyes that felt hot with anger and frustration. Where was the, *"Sorry we left you in the middle of nowhere but there was this really good reason"* or *"You had to walk all that way?"*

"I see you've lost your horse again," Lone Elk said with an almost casual air. "It is good you've returned, however. The snow gave us time to rest from our hard ride but we must leave soon."

"I guess it's good I showed up when I did then," Jack ground out between clenched teeth, but Lone Elk had already turned away and motioned for One Shot, speaking in rapid Blackfoot.

As Jack followed the warrior into camp, he tried to decipher Lone Elk's attitude. It galled Jack to no end that he hadn't asked what happened to him or even showed in the slightest way any type of concern over Jack's weakened condition, but Jack was determined not to let his anger show until he had seen all the cards.

Truth was, he was never so glad to see a bunch of Indians as he was at that moment, and it appeared the rest of them were glad to see him as well. Some of the warriors had come up long enough to slap him on the back as One Shot hurriedly dug a hole to start a small fire in and helped Jack get seated, taking care to cover him with an extra robe for warmth, then handed him a stick with what looked to be cooked rabbit.

Lone Elk remained silent as Jack ate, smiling patiently as clusters of warriors began to trickle in little by little around the fire, all appearing to be waiting for something.

Jack waited, too. He waited for some sort of explanation from Lone Elk or the others but all he got was watched. After awhile, the longer he sat, filling his stomach, the more his thoughts began to fade until his only thought left was to get up from the fire and find sleep in the warmth of his robes. He nearly nodded off at one point and as his head jerked up, he glanced around the fire at the group and was caught off guard by the beaming smiles. When he turned to Lone Elk, he noticed his was the largest.

Hearing a familiar whicker, Jack looked up in time to see Big Black lope slowly past the fire, reins trailing in the dust as he casually headed in the direction of the herd.

"You still have much to learn about keeping your horse," Lone Elk said. A few chuckles started around the fire, quickly mounting into hearty laughter, and as tired as he was, Jack wasn't so tired not to realize he had been duped.

Montana Territory
Winter, 1864

Mrs. Callie McGregor
Plumas City, California

Dear Callie,

I got my first dose of "Indian humor." Believe it or not, I think these fellows enjoy playing a good joke more than an all-out fight.

The "joke" happened not long after our horse raid I wrote you about. I guess they thought giving me some kind of sleeping potion and leaving me out in the middle of nowhere with nothing to get around on except a dirty pair of moccasins would be funny. Well, my two days of fun got me half-starved to death and a bad case of frostbitten feet. I guess I lost my sense of humor, too. Lone Elk seems put out about that.

I guess it gave him a case of the guilts because he admitted he was the one who thought up the whole scheme. He confessed it a bit too proudly if you ask me. He said that playing these kinds of games on each other tests a man's worth—that Blackfoot know at the end of a game just what kind of man you are. What they don't know is our family's love of games.

Might be time I showed these fellows what we Wades are really made of.

Jack

Fifteen

The sound came like distant thunder at first.

Raven glanced up at the sky as she shifted her bundle of wood in her arms. There was nothing different about the sky, only the swollen promise of more snow ready to fall when Cold Maker waved his arm, so she squinted her eyes and looked off in the distance, trying to place the sound. At first she saw only small, hopping drifts of snow, like you might see caught by the wind every once in awhile, but soon she noticed the drifts getting larger, the snow flying up higher, and she spotted dark legs and hooves, hundreds of them, moving closer and closer toward the village.

The scouts had spotted the herd, too. Raven heard the cry uttered and the camp came alive, people spilling out of the lodges to greet their loved ones. She stood where she was, her eyes fixed on the horses and searching for the riders who would be bringing up the rear of the herd. Even as she searched, she knew there was only one man she was really looking for. When her eyes finally fell on the lone rider, she thought her heart would die a thousand deaths. *One man? Was that all that was left?*

Raven dropped her bundle of wood and raised her hand to shade her eyes from the harsh glare of snow, and the grief that flooded her being left as swiftly as it came as the lone figure became clearer. Even with the distance, she couldn't mistake JackWade's outline: the wide shoulders, the long, wavy hair—too wavy to be Blackfoot—but what she recognized most was the smile. Even surrounded by a beard encrusted by snow, the smile was the same and she knew that wherever the others were, they were well.

"Raven!" the deep voice called, and she felt the same tremor of excitement go through her that she felt the day he had left when he had spied her in the river. Without thinking, she quickly smoothed her long hair back from her face and dusted off her snow-specked skirt as JackWade dismounted from his sweat-coated horse. There was a sudden swarm of activity around them; young boys herding horses away as the crowds pushed forward, shouting questions, but Raven felt everything slow down around her and fade. She felt as if suddenly it was only the two of them standing there.

"The others?" she asked, looking up into his face. The crowd pushed harder, pressing her against him, and she felt her cheeks grow hot from their closeness. She took a deep breath and looked into his eyes again. She saw he had gone still as well.

"The others?"

"Oh, they'll be along shortly," he said, his green eyes filling with laughter, but there was something else, too. A look that said he'd missed her as much as she'd missed him, and a part of her heart that had been hiding peeked out.

In the push and pull of the crowd, Jack's hand touched hers and he felt the change, too. *How did it come so quick to this?* he wondered, feeling a bit shook up. The exhilaration of the ride paled compared with the confusing feelings that swirled through him; how many times during the final push home had he seen Lillie's face before him? And how could that all change when he saw Raven standing there? Before he could think of much more, Medicine Weasel appeared, parting the crowd with a look of supreme worry on his face.

"Where are our warriors?" Medicine Weasel called above the noise of the crowd. The people fell silent, waiting. Jack looked around to all of the wary, expectant Indian faces and he knew what they were thinking: *How is it that the white man has returned with all of these horses and our men have not?* Their mood surrounded him like a Norther blowing in, dropping the temperature so suddenly you could barely catch your breath, and he hesitated until his eyes fell on Medicine Weasel and Raven once more.

Like a grieved family hoping for a last-minute pardon, they pleaded to Jack with their eyes.

"They are safe. They will be here soon," he began in halting Blackfoot. He saw the confused looks on their faces as they glanced to each other and then back to him. A few of the young warriors moved toward him anyway until Medicine Weasel held his hand out to stop their advance. The older man stepped closer and peered into Jack's face—more for show than anything. Jack hadn't missed the sudden light of humor that came into the black eyes, as if it had dawned on him what had happened.

"Is it a good story?" he asked, placing his hand on Jack's shoulder, as Jack couldn't help remembering how his pa used to do the same. He grinned at the man who had become more than a friend.

"It is a good story."

Medicine Weasel threw his head back and laughed, surprising the crowd until he waved, instructing all to follow them as he and Jack made their way towards his lodge. Raven walked happily beside them, and Jack watched with a kind of happy amazement, as the whole band began to take on a festive air. They were a funny bunch, he thought, shaking his head. One minute ready to scalp him, the next ready to throw a party.

By the time Lone Elk and the other warriors did ride in, the Blackfoot were in high humor. Jack had been made to tell the story nearly a dozen times already. The parts he didn't know how to say in Blackfoot, he mimed: sprinkling Lone Elk's sleeping herb into all of the warriors' water pouches, how they got all slow acting when it started working, tying the shredded moccasins above Lone Elk's head, then leaving only enough bony horses behind so they would have to double up on them. So when the weary party trailed in, the Blackfoot naturally were ready to rib them. Medicine Weasel even forgot about his sore toes enough to do a little jig around the men before he invited them to sit around the fire so they might hear Jack tell the story one more time.

With this last telling, Jack felt as if he had grown bigger in the Blackfoot's eyes—especially Raven's. He could tell that she thought the part about him leaving his hole-ridden moccasins for Lone Elk was pretty clever and couldn't help chuckling as she prodded Lone Elk to show the moccasins for all to see.

Lone Elk grimaced, then thrust his long leg into the air, wiggling his dirty toes through the large hole in his moccasins, which caused the band to go crazy with laughter. Even Lone Elk laughed, his humor being restored since being promised the return of his horses.

When the laughter finally died down a bit, Jack leaned forward and winked at his weary adversary. "So, how did I do?"

"You played well," Lone Elk admitted. As they both began laughing, Jack felt a change take place around the lodge in the way the people considered him. As if he wasn't just a visitor anymore but a part of them. When Raven gently touched his shoulder to pass him yet another bowl of food, their eyes met once again and he felt as though all of the unknowns of his life had faded away in the welcome of her smile.

Medicine Weasel, who had been sitting quietly by his side, leaned over to Jack and peered deep into his eyes.

"What are you looking for now?" Jack asked. The old man straightened up and smiled a wide grin of pleasure.

"It's your spirit, JackWade. It has returned."

Blackfoot Encampment,
Montana Territory
Winter, 1864

Mrs. Callie McGregor
Plumas City, California

Dear Callie,

You would be pretty proud of your ol' bro' tonight. I wish you could have seen Lone Elk and the other warriors tumbling into camp, still drowsy with their own potion and sore bottomed from doubling up on the nags I'd left them. The best was seeing their faces when they realized I'd driven the herd in myself. There ain't no better feeling than winning a good game.

I know it might sound pretty impossible—me driving a whole herd of horses into an Indian camp alone. Truth is, I was purely nervous the whole time (I had to go after strays so many times I got the shakes), but I was hard-headed determined to make it, too. You know how we get when we get set on something we want to do.

Anyway, I made it. Much to the entertainment of this bunch. They must have made me retell the story of how I paid back Lone Elk and the fellows a hundred times. I admit the boys have been good sports about it all. Especially Lone Elk. He even invited me on a hunt with him come morning.

Wasn't it Mama who was forever saying a person's life could change in a moment? Seems like that's what's happened here tonight. I went from being the enemy to the entertainment in a matter of seconds. They call me "Jack Wade" like it's one name, slap me on the back, and pass the pipe to me almost as if I'm one of them. I don't know about me being one of them, but you might be hard-pressed to recognize me with this garb. My hair is about as long as an Indian's now, too. Lone Elk has been rib-

bing me all night long about how much the Crow would pay for my hair. I didn't take it too seriously. I think he's just trying to get some of the ol' ego back.

I think I'll stay here for awhile. The snow is piling up pretty quick. Not to mention the cold. I can't ever remember a winter in Missouri being this cold. Medicine Weasel says men have been known to freeze right where they stand out in weather like this. I figure I've had all the cold I can handle. My toes still have a bit of blue to them, though Raven says I won't lose them. Cold like this can make you rethink a lot of things, I guess.

Jack

P.S. The moccasins are for little Rose. Tell her that Uncle Jack has walked many a mile in a pair much like them. Only hers ain't used.

Jack shook the snow from the large jackrabbit carcasses as he trudged back into camp. Lone Elk's kill hadn't been much better, but he had hoped for something larger than a jackrabbit his first time out, especially knowing Raven would be waiting to see what he brought for her to cook.

"It is good that you bring food to Medicine Weasel's lodge," Lodge Skins commented. Jack was startled to see he had nearly walked right past the old man crouched by his small fire. Lodge Skins enjoyed any kind of weather and so was found most of the time sitting outside his lodge. Jack worried the old guy would freeze to death, but he appeared just as spry as he always did, as if the cold had no effect on him at all. "I was saying only the other day how sorry I felt for my old friend, having no son or son-in-law to help him hunt."

"Well, these derned jackrabbits ain't more than nothin'," Jack chuckled halfheartedly. Lodge Skins grunted, motioning for him to sit. He did so, wondering as he always did with Lodge Skins, where this new conversation would take him.

"When I heard you and Lone Elk were off on a hunt, I told Medicine Weasel it was a good sign and that everyone feels you would make a fine son-in-law. Maybe I was foolish for making such a suggestion, but I wanted to cheer up the old man."

Jack smiled in spite of the bomb that had just dropped, studying the cracked, weather-beaten face of Lodge Skins, a man twenty years Medicine Weasel's senior, if a day. *Cheer up the old man, my eye,* Jack thought.

"I'm white if you ain't noticed. 'Sides the fact that Raven ain't interested in me. I figure I'm more like a brother to her than anything."

Jack finally managed to glance up from the lie and was met with a frown of disbelief. That he had failed to fool a blind man was a sorry thing.

"I suppose we can all be blind sometimes," Lodge Skins said, then shrugged. He sucked on his pipe and seemed to stare hard at the fire that hissed and crackled before them. After awhile, the old man rose from his fire, a small groan escaping him as he made his way to the doorway of the lodge. He glanced one last time over his shoulder, his cloudy eyes squinting right at Jack as if he could still see, then he shook his head.

"Sometimes I wonder how you whites became so many."

Stinging a bit from Lodge Skins' barb, Jack made the walk back to Medicine Weasel's lodge a long one. There was no denying the warm feelings he had for Raven. He was pretty sure she felt something for him, too. But how could he do anything about it when he wasn't sure where his future would be? And would it be fair to her to ease his loneliness, when he knew his heart was still with Lillie? But when he opened the flap to the lodge and saw her standing there, hands on hips and her head cocked in a jaunty angle, he couldn't help smiling. It had been this way between them ever since he had returned from Crow country, teasing each other, laughing. He threw the jackrabbits on the floor with an air of great authority, taking his robe and cap off.

"Woman, fix my dinner!"

"With what?" Raven gave him and his jackrabbits a look of disdain, but he saw the humor in her eyes, too. "Besides, you are not my father."

"You best learn your place," he said, glaring at her, and with that Raven grabbed a small beaver pelt and put it over her mouth and chin, mimicking Jack's beard.

"Oh, I am JackWade, the white man who conquered the pitiful Crow. The one they call Fast Horse!" She dropped the pelt, grinning. As Jack lunged for her and they fell to the floor laughing, Jack couldn't help thinking their laughter sounded so good together, so right.

"It's good you didn't forget who I am. So, are you ready to listen, now?"

"No," she said, laughing again, but her breath hitched in her chest as he brushed a long tendril of hair back from her face and left his hand rested against her cheek. Jack felt his own breath grow short and he trailed a finger down to her lips, tracing them slowly until he was unable to resist anymore. He pressed his lips hard against hers, kissing her with all of the longing he had had to hold in for so long.

It was Raven who finally pulled away, looking up into his eyes with longing—but confusion, too.

"I've wanted to do that for so long," he whispered, wanting to take the confusion away. "I was just afraid I'd do something wrong and scare you."

"You do not scare me," Raven said quietly. "I scare me."

"I know what you mean," Jack answered softly, realizing that she had been caught up in the same storm of not knowing and it took everything he had not to take her in his arms. He scrambled to his feet and grabbed his winter robe and cap, knowing if he didn't leave he would do something foolish, something that might take the hurt away for the moment but not for good. Not until both of them were sure. As he started to go, Medicine Weasel came into the lodge and, suddenly alert to the tension in the room, he glanced from Jack to Raven. Jack avoided his friend's eyes and looked over his shoulder at Raven and tried to smile.

"I'll be back, I promise," he said and he threw the flap back and stepped out into the cold, wishing its bitterness could drive the terrible confusion from his mind. He had no idea where he was going as he began to walk, but he knew he had to distance himself from their feelings, for he knew now that Raven's ran as intense as his.

She had been married, so she wasn't a maiden, but he also knew some of the Blackfoot custom and the disgrace that would come to her if he had gone any further. No matter how much he wanted her, truth was, she deserved more.

Lillie had deserved more than that . . .

Whether it came from being around the Blackfoot and learning their ways or the old seeds of his raising beginning to bloom, Jack felt the way he had always looked at life start to change. He wanted to do what was right, to have something to hold on to that would last. He wanted a home.

He thought of Lillie and felt a sharp pang of regret. He had told her he loved her, that he would be back. But what if Lillie had already let go of believing that? Lillie *was* his confusion. If he stood with Raven, he would *have* to let go of Lillie, of all that had been between them and what might have been.

But could he? There was so much left unsaid, unsettled: Lillie, his vendetta against Frank . . . He needed to sort it out. But even more than that, he yearned to find some peace with it all. He was so weary of running and never knowing what he was running to. Jack walked and walked far into the night—not running from himself this time but searching deep inside to find the man he was meant to be.

He found him just as the sun began to rise. Jack crouched down on the hill that overlooked the camp and heard the sounds of morning life stir the cold, still air. Not foreign sounds, but familiar now:

children laughing, a woman singing a song to the sun, smoke wisping up through the tops of the lodges, and a sweet feeling of peace came over him like it used to when he would be walking home and spot the old farm in the distance. *I have a new home now, even a new name,* he thought, remembering Raven's words. *This is my life.* Jack was filled with wonder at how easy it seemed his decision had been made. Maybe, because this time, he had allowed his heart to make it.

As Jack quickly made his way down the hill, he felt suddenly light, like a few hundred pounds of weight had been left behind. He turned around half expecting to see the weight scattered along the hillside, but all that remained was the snow and his hurried footprints that were headed for home.

There were no arrogant speeches of wealth or boastings of power, but not because Fast Horse wasn't familiar with their way, Medicine Weasel thought, for the white man studied the people like a warrior would study the land for signs of an enemy, never missing a thing. Instead, he appeared at the door of the lodge that morning with Lodge Skins by his side, smiling a proud, toothless smile as if the idea were all his as Fast Horse humbly asked for Raven to be his wife.

A crowd had gathered by then; some saying it was a good thing, some wondering out loud if the white man would take Medicine Weasel's daughter away, but the medicine man knew as he looked between Raven and Fast Horse, the choice had already been made. He wondered if Grandfather were smiling somewhere, knowing his plan had worked. Medicine Weasel looked at Fast Horse, seeing nothing but goodness in his green eyes. He remembered with warmth the day he had found him, the nights he had sat talking with him, and the sorrow he felt for his lost spirit, then watching him come alive again.

"I accept you as my son-in-law," he declared for all to hear. "But in my heart you will always be my son."

"My pa isn't here anymore," Fast Horse said, his voice gruff with emotion. When their eyes met, Medicine Weasel sensed some final wall had come down in the white man's heart. "But I would like to imagine he's up there somewhere and your words have made him smile."

Preparations for the wedding grew as the day went on. Part of it, the medicine man knew, was the dullness that had settled in over the winter camp. But the main reason was Fast Horse's popularity; he had become a much respected member since besting Lone Elk.

Lone Elk had a good time of trying to make Fast Horse's proposal as difficult as possible, running like a crazy person back to his own lodge to gather as many lavish gifts for the bride's side to make the groom's job of returning equal gifts harder.

Undaunted, Fast Horse left and returned with fifty of his finest horses, nearly half of what he had taken from the Crow, and the crowds howled with laughter seeing Lone Elk's disappointed face. But as was Lone Elk's nature, he took the ribbing good-naturedly and wished the couple well.

The celebration that followed seemed lengthy, even to Medicine Weasel. Most of it was due to the long speeches given by Lone Elk and his friends. Naturally, they were having a good time of it, drawing the night out as long as possible, whispering jokes about the pain on Fast Horse's face. But when the looks between Fast Horse and his daughter said they could take no more waiting, Medicine Weasel called an end to the festivities, feeling a swell of happiness for his daughter as he watched Fast Horse gently take her hand and lead her out of the lodge. He prayed to the Above Ones for their happiness and long lives and for the grandchildren that would make his life whole again. Finally he prayed that the white man would be at peace in their world and would never want to leave.

He watched the happy couple finally step into their large lodge, painstakingly painted with the beautiful figure of a horse in full stride, then turned to Lodge Skins questioningly, knowing all too well how long it took to prepare such a lodge. As he opened his mouth to speak, the old man held a gnarled hand up to silence him.

"You are not the only one Grandfather speaks to, old friend," Lodge Skins said with a smirk, and both men laughed.

Blackfoot Encampment,
Montana Territory
Winter, 1864

Mrs. Callie McGregor
Plumas City, California

Dear Callie,

When I first set down to write this letter, I wondered if it might shock you that I married an Indian woman, but I got to thinking that there probably ain't much I could do that'd shock you anymore.

Besides, I think you would like her. Raven is about as good as a person comes, Sis. She's funny and smart to boot. She's got more patience than anyone I've ever known, too, which is a good thing for me to be around being that I don't have any. But I guess the thing that drew me to her the most is something you are forever telling me to learn and that's peace. I think you were wrong though about learning peace—I think it has to be something you find.

Does it seem as strange to you as it does to me that I would find it in this Indian camp? If it was God that led me here, I thank Him for it and this time I don't intend to mess up. That's why I hope you'll understand when I tell you I'm staying, Sis, and making my life here.

For once, I feel like I'm doing something good, something right. You know, as I was standing there being married, I had the oddest feeling Pa was watching somewhere and he was proud of me. I guess I would've given anything to have turned around and seen him there.

Well, I best end this. I'd sure like to hear from you before we're both old and gray.

Jack

Jack opened the flap of his and Raven's lodge and stepped out into the night, pulling the cold winter air deep into his lungs. He stared at the figure of a large red horse that Lodge Skins had painted on their lodge for them as a wedding gift. *Sometimes we are all blind,* he recalled the old man telling him, and he couldn't help thinking that the words had suited near his whole life. How many years had he run blind, never taking the time to wonder what would happen if he stayed? It had taken nearly dying and falling into the laps of a band of Indians to change him. That and Raven's love.

She and her people had brought a peace to him he had been looking for his whole life and even though deep down he knew the truth of what he had done, that he had traded peace for passion, he felt the decision was the right one.

Jack glanced back toward the lodge. The choice to marry hadn't been a light one. But there was something about being with the Blackfoot that helped him to lose his worry about getting too close. Maybe, he thought, it was that they were different and that meant his luck might be different, too.

After awhile he grew weary of the thoughts and doubts that filled his head, and he crept back into the lodge where the ghost of Lillie couldn't haunt him anymore. He relished the warmth of Raven's soft body greeting him as he slid beside her under the thick buffalo robe. As he pulled her sleeping body closer to his, he reminded himself to count his blessings, to be thankful for the beautiful woman who lie beside him.

But when he finally drifted off to sleep, it was Lillie he dreamed of.

Sixteen

Lillie was never so glad to see dawn begin to peek up over the mountains.

Ignoring the cold, she stood on the front stoop of the Pair-O-Dice and watched the fingers of light spread across the snowy hillside, knowing without checking the time that once the light reached the cluttered streets of town it would signal quitting time. It was the time of day she liked best because it was her own; no one expected a smile or funny remark. Truth was, she felt she had about run out of things to say. She found it hard to talk lately, even though she knew she was lonely. It was a strange feeling to always be surrounded by people but still feel alone. Lillie frowned at her own poor frame of mind and knew without having to be told that her mood had gotten worse after hearing of Jack living with the Indians from two skinners who breezed in one night.

If that news hadn't been enough, having to deal with Frank and his men all night had topped it. There wasn't anything worse than watching Frank's boys pretend to get all misty over a dead friend—especially one they hated. And everyone knew they hated Frank's brother, Jude. Hearing Frank go on and on all night about how Jack had done his poor brother wrong was like reopening a wound that started to heal, throwing a bunch of salt on it, and then rubbing it hard for good measure.

As she stepped back through the door, her frown deepened as she noticed one of Frank's boys curled up in a corner on the straw bed usually reserved for Ely's old miner buddies. If she could have guessed his age, she might have figured sixteen or seventeen but that didn't mean much. Youth never lasted long around Frank. He made boys too evil to be young anymore.

Lillie moved closer to where he lay snoring in a drunken slumber and leaned over to study him, more out of curiosity than anything else, and was startled to see his bleary, dark eyes open and stare up at her. The mean look had been temporarily replaced by a look of puzzlement.

"Kin is kin, ain't it?" he asked, his voice slurred but hushed, like he was talking in church. "My brother Jess always said you ain't never to kill kin." He blinked a few times, then his head hit the floor with a soft thud and he began to snore again.

Lillie felt as if she had been splashed with ice cold water as she stood staring down at the sleeping kid. *My brother always said you ain't never to kill kin. . . .* The words ran over and over in her head as she recalled the casual way Frank had acted when he and his boys had strolled in just after burying Jude. She remembered him laughing and buying drinks, then later on how he had stared after her as though he might consider claiming her—but she couldn't recall any grief on his face. *It was Frank,* she thought with sudden awareness. *Frank killed Jude. He killed his own brother for money.*

Lillie sat down on the floor next to the kid as it all began to sink in. She wondered how long Frank had known that Jack didn't have the money. Was it before or after Jack left town? Or better, did Frank know when he had Duel killed? If Frank *had* known before, then the rest of what happened was her fault. *Hell hath no fury like Frank Monroe scorned.* But she could have told him that was nothing compared with the fury that came from wrecking a girl's dreams.

Her eyes went to the kid again. She knew Frank had most likely been a partner to Jack's leaving—not to mention Duel's murder—and it turned her stomach to think of looking at him too much, not to mention dealing with him. But she knew all too well that eating the bad apple sometimes meant all the difference between living and dying.

"Hey, kid," she said, shaking him gently as a plan began to form in her mind. "You best stay here a bit till I can figure out where to hide you."

He rubbed his eyes a few times, then sat up and looked at her curiously as he tried to steady his wobbly head. "Hide me?" he bleated. "What for?"

Lillie stood up and dusted off her skirts in an effort to hide her dislike. "Frank ain't going to like your spoutin' off about him killin' his own brother," she said as evenly as she could manage. She saw real fear for the first time in Jim's eyes.

"Who'd I tell?" he asked warily.

"Everyone left in the bar for starters. Best thing you can do is sit tight here and let me take care of Frank."

The kid laughed, as though the thought of her taking care of Frank was something funny, but when he looked at her it was with distrust.

"Listen, now I got somethin' that might change things for a friend of mine. And you, well, you might just be able to save your skin if you listen to me."

"Or I could just shoot you and save myself the trouble."

"You'd be dead by sundown and you know it," Lillie said with more sureness than she really felt. "Everyone in the Territory knows Frank's had his eye on me for a long time."

"Had more'n his eye on you from what I heard," Jim retorted, but she saw a bit of doubt in his eyes in spite of the shrug. "Maybe I'll stick around anyhow, might be fun."

He looked at Lillie suggestively and smirked. She wanted to

smack the smirk from his face but she made her way over to the bar instead and poured herself a stiff shot, hoping to calm her nerves. A loud noise that sounded like something between a cough and a bark came but she stared straight ahead; she knew Mabel had heard the conversation but she didn't feel like getting into it with her so she ignored the woman sitting next to her.

"What are you doing?" Mabel asked finally, looking at her as if she'd gone crazy.

"Getting Jack his ticket home," Lillie answered simply as she poured herself another shot. As soon as she downed it, she rose from the stool and started up the stairs.

"You like playing with fire?" Mabel spouted, her voice a bit shrill as she followed Lillie up the stairs. "Even if Frank did kill Jude, don't you know what could happen to you? Jack wouldn't want you to do this, Lillie. It's too high a price."

"Price? You think you can put a price on feelings, Mabel?" Lillie turned abruptly, stopping the other woman in her tracks as they entered her room. Mabel pursed her lips in thought, then slowly shook her head.

"Some do, but it never is enough, is it?" she said with a trembly smile, but there was an aching look around the corners of her eyes, as if she had seen more than she would care to admit.

Lillie glanced away and her eyes fell on the shirt Jack had left behind lying at the foot of her bed. She must have folded and refolded it a dozen times since he had been gone, as if the memory of when he was there could be brought back in the act. *Oh, Jack,* she thought, *why did it have to go so wrong?* When she looked up, she saw Mabel had noticed the shirt, too.

"You let go of that fella before it destroys you," she said softly, but Lillie was already on her way out the door and she answered Mabel by shutting it hard behind her.

Frank Monroe stood at the window in the living room of his home, arms folded across his chest as he watched Lillie trotting off back toward town. In spite of her having her back to him, he knew what she was probably thinking: the stiff way she sat on her horse as she flipped her long braid over her shoulder said she was irritated but he knew she felt a bit pleased with herself, too. He could understand. It wasn't every day that someone bested Frank Monroe.

He smiled without any humor and pulled a cigar from his breast pocket. It wasn't every day he'd allow someone to *think* they had, either, but somehow he'd allowed Lillie to get under his skin. Thing was, he had had his share of pretty women—just none like Lillie. She was one of a kind, alright. He thought of the way she had come rapping on his door, confronting him like a man even though she was only half his size. And when she'd had her say, she left him standing alone in the parlor like some lovesick fool.

I ought to have just killed her, he thought. But since he couldn't, there'd be only one other way to get at her. He wondered what she would think to know she'd set her own trap. Frank stepped outside and hollered at the men hunched around the fire in the yard. Not a one of them would've dared to set foot in the bunk house until sundown, no matter how cold it was. They were a loyal bunch, he'd give them that—loyal or scared. He himself preferred the indoors when it got so cold, but Lillie's visit called for action. When they had all gathered, he gave them the short of what had happened.

"What'd'ya want to do about Jim, boss?" one asked between chattering teeth. Frank lit his cigar and puffed on it while the men waited for him to answer.

"Why, I want you to kill him, of course," he said finally, and a few of the boys looked at each other nervously. "But not until I say so. Dell, you hightail it on down to the post office and tell 'em to let me know when Lillie comes calling with a letter. Tell him to be sure it gets sent right off, too. I aim to be first in line when Wade comes trotting back in town." Frank puffed on his fancy cigar a few more times before grinding it into the snow. "I ain't ever forgot him killing Riley and his horse like he did."

Frank gazed at the men who stood around him. *Avenge Riley but kill Jim?* He smiled at their obvious confusion.

"I always was fond of that horse," he said and began to whistle a tune as he walked back into his house.

> *Pair-O-Dice Saloon*
> *Virginia City,*
> *Montana Territory*
> *December 1894*

Mr. Jack Wade
Fort Benton,
Montana Territory

Dear Jack,

I don't know if this letter will reach you, but rumor came down from a couple of skinners that blew in here during a storm about a white man living up north with the Indians. I just knew it had to be you. If you do get this letter, it was worth the effort to let you know you're free to come back to Virginia City, now. Jude showed up here not long after you left and Frank killed him—word is he got the money, too. But the best part is that we have someone here willing to tell what he saw, so Frank's agreed to let bygones be bygones. I admit I don't put much stock in his promises, but I have a feeling this is one he'll keep. The only bars he fancies are the ones he can drink at.

I guess you can picture my face when I heard those traders talking about a white man with green eyes riding with the Blackfoot. Remember Duel always saying there were reasons for everything? I think me overhearing them was one of them. After all, how else could I send you the good news? I know you'll be glad to hear you can come home now; I can't imagine you being happy with no card table for miles around.

Lillie

P.S. We buried Duel just like you said. It was a fine turnout.

Jack laughed as he watched Lone Elk's face screw up like a kid's, concentrating hard on the cards he clumsily held in his hands. The young warrior looked up and grinned; they had become good friends since calling an unspoken truce, and with the winter storm blowing all around them since dawn, they had decided to spend the day inside Jack and Raven's lodge, playing the Blackfoot's games of chance. Lone Elk was crazy for any gambling but his favorite was a bit like a dice roll, except they used small pieces of wood carved with the different counts and shook them up in a wooden bowl before throwing them. It seemed the more Lone Elk won, the harder he shook the bowl until Jack couldn't take any more of the shaking and finally offered to show Lone Elk his *white man's game.* Like being offered a new toy, Lone Elk dropped his bowl and leaned forward, eager to start. Jack was just as eager to win back his rifle, so he quickly pulled the old deck of cards out of his saddle bag and started his lesson on the fine art of poker. He was winning so far, but he knew by the set of Lone Elk's jaw that the warrior was deter-mined to master this game, too.

"Now just remember, you make me poor and my new wife here will leave me."

"It would be a difficult thing for her to do since she never leaves your lodge," Lone Elk answered, never taking his eyes from his cards. "There must be something interesting that keeps her but I cannot imagine what it might be."

"Why, it's the fine company," Jack said, finally laying his cards down with a grin as he set to collecting the pot, including his rifle. "Ain't a woman alive who don't like to be entertained."

Lone Elk scowled at the cards and threw them down.

"Lone Elk likes to entertain, too." Laughs-A-Lot smiled, then turned sideways to show off her pregnancy. Everyone laughed, including Lone Elk. Laughs-A-Lot was Lone Elk's *sits-beside-me* wife, his favorite, and could almost pass as Raven's twin if it weren't for the pocklike scars on the right side of her face. Raven had told him about Laughs-A-Lot's illness, how none of the warriors had wanted her because of her scars. She told him, too, about how Lone Elk had fallen for her anyway and had brought many horses to her father on the day that they wed—not because he had to but to honor her. Jack had touched the tears that appeared on Raven's lashes with the telling and she had smiled winsomely. *I cry because Lone Elk showed his true spirit that day, what we humans are supposed to be,* she had explained, looking up at him. *Sometimes I am glad for my baby and husband who are no more because now they are able to see that beauty all of the time. Wouldn't that be something, Jack Wade? To be in a place where there is no more sickness or scars or hate?* Jack hadn't been able to answer her but instead he pulled her to him and held her tight in his arms, overwhelmed by her heart, by the emotion that she had brought back to life in him.

Jack glanced to where his wife and Laughs-A-Lot stood, and when he and Raven's eyes met, he saw her eyes widen a bit at the intensity of his stare. She smiled a little, then turned her eyes from his, a faint blush spreading across her tawny cheeks, and he was touched by her shyness. Still grinning, he happened to glance over at Lone Elk and he saw the warrior had caught the look between the two of them and was smiling broadly.

"It must be time to entertain again," he said with an audible sigh. He rose to his feet to leave and Jack noticed his face sobering a bit as they walked to the door of the lodge together. "I do not wish to take you from your wife so soon, but Medicine Weasel says as soon as the storm passes, we must leave for the Many Houses Fort. The traders do not come here because of the weather but they do not understand the weather." Lone Elk shrugged. "Medicine Weasel says Cold Maker will give us enough time to go and return before sending another storm."

"I'll wager the old fellow is right about it, too," Jack said, shaking his head. His father-in-law spooked him at times with the way he knew things, but the fact he was right made accepting it a bit easier. Though he did worry about bringing trouble to the Blackfoot if he happened to run into anyone who recognized him, being wanted by both sides of the law like he was. In spite of the misgivings, he hadn't missed the eager look on Raven's face when the fort was mentioned, or the way her eyes had lingered most of the night on the dress Laughs-A-Lot wore. And more than anything he wanted to please his pretty wife, to care for her like he never had the chance to care for anyone before.

"I'll be ready to go as soon as the storm clears, though I don't have much to trade," he admitted to no one in particular.

"You have horses," Lone Elk said, wrapping his thick buffalo robe around his shoulders. As if a sudden thought occurred to him, his face became more animated than Jack had ever seen. "And cards. You must teach me more so I can beat the whites at the Many Houses Fort. It will be a long time before they forget the name of Lone Elk."

Laughs-A-Lot rolled her eyes in mock despair and pushed her husband out into the night, leaving Jack to chuckle as he pulled the flap closed to their lodge. "I think he forgets I'm white," he said, turning to Raven. She smiled and wrapped her arms around his waist and he knew she was pleased.

"You are only Fast Horse to him now, his friend."

"I think maybe you should come along to keep me warm," Jack said, nuzzling her neck, and he let his hands wander over her backside.

"They should call you Fast Hands—not Fast Horse," Raven laughed, but when she touched his face with her hands he saw tears in her eyes.

"What is it?" he asked, suddenly alarmed.

"I cannot go. The long ride would not be good for me, now." Raven looked at him as if it should mean something special to him, then frowned when it didn't. She tried to pull away a bit, but Jack held her tight, surprised to see a tinge of fear in the soft brown eyes.

"It is still early, so I did not mention it to you," she said, averting her eyes. "But my heart tells me it is true; I am going to have a baby."

Jack felt barely able to breathe as so many things raced through his mind: *Would he be able to love a baby the way a father should? Would the baby love him? Could he care for it right?* When the thoughts died down to a trickle, he realized his silence had scared her even more. He would rather face down a whole army of men than hurt someone so good as Raven. He turned Raven's chin to look at him, and he smiled at her reassuringly as tears stung his eyes.

"You were afraid to tell me?" he asked and she nodded, her eyes still troubled.

"I was afraid. But not just to tell you. I was afraid if you ever decided to go back to your own people, you would leave us here."

"If I ever leave here, it'll be *with* you," Jack said with such emotion that Raven's eyes filled with relief. "I won't ever desert you or our baby. If I can't promise you anything else, that much I promise you, Raven. I know that ain't much of a promise, but . . ."

Raven put her finger to his lips and finally smiled. "It is enough."

A baby, Jack thought again and again as he slipped under the thick robe next to Raven. He had had little doubts that gnawed at him since they had married—not any doubts that he loved Raven or the Blackfoot—but doubts brought on by being torn between the loyalties he felt he owed to his old life and what he wanted for this new one. But when his hand rested low on her belly and he felt Raven cover it with her own, it was like fate had stepped in and made his decision final. They were a real family now. There would be no turning back, he thought, and the thought gave him the final peace he was looking for.

Blackfoot Encampment,
Montana Territory
1864

Mrs. Callie McGregor
Plumas City, California

Dear Callie,

There's a heck of a snowstorm going on as I write this, but Medicine Weasel tells us it will end soon. He also says that we'll have enough time to travel to Fort Benton and get back before the next one, so we'll be heading out fairly soon. I know it might sound crazy to take such a chance, but you don't know the old fellow like we do. He ain't been wrong once about the weather since I've been here. Anyway, I'll finally get to send you all these letters I've squirreled away. I guess there's enough here to fill a book. I don't imagine they'd be good reading for anyone but you, though. About the only other thing they've been good for is keeping me sane—and reminding me I still have family out there somewhere.

Speaking of families, I got something important I want to tell you. Raven and I are going to have a family of our own. I admit I'm scared. I mean, me with a baby (I got shaky just writing that). I can't remember anything unnerving me so much. I guess I know what you meant now when you said how having a family of your own changes you. It's like I've started worrying more about what's right than what's next. Maybe that's what I should've been doing all along, but like Pa always said, it ain't never too late to start. Been on shaky ground with The Man

Upstairs nearly my whole life; it might be nice to see what it's like to be on His good side.

   I can't help remembering what you wrote that Quinn said when little Rose was born, too—something like it being God's way of balancing the scales—and I'm thinking Quinn might be right about that.

   You know what, Sis? His timing ain't too bad, either. Way I got it figured, we've all seen enough death to last us a lifetime.

Jack

"That ain't no funeral procession; it's a derned show," Ely said under his breath. Lillie pulled her shawl tight and glanced over at Ely, who stood with Mabel just inside the doorway of the Pair-O-Dice, then looked back to the icy street filled with gawkers in spite of the cold. She didn't argue or scold Ely, mainly because he was right. To call it a funeral would have been a lie.

But then Frank Monroe was just doing what he knew best, she thought, shivering a bit as she watched him and his men begin their little parade. Already, the cold had seeped into her hands and feet, stealing the feeling from them, but she stood there anyway because she knew she was the one meant to see it. Frank would have made sure of it one way or another so she chose her own way.

"Come on back in, Lillie, you're going to catch your death out there," Ely said. She knew by the wavering sound to his voice that he was still unsure as to what to do about the whole thing. He hadn't taken to his bed yet, which was a change.

"I guess I know what I can handle and what I can't," Lillie said. She avoided their worried looks. They had been looking at her worriedly for the past two weeks since the kid, Jim, had disappeared. His death shouldn't have made their worry more being that they had been expecting it from the moment they found him gone. As horrible as she felt over the kid being killed, her main concern now was Jack showing up and she being without her bargaining chip. She searched the faces along the street as she did every day, half expecting to see him there, then felt the same mixture of relief and sadness when he wasn't.

"You oughtn't to have sent that letter," Ely said for the hundredth time, but she remained silent. She had been so sure she was meant to send Jack the letter. From the moment she had overheard the traders right down to hearing about Jude, she had felt it was fate.

Then why had fate deserted her? she wondered. It felt like a lifetime had passed since she had sent the letter and still no answer. Before she could think of much more, a loud commotion broke out in the street, and she saw people running and slipping in the snow as they scrambled to get out of the way.

Lillie, Ely, and Mabel all turned and watched in morbid fascination as the wagon carrying the kid they had unsuccessfully hidden skidded sideways across the ice and snow, then hopped a couple of times over the thick ruts in the street before coming to rest a short distance from the Pair-O-Dice. The rough pine coffin teetered, then slid to the street with a thud. A few of Frank's men laughed as they dismounted and helped to right it. Frank loped up just in time to view the spectacle. Although he was leaning forward, watching his men with a concerned look on his face, Lillie knew better. He was preening like a rooster and it galled her to no end.

Frank smiled and tipped his hat, but she pretended not to notice. Instead, she turned and watched the men hoist the coffin back up into the wagon and as they did, the lid slid sideways and she saw one of Jim's hands. It was a small hand, boy's more than a man's, and she noticed there was dirt beneath the fingernails. The dirt bothered her. It was like he was just thrown in the box like yesterday's trash. For some reason she thought of Jack's hands and how strong they were, then the horrible thought came of him lying in the box instead of Jim and she felt like she couldn't breathe. *They would have to bury me, too,* she thought, the feeling too strong to deny.

"Don't look so down, Lillie," Frank said genially. "Business is business. But I'm sure we can work something out."

"Maybe we can," Lillie said, not caring about the smug look that came to his face. When she turned to go back into the Pair-O-Dice, she didn't avoid Ely's and Mabel's wide-eyed looks but stared right back. They had no right to look so shocked, she thought, climbing the stairs with a weariness beyond her years. Lord knows, they were both old enough to know better.

Lillie stared at the ceiling above her, wishing with all of her heart it was the ceiling at the Pair-O-Dice instead of Frank's room. She squeezed her eyes shut, like a kid willing a bad dream away, but when she opened them nothing had changed. She might have laughed at her own foolishness if it wasn't so bad. *How did it get this bad?* she wondered even though she knew most of the bad in her life had come by her own poor choices. *But do we ever get to make it different, or do we just keep reliving the bad; same mistakes just different scenery?* The ceiling and the air below it chose not to answer, and it made Lillie think of what Duel had told Jack about cursing the wind. A bittersweet smile came to her lips, then disappeared as Frank strolled casually into the room and she felt something in her start to wither. It felt as if another lifetime had passed since she had known Frank.

The sight of him smiling filled her with disgust and caused her temper to return, which was good since she had been on the verge of tears; the memory of the girl he had abused hurt in spite of the time that had passed. But the more she stared back, the more she decided he didn't look so big without his men all around him. In fact, he looked weak. The thought made her feel a bit stronger and she stood suddenly, bringing her purse up in front of her.

"Glad you could see me, Frank," she said matter-of-factly and saw his eyes narrow.

"What's that, Lillie?" Frank said, inclining his head toward the purse with a grin. "You plannin' on contributing to our cause or somethin'?"

"No, I thought you might be interested in a sudden increase to your finances," she said simply. "You ain't interested in Jack, not really. Everyone and their brother knows you got the poke from Jude before he died." She could have said a lot more than that, could have told him she knew what he'd done to his own brother and that no matter how much money he had or how many men he bossed he would never be the man Jack Wade was. In her opinion, Frank wasn't fit to shine Jack's boots. Frank must have guessed as much because she saw his eyes flash with anger.

"You know so much, then you'd know money ain't what I want from you," he said between gritted teeth.

"That's not part of the bargain."

"Well, what if I just took what I wanted anyway?" Frank asked slowly.

Lillie's hands went still for a moment from buttoning her overcoat.

"Truth is, Frank, you wouldn't live," she said, and it seemed to surprise them both that she meant it. As she headed for the door, she heard his footsteps behind her and guessed he was following, but she refused to turn around.

"Hey, Lillie. Now, what would a *whore* know about the truth?"

"More than you ever will," she answered simply, then shut the door behind her, resting against it as she tried to collect herself. She had dealt with Frank easily. The hard thing now would be dealing with herself, getting poor Jim killed, and if Frank had his way, Jack.

She took a deep breath, trying to control her fear. As she stepped out onto the porch, she looked over and saw the men who lounged on the front stoop.

"Good night for a game, boys," she said in her best voice and the men grumbled, saying something about Frank making them stay put. Lillie smiled sympathetically, waving to them as she headed to where her mare stood. But instead of mounting, she took the reins and led the horse toward town.

I gotta make this right . . . somehow, some way, she told herself over and over again as the icy wind whipped around her. *Somehow I have to get my chance at happiness back. Once Jack is by my side, I'll never have to even think of my past again. And Frank, he'll just be a dirty memory, thrown out with the wash water. . . .*

She walked and walked and when she saw the first lights of town, she straightened her back and held her head high. In spite of the hour, she knew most of the men would recognize her form.

She was glad for the dark at least.

So no one could see the tears.

Seventeen

~❦~

Lone Elk proved to be the talker of the trip. Almost as much of a talker as his old friend Stem had been, Jack thought, smiling inwardly as he watched the warrior's hands wave through the air with great sweeping motions as he came to the exciting part of his war story. The only other sound came from the jangle of bells Lone Elk had fastidiously tied to each of their horses along with feathers and ribbons when he realized they were nearing the fort; the Blackfoot were fond of making an entrance.

"So, you just strolled in and rapped him on his head while he was sleeping in his tepee?" Jack asked, pulling his horse back to a walk. Lone Elk stopped his, gesturing long enough to give his friend a look of patience.

"To strike your enemy with a bare hand is the greatest of all coups to count," Lone Elk replied.

"I think I'd prefer to count chips," Jack said. "I don't guess there's any feeling that beats pulling chips away from a fellow who thought he had you to the wall."

"I have never heard of this wall you speak of but it is possible they have one at Many Houses Fort," Lone Elk considered. "Perhaps the white soldiers are hiding it so they can surprise me. I think I will challenge them to a game," he said as if he had just come up with the thought.

Jack shook his head. If Lone Elk wasn't talking, he was pushing to play cards. And when he played, he forever talked of beating the soldiers at the fort. Jack worried about that as the warrior hadn't yet mastered the art of smooth-talking. Like everything else, when he won, he let you know it. But at least what he lacked in smoothness, he made up for with enthusiasm, Jack thought.

"You best let me go along the first time," Jack said abruptly. The little hairs on his neck had risen in warning the minute Lone Elk mentioned the soldiers and he couldn't shake the feeling. "Strength in numbers, like my pa always used to say."

"My father taught me that a man's true courage is found when he stands alone," Lone Elk suggested. "When I face them, the white soldiers will not forget who challenged them."

"I'd think they'd have a hard time forgetting you anyway," Jack said, looking pointedly into the face his friend had carefully painted blue, yellow, and vermilion.

Both men chuckled as their horses picked up their pace, blowing warm puffs of steam from their nostrils into the bitter-cold air. In spite of the cold, Medicine Weasel's weather prediction had held and the party had made good time. Jack glanced back to the group of Blackfoot that followed, searching for Raven amidst all of the bodies wrapped and hooded in their buffalo robes. When he finally spotted her horse, he raised his hand even though he knew she probably couldn't see him. He was glad she had decided to come. He was worried about her traveling in her condition, but he would have been more concerned had he left her behind.

"We are here," Lone Elk announced, reining in, and Jack pulled up alongside of him and gazed at the snow-covered basin below.

Like a jagged scar on a beautiful woman's face, the adobe walls of the post gouged the land to surround shabby blockhouses and quarters facing their treeless parade ground. Outside the fort, snaking every which way were the civilian homes, though Jack was hard-pressed to see anything civil about them. What he was struck by was the dirtiness of his own kind's living conditions compared with the Blackfoot camp he had just left behind. Once he got past that, the next thing that boggled his mind was seeing whites again: soldiers, trappers, and traders constantly moving about like worker ants. Jack couldn't help thinking how godawful strange it was that he no longer felt any type of kinship with them. His eyes then went to the stacks of buffalo hides piled high in wagon after wagon in numbers too high to count. Jack guessed the majority came from hide hunters—at five dollars a hide, they were walking gold mines for the boys, shipped on one of the steamers docked at the fort to one city or another for someone's entertainment. For the Blackfoot, they were survival.

"By God, but that's a lot of hides," he said to himself, then glanced quickly over to Lone Elk to see if he had heard. Lone Elk's eyes remained on the wagons—his smile was still there, but there was a pensive look on his face now, too.

"It is this way, always," was all Lone Elk said. Before Jack could think of what to say to that, the rest of the party trailed in, dressed in their best finery to do their trading. Medicine Weasel and Raven pulled up next to him and Lone Elk, dressed just as splendidly as the rest. The old man smiled his greeting, but it was Raven Jack couldn't take his eyes off of. She was wearing her soft antelope-skin dress that hugged her figure just right. In her hurry to catch up, some of her hair had escaped its braid and it blew around her face, rosied by the cold wind. Jack thought she had never looked prettier.

"I'm taking my husband back, cousin," Raven declared, her face shiny with excitement. "It is time to collect all of those gifts he has been promising me."

"What gifts?" Jack teased, then ducked when she smacked at him. The group laughed, their spirits high, and Jack smiled at his wife as they turned their horses and headed down the slope toward the fort. Halfway down, Lone Elk broke out in song, his rich, deep voice carrying on the wind, then Medicine Weasel joined in and the rest of the band soon followed. Jack wanted to join in, but suddenly his heart wasn't in it. The tune had caused a melancholy in him he couldn't explain. In spite of the festive mood and as hard as he tried, he couldn't quite shake the low feeling that had come over him. He wondered briefly if it was from seeing all of those hides—and know-ing his kind was behind it all. But as their group trotted up to the gates of the fort, something down deep told him it was much more than that.

"If I've tole you once, I've tole you a hundred times I ain't takin' no more wolf pelts." Jack studied the man behind the counter dicker-ing with the tall Indian with guarded curiosity. He was a surly fellow who appeared to have lost the habit of bathing somewhere along the same time he lost his teeth. But he did seem to know just how far to push the Indian who stood in front of him and Raven before losing his hair.

"But seein' as you brought a goodly amount of buffler meat in, I'll take'm this time," he said, giving a side look to his two compan-ions behind the counter. "Gotta feed them boys somehow." The two men cackled, then fell silent as the tall Indian's eyes met theirs. He picked up the goods he had traded for and stalked off, a grim look on his face. Then Jack moved up to the counter.

Jack saw the trader hesitate as their eyes met, then immediately went to work sorting through the stacks of hides Jack had set on the counter. "Ain't never seen no squaw man with the Blackfoot 'afore," he said conversationally before spitting his tobacco juice on the floor.

"And I ain't ever met someone who needed to jaw so much," Jack returned, sliding the bundle of letters he had been holding tight in his hands.

"I talk when I know what I'm saying, and I say I know Blackfoot and their ways. They's first to take offense, first to break a truce, and first to murder—seen 'em do all three in a day, too." The man took the letters from Jack, glancing at them as he pulled some sort of ledger out from beneath the counter. He rubbed his soiled fingers over one of the letters and frowned. "Wade? Seems I seen a letter to a Wade in here somewheres . . ."

Jack turned to Raven with a puzzled smile and a shrug to indicate the unlikeliness of him getting mail. He decided to humor the fellow anyway and waited patiently as the trader rifled through his stacks of letters. As he was waiting, he had the odd feeling he was being watched. He looked up to find that one of the men behind the counter had leaned forward to gawk at him. The longer the man stared, the more Jack started thinking he knew him, too, and it finally came to him that he did. The man was the trader he had come across in the Crow camp. When their eyes met again, it appeared the man had figured it out, too.

"Knew the face, jes' didn't know the name," he offered slowly, as if trying to decide whether to say anything further. An excited light came to his eyes all of a sudden as if he had thought of something better, and he grinned. "What say we hold a friendly little game at my tent? If ye ain't got the cash ter spare, we can always work something out with yer squaw."

The last sentence caused Raven to stiffen next to Jack, and he touched her arm gently before letting loose on the fool.

"She's my *wife*, soon to be the mother of my child," Jack said between clenched teeth, wishing he hadn't let the man off so easily back in that Crow camp. "You'd do good to remember that."

"Alright, alright," the trader interrupted. "There's enough of that. Here's your letter. Now, you figgerin' on tradin' or fightin'?" he asked, trying to get his business dealing back on track. "I guess I know why yer with them Blackfoot, now," he added as he looked around for what Jack had to offer.

"What I have is five prime horses tied outside your post here," Jack said, ignoring the insult the best he could. "What I want for them is on this here list." He pulled the list of things Raven had asked for and slapped it on the counter. The whole mess had raised his temper so that it wasn't until the trader stepped outside to inspect the horses that Jack glanced down at the letter in his hand. He looked, blinked a couple of times, and looked again. *Lillie.* How in the world had she found him? Before he could muddle through the questions that ran wildly through his head, the trader stepped back inside and started pulling things from his shelves. He piled the goods high in Jack's arms, and Jack, still in shock, turned wordlessly for the door.

"Wife or no wife, she's still *injun* and yer still white," the trader said, attempting to get in the last word, but Jack didn't even hear him. He walked out of the trading post like he was in a dream, oblivious to a worried Raven trailing behind him as he stared hard at the letter in his hands. *Lillie,* he thought again. *And why now? Why now when he thought he had finally made a decision he planned to stick to?*

Jack felt the light touch of Raven's hand on his arm and as he looked down at her beautiful, worried face, he felt as if he had already wronged her in some way.

"I do not care what they say," she said, still searching his face. "It is only words."

She's so good, he thought. Maybe too good for the likes of him. Jack managed a smile as he shifted the load in his arms. "I'll feel a sight better once we're back home," he said. He was rewarded with a smile that immediately calmed him—and reminded him how very much he loved her. " 'Course it'd do wonders if you were to help me with this load," he added. "Now don't take too much, you might squish my boy."

"Your boy," Raven laughed and as she took some of the goods from his arms, he hastily shoved the letter into his pocket. Raven was his *wife,* damnit. Lillie's letter would have to wait.

In spite of his good intentions, Jack couldn't help remembering his pa teasing him once about money always burning a hole in his pocket. As he shifted the load in his arms again, he thought letters might just have the same effect on him.

No wonder you worried over me, Pa, he thought, seeing maybe for the first time that part of himself that others had always worried over. *Help me, Pa. Help me become the man you'd hoped for. . . .*

"Fast Horse!"

Jolted from his thoughts, Jack turned and looked across the parade ground to the door of the hut where Lone Elk stood grinning like a child as he waved a wad of money through the air for them to see. "I've won! It will be a long time before the *napkiwan* forget the name of Lone Elk!"

Jack smiled, then his smile faltered as he noticed a surly soldier step up behind Lone Elk and he was seized with a sudden cold dread. He heard Raven gasp but before he could make a move, a shot rang out and they both watched in horror as Lone Elk's face crumpled as he pitched forward in the street.

"No!" Jack shouted. He dropped the load in his arms and began running across the parade ground toward Lone Elk and the soldiers who started gathering around the fallen warrior. As he ran, he saw the telltale crimson stain blooming across Lone Elk's shirt and saw the smirking face of the soldier who shot him and the others as they watched him lying there helpless. Something in him snapped. An animal cry erupted from him and he dove for the soldier, striking him full in the chest as they both fell to the ground. Jack pinned the soldier beneath him with such force, he could hear bones in the man's shoulders grind together from the weight. "Where I come from ain't nothin' lower than a man that'll shoot another in the back," he growled, the rage in his heart blinding him to the terrified look in the soldier's eyes. "Might be time you get a taste of what it feels like to have an enemy at *your* back."

Jack flipped the soldier over on his belly as easily as if he were a ragdoll and grabbed him by his hair, yanking his head backwards, and he heard the first real scream of terror as he drew his knife and pressed it against the man's forehead.

"Shoot him quick, Jasper!" the soldier cried. "He's fixin' to scalp me!"

"He's white," a young-sounding Jasper commented from somewhere in the crowd. "I don't think I'm supposed to shoot white folks." Before the soldier could dispute the fact or Jack could cut him, another shot filled the air and the sea of Blackfoot and soldiers parted as the trader, flanked by the same two fellows from the store house, strolled up to Jack.

"Ain't goin' to be any cutting or shooting," the grizzled trader announced with authority. The roar of the crowd quieted and waited for what he would say next. "You get on off of that boy, squaw-man, and we'll call it a day."

The red mist of rage that clouded Jack's thinking began to clear, and he looked over to where Lone Elk still lay and saw Raven and Medicine Weasel hunched over him.

"Is he still alive, Raven?" he called out. She nodded yes, but her and Medicine Weasel's eyes told him just barely.

"Let the soldier go, Fast Horse," Raven urged him in Blackfoot. "He isn't worth Lone Elk's life."

"With any luck, your friend there might make it through," the trader added. "Looks like Aubry will make it, too. Let's be done with this and get back to tradin'."

"I ain't done," Aubry said, touching the line of blood on his forehead with his hand. "He scarred me."

Jack put just enough pressure on his knife to make the soldier squeal again. Then with a loud sigh, he released his grip from the man's hair and watched with grim satisfaction as the soldier's head hit the hard-packed snow with a thud.

"I ain't done, either, but that'll have to do for now," Jack said, rising to his feet. He turned his back to the soldier and walked through the crowd to where Lone Elk was and knelt down next to the friend he had laughed with only a short time ago.

"I don't guess they'll forget the name of Lone Elk, now," he chided gently, and he saw Lone Elk's eyes flutter open. But when he reached out to touch Lone Elk's arm, he saw a flicker of hesitation in his friend's eyes. For a split second, Lone Elk stared at the white of his arm as if it were something separate from Jack—like some sort of disease—and a deep hurt filled Jack that he couldn't quite explain. When their eyes finally met again, Lone Elk quickly recovered and grasped Jack's hand.

"It is the name of Fast Horse they will not forget," Lone Elk rasped, trying to manage a smile. "Get me home alive and I will forgive you for that." Lone Elk's eyes fluttered shut again and he said no more.

Jack hesitated at the door of Lone Elk's temporary lodge that stood just outside of the fort, shivering a bit as he listened to the low healing chants of Medicine Weasel mingling with the muffled groans of his friend. Medicine Weasel had gotten the bullet out, but not without a price; the worried look on the medicine man's face said his nephew had lost more blood than he could really afford. The council that was held after that was quick and to the point as they planned the trip home. That the soldiers would retaliate wasn't a question among the Blackfoot. But every one of them had pledged in their hearts to get Lone Elk home safely—and hopefully still alive. Then they would deal with the soldiers. Jack had waited for the wariness to come back to their eyes when they looked at him but it didn't. Instead, they sought his advice, watching him expectantly as if he would be the one with all of the answers.

Strangely enough, that made him feel worse.

Jack sighed as he glanced up at the huge bowl of sky, at the stars that seemed to hang just above him in the blackness. He felt himself asking for the answers, but nothing came back but the silence, broken from time to time only by tree branches cracking as loud as gunfire in the bitter cold.

Where are You? his mind raged, and he thought of earlier that day when he had found Raven bent over Lone Elk, tears streaming down her cheeks as she had whispered her prayer over and over again. It wasn't until he knelt next to her, listening to her soft voice, that he realized it was the Lord's prayer she was reciting in Blackfoot.

"The blackrobes who came to us during the sickness taught us this prayer," Raven whispered reverently, not taking her eyes off of Lone Elk. "I said it many times for my husband and baby."

"Did it work?" Jack asked bitterly but regretting the hurt he caused to come to Raven's face.

"I thought this way, too." Raven nodded slowly. When she looked up at him, there was no anger on her face, just understanding. "After they went on to the Sand Hills, I asked Him why He did not answer. Then one night as I was lying there crying, He came to me and whispered to my heart that He *had* answered me—that it was their destiny to go. He told me He understood my hurt but to remember it was for myself because they were *free.*"

"What I pray for Lone Elk is that it is not his destiny to go."

Jack looked at the still form of the warrior and felt a hardness come over him. When would all of the death end? If he closed his eyes, it could have been his mama, his pa, Rose, or maybe even Duel. Was that the fate for good people: born to die before they even had a chance to live?

Jack stood up as his anger crashed over him in waves. "I'll tell you what my mama taught me from the knee up about the Good Lord—had more faith than anyone I know, too. But all she got for her effort was sorrow and death, same as most everyone I've known. So, you do your prayin' but I don't think I'll join you. I just don't buy it anymore."

"Fast Horse?" Raven called after him as he pulled back the flap of the door and he looked over his shoulder and saw his wife still kneeling, a thoughtful look on her face.

"How can you be angry at what you do not believe?"

Jack sighed and left the lodge. He didn't know what to believe anymore. He pulled Lillie's letter from his waistband and looked at it once again. He had read it and reread it enough times so as to put it to memory. A memory was all it could be. If he had any beliefs left it was the belief that his pa had been a good man, a man who believed in standing by his family no matter what.

Raven, the baby, the Blackfoot, they were his family now. He knew it the moment he had struck the soldier to the ground. The council meeting had just convinced him of it.

Jack touched the dents in the paper and thought of the hand that pressed them.

"Forgive me, Lillie," he whispered, tossing the letter into the campfire. He turned away and began to trudge slowly through the snow—not to Lone Elk's lodge but to his own. He resisted the urge to look back at what he knew the letter would be now, knowing without looking at the curls of smoke that raised into the night sky and the words that had become scattered ashes, the ashes of his past. As he stepped into his lodge, Raven was there waiting for him, as he knew she would be, and he quickly slid beneath the robes of their bed and pulled her to him, his body craving more comfort than warmth.

"I'm sorry about getting so angry earlier," he whispered into her hair. "I didn't mean to hurt you, either. I think I'd rather cut off my own arm than hurt you, Raven."

Raven sighed and turned to face him, putting her hands on either side of his face. "I know you are sorry," she said simply, then fell silent. Jack sensed there was more she wanted to say.

"What is it, Raven?"

"The letter you have, it was a woman who sent it, was it not?"

Raven asked, her voice falling to a whisper. Jack was shocked into silence by her perceptiveness.

"Do you still love her?" Raven added to the silence.

Jack grunted—a handy thing to do when you were trying to figure out how to answer such a question. He saw the troubled look in her eyes and managed a smile as he lifted her chin with his finger.

She searched his face, and as he stared into the wide, intelligent eyes, he realized he should have known better than to think she hadn't noticed the letter.

"Lillie," he began, wincing at the hoarse sound to his voice but determined to go on, to be as honest as he could. If he was going to be a real husband to Raven, he figured to try to start it off right. "Her name's Lillie. We met back in Virginia City." He wiped a hand over his face, then glanced at Raven before turning his eyes to the ceiling of the lodge. How in the world could he explain it all without hurting her? "I guess we were both kind of like two lost kids; alone and looking for some kind of home. We might have found our way if it weren't for all that happened. It just wasn't meant to be." Jack turned back to Raven and smiled in spite of the pain of the telling. "We are a family now. You, me, and our baby. That's all that counts."

"Had you just left her when my father found you?" Raven asked. When he nodded, her eyes grew solemn, thoughtful.

"I feel sorry for her," Raven said quietly, and Jack propped himself up on one arm to look at the strange and wonderful woman who lay beside him. There was no jealous rage, no hatred, just a tenderness for a woman she had never met.

"Why do you feel sorry for her?"

"You said when you met her you both were very alone in the world. Now she is alone again." Raven swallowed the lump in her throat. "I have been alone, too, and I wouldn't wish that sadness on anyone—not even this white woman."

But she didn't tell him the rest of what lay heavy on her heart. She didn't tell him she pitied the woman because she knew that he would have to leave her someday, too. Not because he chose to, but because her spirit had whispered to her that it would be so. Fast Horse pulled her to him and hugged her tight, as if sensing her fear, and she sighed and sank back against the curve of his body. Most of the time, his arms comforted her, but sometimes she was afraid of how she felt when he held her. Because it made her think she couldn't live without that feeling.

Blackfoot Encampment,
Montana Territory
January, 1865

Mrs. Callie McGregor
Plumas City, California

Dear Callie,
    This will be the last letter I'll be able to mail off for awhile. We are preparing to head back to Blackfoot territory and not a minute too soon. There was a bit of a ruckus at Fort Benton and Lone Elk was shot for winning a hand of poker against one of the soldiers. He is in a bad way but if we don't get him out of here now, it could turn worse . . . a lot worse.
    In spite of all the talk of trading, we are about as welcome here as the cholera. I say "we" because I ain't thought of as much different than an Indian by the soldiers—maybe worse. While we were packing up this morning, one of the soldiers stood at the gate of the fort and stared at me hard. "Hey, squaw-man," he said. "Hope you ain't too attached to them red niggers—they ain't going to be around much longer." I started to make a move for him, but Raven put her hand on my arm and the fellow just sneered. "You'd do good to keep away from that woman, too," he said. "Nits breed nits. We have our work cut out for us as it is."
    And they say Indians are the savages?
    I won't lie. I wanted to murder that soldier where he stood. I proba-

bly would have if it weren't for Raven and the others. They're my family, now, Sis, and I think I'd swallow just about anything to keep them safe. The thing is, I don't know how safe any of us are going to be. Fort Benton is the proof of that. I guess none of this should come as a shock but it has. I've always known what whites think of Indians. Wasn't so long ago that I was one of those mouthy ones going on about the "Red Devils." Ironic, ain't it? Well, like Stem always said, you never know the road a man's traveled till you walk it in his moccasins. Thing is, knowing what's ahead can sometimes make you falter. Soldiers like that fellow are just a drop in the hat to what's coming. I know it and you know it, too. Gold fever travels fast and there's big signs of it here. I think Medicine Weasel suspects more than the rest of them. I saw him stare for a long time at the steamboats docked near the fort and all of the miners and soldiers traipsing around and when he finally turned around and saw me watching him, he didn't say a thing. He didn't have to. The troubled look on his face said it all.

Jack

P.S. Lillie somehow got a letter sent to me here at the fort. She wrote that it's safe for me to come back to Virginia City now. . . .

Might be a lot of things in my life that's changed but bad timing ain't one of them.

Part Three

∽

"Life ain't made by chances, it's made by choices."

—*Jack Wade*

Eighteen

❧

Lillie closed her eyes, relishing the fresh, warm breeze that smelled of baked earth and sun as it played around her, washing the stench of the bar from her nose. When she finally opened her eyes, she spread her blanket on the little patch of ground behind the Pair-O-Dice and settled down to watch the sunset. Sometimes, if she was real lucky, she could get out just in time to catch the sun as it hit the spot between the purple clouds and skyline and flooded the hills beyond the gulch with colored light. Watching it seemed to help settle her in a way nothing else could. Ely considered her evening ritual odd—frivolous, too, if the truth were spoken—with the summer crowds filling the gulch again but he never said much. She wished he would say something instead of forever following her with those looks of his. A few times Ely had ventured out and sat next to her as if he might say something, but he only stayed for awhile and stared hard at the mountains and the sky as if he were trying to figure out what she was looking at. But she knew he had guessed awhile back it wasn't what she was looking at but *for*.

There had been times over the past months that she had almost given up on ever seeing Jack again. Days of watching the snow melt and the mud rise like a river, of seeing the sun paint the gulch warm again and dry up the trails and roads that brought new folks in and allowed the weary to go home. Those were the days she felt she might break under the weight of waiting, of seeing life go on without her. But then something deep within her would stir, tugging at her insides, and she would feel such a sureness he was coming, it would ease the hurt. Lately, the feeling had gotten so strong she found her eyes stray every so often out past the hills to the stands of timber that climbed the mountains, and she could almost see Jack riding out of the trees.

Almost.

Lillie sighed as she watched the sun finally dip down and the mountains loom dark against the wide line of sky like massive soldiers set to stand guard for another night and she stood and shook her skirts out. Shouts and laughter filtered out from the back door of the saloon and she felt a twinge of guilt for dawdling, but as she stepped back into the hazy, crowded room, she saw Ely was surrounded by a bunch of newcomers trying to get the hang of fly-lu. He was so embroiled in the game that he didn't even notice her coming in. Mabel looked up at her from the table she worked and waved her over, fairly shaking with excitement. Lillie didn't know if she would exactly call Mabel *friend*, but at least they had come to understand each other over the past few months.

"These fellows just blew down from Benton," Mabel said with a conspiratorial look at Lillie. "Said they'd like to scare up a game."

From the back, the men were no different from the countless other men who poured into the Pair-O-Dice each night, but as they turned to greet her, she was startled to see the same two faces who had met her all those months back and told her of the white man with green eyes who was riding with the Blackfoot.

Lillie smiled warmly but was careful not to let them see the hope that rose in her like a geyser. She glanced quickly at Mabel, who looked pleased with herself, as if she had just handed Lillie the stars in the sky. Lillie nodded at her and led the men to her table, trying to keep up a casual air as she shuffled the deck and began to pass the cards.

"You sure are a sight for these sorry eyes, ma'am, if you don't mind me sayin' it," the older of the two traders commented as he picked up his cards. "Ain't seen nothin' with your shine since we tumbled west."

"Nothin' but trouble," the younger trader added, and Lillie gave them both her best sympathetic smile. It always paid to lay on the sympathy if you wanted to loosen tongues.

"Why, I'd imagine two strapping fellows like you have seen it all and then some," she said, allowing the first pot to go to the older man. "I seem to recall you two having some stories to tell last time you were here." She glanced up at them through her lashes with a practiced look of awe. "Ever run into that white fellow riding with the Blackfoot again?" she asked casually. The older of the two glanced up from his cards with a startled but bright look on his grizzled face, as if he was pleased she remembered them.

"Oh, we run into him all right. He come strollin' into the post at Benton with his squaw, actin' all uppity and goin' on 'bout his *wife* expecting a baby, like we was supposed to be impressed. Right after his speech, he turns around and mails a big stack of letters to some gal in Californy." The older man sniggered. "Guess he figured the little woman was *expectin'* to hear from him. Wonder what she'd think if she knew he had another woman expectin' somethin', too," he said, cackling at his own joke. "Get it? Expectin'?" he added and his friend gave him a disgusted look.

"I get it. Are you goin' ter play cards or jaw?"

"Oh, you're just sour because his squaw wouldn't have none of you."

"Well, she might have if he weren't so teched in the head. Ain't never seen a white feller try to scalp one of his own kind," the friend said, shaking his head. "I had to wash my hands of it. Even injuns won't mess with someone teched in the head."

"I don't reckon he was teched," the older man said. "He just turned red is all."

Both of the men glanced at Lillie as if expecting her view on the matter of being *teched* but she wasn't listening to them anymore. Not really. Words were flying through her mind so quickly she couldn't hear anything else. Words like *squaw-man, wife,* and *baby.* She tried to stop the shaky feeling that came upon her mainly by talking to herself. *You've been a fool is all,* she scolded herself, fighting the feeling of blackness that threatened to swallow her up whole. *A fool holding on to something that most likely died when he rode out of town. . . .*

Lillie let the younger of the two win, dropping the rest of the cards on the table with a smile that hid the tears inside of her as she pushed herself to her feet. The men looked at her, puzzled.

"We do somethin' to offend ye?" the older man asked. As much as she knew she should answer, she couldn't seem to find her voice.

Every word they had spoken was like a sledgehammer breaking up her dreams, not to mention her pride, piece by piece. She wanted to shout at them, to somehow make them take back all that they had said. *Don't you know what you've done?* she wanted to scream. *Don't you know that having a little hope is better than knowing there's no hope at all?* But she didn't shout or scream. Instead, she walked with great effort over to the bar and sat down carefully, feeling like something in her was ready to break.

At least now she knew. There was no doubt that he had gotten her letter or that he had decided to stay, stay with his *wife,* his *baby.* Lillie felt a pain slice through her like a sharp knife at the thought but tried to fight it. And why wouldn't he want to stay? He had a family now. Something he had always wanted.

Something she had always wanted, too. Lillie looked dully around the crowded room of the Pair-O-Dice and forced herself to face the truth, that the life she stood in might be all she would ever know. *Is this it?* she wondered. *Is this all I'll ever have or be?* She wasn't so sure she could live with that kind of truth. Lillie quickly motioned for Ely to pour her a drink, and she swallowed the concoction quickly as Mabel sidled up next to her on a stool. There was no doubt she had heard the conversation, too—as close as she had been standing. Lillie saw the girl slide Ely a cautious look before she turned to her.

"Lordy, if you could see the look on your face," Mabel said, trying to force some cheer. "We ain't old yet, Lillie."

"I feel like I was born old," Lillie said, her voice almost a whisper.

"Maybe it's time you got on with your life now," Mabel said gently. "Maybe it's just time Lillie did for Lillie and quit being so quiet about it all."

In her mind Lillie saw herself trailing after her pa, then there was Ely and Frank, at last she saw Jack, and as hard as she tried she couldn't remember ever saying much about what she really *wanted*—she had just stumbled along hoping someday someone might care enough to eventually ask. Jack asked once, but then he didn't stay around long enough to help her sort out the whole answer either. "Quiet?" she said finally. A lone tear slipped down her face as she looked up at Mabel. "I don't think the real me has ever made a sound."

Mabel watched Lillie walk away, her small shoulders stooped like an old woman's as she made a slow climb up the stairs to her room, and she felt every painful step Lillie climbed, as if they were her own. In a way they were; she knew all too well how cruel life could be, how it could turn a deaf ear to dreams and give you a nightmare in return.

"You hear what she said, Ely?" Mabel said, her voice husky with emotion as she finally turned back to the bar.

"I heard. A man can learn a heap of things keepin' his ears washed," Ely said, scrubbing the length of the bar like there was no tomorrow.

"Maybe things'll get back to normal now that the truth is out," he added. Mabel put her hand over his to stop his scrubbing.

"Or maybe they won't," she said, the hard sound to her voice forcing Ely to look up. He saw the anger crackle in Mabel's eyes, and it jolted him from the safe place he had buried himself and his thoughts in. Angering Mabel had been the last thing on his mind. He had grown fond of her in spite of her hard ways and had lately even entertained the thought of marrying her. He hadn't yet got up the nerve to ask and now that he had gone and angered her, it looked as if that's all it would be. Ely followed Mabel's gaze to the top of the stairs where Lillie stood and was shocked to see such a change in the girl. She looked plain whipped. *How'd it happen so fast?* he wondered, feeling a panicky feeling begin in his belly. The news about Jack was bad, but she had seemed so sure of everything lately.

Jack is what she was so sure of, you derned fool, his mind said and deep down he knew it was something he had known all along. He just hadn't wanted to admit it. Admitting Lillie might just decide to give up, to quit life, scared him worse than the thought of losing Mabel.

After all, Lillie was his friend. Ely folded the bar rag neatly, avoiding Mabel's eyes as he ducked down and pretended to search for something underneath the bar. *I know. You probably ain't inclined to listen to me, me being the right hand of the devil and all with what I do,* he prayed silently, feverishly, just like he'd done when he was a boy. *But you give Lillie back her hope and I'll reform my ways. If anyone deserves hope, she does. I guess that's all. Thank you, Sir.*

The bottle of rot-gut Lillie had taken from Ely's private stash was nearly half empty by the time dawn came to the gulch. She inspected it a bit before taking another swallow, then gazed out the open window into dusky light. The wind that gusted through the window had a sting to it—like getting smacked on the cheek—but she stood there anyway. *Feeling anything is better than feeling nothing,* she thought dully. She was out of emotions: shame, tears, hope, then tears again. Lillie wondered idly if she didn't have it in her to care anymore, if trouble would leave her alone. After all, how could it trouble you if you didn't care?

She raised the bottle to her lips, then hesitated as she caught a flicker of movement from the corner of her eye. She spotted the tattered figure of Alder Rose haloed by the lanterns along the street as she traipsed through the dusty, rutted street, leaving tiny zigzag prints behind her like a wobbly bird with a broken wing. She watched the woman for a good while stumbling along, her silk rose flopping up and down from her dark bird's nest of hair. Lillie hadn't realized she had been holding her breath until the wind carried the sound of Alder Rose's odd laugh up to her and she felt all of the air rush out of her

She put too much hope in someone else, too, she thought. *So much that she gave up on herself. . . .*

For the first time since hearing about Jack, she felt something like the urge to survive fill her. *That ain't gonna be me,* she thought as she backed away from the window and put the bottle down as if it burned her fingers. *That ain't gonna be me.*

Lillie sat down heavy on her old shuck bed in the little room above the Pair-O-Dice and reached for Duel's Bible that lay on its cherished spot on her dresser. Slowly turning it over, Lillie ran her fingers gingerly over the scarred leather cover, feeling almost too tainted to open the book. When she finally did, her eyes widened, then began to tear as they followed the flowery script.

It wasn't Duel's Bible—it was Jack's. All of the marriages, births, and deaths written with such care, all by a family she would never know. Charles and Amanda Wade were the first names, written with what she imagined was girlish pride on a wedding day. Later was the date of their deaths written by a man's hand and she wondered if it was Jack's.

There was a baby who had died shortly before Jack's mother. Next she saw Jack's, Callie's, and Rose's births . . . then Rose's death written in a shaky girl's cursive that she imagined was Callie's.

Lillie pressed her fingers along the cursives, then hesitated, feeling as if she were prying. She quickly thumbed through the rest of the book, stopping abruptly as the pages fell open to a spot where a small dried flower had been tucked for safekeeping. Next to the flower, three underlined words loomed large before her: *Love never fails.*

Through her tears, Lillie smiled, really smiled for what seemed like the first time in a long time, and she touched the words, touched the dent of ink that ran beneath them, no longer feeling as though she were prying. For she knew the words were meant for her.

Blackfoot Encampment,
Montana Territory
August, 1865

Mrs. Callie McGregor
Plumas City, California

Dear Callie,

I have a son. We named him John-Charles after Pa. He's got Raven's coloring and my eyes, but his disposition is his own. I swear, Callie, the way he moves his little fist through the air, it's like he came out ready to do battle. Raven laughed when I told her. She says all babies do that but I ain't so sure. Not that I'm some expert on babies, but I ain't never seen a baby look so hard at people . . . like he can see right through you. I guess I'm just worrying for nothing but I can't help it. Odd enough, it makes me feel like I know Pa better now than I ever did.

It's funny ain't it, Sis? How I bucked being anything like him for fear of failing. Fool that I was, I saw only Pa's struggles and never realized it was us that he was struggling for . . . giving his life for.

When I held John-Charles in my arms I felt all of that. When Lone Elk's wife handed him to me, I just stared and stared at him and all I could think was I was never so glad to see anyone in my life. Like I was a part of something good for a change, if you know what I mean. It's like I have a whole new chance, Sis. Like I got someone who I don't have to ask to forgive me because I ain't disappointed him yet.

I told Lone Elk as much when a few of us got together for a smoke. He grinned at me but there were tears in his eyes, too, which surprised me. He said what helped him mend so fast was hearing his boy's first cry not long after we got him back to camp. He then gave me a little beaded buckskin case shaped like a snake, and told me it had part of John-Charles's life cord in it. He said Blackfoot believed snakes weren't ever sick and most had long lives.

"Both of your sons will have long lives," Lodge Skins announced out of the blue as he passed the pipe to Medicine Weasel and we all looked up as we heard a baby begin to holler and another join in. My father-in-law grinned like a cat and said, "And both will make sure their voices are always heard—much like their fathers." We all laughed at that.

You know what, Sis? Just when you think life ain't got nothing good for you, it calls you a liar.

Jack

Nineteen

⟋⟍

Raven sighed deeply as she snuggled next to Jack and they gazed up together at the white moonlit sky. The night was warmer than usual, so much so that they had decided to sleep out on a high cut-bank near the river instead of in their own lodge. Jack was glad they made the choice. The wind felt good on his sun-baked skin, the sound of the water below easing the tired ache in his muscles brought on by the lance-throw game he had joined in with Lone Elk and the others. He glanced over at the little bundle that was John-Charles, only an arm's reach away, and smiled as he thought of the games he and Raven would watch him learn to play. *Games I can handle, little fella,* he thought wryly, *but life, well, thank God we have your mother to lead us both on that one.* John-Charles cooed in his sleep and Jack chuckled, thinking it the finest sound he had ever heard.

"Your son was very loud at the games today," Raven murmured. "I think he tires of being a baby already."

"A born fighter is what he is," Jack said, swelled with new fatherhood, but when he looked at Raven something in him softened, too. "A good thing he has a mother who can teach him what fights to choose." Jack wondered if it was a trick of the moon or if his wife's smile had really dimmed. She turned and looked back up at the sky. She had been doing that a lot lately, going distant on him, not in a hateful way, he thought, but as though she were just somewhere else.

"It's so beautiful here," Raven whispered finally as she stared up at the stars. "I do not remember it being so beautiful last summer."

"That's because you didn't have me with you," Jack teased and Raven laughed softly. When she turned to him though, there was a sudden earnest look on her face.

"Promise me we will never leave," she said with a soft kind of urgency. "Promise me we will watch our son grow into a man here and see his children born, that we will grow old together, and when we die, we will be buried next to each other on this spot."

Jack repeated the promises, feeling all of the sureness that new love granted as he lay head to head with her watching the stars. But in the short silence that followed, he started thinking of Lone Elk's dream—not to mention a particular soldier's threat—and he wondered if he would be able to keep every promise he'd made to his wife. Rising up on one elbow, he looked down at Raven, brushing her hair back gently with his hand. "I'll do what I can to keep us here, Raven," he whispered. "But never doubt wherever we are, we will be together."

Raven's pleased smile faltered and he saw a brief flash of fear before she recovered enough to look at him once again and smile. "Just so we are together."

"Well, I don't have any plans on going anywhere without you or our son," Jack said, wondering at her turn of thought. He leaned over and kissed her on her forehead, then on her lips, and she smiled at him with pure love in her eyes.

"The blackrobe I told you of? He told us that even when we die, we will all go up into the sky together to live with the World Maker." She fell silent again, as though she was waiting for him to say something. When he didn't, she looked at him a bit more closely. "Do you believe this?"

"Preachers say it's so," Jack answered a bit evasively. "Their Good Book says it's so, too."

"I think this must be right," Raven considered. "If the World Maker would allow the stars to be together for all time, He must surely allow us the same. That would only be fair, wouldn't it, Fast Horse?"

"Yes, it would," he answered quietly, feeling his heart ache for her innocence. He didn't have it in him to tell her that the God he knew hadn't exactly been so fair at times. At least John-Charles coming into the world had made him reconsider his anger. Sometimes he wondered if it didn't really have anything to do with Him being fair but about folks learning what was important along the way. Jack was just starting to figure that with someone as stubborn as himself, he had to be all but killed before he knew how to live. He had started wondering if maybe God had been there all the time and was just waiting for him to get the hang of it all.

Jack felt Raven stir and he watched her gently lift John-Charles into her arms, cradling him to her as she began to sing to him softly. Her lilting voice sounded so sweet and tender in the still summer night. He felt his emotions swell up in him like a great wave and a voice seemed to whisper to him then, telling him how lucky he was to have the moment and that he should never forget all he saw and felt. Jack suddenly felt an odd urgency come over him to say the words in his heart aloud, to let Raven know how he felt.

But he couldn't seem to find the words to say how grateful he was to her for his life, *for his son.*

Raven glanced up from John-Charles and saw him watching her; the look on her face said she understood.

"I know, Fast Horse," she said haltingly, for there was no word in the Blackfoot language for *love*. Living amongst them had taught Jack there wasn't really a need for the word as they loved just as fiercely as they fought and he had to wonder if they might have the right idea. Talk could be cheap after all, he thought, watching her lay John-Charles down to sleep. Without another word, he pulled Raven to him and she turned in his arms, snuggling close as he stroked her hair, her face, with all of the feeling he had deep inside. The sigh that escaped her was unlike anything he had ever heard. As if she had been waiting for this moment for so long. He touched her face first, smoothing his hands down over her neck and shoulders, finally to her hips and legs as he gently tugged her soft buckskin dress up over her head. When he pressed her back against the blanket and took her body to his, he felt everything become sharp, as if every touch, every breath between them had become one, and he realized a part of him that he had kept hidden for so long had been waiting for this moment, too—to not only feel needed, but to need.

They made love long into the night, over and over again, neither of them wanting the feeling to end, until finally somewhere near dawn, Raven began to drift off to sleep, her long legs entwined in Jack's. He watched her sleeping for a long while, awed by the pure feelings that came out of him so freely now. When Jack finally began to drift off to sleep, he felt almost weightless, as if nothing else mattered but those feelings and the soft sounds of sleep coming from his wife and son as he stared up into the immense sky washed by the light of a new day. He smiled, for when he thought about it, nothing else really did matter. *Maybe I am getting the hang of this after all, God,* he thought just before sleep found him.

Raven glanced up from the hide she was scraping, sensing something was wrong. Overhead, the sun beat down upon her neck and shoulders and she felt a line of sweat bead up on her forehead, threatening her eyes, but she remained still, listening, but no sound ever came. The usual chatter of birds was oddly absent. Even the children who had been wading down by the river whose shouts and laughter she had heard only moments before had quieted, as if they sensed something, too.

Feeling uneasy, Raven quickly scooped John-Charles into her arms and headed for her father's lodge; the men had gone off to hunt and would be far away from the village by now. As she picked up her pace, she tried to quiet the fear that welled up in her, telling herself the danger may only be imagined and not real, but she thought of the feelings of foreboding she had been having, too, and wondered if she had foolishly ignored a warning.

Surely Grandfather would not be so cruel, she thought, picking up the pace of her steps. *Not now, not when I have just begun to live again. . . .*

Her father stepped from his lodge just as she was ready to enter. Without a word, he took John-Charles from her arms, holding him to his chest protectively as his eyes searched the distance.

"What is it?" she asked worriedly. He turned and looked at her, his face looking older than she ever remembered, and she had the oddest feeling that he had known something was coming.

"Trouble," he answered simply. Before he could say any more, the sound of horses thundering close broke the silence, and they both turned to see a dozen or so soldiers enter the encampment. The women and children who had been so still startled into action, running to hide in the brush, their eyes wide with fear. As the white men neared, Medicine Weasel raised his hand in the universal greeting. What appeared to be their leader reined his horse in just short of running them over.

"We need someone to speak English, old man," he said. "I ain't in the mood to play patty-cake." He took his hat from his head, wiping the sweat from his brow with a kerchief. His forehead was pasty white compared with the rest of his face, which had been scorched a painful red by the sun. As he wiped his face, his eyes suddenly went to John-Charles, who had been suspiciously quiet through it all. "That white fellow still with you all?"

"I speak English," was all Medicine Weasel offered. He turned and calmly handed John-Charles back to Raven, then stepped in front of them as if to shield them with his own body.

"Not as well as I do," a familiar voice called. Raven's body nearly shook from relief as she turned to see her husband step out from behind one of the lodges and stroll boldly over to where the soldier sat mounted on his horse. The soldier-chief appeared confused at first, staring at Fast Horse dressed only in buckskin trousers, his bare shoulders and chest gleaming brown. But when their eyes met, the soldier-chief laughed a laugh that sounded much like the bark of a dog to Raven's ears.

"Never thought I'd see the day I couldn't tell a white from an injun," he said, peering down at Fast Horse with a smile that was not real. "You on the run from somethin', boy?"

"Maybe *to* something," Fast Horse said with a wide smile that Raven knew wasn't real either.

"Well, that's just fine. Yessir, just fine. To each his own, I always say, right, boys?" The soldier-chief leaned over the pommel of his saddle, still smiling, but Raven noticed a hard look come to his eyes as he stared down at Fast Horse, and the little relief she had felt earlier disappeared. "The thing is, son, I'm not sure we can let you stay. See, we have a soldier missing now, and word is you got to know him pretty well at Benton—well enough to offer him a haircut, right, boys?"

A few of the soldiers laughed, and as Raven pulled John-Charles to her chest, she caught a flash of movement to her right. She saw the rest of the warriors creeping closer to where she stood. Just beyond camp, another group sat mounted and ready, and Raven forced her face to remain expressionless. Inside of her, the words of the soldier-chief drummed through her head, over and over again: . . . *not sure we can let you stay.* . . . She looked to Fast Horse, whose face appeared just as expressionless, but she caught the slight twitch of muscle along his jaw and she sensed his stillness was more like the stillness of a coiled snake, judging when to strike.

"If I was going to finish your man, I'd have done it back at Benton," Fast Horse said finally, his tone hard. "As far as you taking me anywhere, you might want to reconsider the threat, Major."

Raven watched as the soldier-chief's eyes followed her husband's, his eyes widening in surprise, his face becoming an even darker shade of red as he spotted the warriors who now stood in front of their lodges, then further to the distance to the line of Blackfoot that dotted the ridge just beyond the river.

"I got a wife and child here, Major. And whether you like it or not, *friends,* I'm telling you there ain't nothin' that'd make me risk their lives. Not even a fool who has no business wearin' a uniform, let alone packin' a gun. Those warriors you see all around you? They know that—that's why they're here. I really don't give a good damn what you think but I'd hate to see blood shed for no reason."

In the tense silence that followed, Raven watched the soldier-chief's face for signs of understanding but there were none. She looked for anything familiar, some kind of *humanness* like she had found in her husband when he first came to them, but all she saw in his eyes was hate. He leaned over his horse and spit out a large amount of foul-looking juice, wiping his mouth with the back of his hand.

"I say a man who lives like a savage will die like a savage."

The words caused the dam of tension to break on both sides, the soldiers scrambling for their weapons as the warriors advanced, shouting insults that no one needed to have interpreted. With all of the shouting, no one noticed the flap of the largest lodge snap open or the old man called Many Horses who stepped out, his long, white hair hanging in wisps from beneath the buffalo cap he wore to hide an unfinished scalping. Time had eroded the large frame and slowed his steps, but it hadn't touched the spirit inside that was born to lead men. A silence fell upon the crowd as the old chief walked forward, parting them quickly as if some great hand had swept them aside. His black eyes were mere slits in the folds and wrinkles of his face but sharp as he studied first Fast Horse, then the soldier-chief.

"Fast Horse has said he did not harm your man and I believe his words," Many Horses said, his deep, gravelly voice commanding respect. "I do not wish to anger our Great Father and so I will offer you this: I will question my warriors and they will tell me the truth. If any of them tells me he is the one you seek, I will hand him over to you." Raven held her breath as the old chief paused, his eyes remaining fixed on the soldier-chief. She thought she saw an odd light suddenly come to Many Horses' eyes. "I ask you to trust me just as I trusted my white friends at the treaty signing."

At first the soldier-chief seemed at a loss for words, as if he didn't expect such talk from the old man. But then Raven saw him look down at Many Horses with a feral look like that of a fox.

"We'll set up camp about two miles out from you folks—that's as far as *my* trust is going," the soldier-chief said. "You have three days."

The soldier-chief started to say something more but Many Horses had already turned his back to him. As Raven watched the old man walk away, she saw that his back was straight and his silver head high as if telling them all to remember who they were. *We are Blackfoot,* she thought as if hearing Many Horse's voice inside of her. As she looked around the camp at the warriors and the women and children who trickled back to their homes, laughing with relief amongst themselves at the foolish white soldiers who were trailing out of camp like dogs with their tails tucked between their legs, she felt proud to be Blackfoot.

We are Blackfoot, she thought again, and as she watched her father slip into Many Horse's lodge with the other elders of the tribe, she remembered the words he had spoken when she was young. *A thief can take only what he is given.* She hadn't really understood the words until now. But Many Horses had understood; he refused to give them what was not theirs.

Raven hugged John-Charles, kissing him over and over on his face, and she felt the last of her fear fade as he erupted in a deep belly laugh that filled her heart with joy.

"Look, Fast Horse, your son laughs at them, too," she chuckled, but when she glanced up at her husband she was startled to see him standing alone in the center of camp, the heat wavering around him in the still of the afternoon as he watched her and John-Charles with a look of deep sadness.

Blackfoot Encampment,
Montana Territory
1865

Mrs. Callie McGregor
Plumas City, California

Dear Callie,

The trouble at the fort I told you about some time ago has come back to haunt us. A bunch of soldiers came riding in asking if we'd seen the fellow who shot Lone Elk, saying he's missing, and the kick of it is they think I'm to blame. It was on the tip of my tongue to ask what kind of fool would go sniffing around an Indian camp alone, but their major started threatening to take me back with them until dern near the whole Blackfoot nation stepped in. Truth is, I'm not sure if we should stay now. Everything went from bad to worse at the powwow they held tonight when Lone Elk confessed to killing the man after finding him sneaking around our camp. Many Horses, the chief, promised the soldiers he would find the culprit and turn him in, but when I reminded him of this he just shrugged and said, "I asked them to trust my promise as much as I have trusted theirs." That seemed to settle it for everyone but me. They don't know whites like I do, Sis. That major is the kind who'd hunt his own mother down for the glory of it.

My thought is if I go them soldiers will think it was me who killed their boy and I ran off before Many Horses could turn me in. I think I'd have a sight better luck at fading into the crowds somewhere than Lone Elk. I guess the only thing I worry for is how Raven and John-Charles would be treated in our "white world" if we choose to leave. I ain't so ignorant to think we would be welcomed with open arms, but I do think I might have a better chance at protecting them where there's some kind of law. There ain't any kind of law out here—at least not for the Indians—and I ain't seen as any different than Indian by the soldiers— other whites, too, for that matter. The folks coming through this land ain't like we were when we came west. Gold has them in such a lather they're willing to run roughshod over anyone or thing that'll stand in their way. I figure the war has done part of it. Once you've lost every-thing, you're apt to gamble your soul, too.

The sad thing is the Blackfoot don't understand this thinking.

I don't know why I thought we could live in peace. I guess happiness can cloud a person's thinking for awhile. Of all people, I should have known better, though. Sometimes I think my life is like a string of bad poker hands and just when I think I'm ready to rake in the pot, some joker lays down an ace he had up his sleeve.

I sure wish you were here so I could bend your ear a little. I know I've always acted like I didn't need anyone else's view on things, but the truth is, that's all it was, an act. Why is it the hardest choices are the ones we have to make on our own? I guess the answer to that doesn't matter because I'm going to have to make up my mind on this and soon.

Choices are funny things, Sis. You can think a choice is too hard but then, the way I see it, if you decide to do nothing, that's a choice, too, ain't it?

Jack

Jack startled awake at the sound of his lodge door being thrown open and had his gun aimed and cocked before he realized that the shadow standing in the doorway was Lone Elk. Before he could ask him what was going on, Lone Elk slid a grim look to Raven, who stirred in her sleep, put his fingers to his lips, and motioned for him to follow.

Outside, there was only a feather of a breeze working against the heat and Jack squinted at the sky, judging he and Raven had slept later than usual. The rest of the camp was just beginning to come to life as well, but there was none of the usual laughter or talking, which made him think his lodge wasn't the only one kept awake by the threats of the white soldiers.

"There is more trouble," Lone Elk said, turning to look at him over his shoulder as he mounted his horse.

"Seems like that's all we're good at finding lately," Jack said, hitching himself over Big Black's back. They trotted out of camp in silence, both lost in their own thoughts. The silence stayed between them until they climbed up out of the deep coulee they had been following, pulling up short of the clearing just beyond the trees.

"Look there," Lone Elk said, pointing fifty yards or so just beyond them where the trees had thinned away to nothing. Jack was filled with dread seeing the soldiers from Fort Benton milling about. A few of them had taken their shirts off in the heat and were listlessly kicking around an abandoned campfire, then the major leaned over and picked something up from the pile of ashes and started shaking it, hollering excitedly. Jack squinted, trying to make out the object. As the major shook it again, he realized it was a canteen; army issue from the looks of it.

"Hell," Jack whispered.

"They are standing on his grave," Lone Elk added, and the two friends looked at each other with eyes that were sharp and full of worry. Lone Elk swung a leg over, dismounting from his horse, and handed Jack the reins, motioning for Jack to lead the horses back to the dense thicket of trees from where they came. Using his moccasins, he toed-out whatever tracks they had made in the dust, carefully backing his way toward Jack. As Lone Elk swung onto his horse once more, Jack noticed the warrior's knuckles had gone white as he gripped his reins in one hand. But it was his eyes that spoke his feelings; black and foreboding and asking the question Jack had asked himself too many times to count, too many times to forget. *What have I done?*

"Many Horses will want to know of this," Lone Elk said, looking around him as if he could find the rest of the words he searched for.

"They will have to turn me over to the soldiers," Lone Elk said finally. Jack heard the hollowness in his voice and he knew the warrior was trying to imagine being stripped of his people, his family . . . *his life.*

"No," Jack said with such force that Lone Elk didn't argue but managed a sad smile that seemed to say he trusted Jack's intentions—just not life's.

The two turned and rode back to camp without another word.

Raven tried to sleep but couldn't, so she lay on her back like a sick person, staring up at the dark hole of night at the top of the lodge. She knew something had happened from the time she had woken to find Fast Horse gone and she knew it was bad—even before she had heard the cry go out about their village for medicine pipe men, mature hunters and warriors, and wise old men to gather. She had peeked out of her doorway and seen Lone Elk and her husband slipping into Many Horse's lodge with grim looks on their faces. Laughs-A-Lot had been watching, too, and they had smiled wanly at each other before ducking back into their own lodges. As she lay there, Raven wondered if Laughs-A-Lot felt as scared as she did, if her body hummed with warning, too, but she couldn't bring herself to go ask her.

When he finally sat down next to her, he didn't look at her at first but stared at John-Charles' sleeping form for a long while. Raven remained quiet, sensing the struggle inside of him.

"The soldiers found the spot where Lone Elk killed that fellow. They start digging and it won't be long till they find the body, too," Fast Horse began, his voice dull. "Many Horses wants to leave for the new camp come morning. We'll be going with them but we can't stay. The soldiers won't quit hunting the Blackfoot unless they find out that the white man they're hunting has run back home."

"When?" she asked, stifling the sob that rose up in her as Fast Horse turned to her, his green eyes filled with both love and pain.

"We'll go after everyone settles so we can say our proper good-byes. I'm thinkin' a week—but no more than that," he said, a deep sadness in his voice as he sank down next to her and slipped the blankets back over them that she had kicked aside in her tossing and turning. *A week.* Raven tried to imagine saying good-bye to all she had ever known in a week, of leaving her relatives and friends behind to face a world she couldn't even imagine.

"You know I wouldn't choose this if there was any other way," he said softly, and Raven nodded her head, unable to speak.

"You and John-Charles are my family—all that matters to me," he added and she nodded again, this time trying to smile as Fast Horse pulled her against him and they clung to each other like two tiny birds caught in a storm neither could fly free from.

Raven allowed herself to be lulled into the comfort of his arms and tried not think of the bad feeling that followed her like a big shadow lately. Leaving her home was a small price to pay to keep her family together, she realized. It was probably just her worry that brought the bad feeling to her anyway. Worry always gave small things big shadows.

Blackfoot Encampment,
Montana Territory
1865

Mrs. Callie McGregor
Plumas City, California

Dear Callie,

One of the hardest things I've ever had to do was make the choice I made tonight . . . to take Raven and John-Charles away from here. As much as it pains me, I know that I am doing the right thing. So, why do I feel so lousy?

As luck would have it, the soldiers found their man—or soon will—and we are sure to be next on their list. I've had a hard time of it con-

vincing the Blackfoot how serious this is. Fear ain't exactly common to them. Many Horses is a wise old fellow but is stubborn, too. He figures we can move camp and the soldiers will eventually give up the chase. Like I said before, he doesn't know them like I do. I aim to stick to the plan I told you about before. It's the only way out I can see for all of us. But I figure I'll wait until everyone's settled in at the new camp before I announce my plans so that way we can say our good-byes right. I owe the Blackfoot that much—not to mention Raven.

She's a strong woman, Sis, but there's something fragile in her eyes now, too, as if she's not sure where she fits in this world anymore. A lot like someone else I once knew. Which is why I aim to do right by her. I can't go back and change the past but I damned well can choose to do different this time around.

After all, if we can't learn from our mistakes, then what's the sense of it all . . . of life?

Jack

"Even God Almighty took a day to rest, " Ely huffed, carrying a large basket filled with food on one arm and a little table on the other. A bead of sweat ran down his thin nose as he glanced over at Lillie and she couldn't help chuckling at the pitiful sight.

"It ain't Sunday yet," Mabel piped up, several strides ahead, carrying two chairs from the bar. "Not until we find a spot to put our things down. Then we'll call it Sunday and you can rest all you like." Lillie watched Mabel swipe a strand of hair from her flushed face as she looked around for a good shade tree. With the sun high overhead, the heat was almost unbearable but it didn't seem to touch Mabel, Lillie thought. She looked happy—and in charge; two traits that had suddenly appeared since she and Ely had married. All in all Lillie was happy for her. She had turned out to be a good friend, just when she had needed a friend the most.

Which is why she agreed to come to the church picnic even though it gave her a bad case of the nerves. It had been so long since she had done anything normal she wasn't sure how to act.

"I know that woman from somewhere," Mabel said, narrowing her eyes toward a crowd of picnickers as she set the chairs down.

"You always say that," Lillie chided, draping the quilt she brought over her own chair. "If you knew so much you'd know that's the preacher's new wife."

"No, I know *that*. I'm tellin' you I know her from somewhere *else.*"

"I guess I worked up a thirst," Ely announced abruptly.

"Well, go get yourself a drink, then," Mabel said. The corners of his mouth turned down in what Lillie imagined to be a pout.

"I suppose you want me to hold your hand, too," Mabel said. "Well, come on. Lillie, you need anything?"

"No, not right now," Lillie laughed and watched the two set off down the hill to the little stand where the preacher and his wife stood with the rest of the crowd, slicked up and proper. Lillie shook her head. Virginia City had changed.

I've changed, too. Lillie smiled, thinking of how far she had come over the past several months and of a past she had finally put to rest. The bad choices she had made she had thought at the time were made in the name of survival or sanity, but now she knew better; they had been done in the name of love. And she had finally put that to rest, too. Oh, the ache of losing Jack was still there at times, but there was also a kind of gratefulness she felt, too. A gratefulness to have learned that the old saying of hard times not killing you but making you stronger wasn't just a saying, but truth. Lillie inhaled a deep breath and smiled again. She *felt* stronger.

Turning all her hurt into work had paid off, too. Soon she would have the little house she dreamed of and maybe one day, someone to share it with. But for now, she had friends, good ones.

As Lillie turned to sit, she saw Frank Monroe plain as day heading her way. She felt herself tighten, as if preparing for a fight.

"Why, Frank, I'm surprised you'd show up here, this being a *church* social and all," she said, fear putting a bite in her words. "Ain't you afraid of lightning striking you or something?"

"I ain't the only one that'd be ducking," he sneered. "I'm just wondering what's got you so interested here. Is it that churchy feeling? Tell you what, next time you come calling, we'll pass the hat around and make it feel just like Sunday."

"There isn't going to be any next time," Lillie said, her voice strong but shame heated her cheeks anyway and she hated Frank for it, hated him for trying to rip apart the life she had worked so hard to piece back together. But instead of letting him goad her into an all-out fight, she turned her back on him and fell silent. Frank didn't quite know what to do with her silence and finally stalked off. Lillie glanced down at the quilt she had sewn, wondering if she had been foolish to bring it. It wasn't much of a quilt.

She didn't know a lot about quilting, but what little she did know was culled from her memory as a little girl sitting with her grandma and her friends as they sewed the day away, laughing and talking. The memory had come back to her the night she found Jack's Bible and she had started sewing that very night, choosing scraps from the meager collection that summed up her life: an embroidered handkerchief of her mama's; pieces of her pa's overcoat; scraps of an old linsey-woolsey dress Ely had given her and another dress that Frank had store bought. Out of all the confusion she had sewn two wildflowers in the center—one yellow and one blue—for each of the dresses that Jack had given her. She had brought it to sell at the church raffle. A kind of sendoff to her past.

"You made a fine choice with those colors," a voice said from behind her. She turned to see the preacher's new wife watching her closely. Lillie cringed inside wondering how much of Frank's comments the woman had heard, wondering if she was a fool to think her life could change.

"I used to think it was so hard, you know, choosing the right colors, but an old friend told me a good quilter doesn't choose with her eyes, but with her heart. She said that way no matter how ugly it might seem, it always turns out good in the end."

"It's my first try," Lillie said awkwardly. "I don't know much about it."

The woman ran a smooth, slender hand lightly over the two flowers, then looked at Lillie and smiled. There was something about the smile that made Lillie want to cry but feel good, too.

"Oh, I think you do," the preacher's wife said but before she could say any more she was joined by her husband, who was in a rush to introduce her to someone. The preacher smiled nicely at Lillie before he led his wife off down the hill. Soon after Mabel and Ely were heading back toward her at a good clip.

"I brought you a drink anyways. Here," Mabel said a bit shakily as she sat down next to her, then she lowered her voice to a bare whisper. "I know where I've seen the preacher's wife before. She was one of them girls at the hog ranch I worked."

Both of them glanced over to where the preacher's wife stood.

"Did you hear what I said?"

"I heard you," Lillie said. She didn't care what the woman had *been*—she admired what she had become, *who* she had become. Lillie looked down at her quilt. She didn't much feel like selling it anymore. She felt like keeping it and remembering the preacher's wife's words. *Choose with your heart,* she had said. *No matter how ugly it might seem, it always turns out good in the end.* They were good words.

Lillie hugged the quilt to her chest and looked out toward the mountains in the distance—not searching this time. Just looking and wondering about choices.

Twenty

Medicine Weasel had always believed in being the kind of parent who kept his nose out of areas where it did not belong—but only up to a point. He had found himself more and more troubled by the silence that had fallen over his daughter and Fast Horse since their move to the new encampment. He had his suspicions of course, but he decided it was his right as a father to see for himself.

As he neared their lodge, he saw Fast Horse's buffalo runner tethered to the pole outside, but the medicine man knew his son-in-law was gone. He had seen him riding out of camp with Lone Elk earlier that evening, which is why he chose this particular time to visit. Medicine Weasel scratched at the door of the lodge, heard his daughter's muffled invitation, and stepped inside.

"I see you have settled in well," Medicine Weasel said as he forced himself to look about his daughter's lodge. "This is a good home. It smells good, too."

Raven's answering smile didn't touch her heart and it sent off a warning in him. "I was just getting ready to bring you your meal."

"I think I will sit for a minute," he said casually, waving off the bowl of stew. "Sometimes when you get old, being comfortable is better than eating." He waited for Raven to settle next to him and he turned to her and smiled. "So, tell me. How are you doing?"

If she hadn't been his daughter, she would have allowed the tears in her eyes to fall. Instead she forced another smile.

"I am well," she said, then rushed on. "Fast Horse is a good husband; he provides well for me and his son. He would give his life for us."

"Yes, he is a good husband."

So, it was to be. Medicine Weasel closed his eyes for a moment and allowed the knowledge that his daughter was leaving to sink in. When he opened his eyes, he saw his daughter's worried expression and patted her leg reassuringly. For whatever reason, they had decided not to tell anyone yet and he would respect their decision. But that didn't stop his worry.

He remembered a premonition he had had when she was but a girl of her giving out pieces of herself until there was nothing left and she disappeared before his eyes. *"She chooses too much with her heart,"* he had whispered to her mother under their robes one night. *"I'm afraid for her. That one day she will choose wrong." "How can a heart's choice be wrong?"* his sits-beside-him wife had asked. *"It is how I chose you."*

The memory of losing his wife not long after that came and he grunted, pushing the memory and the pain aside as he reached over and picked up a long swatch of his daughter's hair and twirled it around his finger as he had done when she was small. Raven's eyes became wide with anxiety and he knew she remembered the gesture, too.

"I must go," he said, suddenly standing, and Raven stood, too, looking lost.

Don't go with him, he wanted to say but he didn't because he knew his daughter's destiny was not his choice. His grandson began to cry and he watched his daughter scoop him up in her arms to comfort him. He thought of when she had once been that small and how he had held her in his arms. Unable to resist, he took them both in his arms and hugged them tight. When he finally stepped back, they both had tears in their eyes.

"I hope you don't mind an old man's foolishness," he said, trying to joke. And because he didn't wish to cause her any more pain, he stepped out of her lodge and back into the night.

"Father?" Raven called after him. He turned back to see her standing at the door of her home, her pretty face marred by a single tear that traveled down her cheek. "You are not so foolish."

"By God, she makes me nervous doing that," Jack said, glancing at Lone Elk, who offered him a smile of understanding. Both men turned again to watch Raven as she rode on in the shaggy sea of running humped-back giants. They had planned just a leisurely ride but it turned out the pony he had chosen for Raven wasn't a tame little pony but a trained buffalo runner. No sooner had he and Lone Elk circled to the back of the herd than Raven's pony darted into action, passing their horses as if they were standing still. Jack had shouted out a warning to her, but it was lost in the thunder of hooves. Instead of being afraid, Raven had laughed and quirted the pony faster, glancing back once to grin at Jack, her eyes wide with excitement. From their spot on the little butte, he watched her riding along with a mixture of fear and awe as she stayed with them, riding the tide of buffalo, inky hair flying out behind her in waves, her look wild and careless, as if it were her last day on earth. Jack felt as though he had never understood her better or loved her more than in that moment.

"It is what makes you glad to be her husband, eh, Fast Horse?" Lone Elk said, as if reading his thoughts, and Jack managed a smile. He had yet to tell his friend of their decision to leave. Sometimes he wondered if his holding back was his way of stalling their departure. There was still no sign of the soldiers, but he knew the quiet wouldn't last.

"She's something all right. But I don't think I'll be giving her that pony to ride again anytime soon. You think she's safe out there?"

"They will tire soon," Lone Elk said, and no sooner had he spoken the words than Jack saw the front of the herd slowing to a trot as they tried to climb the long slope that took them to the outlying ridge of the mountains. He took a deep breath, feeling his nerves settle a bit as he watched Raven finally turn her pony and head in their direction, snaking through the tail end of the massive herd that painted the prairie black clear to the breaks of the Missouri. He felt awed by the scene. He figured if he lived to be a hundred he would never forget such a view or the wonder it filled him with; the wide bowl of blue that seemed to light the way to forever, reaching past the rolling prairies and immense mountains that seemed to stand watch in the distance. *God's backyard,* folks called it, and he thought the name most fitting. There was something in the greatness that made it hard to put to paper, as if you had to see it yourself to believe there was such a place.

That they had to leave it soon made him want to linger a little longer, so as to be sure to put it to memory right.

"I had a dream once," Lone Elk said, breaking the silence as his eyes remained fixed on the herd. He appeared to hesitate, as if he were trying to decide whether or not to continue, but when he turned to Jack and their eyes met, it seemed to settle the matter. "I was chasing a great buffalo, probably the largest I have ever seen. When I finally cornered it, the great buffalo shocked me by hunkering down like a whipped dog. He spoke to me then, saying, 'I am the last buffalo. When I am gone, you are gone.' When he said this to me, I looked down at myself and I was white—like the pale white of death, even my horse was white. It scared me so that I asked the buffalo what this meant, but when I looked up he was gone." When Lone Elk glanced over to Jack, his smile was grim. "The vision made me so sick I could not eat buffalo for many weeks."

Jack didn't know what to say so he remained silent. Lone Elk chuckled after awhile and swept his hands through the air. "They are plenty, huh, Fast Horse?" He nodded then, as if satisfying his own worry. "Blackfoot land will never change." When he turned to Jack, his face was wide-open innocent as a kid's.

"It was a foolish dream, eh?" he said, more telling than asking, but there was a questioning look in his eyes that Jack had never seen before, too, as if he wasn't as sure as he acted. Jack smiled, but his heart wasn't really in it. How could he tell Lone Elk what he knew, of what was coming? When Medicine Weasel had asked at the meeting about the white soldiers and those who were coming west, he had tried to answer honestly, but when he realized what would be taken from the Blackfoot by his own kind, he had fallen silent.

Ever since leaving Fort Benton he had grown more and more ashamed of being white. He caught himself speaking more in Blackfoot, taking extra care to shave the hair from his face so it was as smooth as the other braves', anything to keep his whiteness from the people he had come to care for. Soon enough the color of his skin would be hated by them. And for good reason.

Jack looked at the Blackfoot warrior he called friend and he wondered what would become of their friendship when he was gone. Jack saw a sudden wary look come to Lone Elk's eyes and his smile faltered as if he sensed something was wrong. *I'm sorry, Lone Elk,* he wanted to say. *I'm sorry for what my kind have done and for what they will do.* But Raven came trotting up, flushed and laughing, and the words never came.

Blackfoot Encampment,
Montana Territory
1865

Mrs. Callie McGregor
Plumas City, California

Dear Callie,

I've asked for the council members to meet with me tomorrow. As much as it pains me to tell them of our leaving, neither Raven nor I can go on keeping it from our family and friends any longer. I guess waiting for the right time was just foolishness. There's never a right time to say good-bye to folks you care for.

Lone Elk told me of a dream he had today, a premonition, really, and it has chilled me to the bone. He was chasing a great buffalo and when he finally got it cornered, it hunkered down like a dog and said, "I am the last buffalo—when I am gone you are gone." He said when he looked down at himself, he was white. "The pale white of death," he said. He tried to make light of the dream but I could tell he was worried. The worst part was there was nothing I could say to make him feel any better.

This land is their home, Callie, the only life they've ever known. Who gave us the right to take that away? I wish there was one person I could see and say, "That's him," and wrestle him down until he gave in. But how do you wrestle a nation? None of this makes any sense.

I wonder if anything will ever make sense again.

Jack

Jack glanced around the lodge at the circle of familiar faces red-lit by the fire that peered back at him questioningly and he felt a sadness come over him, remembering happier gatherings. There was no happiness in his heart for what he had to do now.

Somewhere out beyond camp he heard a lone wolf howl to the coming night, and the tone, so lonely and forlorn, seemed fitting. When he finally found his voice, the sound that came out was so low that the warriors had to lean forward to hear his words.

"The soldiers who came to our old camp think I killed the one they call Aubry," Jack began. "I *wanted* to kill the hair-mouth who shot Lone Elk, but I spoke the truth when I told them I did not. Even so, they think I did, which doesn't matter much, but now that they have found the body there will be much trouble for the Blackfoot."

"Their trouble is not so much," Many Horses interrupted as he carefully filled his pipe. The old chief adjusted his buffalo cap, making sure his bald patch was covered, then turned to Jack, his eyes glittering like two bottomless pools of black. "I have fought and killed many whites," he said with no apology. "Their weapons impressed me but they did not. " He shrugged his stooped shoulders "Does a buffalo concern himself with the tiny flea bite on his back? Blackfoot should not concern themselves with such things."

Jack watched the old chief take a tentative puff on his pipe, feeling the bittersweetness of being handed a gift that you knew you couldn't keep; the old fellow had as much as called him Blackfoot, declaring him one of them, which made his decision to tell what he knew all the more important now. "What if the flea grew in such numbers that it could consume the buffalo? The whites you see now are only the beginning. More are coming, too many to count." Jack looked around the fire at the expressions of alarm and took a deep breath before he went on. "Way I see it, the buffalo might be wise to shake that first flea. There will be others, I won't lie to you. But if I go now, the soldier-chief will believe it was me who committed the crime. It would be easy for him to find a white man living with the Blackfoot and no one would say much if he hurt the Blackfoot who protected this white man. But it would not be so easy in the white world. I won't risk your lives—or my wife's and son's. It will be better for all if I take my family and go."

Some of the warriors glanced up, looking startled or genuinely grieved. Others tried to politely mask their relief to be rid of him, but it was Lone Elk's reaction that caused him the most pain. The fierce-looking warrior who had become more like a brother laughed in disbelief. He turned to One Shot sitting next to him and slapped the young warrior on the back, acting like it was a fine joke.

"Fast Horse will go back to the white world," Lone Elk laughed again as if the idea were too crazy to even consider as serious. "He will wear starched shirts and his hands will grow soft as a woman's again. He will—"

Many Horses coughed, interrupting the banter, and in the silence that followed, Lone Elk's expression began to sober. He stared hard at Jack, his eyes asking the questions he didn't appear to want to say out loud. Jack avoided his friend's eyes for fear he would lose control of his emotions. Instead, he turned his arm over and stared at the pale skin, unchanged by the sun.

"You forget your dream, friend," he said quietly, not looking up but staring into the fire. Lone Elk flew to his feet, a look of despair on his face as he raised his hand and pointed at Jack.

"You are Blackfoot," the warrior declared, then stalked out of Many Horses' lodge before anyone could stop him.

When Jack managed to look up, Many Horses was studying him shrewdly. "Have you spoken to your wife of leaving?" the old chief asked unexpectedly. Jack's eyes flickered briefly to where Medicine Weasel sat, his face drawn down in sadness.

"Yes," Jack answered finally. "She will go with me as will our son."

Many Horses filled the silence with the quick tapping sound of him emptying his pipe. "Then it will be," the old chief announced. "Go in peace, Fast Horse. But take these words to heart. You are not an orphan, you have a home and a people."

As the meeting broke up, Medicine Weasel caught up with Jack and invited him to walk with him. Jack slowed his pace, glancing at the medicine man. He looked older and a bit lost, and Jack felt guilt flood his body. Taking his daughter and grandson off was a hell of a way to thank a man for saving his life.

But when Medicine Weasel turned to him, it seemed his thoughts were on something else.

"Lodge Skins had a dream two moons ago that you would come and tell us of your leaving," Medicine Weasel began. "I knew before this, but I also knew you would tell us in your own time." Jack felt there was more so he waited.

"In this dream of Lodge Skin's, you did go, but he said you came back to us when your son was still a child. He said that two rivers run in your heart, one white, one red, and you will have to endure much because of this."

"I think I'd trade life itself to keep Raven and John-Charles safe,"

Jack said, feeling the hopelessness of it all. When he turned and looked at Medicine Weasel, his father-in-law merely nodded, his face grim.

"I'm going to miss all of this," Jack added, emotion making his voice raspy and raw. Both of the men paused to look out over the land.

For a brief moment, Jack felt peace settle over him, as it always did when he took to the country; slow and thick, like taking a long draw of good whiskey and feeling it ease through his veins. Here, he had had everything a man could want: a woman to keep camp with, good company when he wanted, and a freedom he could never explain to anyone who hadn't lived it.

But he knew in his heart that he would trade it all to keep his wife and son safe, to keep the Blackfoot safe. Even knowing that didn't stop the tug of loss as he looked out past the last of the lodges over the land, to the plains that seemed to rim the sky and the great mountains beyond, land that suited him better than anything he had ever known.

"I wonder if I'll ever see this place again, the way I see it now," Jack said, almost to himself.

"You will be back," Medicine Weasel said with great conviction. When he turned to Jack, his eyes were not hopeful but calm and shining with the knowing of age. "It's not just my daughter that's claimed you, JackWade. It's this land."

Blackfoot Encampment,
Montana Territory
1865

Mrs. Callie McGregor
Plumas City, California

Dear Callie,
Well, the deed is done. I know the Blackfoot don't exactly agree with our leaving, but they have accepted it.

Raven asked me tonight where we were going and it struck me that I don't even know. A farm might be the answer; close enough to town but far enough that I could keep my family from the judging I know is sure to come. Or maybe a ranch. I'm taking most of my horses with us as we'll need to sell some to make a good start of it wherever we go. There's an old fellow I know in Deer Lodge who might give me a square deal on them, too, if he's still alive. I hope so, because I don't have a dime to my name.

Callie, I don't know why I'm still sitting here writing this. I'm so torn over the whole thing. It's like I'm caught; I'm worried for Lone Elk and Medicine Weasel and the rest of the Blackfoot, but I'm worried for us, too. Raven and John-Charles are all that I am. I think I'd rather die myself than have to live without either of them. Yet I'm taking them from the only home they've ever known—the first place I've called home in a long, long time.

Ah, well, what was it Pa used to say? "Trouble gives a fellow a chance to learn his strength—or lack of it." I guess we'll soon see what I have, Sis.

Jack

Blackfoot Encampment, Montana Territory 1865

Mrs. Callie McGregor
Plumas City, California

Dear Callie,

Just woke up. I had the oddest dream. I dreamed I was walking down a street and I saw this body lying in the middle of the street wrapped in a winding sheet. So I walked over to the body to see who it was that died, but when I pulled the sheet away from the face, it was me that'd died.

I ain't ever put much stock in dreams, but this one was so real the hairs on my neck are still raised.

Maybe it is a good thing we are leaving here now.

Jack

P.S. Say a prayer for us, will you, Sis?

Jack had forgotten how ferocious Lone Elk could look, but as the warrior skirted the high ridge above them, pushing his horse to catch up to them before they left, the emotion on his face was plain to see. Pebbles and rocks danced and clattered down the steep embankment as the horse turned around a sharp bend in the trail but Lone Elk appeared not to notice, so intent was he to reach them before they were gone.

"Blackfoot do not run, Fast Horse," Lone Elk called down, prodding his horse to keep up with their pace below.

"Blackfoot protect what they love," Jack answered back, his voice carrying in the still summer morning. He glanced to Raven, who rode beside him with John-Charles, but her face was hidden by her dark curtain of hair. He *wasn't* running this time, he thought. Not really.

"Not alone," Lone Elk called down with childlike stubbornness. "Blackfoot stand together, not alone." In spite of the heaviness in his heart, Jack smiled, shielding his eyes from the sun as he looked up at the warrior he called friend and was glad Lone Elk decided to see them off. Jack thought of the last night he saw Duel alive and how he had wanted to say more than what he had—and later wishing with all his being he had. *Mistakes are better than any schoolhouse you'd set in—if ye learn from 'em,* Stem had told him once, and Jack thought it was a shame that he hadn't really understood those words until now.

"I am not alone," he shouted up to the warrior, his voice catching a bit. "As long as I carry the Blackfoot in my heart, as long as I remember I have a brother, Lone Elk, I will never be alone."

Lone Elk stopped his horse suddenly, his body so still he appeared like a proud statue carved out of the hillside as the sun blazed behind him. Although Jack couldn't see the expression on his face, he figured that Lone Elk, like he, knew there were no more words left to say. *Go in safety, brother,* Lone Elk finally signed. Without another word, he slowly turned his horse along the narrow trail and headed back toward camp. As Jack turned to Raven, he saw her pretty face streaked with silent tears.

Seeing her tears brought back another memory of another time and another family forced to leave their people, their home. He saw again his sister Callie's tear-streaked face and his pa's jaw hardened by the choices he had to make. *This ain't a mistake. I'm doing the right thing,* he told himself, hearing the echo of his father's voice in his own. *No matter how hard this is right now, I'm doing right by them.*

Jack sidled up next to Raven, leaning over as he gently brushed her tears away.

"Trust me," he said, his voice soft with understanding. "I know it is hard for us now, but you'll see, Raven, we're going to have a good life."

But when he looked at his son, silent as a grave in the robed cocoon on Raven's back, the green eyes so much like his own that stared back at him with such a steady look of foreboding, he had to wonder.

Twenty-One

The valley made him think of Duel. Or maybe it was the wind, blowing softly and warm and parting the knee-high buffalo grass in such a way that made Jack feel as if they were expected. Jack hawed and whistled, pushing the horses on through as Raven quirted her pony to catch the front of the herd, her long black hair waving behind her as she looked about the settlement of Deer Lodge with childlike wonder. Earlier, she had been so full of questions: Were there many white women in this place? What do they wear? What should she do if one speaks to her? Why do they have their homes so far apart? Do your people not wish to be near each other?

For Raven it was all new, but for Jack, it felt like he was tiptoeing back into his past as wary as a boy stepping into a house that might have a haunt. If a heart was able to hold haunts, Jack felt his must. Memories and faces rose up before him so clearly he felt for a moment he was back in that time again but he forced the memories down, telling himself they were things of the past, laid to rest with the man he had once been; running without knowing where he was running to. At least this time he knew what direction to take—or at least he hoped he did, he thought, watching his son bounce and sway in his little cocoon on his mother's back.

A little while down, they passed a white woman out in front of a hovel no bigger than an outhouse, scrubbing what looked to be rags against an old scrub board. The woman glanced up briefly as they passed, then went back to her scrubbing as if they were not worth the effort to lift her head again. But Raven was entranced by the woman. She fell behind, watching the woman scrub and then dip the clothes back into the dirty water, over and over again. Jack saw a frown knit her brow, her eyes taking everything in. Lastly, she looked at the woman's appearance and he saw her unconsciously smooth a hand over her soft antelope-skin dress, her fingers brushing the intricate beadwork. He could see in her eyes that she didn't think much of the disheveled white woman, and he could almost hear her thinking: *And I was afraid of what they would think of me!*

Jack grinned to himself, heartened to see some of her confidence return. She had been so quiet since they left the Blackfoot and edgy too, glancing over her shoulder from time to time with a tense look on her face that said she expected danger of some kind.

They followed along a stream that cut left out of the valley, past the few huts and cabins that Jack thought he recognized and more he didn't. It appeared Deer Lodge had grown some since he was last there, and it made him wonder if the old man would still be around; he'd seemed the type who didn't like being crowded in on. His worries were for nothing, he soon realized as they rounded a dense stand of trees, and he saw the familiar cabin come into view. Jack whistled and Raven trotted her pony forward, heading the horses off until they finally came to rest near a wide lip of the stream. They quickly dismounted and headed for the cabin.

Nothing appeared to have been touched since the day Jack rode away from the place except that one of the tepees looked to have been abandoned a good while back. The old-timer was sitting in the same chair on the porch, but this time he was wide awake.

"Come on up and set a spell. Dinner'll be served shortly," he announced, as if no time had passed at all, smiling as he struggled up from his chair and immediately reaching his arms out for John-Charles.

Raven glanced at Jack hesitantly and Jack nodded, liking the old guy's familiar disposition. "Mind if I hold yer boy?" he asked, though in fact he already had John-Charles wrapped in his wiry old arms as he turned to Jack. "I suspect he's yers, ain't ever seen no Blackfoot with green eyes, tho' I did see one as white as snow, albiner I'm thinkin'—say he became a killer when the whole tribe disowned him but I figger he was jes' mean." He studied Jack for a long moment or two. "Figger you heard I got yer friend buried jes' like you asked," he said. When Jack nodded his thanks, the old man grunted as if satisfied. "Well, bein' we're old acquaintances and sech the polite thing to do is trade names. Constantinople is my name, Connie to my friends. I know your name, young feller, but I ain't ever had the pleasure of meeting yer wife 'afore."

"Well, Connie, this here is my wife, Raven, and the boy you're holding is my son, John-Charles," Jack said hurriedly in an effort to keep up; the man talked more than anyone he had ever met in his life. But there was a general feeling of goodness and cheer that made you want to be around him, just to listen. He even had Raven charmed into a full-blown smile. She looked a bit dazed, too, but Jack could see she was enjoying it all.

"Glad to meet ye, missus. I'd shake if my hands weren't so full."

Connie jiggled John-Charles a bit and laughed as the baby stared wide-eyed at the long, white beard that hung clear to his chest. John-Charles glanced from the old man to Jack, to Raven, and it was his mother his gaze locked on, his lower lip trembling. Before he could start to cry, Connie quickly handed him back to Raven.

"Thankee, ma'am. Nice to hold a little one again," he said, a sad look in his eyes. Jack wondered if it had anything to do with the empty tepee. "Once they get big and ye can't even hold 'em home—let alone in your arms."

"Little Woman?" he hollered abruptly. "You come on out here and meet our company."

The Indian woman who stepped onto the porch was anything but little, but she had a comely face and eyes that were kind—if not a little shy—as she glanced from her husband to the three of them. Jack heard Raven's quick intake of breath and turned to see her studying the woman's dress with an excited look on her face.

"She is *Cree,*" Raven said. Without further explanation, she turned and began speaking to the woman in what Jack guessed was her own language. He glanced at Connie, who smiled and shrugged his thin shoulders.

"Ain't nothin' that'll stop women from havin' a hen party. This here just proves my case."

Jack laughed. "Well, what 'say we leave them to their party and go take a look at them horses of mine?"

"I'd like that. Don't do much buyin' anymore but I know them that do," he said as they made their way down the stairs and out to the yard, then raised up a bony finger of warning. "Step lively, Jack. I got my mother-in-law in that second tepee and she's likely to spit at ye when ye walk by. She don't do nothin' else but spit, but she's got a deadly aim for an old woman."

As they skirted the tepee, the flap indeed slapped open and Jack caught a glimpse of an Indian woman no older than Connie himself peering out, salt-and-pepper hair plaited against a wrinkled face that had drawn up in a pucker. They both sidestepped at the same time, but Connie ended up the loser.

"Dernit," Connie said, wiping his boots off in the grass. "That's the third time she's hit my boot this week."

Jack shook his head in amusement. It was no wonder Connie liked the porch so much. The visit wasn't turning out anything like he had expected but maybe better in an odd, confused kind of way. He looked over his shoulder and saw Raven still standing on the porch with Little Woman, laughing, and the scene looked so natural it made him glad he had brought her to Deer Lodge.

Raven was thinking much of the same. There was something

about the Cree woman that reminded her of Laughs-A-Lot—but even more than that, she reminded Raven of herself, living in a world she wasn't born to and hoping for a friend to help ease the lonely feeling . . . to understand.

"My mother believes in putting men in their place," Little Woman said apologetically once she had contained her laughter, but her eyes crinkled mischievously. "Would you like to meet her?"

"Yes, I would," Raven answered, still laughing. Little Woman's eyes rested briefly on John-Charles, who had fallen asleep in her arms, a wistful look on her face, then she met Raven's gaze again and she smiled warmly.

"Follow me, then. She always comes to the house after Connie leaves." The cabin was dark compared with the blinding afternoon sun, and Little Woman lit a lantern, leading the way as Raven looked around her with interest. She wasn't sure she liked the closed-in feeling of the wood home, but Little Woman had managed to make it inviting all the same; everything was clean and orderly, the floors were spotless, and the windows sparkled. In the main room, she saw a sewing machine and a table, both covered with pretty cloths. Against the far wall hung cooking utensils and pots and pans, and below was a cookstove with a large pot boiling with what smelled like some kind of stew. There were two bedrooms off to the right that had bright-hued blankets covering the rough beds. Raven tried to imagine herself and Fast Horse sleeping in such a room, but all she could think of was their lodge. *It is a good home,* her father had said, and the memory of his words caused an ache in her breast.

"I hope you will forgive my bad manners," the older woman announced as she entered the room. "I have no patience for men." She smiled and Raven saw the same mischief around her eyes as she had seen in Little Woman's. "Besides, I like to see my son-in-law jump." She took a bite of the stew that was simmering in the pot, rolled it around in her mouth, then nodded, wiping her mouth with the back of her hand. "Here, let me see your boy. It is a shame you are only visiting—the three of us could raise him up properly. He will be a very handsome man and handsome men need to be raised properly, otherwise they turn vain."

"He looks like his father," Raven said, feeling as though she needed to say something in Fast Horse's defense.

"Yes, he does look like his father," the older woman admitted. "It is wise to choose a good-looking man, that way your children will not turn out ugly. It is good if the man keeps his looks, too, that way you have something pleasant to look upon. When you get to be my age, all you have energy for is looking."

Little Woman and Raven looked at each other, laughter erupting from both of them at the same time and as Little Woman's mother joined in, Raven thought their laughter sounded good together. Sitting in the little cabin with the two Cree women, she felt happy in a way she hadn't felt in a very long time. A time long before Fast Horse came, when she still had a mother, and she suddenly felt the strange feeling that she was being given back something—a gift—in the midst of all that she had lost.

John-Charles woke in the older woman's arms and let out a wail of distress, seeing the strange woman looking down at him. As Little Woman's mother quickly brought him to her and she began to nurse her son, Raven felt a rush of love, looking down at him, and a sudden hope for their future. Maybe she could ask Fast Horse if they could stay in this valley. Surely they were far enough from the soldiers now. Heartened by the thought, she planted a kiss on her son's forehead. *Sometimes, little one, even when we think all is lost, it is not,* she thought. How she wished he could understand now. *When you are older, there are so many things I will teach you.* Feeling the older woman's eyes still upon her, she raised her head and saw that the woman seemed to understand.

"Grandfather is always with us, even when we believe he is not, huh, daughter?" she said and Raven nodded, not trusting herself to speak. The woman then lifted her nose to the air, as if smelling a change, and abruptly took her leave.

"The men will be returning soon," Little Woman explained, smiling as she sat down next to Raven. "I have something for you. I made it when I first came here, when I was *Little Woman.*" The Cree woman laughed at her own joke as she pulled the dress carefully from the box it had been stored in.

A white woman's dress, Raven thought, brushing the strange-feeling material with her hand as John-Charles suckled. It had been made with great care, the stitches so fine she could barely see them. There was a long row of buttons that ran down the length of the back, and as Raven touched them she wondered what Fast Horse would think of her in such a dress.

"Has it been hard, living away from your people?" she asked, looking up from the dress. Little Woman seemed to consider the question for a moment.

"It is hard sometimes," she nodded finally. "But it would be harder to be without my husband."

"Maybe your man, he would like to stay here?" Little Woman asked shyly. Raven smiled, knowing Little Woman was lonely for a friend, too.

"I was thinking of asking him tonight," Raven said. "When I wear this dress."

"I was thinking the same," Little Woman said, her dark eyes large and very serious. Both women smiled at each other, taking joy in sharing a small joke between friends.

Raven didn't really care for the dress; it made her feel hot and confined, like a prisoner bound in scratchy material. She glanced around the room and on impulse, she touched the walls and they felt scratchy, too. *Was everything so unyielding in the white world?* she wondered, shaking her head. In spite of her thoughts, she smoothed a hand over the dress and listened to the muffled sound of the men talking out on the front porch, waiting for the time when Fast Horse would come to find her and wondering what he would think when he saw her dressed as she was. She heard him laugh at something the old man had said and his laughter caused her to smile.

She was glad they had come to Deer Lodge. Everything felt better since they had arrived and she thought finding a friend in Little Woman was a good omen. Now all she had to do was talk her husband into staying. . . .

Jack found her like that, staring out of the little window with a thoughtful look on her face, with what looked to be a store-bought dress on, and it stopped him in his tracks. She looked beautiful, of course, and had even pulled her hair up into a bun that hung loose on her slender neck, but something about the dress bothered him. It was as if a part of Raven had been taken away. He stepped into the room and closed the door softly behind him.

Raven turned from the window and seeing him standing there became suddenly shy, her hands smoothing the skirt of the dress nervously as she smiled at him. "Little Woman gave me the dress. I think it fits pretty good," she said, looking at him expectantly.

"You are beautiful no matter what you wear," he said gently, brushing a thumb across her brow and her brow furrowed suddenly beneath his touch.

"You do not like it?"

Jack didn't know what to say. As he tried to form the words that would make sense, he saw tears well up in Raven's eyes and he realized she mistook his silence for anger. He pulled her to him quickly, putting his arms around her.

"Aw, don't you see?" he whispered into her hair. "Already you're worrying about things you shouldn't. I remember the woman who stood out from the other women in her antelope-skin dress, proud and unashamed as she danced before me. That is the woman I married." He tipped his finger under her chin. "I don't want you to change, Raven. I don't want you to forget who you are. We had to leave our home and come to this place, but we don't have to change who *we* are."

"Can we stay here?" she asked suddenly, catching Jack off guard for a moment.

"Well, I was going to ask the same." He smiled, seeing the delight in her eyes, and wished with all of his heart he didn't have anything else to say but he did. He took a deep breath and went on. "I might have to make a quick trip to Virginia City to sell the horses—Connie says there's an auction that's going to take place down there fairly soon."

"This Virginia City, isn't this the place that caused you so much trouble?" Raven asked, her eyes clouding over. He saw her glance at John-Charles, who lay on the bed sleeping.

"Yes, but I think the trouble is finished," he said with more confidence than he felt.

He had wrestled against thinking of Lillie, of wondering how she would take seeing Raven and John-Charles, but the wrestling seemed a losing battle.

I love you, Lillie. The words caused him to shut his eyes in shame, and he tried again to will her memory away.

"Jack Wade?"

He opened his eyes to see Raven watching him curiously and he felt his resolve return. He would do right by her and John-Charles, no matter what the cost. They deserved that much.

"We need the money from those horses to make a go of it," he said finally. "I was thinking though, if you want, you and John-Charles could stay here with Little Woman while I go. Maybe look around and pick out a spot where you'd like our home to be."

Raven looked at him for a long time as if she were weighing the tuggings of her heart, then she finally shook her head no. "We must stay together," she said and Jack nodded, though he was still unconvinced that it was such a wise move to take her along. But the truth was, he didn't want to be without her or John-Charles, either. Surely there wouldn't be any harm in going for one day, not after all this time. They would get in and out just as fast as they could, he told himself. With the auction going on, it wasn't likely they would even be noticed.

"I guess it's settled then," he said finally.

Raven quickly dried her eyes and with a smile as wide and open as a child's, she turned her back to him. "Good," she said, glancing over her shoulder. "I'm glad that it is settled then. Now, can you help me get this dress off?"

> Deer Lodge,
> Montana Territory
> October, 1865

Mrs. Callie McGregor
Plumas City, California

Dear Callie,

I feel like I'm following the steps of my life backwards. Like some invisible hand is leading me back to where it all started and I'm not sure if it's good or not.

We've only just arrived in Deer Lodge to find out that old fellow I told you about doesn't deal in horseflesh anymore. Connie (that's his name) did tell me of a livestock auction that's due to take place in Virginia City in a couple of days and he seems to think it would be my best bet. Virginia City. I would've laughed if I could have. Fate doesn't pay much attention to our worries, does it? Truth is, I ain't as worried about facing Frank Monroe as I am Lillie. I sure never planned for things to turn out like this, Sis. But Raven and John-Charles have to come first now, so I'm going back. The more I've thought on it tonight, the more I realize it's my only way to get the ready cash we need.

Callie, why is it that the older we get, the mistakes we make are harder to live down and the choices more painful? Seems like it would be the other way around, doesn't it? I did ask Raven to stay in Deer Lodge while I go, but she's determined to keep us all together. She admitted to me tonight that she has been afraid of everything being taken from her again . . . like before when she lost her husband and baby to the pox. Can't recall if I ever told you about that. Seems like there aren't no strangers to grief anymore, does it, Sis?

I know one thing, I want to give Raven and John-Charles back better than what I took them away from, and if that means facing some demons in Virginia City, so be it. Makes me think of how Pa felt about us when he decided to take us west; I guess I'd face just about anything for my family.

Jack

Montana Territory
October, 1865

Mrs. Callie McGregor
Plumas City, California

Dear Callie,

We are now only a day or so out of Virginia City, so I thought I'd sit and write you about what happened today. I guess most would look at it as a small thing, but I'm finding out more and more that little things can mean the most.

I recall telling you that I had a feeling that this land would make me, but I might have been wrong, I think—oh, the land is part of it, but it's what you can see through your loved ones eyes that changes the way you look at things. I never believed that so strongly as I did today. See, Raven and I were riding along the cut-banks of a river when we both spotted an eagle soaring high above us, then another appeared. Raven pulled her horse up quickly to watch and just when I was about to remind her that we didn't have time to stop, I noticed the strangest look on her face. It was like she was up there with them eagles, too. Those eagles circled around each other then kind of crashed together, locking claws, and all of a sudden they were falling down through the sky, just falling. It was a sight to see; four huge wings beating, claws locked in a kind of death grip as they looped down toward the river, then just as I was sure they were to hit the water, they broke apart, one flying back up toward the bluffs and the other following. I told Raven I'd never seen anything like it, eagles trying to kill each other like that, and she smiled. "They were courting," she told me. "She was testing his courage; the mate she picks will be the one who holds on the longest, until the very end, and that mate will be hers for life."

She told me tonight it was a good omen, us seeing that. "It is how we will be," she said, "holding on until the end." Callie, never in my life have I felt the urge to thank someone for showing me something like that, but the thank-you died on my lips because they seemed too small of words for what I felt. By the time I did start thinking of what I might say, I looked over and she had already fallen asleep with John-Charles in her arms, and now I feel like tomorrow can't come soon enough.

Jack

Part Four

〜

"Let the end try the man."

—*Jack Wade*

Twenty-Two

Virginia City hadn't changed much. The dusty streets were still filled with peddlers and prospectors and just about any other fortune seeker you could imagine. But there was none of the excitement he had felt when he had first come to the crowded, bustling little town. All Jack felt was apprehension; the ghosts of his past weren't ghosts but very much alive and with every minute that passed, he felt himself grow edgier. Now that the auction was over and he had a bankroll in his pocket, it was time to leave town. And soon. Jack lifted his eyes to the leadened sky as a north wind blew across the tatters of clouds.

"We ought to head out now before this weather gets worse," he said, looking down at Raven as she tried to shield John-Charles from a sudden gust of wind. She looked so pretty standing there like that with the wind in her hair, her smile so sweet and trusting. He had watched her dress so carefully that morning, making sure her hair was brushed until it shined, switching to her best moccasins, and he realized as he had watched her that she had been thinking of his past as well. With the auction going off without a hitch, she grew bolder, though, even venturing into some shops, chattering excitedly about what they would have in their new home. But now, as she looked up at him, he saw something flicker in her eyes that made her look unsure . . . apprehensive, too, and he wondered if it was the weather or something else.

"Unless you want to end up carin' for a husband with a broken back," he said with a pointed look to the mountainous stack of purchases he carried in his arms, trying to tease away the worry on her face.

"I would not mind that much," Raven shrugged, mischief suddenly appearing in her eyes. "You were much easier to handle when you were sick."

"That's only because I saw who was going to be nursin' me," Jack laughed, winking at her. He lifted his eyes from hers only for a moment to study the crowds, and the laughter in him died as he saw the familiar figure that was walking toward him.

"Well, Jack Wade, I almost derned near walked right past ya," Ely said, unable to hide his surprise as he surveyed the long hair, buckskin britches, and moccasins. "Dern, it's good to see ya," he added, finally grabbing Jack's hand and pumping it with all the strength he could manage, as if to show Jack things were different with him, too.

Jack turned to Raven, fighting to maintain his composure as she searched his face, curious. "Raven, this is Ely, an old friend of mine," he said easily, instinctively drawing upon all his years as a gambler. "Ely, I'd like you to meet my wife."

"Missus." Ely took Raven's hand, staring at it a bit longer than what might be considered proper, then managed to get a hold of himself and smile. "Looks like we both tied the knot. Remember Mabel? You ought to come by and see what she's done to the place—you wouldn't recognize it. Why. . . ."

Whatever Ely had meant to say faded off as both men turned to see what had caught Raven's attention so suddenly, and they both spotted Lillie at the same time, standing frozen to the spot not five paces from them.

Jack felt as if all of the air had rushed out of his body as they looked at each other. Lillie was the same beautiful Lillie who had haunted his dreams—but different, too. She seemed stronger, somehow. Jack tried to read what might have happened to her while he was gone, but she hid her secrets well. But when he saw the dimple in her cheek suddenly appear, it tore at his insides.

"Good to see you, Lillie," was all he said, and Lillie was struck with the fear that she was going to have to say something back. Months that had seemed like years faded to nothing as she felt the old memories and yearnings come alive, fresh as the day they were born. She thought she saw the same emotion in Jack's eyes, too, before he turned away, and she remembered an old gambler telling her once that the face sometimes had cards it didn't want to show.

Jack looked down at his Indian wife and his son and smiled. Lillie suddenly felt like she'd been dunked into a bottomless well of cold water. Somewhere in the distance she thought she heard him making introductions and she tried to get her thoughts together, tried not to hate the pretty Indian woman. But when their eyes finally met, she was struck by the deep fear in the woman's dark eyes. *She knows who I am,* Lillie thought. *She knows and she's as scared as I am.* As jealous as she was, she couldn't help but admire the woman's pluck as she took Lillie's hand in her own and smiled shyly.

Was there anything that made sense anymore? Lillie wondered wearily after she had made her excuses and walked away from them, heading in the direction of the Pair-O-Dice. As she stepped through the doors of the saloon, she saw Mabel standing at the window, but she jumped back from it, looking guiltily at Lillie.

"Get a good look, Mabel?"

"I guess I got a right to be curious with everyone talking about him living with the Indians. He looks like an Indian himself with that long hair and all," Mabel said defensively but her look was contrite. "Guess you must hate that squaw."

"Hate her?" Lillie looked at Mabel for a long moment before turning to look out the window to the street, her smile bittersweet. "No, I don't hate her. Might be I wish I did, though."

Jack lifted his eyes once more to the darkened sky as Ely took his leave, feeling as though the heaviness of it had settled right down over him as the tumble of memories and emotions played through his mind. He had never intended to hurt anyone but he had. *How did everything go so wrong?* he wondered but no answer came to mind. He glanced down at his son and he found himself smiling in spite of it all, seeing John-Charles looking up at him like he did. The baby's green eyes watered and blinked against the chilled gusts of wind, and Jack suddenly took him from Raven, rewrapping the blanket so all that could be seen was a tiny nose peeking out. Raven gave him a tolerant smile.

"She is very beautiful," Raven said as Jack offered her his arm to help steer her through the heavy crowd in the street, and he looked at her closely. Whatever touches of sadness or regret were for him to feel, but he wouldn't have Raven suffer for his doings. He saw only honesty in her eyes, and as her dark head bent over their son, kissing his chubby face until he laughed, Jack felt his heart swell with love for her. She was so good, he thought, and he resolved himself not to look back. What was done was done.

"My *wife* is beautiful," he countered and was glad to see the happiness shining in her eyes—and the humor.

"You've become a wise man," Raven laughed and he joined in, feeling the love for his wife and son soothe over the old hurts. *We're going to make it,* he thought with a tug of relief. He glanced over his shoulder one last time at Virginia City—this time in farewell—then frowned as he felt the hairs on his neck raise. A sudden feeling of foreboding started low in his belly and he searched the street. He then caught a glimpse of Lillie, running through the crowds toward them, and real fear snaked through his body when he saw the gun in her hand.

"What in the hell is she up to?" he asked almost to himself. When he turned back to Raven, he saw Frank Monroe materialize out of nowhere, aiming his gun at him with a hard look in his eyes. Raven saw him, too, and in the next instant everything seemed to turn into a slow-moving dream. Jack fumbled with John-Charles, meaning to pass him off to Raven so he could draw his own weapon, but he knew he was too late—even before the loud crack of the gun being fired filled his ears. Raven flung herself in front of him and John-Charles, and just as Jack cried out, he felt her body thrown back into his own. They both dropped to the dusty street as John-Charles began to wail, arms and legs pistoning against the tight grip of Jack's arms. Jack felt his body begin to shake as he pulled Raven to him, cradling her head in his free arm. Somewhere another shot exploded in the street and he heard people running, but his eyes were on Raven and the blood pouring from the wound in her chest.

Raven's eyes sought his then, hurt and startled as if she hadn't expected life to be so cruel, and he knew in his being she was dying. "The baby?" she rasped and Jack swallowed thickly, brushing her long hair from her face, then propping her up with one arm as he laid John-Charles on her chest. *I'm afraid,* he remembered her saying. *I'm afraid that everything will be taken from me, like before. . . .*

"He's fine," he said finally, feeling his heart shatter into thousands of tiny pieces. "We're both fine."

Raven looked down at the baby wistfully, but when her eyes met Jack's again they were calm, almost proud.

"My son," she whispered and tried to smile, but her eyes focused on the sky to somewhere far away. Before he could tell her that he loved her she was gone.

I never told her I loved her, he thought, anguished. *She took a bullet for me, for our son, and I couldn't even tell her I loved her.*

Jack kept her tight to his chest, rocking back and forth, thinking somewhere in his heart if he didn't stop rocking, it wouldn't be the end. *It is how we will be,* she had said, *holding on until the end. . . .*

A quiet fell over the crowded street and all that could be heard was the empty click of the pistol Lillie held as she pulled the trigger again and again, standing over Frank's body with the wary look of a caged animal that doesn't believe it's been freed.

"No more," Lillie said to no one in particular. "No more."

Jack looked down at the still figure of his wife and touched his finger to her cheek. The tears of happiness that shined in her eyes only moments ago trailed down her lifeless face as if to mark the end, and he felt a horrible helplessness build in him. It was all his fault. He'd thought he could take her away from the danger, but all he'd done was walk her straight into the arms of it.

It was only going to be for one day, he thought desperately. *We're not through yet. . . .* He looked around at the crowd of gawkers that surrounded them in the street for someone to come and take it back, to undo what had just been done, but the only eyes that met his with understanding were Lillie's. She stood, tears streaming down her face, still limply clutching the gun that she had used to kill Frank Monroe, and suddenly something in Jack snapped.

The sound that came out of him was so primal, so filled with vengeance, that the crowds parted an instant before he shoved past them to where Frank's body lay on the other side of the street. Jack dove on Frank's back and some of the women screamed and men shouted for him to stop, but Jack heard none of it as he savagely yanked Frank's head back by his hair, his knife slicing with deadly accuracy. He uttered a hoarse cry, filled with agony and rage as he held the scalp up to the heavens as if to show proof of what had been done to him, to his life.

"Lord-a-mercy," a miner in the crowd declared, breaking the hushed silence.

"Yeah," his friend said in agreement. "I ain't never heard nothin' like it. You'd think he was the one that was scalped."

There were other things said, too, but the only thing that broke through his rage was the sound of his son's anguished cries as he lay in the dusty street with a mother who could no longer hold him. The undertaker, seeing Jack's attention diverted, quickly grabbed one of Frank's arms and started to drag him away as Jack headed for his son until the figure of a man blocked his way. There was a star pinned to his chest.

"I got to take you in, son," the man said. His eyes were wary but determined and his voice dipped down lower. "Just till I can get them cutthroats of Frank's that are standing across the way hustled out of town. If nothin' else, think of your boy; he's already lost his ma."

At the mention of John-Charles, Jack made a move for the man but grief made him slow and the sheriff pulled his gun and aimed it level at Jack. "I ain't never liked Frank Monroe myself, so don't make me do something I'll regret."

"My boy," Jack uttered finally, and the man's eyes flickered understandingly. As they glanced back to the street, they both saw Lillie gingerly pick up the frightened infant and hold him to her chest.

"I got him, Jack," she said, tears streaming down her face. "You just go on with the sheriff."

Jack remained silent as a grave as the sheriff quietly began to lead him away and he looked over his shoulder. The crowd had died away and he saw Raven's body lying in the dust, like a forgotten doll, as the wind rushed and whistled around him, vengeful and loud—but not loud enough to shut out the silent screams of his heart.

"Lillie? Don't let them leave her like that, like she was nothin'," he called, his voice breaking with grief. Lillie nodded, the raw anguish in his face causing her eyes to fill again. The horrible, senseless tragedy had brushed everything aside that had been left unsaid between them, all of the questions and hurt and anger, leaving only compassion in its wake. But even compassion couldn't shield her heart from the words he spoke next.

"She was my wife. She was my wife. . . ."

Jack stood in the dank cell of the jailhouse, gazing through the bars on the window into the night, searching the dark like a child lost and hoping for someone to take his hand and bring him home as the gulch started up another night, oblivious. Somewhere in the back of his mind he could hear the piano banging, people laughing, and Jack hated them for their laughter. He had tried to bargain with

God—mainly because he didn't have the strength to argue with Him anymore—then he turned to begging.

Just let her come tell me she's all right, he silently pleaded. He waited and waited, staring hard at every shape and shadow until the sun finally began to peek over the mountains again and he felt his childish hope fade with the new day.

There would be no bargaining or begging with God, he realized hopelessly. For whatever reason, Raven had been taken from him and was never, never coming back. Maybe even somewhere down deep inside of himself he had known it but hadn't wanted to accept it.

One thing he did know for sure was that he would go to his own grave wondering how God could allow so much pain and no way to escape it.

It was then and only then that he dropped his head into his hands, allowing his broad shoulders to sag under the weight he couldn't bear anymore, and he began to cry.

The procession of Blackfoot that rode into town four days later was bound to be noticed. It wasn't every day that the gulch witnessed fifteen somber Blackfoot warriors, dressed and armed to the hilt, riding through the main thoroughfare of their town. People whispered and pointed but all gave the group wide berth for they had sensed an underlying current of rage beneath the somber expressions. Even the reporter from the *Montana Post* kept his distance as he furiously scribbled his notes, watching with rapt attention as what appeared to be the elder of the bunch dismounted and slowly walked toward the jail.

Jack heard the commotion and scrambled to the window to see what was going on, and he saw Medicine Weasel walking toward him with a look on his face that no parent should ever have. *I've done this,* he thought, anguish and guilt welling up in him fresh. *I've done this to us all.*

Unable to bear facing the man he loved like a father, he dropped his eyes in shame.

"It is not your fault, Fast Horse, lift your eyes," the old man commanded in Blackfoot. Jack felt every emotion he had tried to push down break free and well up in his eyes.

"Aw, God, she was so happy," he said as the dam of all he was feeling and thinking burst. "She even picked out things for our new home. The bullet was meant for me, not her. She just jumped in front of me . . ." Jack looked at Medicine Weasel, misery keeping him from going on. He saw the medicine man's eyes were bright with unshed tears—but something else flickered in the dark depths, too, like pride for his daughter.

"How did you know?"

"The Above Ones came to me in a vision and told me that she would die so that you would live. They whispered of her bravery to me, comforting me as I cried out to them." The old man glanced away briefly. On his face, Jack saw acceptance of his daughter's fate, but no comfort.

"I am taking her back to our people for burial," Medicine Weasel said finally, as he turned back to stare at Jack through the bars of the cell. "She would have wanted it this way."

We will grow old together and when we die, we will be buried next to each other on this spot. . . . Jack squeezed his eyes shut against the memory. No, no, no, he chanted over and over in his head, trying to shut it away but he couldn't. *We will watch our son grow into a man and see his children born. . . .*

"You can't have the boy," Jack said suddenly, his eyes snapping open. He would die before any more was taken from him. But Medicine Weasel didn't appear to want to argue over John-Charles. He looked sad.

"No," he agreed solemnly. "The boy and you have a different journey, one you will make together. Raven was just the beginning for the two of you."

"By God, she was your daughter. Is that all you thought of her?" Jack asked, his anger returning fresh, but the medicine man seemed to understand.

"She taught you peace, how to live again. The Above Ones have decided it was enough," Medicine Weasel answered, his voice even but his eyes were unreadable and Jack wondered if he was trying to convince himself of the words as well. Even if he had thought of arguing about it, he didn't. The medicine man's face was set with finality.

"They have her laid out at a place called the Pair-O-Dice," he said, knowing there was nothing else left to say. He reached over and grabbed the letter that lay on the rickety table and handed it through the bars to Medicine Weasel. "I'd be obliged if you could take this. There's a lady at the Pair-O-Dice by the name of Lillie who's looking after John-Charles; she'll know to mail it to my sister."

The medicine man took the letter from him and as he did, their eyes met through the bars one last time. "We will see each other again," Medicine Weasel said. "Until then, remember Many Horses' words and keep them in your heart."

A little while later, Jack watched from the window as the Blackfoot warriors he had once called brothers passed him by as they made their way out of town. Medicine Weasel was at the end of the line, leading the horse that carried his daughter's lifeless body. He felt his life leave with them.

Many Horses was wrong, he thought. He didn't have a family anymore or a people. He was an orphan.

Virginia City,
Montana Territory
October, 1865

Mrs. Callie McGregor
Plumas City, California

Dear Callie,

I finally got this paper here from the sheriff so that I could write and tell you what has happened. They got me locked up here so Frank Monroe's men can't get at me—not that I care.

Raven is dead. Frank tried to shoot me down, but Raven jumped in front of me and took the bullet herself. Death stole her so quickly I found myself sitting in the street, looking for her in the crowd that stood gawking at me, even though I held her in my arms.

It's all my fault, too. My idea to come back here, my enemies. But you know what, Sis? Of all the enemies I've had I'm beginning to think I'm my own worst enemy.

What kind of fool was I to think bringing her and John-Charles back with me could keep them safe? Medicine Weasel and his band will take Raven away for burial. I wish they wouldn't take her so soon. I need more time. I need to see her again, but now it's too late. You know, tonight I've tried and tried but I can't remember how her voice sounds. Why can't I remember her voice?

I know I should be strong for John-Charles, but I feel like it's taken all my strength just to write this. That dream of mine has come true. It's like I'm dead now. Only difference is I'm breathing. I'm a breathing dead man.

I wish I could die. How can I live in a world I hate?

Jack

P.S. Lillie shot Frank dead after he killed Raven. No one is talking much about it, not even the law. I think they're all grateful. I ain't. It should have been me who killed him.

Lillie laid down Jack's letter to Callie and stared out of the window of her room. She hadn't meant to pry, but she was desperate for answers. The Jack she knew seemed to have disappeared when the sheriff let him out of the jail cell.

The letter wasn't anything like she had expected. His words were raw and soul-baring . . . and scared. Nothing like the words that had come from him as he stood in her room only hours before and told her in a dead-sounding voice that he needed some time to think, that he would be back . . . could she just watch his son for a little while longer?

But she hadn't missed the way he had refused to look at her or his son directly . . . or the pure anguish on his face as he turned and stiffly walked back out the door. He was like a bomb ready to go off with nobody to help put out the fuse. He couldn't seem to talk to her about any of it, she thought, swallowing the hurt.

Lillie picked the letter up, then on second thought added the article she'd clipped from the *Post* that captured the awful day on its front page.

If his sister was anything like Lillie hoped, she knew Callie couldn't read that letter and see that article and not come to her brother's aid. If anyone needed family right now, it was Jack and his son.

She glanced over at the sleeping child and gently brushed the baby's hair back from his forehead, pity welling up in her for the motherless baby. She didn't know much about babies, but she thought it was odd that he hadn't cried since his mother's death.

John-Charles had awakened at her touch and was staring up at her solemnly.

He was an uncommonly handsome baby with his mother's skin and those green eyes like Jack's. Lillie ran her finger softly down the side of his cheek and was greeted with a sudden intense stare. *Those eyes seem so old, like they know the secrets of the world,* she thought. *What secrets do you know, little one?* she wanted to ask. Instead, she gathered him in her arms and went to stand by the window again. Ely had told her he had seen Jack up at Duel's grave, staring up at the angel as if he were waiting for some kind of answer.

"Your daddy, he'll be back," she whispered thickly. "There ain't nowhere to run to now."

Virginia City,
Montana Territory
November, 1865

Mrs. Callie McGregor
Plumas City, California

Dear Callie,

I'm holed up here in Duel's old cabin—have been for the past couple
of days. I thought I needed quiet but that has gotten to me, so if you
don't mind I'd like to bend your ear for awhile. Things ain't too good.
Lillie's got John-Charles. I know I ought to go get him but I keep thinking, I can't even take care of myself right now, how am I going to take
care of a baby? I just need to get everything straight in my mind again,
then I can go get my son. My hands are shaky, I hope you can read this.
My mind has been playing tricks on me; when I wake up in the morning, when I try to find sleep, sometimes even when I'm walking, I'll get
an idea in my head and think, I got to go tell Raven about that or I
wonder what she'll think of this, then I remember.

Death is harsh. There ain't no making up for it, nothing you can do
to make it better, no way to ever get back what you had.

Oh, why did I take her back to this godforsaken place? Why didn't I
see Frank Monroe coming? I ought to have been able to save her. I keep
going over and over that day but I can't find the answer.

Why can't I find the answer?

Jack

Twenty-Three

"Never thought I'd see so many mourners for Frank Monroe," Mabel said with a sniff. She and Ely were watching the funeral procession from the saloon window slowly trail through town, picking up followers like a snowball gathering more snow as it rolled downhill, each silently hoping with Frank's burying that life might now get better around Virginia City. It had been an odd week; first the Indians, then Jack shutting himself off in Duel's cabin, then Lillie shutting herself off in her room with the baby. Mabel wondered if Lillie's attachment to the boy was her way of staying close to Jack. Not that she thought it'd work—the gambler had turned strange. The memory of him holding up that scalp and the cry that followed flashed through her mind and she shuddered.

"Why, them ain't mourners, they're checkers," Ely volunteered as he peered out of the window.

"Checkers?"

"Yes, checkers," Ely said. "Them fellows were sent by Frank's enemies to make sure he's dead." He set up two glasses on the bar and poured them both a small drink and as he did, Mabel noticed his hands looked worn. He works so hard, she thought. Even if his slowness aggravated her at times, at least he was steady and that counted for something in a husband.

"Checkers, huh? Well, that makes more sense," Mabel said, smiling at him softly. They both turned, hearing footfalls on the stairs, and saw Lillie coming down with the baby in her arms. There was a stiff look on the girl's face, almost as if her mind was making her body do something she didn't want it to. She went out the door quickly, without a word to either one of them.

Mabel picked up her drink, a thoughtful look on her face as she walked over to the window and watched Lillie weaving down the street toward the stables. She used to envy Lillie; envy her looks and her life that always seemed so full of excitement.

But the excitement she had seen lately could kill a person—or make them wish they were dead, she thought. Mabel shook her head. No, she'd take the slow and steady type over that. She watched Lillie's small form fading and she couldn't help thinking how vulnerable she looked, how alone as the crowds pushed past her like she wasn't there, and her heart went out to the girl.

Life hadn't been so easy on Lillie so far. Mabel said a quick prayer that Somebody Up There might take notice of that and have some pity.

"What are you doing here, Lillie?"

The words bit into her resolve and she forced herself to take a deep breath before she looked at Jack again. He looked like a wild . . . *Indian,* his long hair loose, hiding his face as he sat cross-legged in the middle of the floor, rocking to some silent beat. She stole a quick glance to the bed where she had laid John-Charles and then met Jack's glare head-on.

"I brought you some food because Ely said you haven't eaten anything he's left outside the door. And I figured you might just want to see your son."

At the mention of John-Charles, Jack's eyes became wild—not like himself—and Lillie saw such bare pain and emotion on his face that she wanted to turn away from the nakedness of it.

"I don't want you here!" he shouted, as if sensing what she saw. He jumped up and picked up a small pitcher and hurled it across the room, where it fell in a tinkling pile of sharded glass along with the countless pieces of other things he'd obviously thrown against the wall.

"You think that's the worst I can do?"

"I think it's the worst you will do," she said quietly. She could have argued, maybe given him what for because he hadn't cared for his son right, but her mind was filled with the thought that Jack had somehow become small.

He wasn't *small*, though—not really—if she looked at him right. Lillie realized it was only when she looked in his eyes that he seemed to disappear.

Don't disappear, Jack, she wanted to plead, but the baby picked that moment to kick up a fuss; arms and legs pistoning in the air wildly, his cries freezing Lillie where she stood.

"He hasn't cried a peep since I had him," she said almost to herself. Lillie started for the baby until she saw the look in Jack's eyes change for a moment. Lillie watched Jack glance down at his son as if remembering where he was—*who he was*—and she knew then that it would be the boy who would pull Jack through. Whether Jack could see that now or not.

"Pick him up," she said. "He won't break, Jack."

"Yeah, I guess he's too little to know about breaking," Jack snapped. Lillie steeled herself against going to him and taking him in her arms. It was too soon, for both of them.

"I ain't as strong as you, Lillie," he said, so quiet she almost didn't hear the words, but something in his giving up made her angry. Did he think he was the only one who had loved and lost?

"Life *forced* me to be strong, Jack—ain't no one that's born to it.

We're just made strong by what happens or we quit life. You can't run from this. He's *yours.* He's your son, Jack. It's about time you started acting like his pa," she said with a hard sound to her voice. Then she turned and walked out of the cabin, fast, before she could change her mind.

When the door shut behind her, she leaned on it, letting the tears come.

No matter how ugly it seems, it always turns out good in the end.... Lillie let the words roll over and over in her head, hoping what the preacher's wife said might be true. Everything seemed so ugly now. Jack probably thought she didn't care about him or his grief but the sad thing was she did care. It was the only way she could figure out to shake him out of the hole he had crawled into.

But if it worked, maybe one day she'd be able to tell him what she knew about love. And that sometimes kicking someone you love when they're down is the only way to help them get back up.

Jack stared at the closed door. *What has she done?* he thought. *Why did she leave me with the boy when she knew I ain't able to care for him?*

When he finally looked at his son, he felt the grief well up in him so thick he wasn't sure he could move. It was like his body was alive but his insides were dead. He looked around the room, trying to avoid John-Charles, looking for something to take his mind off all of the hurt.

John-Charles cried again and the sound nearly undid him. Jack looked at him for a moment before picking him up, feeling his heart tearing; the little face that stared back at him looking so like Raven. Realizing his father had him, John-Charles gurgled happily. As Jack held him in his arms, he remembered the first time he ever held him and what he had thought: *It's like I have someone I don't have to ask to forgive me, because I haven't disappointed him yet.*

A tortured groan escaped Jack as he hugged the baby to him and he suddenly caught their reflection in Duel's old mirror. One face filled with helplessness, the other, understanding. Jack wished John-Charles could speak so that he could give him the answers.

John-Charles smiled toothlessly into the cracked mirror. The crack separated his features and for a moment Jack saw a glimpse of himself, then his pa, and finally Raven and he suddenly realized he wasn't alone.

He glanced to the pile of things Lillie had left on the bed and he was shocked to see his mama's Bible sticking up out of the midst of it all, the same Bible he had given Duel all that time ago. Jack smiled, really smiled, and as he did, he thought he heard his mother's voice somewhere in the shadows of the room, at first so soft he had to strain to hear, then stronger, echoing a song from his past. He was six or seven again, listening to her voice rising and falling with the music as he held her warm, comforting hand, the sun streaming through the stained-glass windows of the tiny church she loved.

Jack looked at his son again and then he did what any world-weary man would do in such a time. He got down on his knees and prayed.

Virginia City,
Montana Territory
November, 1865

Mrs. Callie McGregor
Plumas City, California

Dear Callie,
　　Are you still out there somewhere?
　　I'm still at Duel's cabin but John-Charles is with me now. These past couple of weeks have been a learning experience that I ain't likely to for-

get, either. I never knew babies could be such hard work—or so fun. I was real mad at Lillie at first, leaving John-Charles with me like she did, but now I know her reasons were good ones. I guess I went a little crazy there for a bit and in my craziness I had it worked up in my head that I couldn't handle having John-Charles around because he reminded me so much of Raven. It wasn't until Lillie left him with me that I realized I need him more than anything, maybe more than he needs me. It's like when I look at him I remember I haven't lost everything—he's the part of her that didn't get taken away.

I'm sorry you didn't get to meet Raven, Sis. She was one of those rare souls who could make you believe in people again, in life. She taught me more about peace in the short time I had her with me than anyone I knew my whole life. But I guess even that short time was a lot for this unmerciful world.

I miss her something awful, Sis. Trying to imagine my life without her is too much. . . . John-Charles growin' up without a ma. . . .

Lillie says we're either made strong by what happens to us or we quit life. If I've learned anything from all of this, it's that I can't beat this horse that carries me anymore. But maybe that's the way it should be. Maybe the only way any of us can make it through is to just learn how to ride it out.

Jack

Jack went to the graveyard, mainly because he needed a friend to talk to. And there was no way he could talk with Lillie about what weighed so heavily on his heart. The grief of living when Raven was gone and the guilt of realizing he still cared for Lillie was too much to hold inside anymore.

Jack sighed heavily as he carried John-Charles through the wobbly rows of graves, holding him easily, as if he were born to hold a child at his hip—not carry a gun. He thought of all of the lives that had started out so happily, so fresh with smiles and folks celebrating only to end up here.

. . . When we die, we all go up in the sky together, Raven's words echoed in his head as he glanced up at the clear blue bowl of sky.

By God, Duel, if you are up there you take care of Raven, you hear? he thought. *Take care of her good . . . like I should have. Make sure she's happy. . . .*

Wouldn't that be something, Fast Horse? To be in a place where there is no more sickness or scars . . . or hate? Raven had said not so long ago and he knew the place she spoke of must be heaven.

Jack remembered something his mama told him about heaven. What was it? Something about the folks up there cheering you on as you run your race. . . .

But I don't know if I can run anymore, he thought wearily and that's when he saw the big man standing at the grave with his back to Jack, gazing up at the angel of Duel's as if he too were looking for answers.

John-Charles let out a howl, and the man glanced back at them. Jack was struck by the friendly way the stranger looked at them, as if he had known them all his life.

"I heard some say he was a kind of lawman in these parts," the man said, worrying the brim of his hat as he glanced over his shoulder at Jack, looking almost hopeful. "Even a hero."

Jack smiled, thinking of his old friend. "I guess you could say he was all of that and then some."

When the stranger turned full around, Jack saw a twitch that might have been a smile form on his lips, and in that instant he realized who the stranger was. It was the smile that gave it away and he felt foolish he hadn't seen the resemblance right off: the big, broad shoulders, the dark eyes that took everything in, serious but kind. Jack felt his throat tighten with the memory but he felt good, too. Like he had been given back a part of something he'd thought gone forever.

"You're Duel's son," he said when he finally found his voice. After a brief look of shock, Coy Harper laughed, pushing his hat back on his head, and they shook hands.

"You must be Jack," he said. "I've heard folks speak of you in town."

"Well, don't believe everything you hear," Jack said with a mock look of distress.

"Don't need to say another word," Coy said, his eyes suddenly full of humor. Eyes so much like his father's, Jack thought. "Ain't nothin' like a bunch of facts to spoil a good rumor."

Anything ever happens to me, Jack, and the mine is half yours—the other half is my son, Coy's, if he ever decides to come back. It was almost as if Duel knew, Jack thought. *You and my boy seem to have a powerful lot of wantin'. . . .*

"Ever done any mining?" Jack asked. Duel's son laughed again as he leaned forward and reached for John-Charles' hand, looking at the boy as if he'd never seen a baby before.

"No, but I have a feeling you could teach me," Coy said wryly, looking up at Jack.

"Well, it could take a spell, teaching someone as green as you."

"You got anything better to do?"

"Do you?"

Laughter filled the quiet little cemetery and as the two men headed down the hill toward their horses, Jack could've sworn he heard his friend chuckle, the wind whispering his voice. *Always be another game, Jack. . . .*

Twenty-Four

Jack threw himself into mining the Celie-Mae like a man who had been given a pardon but wasn't sure how long it would last; sunup to sundown, he worked the claim as if he were wrestling the mountain itself for its treasures. Coy leaned against his pickax, wiping his brow as he watched Jack swing the hammer again and again, ignoring the sweat that ran down his own face. Coy had been trying to keep up with him all morning, but the pace was starting to take its toll and he thought he might like to head for the Pair-O-Dice— if he could talk Jack into taking a break. He didn't mind hard work, but he liked pleasure, too.

He had thought of gambling a little in the evening, but Jack wasn't interested—something that had shocked Coy since he had heard his pa's friend was one of the best anyone had seen at the tables. *Gamblin' ain't never brought me anything but trouble,* he'd said in a voice that meant he didn't want to discuss it any further, so Coy had dropped the idea. Besides, he liked Jack, he thought, chancing another glance at the man working next to him; long hair and buckskins and eyes that looked a hundred years old. At a first look you might be inclined to step out of his way and just keep going. But there was something about him, too, that he thought he could learn from. He had all the book learning he figured he needed back in Kansas, but life, well, he had a feeling he could still learn a thing or two about life, if Jack ever decided to talk about anything besides mining. Coy had heard other folks whisper about Jack's life: the card game that had led to his own father's death, living with Indians, his Indian wife's murder, and the scalping of Frank Monroe. He shook his head. The man had lived and seen more than anyone he knew.

"You think we'll ever see any color?" he asked, more out of wanting to talk than anything.

Jack stopped his hammering, looking over at Duel's son consideringly. It was good having Coy around, Jack thought. There was so much in him that reminded him of Duel.

"Not if you keep jawing, we ain't going to see color," he replied, his voice thick with amusement. "I guess you're hungry again."

"I guess I am," Coy said defensively, then he grinned and tipped his hat back. "Like my daddy always said, you feed the inner man and the outer will be obliged to follow."

"Well, I ain't one to dispute such wisdom." Jack gave Coy the once over, shaking his head. "You're about as big of an eater as your daddy was, too. It's no wonder he left us this mine."

"Money might buy a fine dog but it's feedin' him that makes him wag his tail."

"I'll have to agree with Coy on that," Lillie said, laughing as she came up behind them. Jack saw she was carrying a basket in one hand and had John-Charles perched easily on her other hip. He felt something both painful and pleasing seeing them together like that. He had had to argue with her about taking money for watching the boy, but for him there was no other way. It seemed right that the money from his and Raven's horses would go to care for their son.

Besides, paying her eased his mind, eased the guilt he felt every time he saw her looking so pretty and fresh and felt the old feelings stir in him that were always followed by the pain of knowing Raven could never hold her son like that again. Jack looked away as she drew near, wishing he could just be numbed of it all. They had formed a kind of fragile friendship since Raven's death, neither of them talking about the past, but he wasn't so foolish to think it would last forever.

"I thought I'd bring you some grub since it didn't look like you were going to make it into town today," Lillie said, trying to ease the tension. "There's plenty here, so don't be shy."

"Well, I ain't shy," Coy announced, nearly falling over himself to help. There was something needy in the younger man's wanting to please Lillie, something that made Jack think he was lonely for a family, too. He watched the two of them spread the blanket and saw the way Lillie's eyes lit up like a kid's as Coy made over all she had brought them. *Something's changed her,* he thought, remembering a time not so long ago when she had been scared as a jackrabbit to venture much farther than the Pair-O-Dice. He couldn't help thinking how tricky life could be; just when you think you know what you want or feel, life steps in and changes the game.

You and my boy Coy seem to have a powerful lot of wantin'. . . . Duel's voice whispered to him again. He squinted his eyes against the sun and looked at the mine, remembering the look on his old friend's face when he had said that.

You were right, Duel, he thought. *It just ain't money none of us are needing, not really . . . but I guess you knew that even then, didn't you?* Jack trudged over to the blanket and sat down, scooping John-Charles up in his arms to comfort himself. His son looked up at him with his solemn eyes as if he understood.

"He's already been fed and dried, Jack," Lillie said softly. "You ought to set him down and eat something yourself." Lillie handed him the napkin filled with biscuits but when their eyes met for the briefest moment, the hurt and pain showed like twin mirrors before he turned and laid the baby back down on the blanket. *Would the pain of the past ever go away for either of them? Or the longing?*

In the silence, Coy reached over and tickled the baby and John-Charles laughed, shocking them all with a full-bellied kind of laugh that sounded too big for his body and it got them all laughing, too. When they all looked at each other, it was with shy smiles, as if the laughter had coated each of their hurts with a kind of magic balm none of them expected.

Sometimes God can take what was meant for bad and turn it to good, Jack recalled Lillie saying not so long ago, and he suddenly had the eeriest feeling that this was one of those times.

This is what it's all about, Jack thought. Learning to find laughter again and letting go, like a baby with a laugh that seemed too big for its body.

"He's some baby, ain't he?" Jack said, shaking his head and smiling down at the gift he had been given. He didn't even have to look up to know Lillie and Coy agreed.

Virginia City,
Montana Territory
March, 1866

Mrs. Callie McGregor
Plumas City, California

Dear Callie,

Duel's son Coy showed up in town a couple of weeks back and we've been fast friends ever since. Coy is so much like his pa it just seems natural that it turned out that way. It's derned near eerie that we'd meet up like we did . . . and just when we needed this the most. "Ain't nothin' better in life than finding a good friend and a warm fire on a rainy day," I can hear Duel saying. Truth is, I've been thinking a lot of friends and family these last few months.

Sometimes when I close my eyes at night, I can almost believe I'm back in my lodge, that old Lodge Skins or Medicine Weasel or Lone Elk will come to shake me out of this dream. I miss the Blackfoot, my friends. I miss Raven.

There ain't a day that goes by that I don't still think of Raven and that I don't miss her, but I guess that's how it will be. John-Charles is my saving grace, even if he's a handful. Lillie lets him play with the faro chips, and he draws a crowd the way he chucks them across the table— some even bet on the cards they fall on. Ely swears he'll be gambling before he walks, but I want more for him than to go through what I did, Sis—I know Raven would, too. I guess all parents want better for their kids. I sure wish you could see him. Just today, Coy got to tickling him and he laughed so big that I busted out laughing too, and the sound gave us all a shock, being that I haven't really laughed in so long.

You know, I always held onto Grandma Wade's promise to keep me out of hell—even if she had to throw an apron string down from Heaven to yank me out herself. It's been one heck of a trip, Sis, but it appears the old lady has kept her promise.

Jack

Twenty-Five

Lillie was nervous and fidgety as she finished dressing, and her reflection in the mirror only confirmed her state. Her eyes, wide and fearful as a startled deer's, stared back. Mabel sat on the bed behind her, her head bowed as she read the letter Jack had written, telling her to meet him up at Duel's cabin. The letter worried Lillie. For Jack to send something so formal instead of coming into town himself, it had to be serious. She tried to imagine what might have changed in the last day or so. They had been getting closer again, their talking easier, even laughing together sometimes, but there were still bridges neither of them had crossed

Maybe he was going to tell her he was leaving again, she thought, her hands pausing on the buttons of her dress as she felt the old dread fill her. Maybe she didn't *want* to know what he had to say. . . .

"I ought to just stay put," she said, thinking aloud. "There's a lot of work I should be catching up on anyway before opening tonight." As she turned from the mirror, Mabel looked up at her with a thoughtful look on her face.

"Sometimes you just gotta do what's first on your mind, just say that's it and stick to it," Mabel said, laying the letter back down on the bed, a frown knitting her brow. "Sometimes thinking about it too long will take your choice away."

"But what if what he's got to tell me isn't good? Or what if I think it is, but it don't work out again?" Lillie sat down next to Mabel on the bed and felt all of her pent-up fears want to come rushing out. "I keep thinking *why,* you know? If me and Jack were meant to be, why did all of those things happen?"

Mabel pursed her lips, considering, and when she finally spoke again, Lillie had the feeling what she was about to say shouldn't be taken lightly.

"If I ever stopped long enough to really look at my life, to ask myself *why not* to all those choices I never made, thinkin' it would be easier just not to make 'em . . . Well, I guess I'd go and get me one of the biggest bottles of laudanum I could find and forget it all. But sooner or later there ain't enough laudanum to do the trick." Mabel smiled then, and there was something in her smile that made Lillie think of a tiny bird that had just found the cage door wide open. "Besides, I ain't asking *why not* no more. Because this time when I had a choice to make, I made it."

Lillie rose from the bed and hurriedly gathered her things for the ride out to Duel's. Mabel was right after all—even if she did fear losing herself to Jack again after fighting so hard to get strong. If anything, she needed to finally find out for herself if Jack was really *who* she wanted and not some distant dream that was always held out of reach. She put her hand on the door to open it, then hesitated, looking back over her shoulder at the woman who had become such a dear friend. Mabel smiled with unshed tears glistening in her eyes.

"Ever think that the Good Lord had to knock some sense into you two before He could see fit to put you together again?"

"He looks a lot like her, doesn't he?" Lillie asked, sitting next to Jack in Duel's cabin, watching him finger a tuft of inky hair on his son's head. The tiny features were so like his mother's: same color hair, same tawny skin. But from the Indian face, curious green eyes shaped like tiny half-moons stared up at his father with love.

"Yeah," Jack answered quietly and the look on his face told her he wasn't sure he could say any more than that. As hard as she tried, Lillie couldn't help feeling jealous of the dead woman and the feeling made her ashamed. But something had to give, if they were going to make it. If they *could* make it. Lillie closed her eyes for a moment, trying to push down the hurts and fears. The look on her face nearly undid Jack.

Why do I keep hurting her when all I want is for things to be good between us again? Jack thought. Every time she was around, the emptiness in him was filled and he found more and more he didn't want her to leave, didn't want the emptiness to return. He had sent the letter to town because he knew it was time to tell her everything. For so long, he had tried to ignore his feelings for Lillie because they made him feel guilty, but even the guilt couldn't make them go away.

"We got to talk, Lillie," Jack said, breaking the silence. When he looked at her, his eyes were both happy and sorrowful. "I love you, Lillie, I think you know that—"

"You loved *her,* Jack," she interrupted, tears of hurt filling her eyes. "You can't tell me you didn't."

"I loved her, but not the way I should have—not like I loved you. I didn't aim for it to happen, Lillie, but it did." Jack fell silent, trying to find the right words, afraid if he didn't, he would lose her for good. "She taught me peace, Lillie, something I didn't ever think I'd have after what Frank did to us, to Duel. But you were always there. Even when I married Raven, you were still in my heart. It shamed me sometimes, you know, like I was living two lives. But I tried to do right by her because she deserved that much." Jack brushed a hand over his face, taking a ragged breath. "Hard as I tried I think she knew anyway," he said, sighing. "She was my peace, Lillie. But you, you've always been my passion."

Jack watched her squeeze her eyes shut to try to hide her tears. He saw the emotions roll from joy to anger and *felt* them as if they were his own.

"I loved you nearly forever, Jack," Lillie whispered, angrily brushing off the tears that had broken free. "I would've done just about anything for you." She shut her eyes to the memory, to the hurt of seeing Jack and his Indian wife that first time. "I don't think I can forget the past."

Lillie's smile was filled with pain. "Sad thing is I wanted to so bad. When I came to Ely, I was just a bit more than a kid—and seems even when life deals rough with a kid they can always find some hope. I was ripe for the picking when Frank Monroe came along, ready to believe when someone said they loved me, they meant it."

Lillie looked in Jack's eyes and he thought he saw a part of the girl she had been. He wanted to hold her so badly, but knew in his heart she had to finish.

"Frank didn't kill me outright—he just killed my dreams." Lillie swallowed hard. "He took me and he used me, Jack. Then he told me what trash I was and he didn't stop telling me until he rode out looking for Jude. That was the first night since I was a real little girl that I got down on my knees and thanked God."

Lillie laughed softly. "Next time I was on my knees, I was thanking Him for you."

When she finally looked up into Jack's eyes, she felt the pain of loving him swell in her and she clenched her fists to her sides. "You took that from me," she said, nearly whispering, but when he started to deny it, Lillie felt some of her old strength return and she held up her hand to silence him.

"You had someone else," she said, her voice thick with hurt. "Don't get me wrong, I think she was a fine lady, from what I saw. And she gave you a beautiful son. But, Jack, you took someone else . . . when I had nobody." Lillie swiped another tear that had escaped and traveled down her cheek. "You took my hope. How do I get that back?"

She looked off past him, imagining her life without him as she had before he had shown back up again and she saw nothing but emptiness ahead. But what if she could never forget the past? "Maybe the best thing for you to do now is just go. Go back to your family in California," she said softly.

"Maybe you're right," Jack said as he leaned close. "Hell, Lillie, I know you don't need the grief and maybe the noble thing for me to do is go and let you be." He knelt down and she shivered as he traced her face with his fingers. "But the thing is," he whispered softly, "I ain't that noble. Besides, I got something to show you."

Jack turned away from her for only a moment, reaching for his family Bible that lay on the dresser next to his bed. When their eyes met, she was surprised to see a shyness come to his face, and he reminded her a little of a boy kicking his toe in the dirt.

"I ain't ever been much of a Bible reader, Lillie," he began and she kept quiet for fear if she said anything he wouldn't finish. A sigh came out of him and he sat down on the bed, motioning for her to sit next to him. "Well, I got to thumbin' through this book one night after gettin' John-Charles to bed and it fell open to this here page—I guess 'cause of the flower one of them tucked there. Whatever the reason, I read the derned thing." Jack smiled at her and she smiled back in spite of her heart hammering hard in her chest. She looked down at the dried flower he was turning between his fingers, and the memory of the lonely night she had sat on her own bed touching that same flower came rushing back to her. *Love never fails.* It was the same verse she had turned to.

"Whole thing was about love," Jack said, breaking through her thoughts. "What got me though was it saying love never fails. Way I got it figured is *never* is the best odds I've come across in a long time. Like being showed a new game."

When Lillie stared into his eyes, Jack's smile was wry, and she suddenly felt a smile come to her lips in spite of it all. For a moment, they were just Lillie and Jack again. She felt all of the feelings she had tried so hard to bury come bursting up in her easily, as if they had been waiting for this moment all along.

"Sometimes I feel like the game went sour a long time ago," Lillie said finally, not yet trusting herself to believe. "That I should have just been done with it and went off somewhere else."

"But you didn't." Jack got down on his knees beside her and took her hand. As he looked up into her face with fear and hope he whispered, "This is one game I can win, Lillie—*we* can win. Marry me, Lillie."

Instead of answering right off, Lillie picked up the old Bible that lay on the bed and ran her hand over the leather cover, worn soft by years and touch. "Don't you want to go home, Jack? See your family?" she asked with the breathless fear of not wanting to hope too much.

Jack read the fear and the longing in her face and he felt the bittersweetness of regret and time lost between them. *But,* he wondered, *maybe that time lost was for us to learn what we had.* He looked into Lillie's eyes, really looked as he brushed back a wayward curl from her forehead, and he felt an odd kind of change come over him. There wasn't the need to hide anything from her anymore, he thought, least of all himself, and something in him told him he was becoming the man he was always meant to be.

"You're my home, you and John-Charles," Jack said simply. When he took Lillie in his arms, this time she didn't fight it. Somehow that feeling had crept back in her. It had a name.

She called it hope.

Virginia City,
Montana Territory
May, 1866

Mrs. Callie McGregor
Plumas City, California

Dear Callie,
 I'm staying in Montana—marrying Lillie if she'll have me.
 They say you can't ever go back home, and maybe they're right about

that, Callie. See, I think I got that figured out now. After we leave, "home" ain't the same place no more because we ain't the same. Home is a feeling. It's where the people who know you are—the people who love you for who you are.

And maybe stick by you in spite of it.

Medicine Weasel once told me that this land had claimed me. Maybe he was right, but I think this land has made me, too. Made me the man I ought to be. All the running I've done, all the hard-earned lessons I've had to learn have been here and I figure that's got to mean something. Wasn't it Quinn who once said a man's made more by his tragedies than by his triumphs?

I sure do miss you all, Sis. I think I'd give anything to be sitting across from you telling you all of this instead of writing it. It's hard to put to paper all I feel, but I guess I'll just have to let my heart do the talking for now. But maybe one day, Lord willing, we will meet again and you can tell me what you heard. . . .

Jack

Plumas City, California
June 30, 1866

Mr. Jack Wade
Virginia City,
Montana Territory

Dear Jack,

We're coming to Montana. I've stayed away long enough. And don't get it in your head that it's out of pity or sisterly duty—because that's not the case. The truth is, I've missed you since the day you rode away from me in Salt Lake. Families aren't meant to be so scattered, Jack. The Good Lord wouldn't have put us together, just to scatter us. It doesn't seem right that I've never laid eyes on my own nephew, let alone my new sister-in-law.

Besides, I have a yearning to see this picture you've painted of Montana before I'm old and gray and don't have the energy for adventure.

You aren't the only one who inherited Grandma Wade's wanderlust, you know. . . .

> With much love and happiness,
> Your sister,
> Callie

Twenty-Six

*T*hat wind's got a hateful bite to it," Mabel announced as she carried John-Charles through the door.

"Fall is here to stay—however long that is," Lillie replied, watching Jack and Ely laughing and talking out in the yard and noticing every so often how her husband's eyes would look past Ely to the horizon. He was searching like he always had, but this time was different because this day he knew what he was searching for. "Could snow tomorrow. It's a good thing Jack's family's due here today. They'd be lucky to find this place once it snows."

Lillie turned away from the window, glancing around the little cabin that was now their home. *Our home.* It still seemed like a dream; she and Jack getting married so quickly and moving into Duel's cabin. Coy had turned over his share of the cabin the night of their wedding, with his blessings. *I'm more of a city fellow myself,* he had told them with that same quirky grin as Duel's. *It's a derned shame to have so much life going on and me not there to partake in it.* She and Jack had laughed after he had left, his words reminding them so much of Jack when he had first come to Virginia City. They had been doing a lot of laughing lately. A lot of dreaming, too. The closer the time came for Jack's family to arrive, the bigger his dreams seemed to get. Lillie smiled at the thought but her smile faded some as she wondered what the McGregors would think of their home.

She had decorated the cramped little cabin with bits and pieces of all of their lives; some of the nicer things belonged to Duel's wife Celie that she had found packed away in a trunk, like the pretty blue bowl and pitcher and handmade rugs. The quilt Lillie had stitched together from pieces of her past now took its place in her future, cheering up the rough little bed in the corner with its color. Jack's family Bible sat next to the bed on a little stool with the newest entries: John-Charles' birth, Raven's passing, and their marriage.

Lillie opened up the Bible gingerly, turning the pages until she came to her and Jack's names. *You're a part of the family, now,* Jack had told her the night they married, and it still filled her with a sense of awe that her name was really there. *Lillie.* Lillie brushed the pages back and looked at the other names and wondered what Callie and Quinn would be like, and suddenly she felt the old fear of failing to measure up coming to haunt her.

"What if they don't like me, Mabel?" she asked, her voice just above a whisper.

"What'd'ya mean, don't like you? What ain't to like?" Mabel asked incredulously as she put John-Charles down with an affectionate pat to his rump.

Lillie handed the Bible over to Mabel and opened the first page for her. "See that?"

"See what?" Mabel asked, looking a bit unsettled.

"Look at that writing, how carefully all the names and dates were entered. Only good family does things like that," Lillie said with trepidation as Mabel bent over and carefully inspected the book once more.

Mabel looked up at Lillie strangely, as if she hadn't heard right. Then she took the book and set it back down on the stool.

"Ain't no different than us," Mabel shrugged finally. "They lived and they died."

They lived and they died. Lillie grinned in spite of her fears. *Leave it to Mabel to say such a thing.*

Lillie scooped John-Charles into her arms, feeling her spirits lift as he wrapped his chubby arms around her neck, turning to stare out the window with her.

"Da-da," John-Charles announced, spotting Jack. He turned his green eyes to her, so serious, waiting for her to respond. She grinned at him, planting a kiss on his forehead.

"Yes, Da-da," she said and was surprised by the soft pat on her cheek that came next.

"Mom-ey," he said, patting her cheek again.

"Did he just say what I think he said?" Mabel asked with wonder.

Lillie laughed, tears stinging her eyes. "I think so."

"Well, I swear," Mabel said. But Lillie wasn't really listening anymore. She had turned to look back out the window with John-Charles for Jack's family.

Their family.

If there ever was a heart haunted by memories it was Jack's, Lillie thought as she stood next to him in the yard beyond their cabin. She watched Jack's eyes stay fixed on the dusty little caravan as it lumbered up the hill and into their yard. She watched him swallow and blink a few times and she knew he was fighting to keep his composure. Her heart went out to him. *How long had he yearned for this day? How many times have we all wished for a day like this?*

Lillie hastily blinked back her own tears and watched the man who drove the rig as he quickly stepped down. The first thing that struck her was his size; he was as big as a barn. She saw him cock his dark head sideways and laugh at something that was said and something about his laughter made her feel good. *That must be Quinn,* she thought, watching him gently help a little girl of about seven or eight down. She was a pretty little thing and so serious looking. She then took a toddler into her arms and turned to face them. Next, she saw a dark, wiry old fellow with a shock of silver hair step down and offer a hand to a stout-looking woman who slapped it away, and she heard more laughter.

"Well, I'll be," Jack said, his voice just a whisper. "Ol' Stem's come, too . . . and brought Jessie." But the look that came across Jack's face was one she knew she would never forget. If she lived to be a hundred she would never forget that look . . . or the sound of a small sob that escaped his throat.

Her bonnet came loose as she turned to them, and Lillie saw auburn hair and a smile so big, so filled with joy, that it tore at her own heart. *Callie.*

"Jack!" she yelled. She picked up her skirts and began to run.

Jack grabbed Lillie's arm and she held onto John-Charles for dear life as he began to cut the distance between them, his strides long but checked, as if he were forcing himself to keep from running. Then he let go of her arm finally and he ran. Lillie began to cry as she watched Jack and Callie finally hug each other—not say a word, just hug—and then the laughter that came when Jack picked Callie up and swung her around in his arms like two lost kids who had finally found their way home. When he finally put her down, they stood and looked at each other as if they couldn't believe what was happening was real. Then they laughed again and Callie looked over Jack's shoulder and smiled.

"You must be Lillie," she said, tears spilling freely down her cheeks. Lillie thought she was the prettiest woman she had ever seen: small and delicate-looking but there was strength in the green eyes that stared back at her. She reluctantly pulled away from Jack and walked over and hugged Lillie warmly, kissing John-Charles on the cheek. Lillie felt heartened by her warmth.

"I guess you must feel a bit overwhelmed. It isn't every day you inherit a group like us," Callie said wryly. Lillie laughed and as Callie joined in, Lillie noticed the fine feathering of lines at the corners of her eyes that showed both happiness and sorrow.

"I'd advise ya ta run like the wind ma'am, but it 'pears too late," a rough old voice intoned, and everyone broke into laughter as Stem hobbled into the thick of it.

"It's a good thing I married her before you all got here," Jack said, emotion thickening in his throat; the years had aged Stem more than any of the rest of them, making him look a bit frailer than Jack remembered. He didn't like thinking of Stem as old. There was so much lost time to make up for. He felt his heart swell with a happiness that he never imagined existed.

"Gimme your paw you derned rascal. And quit gawking at me like you're surprised to see me standing up." Stem's voice boomed strong, and Jack grinned with relief as he grasped his old friend's hand.

"Surprised to see *me* alive?" Jack asked and Stem nodded, his rheumy eyes filling.

"Can't think of a better surprise."

Jack felt a tug at his trousers and looked down then to see a little girl staring up at him with eyes that were so much like Rose's, it nearly took his breath away. She hiked the baby that was Quinn's spitting image further up on her hip and wordlessly held her dainty hand out, displaying the little gold ring he had sent her, then peeked a moccasined toe out from her skirt and gave him a wide-open grin as if she had known him all of her life.

"Why, this must be Patrick," he said, touching the dark head of curls. "And you . . . you must be little Rose." Jack glanced to where Callie stood and felt the years fade away as their memories came alive again. The emotion that passed between them caused a sudden hush to fall around the group.

"My mama says you call Montana God's backyard," the child announced, looking up at him with those large, serious eyes. "I've looked all over this hill and I can't find Him anywhere. I peeked under the little bushes, too, even tho' I know He's too big to hide behind them. I figure He's got to be here somewhere."

"You close your eyes, honey, and you'll feel Him sure enough,"

Jack said huskily, never more sure of anything in his life as he looked from face to smiling face. He suddenly realized that the sureness he felt in his heart at that moment wasn't just his, but all of theirs, together. All of the roads they had each taken, looking for that pot of gold at the end of the rainbow; somehow they were lucky enough to finally figure out what was worth more than gold . . . family.

"Out o' the mouth of babes, eh, Jack?" Quinn said, laughing as he squinted against the wind and maybe just a tear or two.

"Yeah, it makes you think, doesn't it?" Jack said, putting his arms around his wife and sister as he led the way for the group up the hill toward the little cabin they would for the time being all call home.

Epilogue

*J*ack and Callie looked out over the broad stretch of green valley to the Bear Paw Mountains that stood like sentinels in the distance, and Jack felt his heart swell with pride as he watched his sister's eyes fill with awe, sweeping over the land he had come to love.

"I reread all your letters coming out here," Callie said in a hushed voice. "It's just like you wrote, but more. I think Pa and Rose would have loved it here."

"I think so, too," Jack said and when their eyes met, they smiled. There was no more hiding the past. If anything they had both learned it wasn't just triumph but tragedy that made them stronger, made them a family. To deny the bad would've made it impossible to see the good, for they were woven together tighter than any tapestry made by human hands. Laughter floated up from the grassy picnic area where the rest of the family sat, and as he turned to look, Jack saw Lillie bend her head close to hear something Quinn said and she laughed again, bouncing John-Charles on her hip.

"Days like this can make you real glad to be alive, can't they, Sis?"

"The stuff good memories are made of," Callie replied, her eyes lit by unshed tears.

As he stared into his sister's eyes, it was like a door opening and he saw his life roll out before him—memories of good and bad. He remembered seeing Lillie that first time, all business, then later on, fear and longing on her face as he rode away. He saw Duel with his broad shoulders hunched over the fire, reading over his mama's Bible. Lone Elk grinning. Raven riding through the sea of buffalo. Medicine Weasel as he led Raven away for good, his long, silver hair whipping in the wind. He saw his sister Rose, too, with her impish smile, and this time he didn't shy away from the memory. *"They's the ones you hold real long, the ones you keep in your pocket until it gets too heavy and you have to set 'em back on the road,"* Duel had told him, and Jack felt for the first time he understood what his friend had meant.

He looked at Callie and felt an overwhelming gratefulness to be there with her, together again, and the look in her eyes said she felt it, too.

"Folks back in California thought we were crazy to give everything up to come here," Callie said softly. "But I *knew* it would be like this, Jack. In my heart, I just knew—Quinn did, too."

"It can be a good thing, learning you're wrong sometimes," Jack said when he finally found his voice. Callie turned, looking at him as if he were a little off, and he laughed. "I mean, finding out you didn't know what you thought you did about life or how it'd turn out."

Callie nodded, looking back toward the mountains.

"I always imagined life like seeing that first perfect blanket of snow; covering everything, making the world look so clean. Then folks trample on it, teams dredge up the mud underneath, and it's not so pretty anymore," she said, then smiled that smile he tried to remember when he was lonely, but he realized his memory never did it justice. "Then it snows again and—"

"You get to start over," Jack finished.

Journal Entry

∾

October, 1866

How strange yet beautiful the twists and turns in life's road are. Who would have ever thought our little ragtag bunch would end up together again? I know I didn't. But maybe that's part of the beauty, too—not always knowing just how life is going to turn out.

One thing I do know is I will never forget this day or how I felt having Jack show me the stars tonight, how he grinned like a kid when he took my hand to lead me outside. I think I would walk through fire itself to see him grin like that more after all he's endured. I think Lillie would, too, the way she smiled and swiped at her eyes as we walked out the door.

"Lillie ain't ever had much of a family," Jack told me as we walked, keeping a hold of my hand. "Not like us." He stopped then and pointed up to the wide bowl of sky above us and I felt my breath catch, the stars so thick and bright and hanging so low I felt I could almost touch them.

"No matter where I've been, I ain't ever felt alone when I look up at this sky," Jack said a bit shyly and I squeezed his hand tight.

"Quinn told Rose a story just before she died," I said. "About how the ones you love that are in Heaven are lighting a star in the sky each night to let you know they're there."

"Feels more like truth than tale when you look at this sky," Jack said quietly. As we walked back to the cabin together, I couldn't help thinking how different we were now; a little more world-weary, maybe, and a lot more wise about not taking those you love for granted . . . but still the same in a way. I think down deep, we both had hoped things might end up this way or at least dreamed it.

I'm a pretty big dreamer, but I don't think even I could have dreamed up such an ending—or is this a new beginning? Another crossroads for us to stand at and decide which way to go this time around? I can't help thanking the Lord at least this time we're all standing together.

A new beginning?

I'd like to think so. . . .

Callie McGregor
Montana Territory

Acknowledgments

I believe each book a writer begins is like a new journey of the heart. Without the love or support of friends and family, I couldn't imagine even beginning such a journey. I will be forever grateful to each one of you, but most of all to the Good Lord, so I'll give Him my thanks first.

To my family . . .

My brother, Shawn Becker, who always inspired me to dream big dreams. One fine day we'll meet again, little brother, and you can tell me what you think. Until then, we'll just have to let our souls do the talking.

My brother, Danny Becker. You told me you believed in me when it really counted and I can't thank you enough for that—I guess I don't have to tell *you* where my inspiration for Jack came from. I love you both more than I can say.

My son, Mitch. You are the "wind beneath my wings." I'm so proud of your honorable spirit, of your kind heart. I couldn't imagine a better son if I could have hand-picked one from Heaven myself.

My Mom and Dad, Joe and Diana McClure, who have always been there to pick me up and dust me off when I fell. I love you both so much.

My Grandpa and Grandma, Doug and Dorothy Vance, who have always listened and whose family stories helped shape my writings. I can't thank you two enough for all you've given me.

My nephew, Shawn-Michael Becker, the boy with a "warrior spirit." I miss your funny stories and the way your eyes would light up when you won a game of Nintendo. No matter how much time or miles separate us, know that I love you.

My niece, Raelyn Becker. I miss your sweet, gentle spirit, the way you bring sunshine to even the cloudiest day. I miss your laughter. I pray you never forget how much I love you.

To my friends . . .

Lisa Higdon, "The Voice of Sanity" and a true friend. Your kind words and support came just at the right time. *Same time next year. . . .*

Chris Hughes. Sometimes you can go back home, huh, Chris? Funny how we ran into each other again—just when we both needed an old friend the most. Thanks for always being there. I love you, ol' buddy.

Ann Pals, my guardian angel. Thank you so much for everything: for your kindness, for believing in me, and for your letters that have meant more to me than you will ever know.

Denise Silvestro. You believed in my ideas from the beginning; my first editor, hand-holder, and good friend. I can't imagine you not being a part of this. Thanks, D.

Caroline Tolley, editor and friend. There aren't enough words to thank you for your patience and understanding, for helping me to keep my stories alive, and most of all, your friendship. *Same time next year. . . .*

Laurie White, "Two peas-one pod." Your phone calls have saved the day too many times to count. Thanks so much for listening, for laughing, and for being a true friend.

To all the folks in Virginia City, Montana, who answered my countless questions with such good cheer. You are what has kept the true spirit of the west alive. Hope to see you this summer!

And finally, to all the wonderful people who have taken the time to write me such kind words of praise and encouragement. Your letters have meant the world to me. They have made me laugh and cry, but most of all, they have inspired me to keep writing. And that is the greatest gift I could receive. After all, a storyteller isn't anything without someone to listen to her story.

Author's Note

~❧~

The West, with all of its new promise, scattered families more than ever before—much like the families of today, lured away from their hometowns by better opportunities. But unlike today, the original pioneers were forced to turn to their only means of holding family ties together, of talking out their hopes, dreams, and even their fears: through their letters.

Fortunately for us, letters and journals, unlike life, are timeless. For anyone who has ever come across a loved one's words, they are rewarded with that very feeling of timelessness: shared moments of love, joy, hope, even sorrow, flood our senses as we read those words written by the hand of another . . . and remember. . . .

When I first set out to write *Letters to Callie*, it was important to me that I show the bond of family, that I might somehow help to share what a gift from God it is to put wayward souls together as families for the time we have here—to give us a sense of home. After all, as Jack wrote in one of his letters to Callie, *Home is feeling. It's where the people who know you are—the people who love you for who you are. And maybe stick by you in spite of it. . . .*

Having two brothers of my own and sharing such a unique and wonderful bond with them, I hoped to share some of that feeling in the pages of *Letters to Callie*. It became even more important to share when I lost my brother Shawn, tragically, around the time I began Jack's story—like Jack, I hope to always learn from the things life deals me and to hopefully pass on some little nugget of wisdom that could help another.

For me, the inspiration for my stories is my life, my family. Jack's character, of course, came to life by my having two brothers who have shared their journeys with me—and their hope that what they learn in life could make them better men.

One of the finest lessons I heard my brother Shawn teach was shortly before he died. I recall being with him in his martial arts school, watching him teach a children's class. He was telling the kids that winning wasn't the most important thing. He said, "It isn't who finishes the race first that's important, but how you run it. Did you stop and help someone who fell? Did you shake hands with the man who won—or the man who lost?" Those words still ring in my mind to this day. . . .

I think that's what our lives *are* about, what family is about: not winning the race, but how we run it. I hope I've shared that feeling with Jack; his character stumbles and falls more than a few times, but like any good distance runner, he brushes himself off and gets back in the race.

I hope we can all learn a little from Jack. I hope we can, in the words of my brother Shawn, learn compassion for others . . . cry for someone, see God in the sweet smile of a child, and hear Him in the worn laughter of an old man or woman. Embrace life, and when you look at your family, count your blessings that you have them for that one day, to laugh with, to cry with, to start over with. . . .

Dawn Miller,
Foristell, Missouri